LOST BOY

A NEVERLAND TRANSMISSIONS NOVEL

J.M. SULLIVAN

Bleeding Ink
Publishing

LOST BOY

The Neverland Transmissions Book 2

Copyright © 2019 by J. M. Sullivan

Sale of the paperback edition of this book without the cover is unauthorized.

For information contact:

Bleeding Ink Publishing

253 Bee Caves Cove

Cibolo, TX 78108

www.bleedinginkpublishing.com

info@bleedinginkpublishing.com

Cover design by Strong Image Editing

Book design by Inkstain Design Studio

Paperback ISBN: 978-1-948583-19-0

Ebook ISBN: 978-1-948583-23-7

LOST
BOY

For Grandpa Al
Until we meet in Neverland.

"Wait for me somewhere between reality and all we've ever dreamed."

—J.M. BARRIE. PETER PAN

PROLOGUE
COMMANDER'S LOG

AIDAN BOYCE
IDENTIFICATION CODE #33672

We've been fleet bound for approximately ten days upon completing our excursion to Neverland. Though the planet itself was impressive, Pan's vagabond fleet crew leaves much to be desired. Admittedly, there must be something said for the psychological effects of being marooned and the compounding impact of the Neverland Effect, which froze them in the same physical form for a century. They look like children. And they act the same.

I wonder about the full effects of their trauma.

One would think their thought processes and neuropathic capabilities would remain intact. During our stay on the mysterious planet, I maintained my memories and in turn, learned from the experience. However, these *children* act just like that. They have no responsibility or sense of pride in their decorum that I have yet to find. It's almost as if they didn't *want* to

1

grow up. I wonder what will happen when they return to the Fleet. Will they rejoin the ranks? I have yet to determine any other marketable skills they have to offer society. I doubt they will have much of a choice. But for now, I tire of their games.

There are more serious matters to consider.

The ship flies heavy. Like tired flesh wrapped around a dissolving skeleton. Though it was crowned the height of technology in Hooke's time, it is dated—an antique. It didn't take long to recognize the *Roger's* deficiencies. And while a viable vessel is obviously better than a downed bird; in this case, I wonder how much.

Compounding on top of minor glitches and partial functionality within the ship, we've run into larger issues. The HyperShot technology that enabled our expedited arrival to Neverland is out of the question. It is nonexistent. The capability lies deep inside the abandoned *Fiducia*. Our return voyage will be laborious—if we last that long.

The ship creaks. She groans as she flexes long forgotten muscles. Thus far, she has maintained her integrity, but compared to the way the *Fiducia* sliced silently through the air, the rattling bones of the *Roger* unsettles even the steadiest of heart. Paired with the dark whispers that howl angry secrets through her rusted grates, it's enough to make a man release the airlock just to give the insides a good sweep.

~~I wonder how long it would take to clear out the entire crew.~~

Excuse me. I've been feeling unwell. Not quite myself.

Not surprising considering the general fatigue that has settled over the crew. There's not one soul on board that wouldn't benefit from a solid week's sleep. Except the captain. She looks as though she could use two or three.

Even through her evident exhaustion, she is a wonder to behold. There's not been a day where she fails to inspire. Her dedication to the crew—even its newest additions—is unwavering. She is as determined in her mission as ever, though I worry her attention is pulled to the past.

To *him*.

But he is not here. He cannot support her the way that I can. The mechanic, Pan may have held the upper hand on his infinite planet, but here, I have the advantage. Here, ~~I am in control.~~

[Recording interrupted — Entry <<897/23://>> Not logged]

RETURN FROM NEVERLAND

1

THE JOLLY ROGER

CAPTAIN WENDY DARLING

"Dawes, report. Have there been any changes to our current course?"

Captain Wendy Darling hovered over the helm of the *Jolly Roger's* dated command system. It had taken a few days to acclimate to the ancient vessel's crowded panel of blinking lights, but now she could navigate her way through the StarBoard's multitude of switches without eliciting a string of creative language. She didn't normally swear, however, she also wasn't normally the captain of a centuries-old ship that had been reconstructed from salvaged parts and sheer will. Her pilot, Arielle Dawes, commended her on the accomplishment greatly.

"Not since the last time you asked, Captain," Dawes answered, fixing Wendy with a teasing grin. "But that was only five minutes ago. Maybe if you ask me again, something new and exciting will happen." Dawes' playful wink fell flat against Wendy's frown. Reading the hard lines on Wendy's face, the pilot cleared her throat and nodded at Wendy's charts. She flipped her braid and continued in a more serious tone, "I imagine it will probably be the same, unless you are going to change it up on me."

"No," Wendy sighed, looking at the mess. The scattered charts hovered across the StarBoard adding to the cluttered grid. "No changes yet. We need to await instructions from the Fleet before we consider altering course. Which, by the way—"

"No updates there either, Captain," Dawes anticipated Wendy's question with a delicate laugh. "Not since you asked *six* minutes ago."

Wendy released an impatient huff and stalked across the room. She knew Dawes' teasing was meant to ease her stress, but it only exacerbated her already keyed nerves. She tread across the room until she realized her pacing and forced herself to a stop in front of the ornate mirror, a relic of Hooke's former residency. Her nose turned as she took in the petite girl dressed in a captain's suit. Her hazel green eyes narrowed in an accusatory glance as they traveled from her disheveled hair to her worn-in uniform, ending her gaze at the sleek brace encasing her right knee. Breathing a soft sigh, she swept her hands over her chestnut bun to tame the stray curls that had escaped. She was pretty enough, she supposed, with delicate features that neatly fit her heart shaped face, but being pretty had never been her priority—being captain had. And now, she felt more like an imposter than anything.

Chasing the thought with a groan, Wendy whirled from the mirror and tugged anxiously on her jacket to channel her nervous energy. She didn't like to fidget, but Dawes had already pointed out the path that her nervous pacing had worn in Hooke's plush carpeting. Wendy frowned at the stamped treading and glanced around the captain's quarters. Though the room was decorated entirely too lavishly for her taste, she had already spent the better part of the last two weeks streamlining the space to make it a better suited Navigations center. It was still rather pretentious, but now at least, more efficient than elaborate.

"Really Captain, everything is fine," Dawes assured her. "The skies are clear and it's been smooth sailing. You've got this handled—even with a half-cocked pilot." She tapped the obnoxious bandage on her head. Wendy couldn't help but laugh.

"You know, those aren't standard uniform protocol," Wendy nodded at the bright yellow fish splashed across the oversized bandage. Not that it mattered. Even with the ridiculous accessory Dawes was still stunning. Wendy wondered how she made it look so effortless.

Dawes laughed. "It'll be gone before we meet the Admiral. Besides, it's this or a serious bride of Frankenstein vibe, and I for one, prefer Flounder."

Wendy's stern disapproval twisted to a wry grin. She had missed Dawes and her easygoing attitude. Although it was hard to tell now, a few weeks ago the pilot was in pretty bad shape. She had been bedridden for the majority of the Neverland mission after sustaining severe injuries in the crash that had trapped them on the ageless planet. If it hadn't been for the expertise of their medic, Marisa DeLaCruz, Dawes might not have made it, let alone be in commission. Now, only the brightly colored bandages plastered on Dawes' forehead betrayed her injuries.

Wendy was glad to have her friend back.

"Are you ready to hail the Fleet?"

"Hmm?" Dawes' question interrupted Wendy's quiet musing, pulling her to the present. Her eyes rounded as she registered Dawes' words. "Yes." She asserted. "Thank you for the reminder."

Dawes nodded and muted her music, silencing the bright reggae track as Wendy initiated her comm. It hummed as the transmission spooled, giving her a chance to exhale a shaky breath as she considered her newest message. Since the start of their homeward voyage, she sent communications on the same day and time each week. It was nothing more than a short hailing message that Michaels rigged to play on loop until the recording expired and faded into the depths of space. The hope was that the message would ping a station within the TerraGalactic Union and be redirected to the Fleet, so they would no longer be classified as lost in space.

This was the fourth message Wendy had sent, and they had yet to receive any indication that they had been heard. In her head, she knew it would take time to reach Union satellites, but in her heart, she worried that time wasn't on their side.

"Gonna say anything new today?" Dawes asked with interest.

Wendy shook her head. "Same as always," she sighed. "Maybe one day they'll get so tired of hearing the same message over and over, they'll actually respond."

Dawes snickered. "Well in that case, maybe loop in a recording of Johns singing in the shower," she grinned. "That would speed things up."

Wendy laughed knowingly, remembering the original voyage to

Neverland. The walls between the cabins and the facilities in the *Fiducia* hadn't proved strong enough to keep out Johns' emphatic falsetto. "That or it will make them think we've enacted some sort of satellite scrambling tech," she snarked.

Dawes snorted and shrugged. "Or that."

Wendy's laugh morphed into a heavy exhale as the levity of the moment dissipated, leaving her to face the reality of what would happen if their transmissions were never received.

"They'll find us," Dawes assured, intuiting Wendy's fears. Wendy's lips curled in an unconvinced smile, but the pilot's words were the encouragement she needed. Squaring her shoulders, she cleared her throat and leaned into the comm, speaking slow and steady as she repeated her memorized message.

Hailing the Londonierre Brigade. Hailing the Londonnierre Brigade. If intercepted, please direct this transmission to Admiral Renee Toussant of the Londonniere Brigade. This is Captain Wendy Darling of the Fede Fiducia, *status: homeward bound.*

We were sent on a rescue mission to recover the Expeditionary Vessel the Jolly Roger, *presumed lost in the Neverland Sector. En route, we experienced interstellar turbulence and our ship pulled into the planet's atmosphere. While grounded, we discovered the fractured remains of the* Roger *and Captain James Hooke's crew. We were able to recover some of the* Roger's *original crew, but Hooke's betrayal resulted in the loss of many fleetmen. Using our available resources, we got the* Roger *spaceborne, however, the viability of flight is uncertain.*

We have charted a course home, based on the Roger's *capabilities. Our estimate places us at ten months without Fleet assistance. I am unsure we will last that long.*

Our hopes remain, but we need help. This message is an official mayday requesting assistance from the TerraGalactic Union. Immediate transmission requested to the Jolly Roger, *communication code xv1543f7-9, hailing the Londonierre Brigade. This is Captain Wendy Darling, signing off.*

Wendy ended the comm and sat in silence, imagining the transmission dispersing into the depths of space. She glanced at the charts before her, feeling the weight in her stomach sink further. Harried, anxious thoughts crashed through her mind, all working as a single unit to strangle her hope.

From the corner of her eye, she saw Dawes' intent stare and she stretched her forehead to unknot the look of concern tangling her features. "Let's see if they respond this time," she offered, forcing a smile.

Dawes nodded slowly, cased in a rare look of sobriety. They sat quietly for a moment before the pilot brightened. "And if not, we get Michaels to bug the showers."

A begrudging laugh escaped Wendy's chest. "Deal," she agreed. "But not a word to Johns, or I'll never hear the end of it. He's already convinced he could be an international pop star—let's not make his ambitions intergalactic."

Dawes grinned, then glanced at the blinking transmission light. "That's one message down, Captain."

Wendy's heart clenched as she met Dawes' meaningful gaze. After Michaels had ensured he could loop the outgoing transmissions, she had instituted a strict rule to hail the Fleet sparingly to conserve energy on the *Roger.* While the outgoing messages utilized little in the ratioed outputs, she was determined to preserve as much energy as she could.

With one exception.

Each week, after hailing the Brigade, she recorded an additional transmission that only Michaels and Dawes knew about—a message that returned to Neverland. Each one containing a promise that she would return.

Wendy glanced shyly at Dawes, whose lips twisted in a knowing smile.

"I'm going to go take a walk," Dawes stood and stretched. "Page me if you need anything." She saluted, then turned to leave, her braid swishing after her like a mermaid's tail.

Wendy waited until the doors whizzed shut, then gazed at the comm, her mind feeling strangely blank. It was a sensation she felt only before her Neverland transmissions. There were a million things she wanted to share, yet none of them seemed important enough except what she really had to say.

I love you.

She nibbled the inside of her lip as she gathered her scattered thoughts, then slowly activated the comm. Her breath shook as she spoke into the receiver, but she soldiered on, her heart's unsteady cadence spurring her onward.

"This is Captain Darling of the *Fede Fiducia*—but if you're listening, Peter, it's just me, Wendy. It always feels so strange to begin these transmissions. Formal seems more appropriate, but then—these are intended solely for you, so… formal also seems strange. I never thought I'd experience a time where formality would be in question. It's been my home for so long that…well, formal is comfortable. Except with you."

Wendy cleared the lump in her throat with a nervous laugh. "But, that's a discussion for another day. Our return is proceeding well, at least, as well as can be expected. The modifications to the *Roger* are holding, considering her age. If it weren't for the care you put into her prior, I doubt we'd have even made it this far. But she misses you. And so do the Boys. They're adjusting to the crew, some better than others. Their spirits have remained intact, but they'll all be happy to land home. And as soon as we do, I'm coming back for you."

A guilty twinge pulled her chest as she spoke those words. She wanted to assure Peter that she was on her way, but her conscience couldn't promise it. She would do her best—it was all she could do.

"It's strange to think we aren't just stretching in distance, but in time. When I return, you will be exactly the same as I remember—to the day—I worry what you will think of me."

Her voice broke and she dipped her head as she collected her breath and chased the traitorous thoughts threatening the edges of her sanity. She forced a smile to brighten her voice, determined to reassure the last Lost Boy.

"I will return. After your men are home safe, I will come for you. Be ready for me."

Wendy pressed her thumb against the button, ending the comm. She dropped her gaze to the blue mission file and slowly flipped it to a half empty page with a few simple lines of text. In the top right corner, a small photo was glued crookedly to the page. From the frame, a handsome young man in a mechanic's suit flashed a challenging smirk under a crop of dusty red hair. Wendy brushed her fingertips over his smile, remembering the warmth of his lips pressed against hers.

"I miss you," she whispered, then glanced at the StarBoard's charted course. They had only been traveling four weeks, and already they were a million miles away. Wendy sighed and cast her message, releasing it after the others, wondering if Peter received them.

She hoped he did.

2

The transmission finished spooling, and a low whine groaned through the *Roger* followed by a tired shudder, sending her teetering. The sudden turbulence jerked her from her brooding and set her storming across the room to the illuminated StarBoard.

Wendy shoved the mountain of yellowed charts to the side, revealing a grid of angry flashing lights proclaiming the *Roger's* distress. Wendy attacked the board, adjusting the dials she had familiarized herself with while praying the ones she hadn't learned were nonessential. Beside her, Dawes struggled to man the helm as the lock engaged, denying her control. Wendy reached for her comm to interface Michaels, when the ship released another tired moan and the jarring stopped, leaving the StarBoard blinking innocently under Wendy and Dawes' incredulous stares.

Wendy slumped over the massive panel and let out a relieved sigh while

Dawes slowly eased from the grid with a nervous laugh. They sat in stunned silence until a series of loud pops crackled through the room and everything dimmed as the captain's lamp flickered and burst. Wendy's heart ricocheted, shooting a painful surge of adrenaline through her system as she let out a flurry of Johns-sanctioned curses.

"Ditto to that, Captain," Dawes chuckled as the color slowly returned to her own drained cheeks. "Although I must say, that's one of the more *creative* uses of expeditionary terminology I've heard. I particularly enjoyed your use of 'jansky' as a verb."

Wendy scowled. "Yes, well. It's one of the more creative times I've used it as well, Dawes. Thank you for noticing."

Dawes grinned. "Anytime, Captain." She settled into her chair and began readjusting her controls. Wendy cast a final, wary glance at the flashing indicators flickering across the grid before deeming it stable. She bent forward to scoop up the charts strewn across the floor and her weight shifted, shooting a sharp pain through her right knee before her leg buckled and she dropped to the floor. The soft burn pulsed through her leg, and she knelt, waiting for the spasming pain to subside. With a grimace, she braced the ligaments, then reached slowly to retrieve the scattered charts.

Gingerly, she returned the charts to the illuminated StarBoard. Although she tried her best to hide it, she had sustained injuries of her own on Neverland. Their battle with the Shadow hadn't left much unscathed, and Wendy's reconstructed knee was proof. It could have been worse, Wendy knew. With DeLaCruz' help, her leg had healed, but still, she was recovering, and with the *Roger's* dated medTech, she would be for a very long time. The limp in her gait was a constant reminder, and Dawes' sympathetic stares didn't help. Aware of the pilot's attention, Wendy straightened her posture, gritting her teeth as her knee strained and cracked in protest.

Noticing her discomfort, Dawes focused intently on the grid, allowing Wendy to settle into her seat before hesitantly breaking the quiet.

"Have you been to physio today?" Dawes forced her attention forward as she asked, but her posturing didn't fool Wendy. Her voice was too bright, the way it always was when Dawes tried—and failed—to be nonchalant.

"No, Dawes," Wendy grumbled, "I've been busy trying to make sure our rig doesn't drop from the sky. Then we'd have a lot bigger problems than a sore leg."

Dawes bit her lip. "I think we've passed the worst of the turbulence. I can handle things here for an hour if you'd like to stretch it out."

"I'm fine, Dawes. Although the next time I require mothering, I'll be sure to ask," Wendy clipped. Dawes' brows knotted in a tight bow and Wendy winced as she realized how callous she sounded. It wasn't the pilot's fault she was broken. And to be honest, Dawes was showing more concern than Wendy's mother ever would. Mrs. Darling's only worry would be the extent of her scarring.

Absently, Wendy leaned forward to massage her aching knee, gingerly prodding the swelling padding the bones. Ridges and divots of newly formed scar tissue dotted the joint, remainders of the incisions DeLaCruz had made to reset her leg. They ran tracks along the side and up into the base of her thigh. Wendy was grateful her uniform masked the worst of it.

Wendy puffed her cheeks. "I'm sorry, Dawes. That wasn't fair. It's just—"

Wendy searched for the proper words. How could she explain? A captain's weakness should never be translated to a subordinate—no matter how kind they may be.

"It's alright, Captain, I get it." Dawes waved Wendy's apology away. "Just let me know when you need a break." She grinned and the movement crinkled her bandage, making the tiny patterned fish swim over her brow. "I'll do the same," she winked.

Wendy laughed. "I appreciate that." She leaned forward to study the charts she retrieved from the floor and frowned. There were so many maps. She had already decoded the ones she needed to find their way home, but several others had caught her eye. Complex, intertwining charts depicting galaxies and plotted coordinates for planets she'd never even seen. All the places that Hooke had been, but had never told the Fleet.

There was so much to learn.

Her eyes traveled over the top chart. It was the one she kept coming back to. On the left side of the chart, a constellation hovered with two married stars nestled in the center. One, a bright white spot resting protectively beside its brilliant green counterpart.

The Second Star.

She bit her lip as she leaned closer, following the chart. Outside the radius of the Second Star, a cluster of small purple wisps had been scribbled in and notated with a pen-scratched question mark. Wendy brushed her finger over the violet lines, chasing the traces of a memory as the crease in her forehead deepened.

"Dawes, can you—"

Her question was interrupted as the doors whooshed open and SMEE rushed through in a tizzy. If it had been anyone beside the cybernetic first mate, Wendy would have described him as disheveled. An artificial flush crept to his cheeks, simulating exertion. He must have been in a hurry to get here. SMEE stuttered to a stop, then glanced around the room, his golden eyes blinking as he searched for her.

"Apologies, Captain. I thought it might be prudent to provide an update on the status of our resources. Currently, we have ample supplies to make the projected return to Earth," he paused as his manufactured features twisted into a scowl. "However, if Lieutenant Johns maintains his current consumption rate of our hydrogenated biscuits, there will not be sufficient amounts to complete the journey. I do know how much you enjoy them. Shall I say something?"

An exasperated smile crept to Wendy's lips. She couldn't help being endeared to the atypical synth. Though many in her crew questioned her decision to allow him freely on board, SMEE was the only one of Hooke's pirates who had been kind to her. It wasn't the manufactured mate's fault he had been designated to a traitor.

"No, SMEE, it's alright." Wendy cast a sideways smirk at Dawes, who covered her giggle with a slender hand. "As long as I have coffee, I can do without a biscuit or two. But for rationing purposes, I'll make sure to speak to Johns. Is there anything else?"

SMEE cleared his throat as he smoothed his uniform. "No, Captain. Nothing pressing. Is there anything I can assist you with while I am here?"

"That will be all for now. Thank you," Wendy said. SMEE's head dipped in a clumsy bow before he scurried out, humming a jaunty tune. The door shut behind the synth's uniformed figure and Dawes let out an amused laugh.

"Pan better watch out, the bot's gunning for his girl."

Ignoring the squeeze in her chest, Wendy offered a weak laugh. "SMEE is sweet, but I don't think it would work," she shrugged good-naturedly. "We're just not compatible."

Dawes laughed again, then stood and stretched. "True. I guess the mechanic should be thankful he's not a real boy, or he might have some competition." She followed the path Wendy's pacing had tread to the door. "I'll be back in ten. You need anything?"

Wendy responded with a quick shake of her head, but her attention was drawn inward. Although SMEE wasn't 'a real boy' as Dawes had pointed out, there *had been* some competition for Peter, and while her mechanic had been left on Neverland, his opposition, Aidan Boyce, was very much on board. Wendy hadn't told anyone about the kiss she had shared with the arrogant Commander—and she didn't plan to—but it didn't stop the guilt that gnawed at her whenever she thought about Boyce's lips pressed against hers.

The door hummed as Dawes departed and Wendy sagged into her chair while her fingers massaged the dull pain throbbing in her temples. She closed her eyes and was met with Boyce's sapphire gaze searching her face, his chest heaving ever so slightly as he gently brushed the smooth skin of her cheek.

A loud hiss startled Wendy from the memory and she twisted toward the door, thankful for the reprieve until she found herself staring directly at the real Commander Boyce—not a conjured memory. He strode across the room purposefully, his dark uniform pressed neatly into place, adhering perfectly to Brigade standards. The banding on his sleek, black jacket offset the blue in his eyes, highlighting them even more starkly against his pale skin. Or, it might have been the unusual flush to his cheeks.

Boyce stopped in front of Wendy and handed her a small, hexagonal tablet. Wendy accepted the tech, careful to avoid grazing her fingers against his.

"Here is the Recording Log as you requested, Captain. I attempted to document my weekly correspondence, but the file is corrupted." Boyce eyed the machine peevishly. "Perhaps Michaels should run a systems check. Once the error is adjusted, I'm happy to complete my report."

Wendy accepted the pad and studied the formal officer. Fine lines traced the edges of his eyes, lines that hadn't been there when the expedition first began. Her gaze traced the hollows of his cheeks, which had grown more pronounced over the past weeks. The added definition didn't detract from the commander's chiseled features, but it was clear he was settling into his age. Away from Neverland's mysterious atmosphere, time had resumed, its brief absence enough to make her acutely aware of her mortality. Each morning she woke feeling its claws wringing out another day of her life, strangling her as it ripped the essence from her soul.

She wondered if he felt it, too.

Boyce cleared his throat, alerting Wendy to her stare. Flushing, she briskly tucked the tablet under her arm. "Thank you, Commander. I'll look into it. Was there anything in your brief that I should note?"

He scowled. "Nothing pressing, unless you've finally decided to allow me to evac Pan's heathens."

Wendy sighed, but a wry smile crept to her lips. The Lost Boys had been a challenge, but for nobody more than Boyce. They seemed to take his proclivity for protocol as a personal challenge, and Wendy had heard of more than one occasion where elaborate pranks were involved. Most of her intel came from Johns, who delivered each story with impish glee. It made her wonder if perhaps the commander wasn't involved in the matter himself.

"What's happened now?"

Boyce's glower darkened with a huff. "What *hasn't* happened is a more appropriate question. They're like children—noisy, smelly, always underfoot," his nose wrinkled with disdain. "We'd have been better off rescuing a rogue horde of space monkeys."

Wendy snorted. "You'll make an excellent father one day, Boyce, I'm sure your future bride will be—" Wendy swallowed her last words, but the shocked look on Boyce's face told her it was too late to recover. She tugged the neck of her coat, which was suddenly too tight against her skin. She coughed to clear her throat, then straightened her shoulders, feigning her composure.

"I'll speak to the boys," she assured, burying her emotions under a wall of professionalism. "But let's not be too hard on them. They were separated from society for a very long time. The evacuation hatch is probably a bit extreme for now."

Her attempted smile fell flat on Boyce's stoic stance. He watched her carefully, his jaw tight before he gave her a stiff nod. "Thank you, Captain. If you have nothing further, I have other things to tend to," he said, a glimmer of hope flashing in his eyes.

Wendy met his gaze. Up close, the lines tracing his forehead were even more pronounced, and accompanied by puffy bags under his eyes. She wondered how the commander had been sleeping. Her lips pressed in a tight line as she shook her head. "If there's nothing urgent, take a break. You look like you could use some rest."

The crease in Boyce's forehead deepened, but he nodded. "Yes Captain," he conceded before quickly turning to go. Wendy's gut twisted, and before she could stop herself, she placed her arm on his, stalling him near the door.

"Boyce, I—" she started, but her words were cut off by the hum of the door. She jumped back, biting the yelp that sprang to her lips as Dawes sauntered in, nibbling a dehydrated fruit bar. She nodded at Boyce, then passed a puzzled look to Wendy, who stood guiltily, her hands clasped tightly behind her back. Noticing her stare, Wendy tugged her jacket in place before loudly addressing the commander.

"That will be all, Boyce" she announced, feeling the strain of her unnatural pitch against her vocal cords. She swallowed to stamp away its shrill. "I'll make sure Michaels inspects the Recording Log. Until then, a manual entry will suffice." She returned her attention to the abandoned charts while Dawes settled in behind the grid. Her pulse thrummed as she listened for Boyce's movement. He stood, silently lingering before his quiet footsteps moved to the door. Wendy strained her ears for the familiar hum of the sliding door. When nothing came, she glanced at the entry, where Boyce stood stiff at attention.

"Commander?"

Boyce wet his lips, then sliced his hand through his hair, disheveling its meticulous styling. His gaze darted to where Dawes studied the grid before resting carefully back on Wendy. A quicksilver shadow flashed through his sapphire stare.

"It's nothing," he recanted, and stalked stormily from her quarters.

Wendy watched as he left, her brow furrowing as the door whirred shut behind him, and his footsteps faded behind the heavy panels. She released a heavy sigh. His kiss had brought a whole new dynamic to their relationship—including her response to his presence.

She dropped into her chair, kneading her burgeoning headache.

"Everything ok?" Dawes' head tipped in a curious stare.

"Yes, Dawes," Wendy swept her hand over her hair to busy her nervous fingers. "But my knee actually is feeling a little stiff. I think I will try some physio. Are you alright here?"

"Of course, Captain."

"Excellent," Wendy clipped. She averted her gaze as she tucked the Recording Log under her arms, hoping a detour to the maintenance bay would free her from Dawes' perceptive gaze. Maybe Michaels could fix it sooner rather than later. Under her feet, the *Roger* let out a low grumble before falling back into its silent course. Wendy glanced nervously at the StarBoard, but its blinking green lights betrayed no concern.

"I'll be back shortly," Wendy nodded, unsure if the nervous twisting in her stomach was caused by the barge or Boyce. "Keep her in the sky."

3

Wendy rushed through the corridor, grateful for the solitude. Her quick movements released her keyed energy, but still, she felt unsettled. Unused adrenaline tingled through her nerves, and she found herself looking forward to physio. One of the things she hated most about her injury was how it had affected her attitude toward the gym. She had always been active, and her efforts had produced a strong, athletic body. Now, her movements were slow and stiff, and infected her training with unwanted weakness.

She hurried through the corridors to the *Roger's* renovated medTech. Though the facility was dated, with Johns' help, DeLaCruz had upcycled the space into a makeshift facility complete with bay rooms and a small physio deck where the crew could train.

Wendy activated the doors and looked approvingly at the humble deck. It wasn't the state-of-the-art facility installed in the Fiducia, but it was functional. A telemagnetic weight set sat in the corner next to the anti-gravity resistance trainer and stretching pads, leaving enough room for a small sparring mat in the center and a sleek physiokinesis machine up front.

In the back corner, Johns' feet pounded a steady cadence on the synTrack. His shirt was discarded on the floor and he ran at full-speed, humming off-key to a popular technogrunge song. Unaware of his audience, he belted a shrill resolving chord, then decrescendoed back into a silent, steady pace.

Wendy snickered. She was glad to see the equipment was working. The synTrack had to be manually extracted from the floor of the *Fiducia*, and then installed into the *Roger*. It was only through Johns' sheer determination—and of course, Michaels' tech-savvy—that the device was operational. They had even managed to arrange its simscreen for simulated terrain expeditions.

Red, craggy mountains covered the screen, emulating a high-altitude trekking excursion while the lower corner displayed Johns' vitals as they streamed from his scanband, proclaiming peak performance. As Wendy crossed the room, she could see why. Beads of sweat streamed down the lieutenant-commander's face onto his broad shoulders before trickling down his torso. His dark hair was just as damp, and it clung to his forehead while his cheeks flushed with exertion. Finally, the simscreen beeped, and he swept the loose strands from his eyes with the back of his hand as the synTrack slowed, indicating his training session was complete.

"You know, Johns, they make these things called shirts," Wendy teased when the deafening roar of Johns' pace slowed to a soft thud. "You should look into them."

Johns turned to Wendy and grinned. "I did once," his expression twisted in a faux grimace. "Not for me."

"Of course not," Wendy snorted a laugh. "You know if anyone complains, I'll have to enforce a dress code."

Johns flexed, emphasizing the cut of his chest. "Who would complain?" he scoffed, then struck an exaggerated pose. "DeLaCruz never does."

"I'm sure she doesn't," Wendy deadpanned before tossing a towel in his face. "Just don't sweat all over the machines. I don't want them to rust."

Johns laughed. "I'm not sure that's quite how it works, Darling, but I'll try and keep my sexy man-drips to myself."

A laugh bubbled from Wendy's throat before she pushed past Johns to claim the physiokinesis machine. She strapped her leg in, then tapped the keypad to summon the electric sensor pads. The machine hummed, then beeped as it dispensed the pads for Wendy to retrieve from the capsule. The compartment clicked open and she withdrew two tiny liquid alloy pads. Wendy pressed them to her medial and lateral ligaments, then shivered as the alloy slithered to conform to the shape of her knee, slicking over her joint like a second skin. Sensors in place, Wendy keyed in the stretches DeLaCruz programmed for her and leaned into the chair as the machine thrummed to complete its regiment.

Under the pressure of the machine, her knee contracted and relaxed, pulling her leg taut against the bands. Wendy gritted her teeth as she watched her weakened muscles work and saw that even with the added assistance, her leg wouldn't fully straighten. She frowned as she studied the gap between the back of her knee and the chair, while her other leg easily rested flush against the padding. Such a small space, and yet, without the sensors' forced pressure, her right leg just wouldn't match its partner. Wendy clasped the side of her leg to massage the muscle as the now-solidified pads pulsed tiny electric pulses through her repairing muscles.

"Still bugging you?" Johns asked.

Wendy peeked through her grimace to meet Johns' worried gaze, and her prepared lie disappeared in a frustrated sigh.

"Yeah," she nodded before dropping back into the chair.

Johns clapped his hand on her shoulder. "You had a serious injury, Darling. It's gonna take time to heal." He motioned around the sparsely equipped cabin. "Especially with our tech at half-capacity. Don't beat yourself up. 'Rissa says you're making great progress."

"Really?"

Johns tapped his chin thoughtfully. "That, or something about the worst patient she's ever had," he shrugged before bumping her shoulder with his. "Seems someone doesn't listen very well and keeps trying to overexert herself when she's supposed to take it easy."

Wendy's laugh was cut short by a sharp tug from the machine's extender. It shot a searing spasm through her knee, followed by a therapeutic pulse from the receptor sensors. Seeing her wince, Johns gripped her shoulder. A wave of impatience surged through her, and she screwed her lips into a scowl.

"I can't, Johns. The *Roger* deserves a fully functional Captain, not an invalid."

Johns sighed. "A limp does *not* make you an invalid. It just means you move a little slower than normal."

"And what happens when I can't afford to move slowly? What if my injury puts you in danger?"

Johns cast an exaggerated glance around the room. "What kind of situation are we talking about," he asked incredulously. "A rogue weight set? Maybe an overzealous sim?" He chuckled at Wendy's deepening scowl. "Because I'm pretty sure I can handle it."

"That's not what I mean and you know it," Wendy grumbled through a begrudging grin. "But if the weights take you down, I don't want to hear a single word."

Johns laughed. "Duly noted. I'll save my whining for DeLaCruz," he grinned. "You wouldn't kiss my boo boos anyway," he teased.

"I absolutely would not."

"And *that's* why you'll never get a date. No sympathy."

"Of course." Wendy scoffed, "Being an entire galaxy away from any potential suitors couldn't have *anything* to do with it."

Johns' lips pursed in consideration. "Nope," he chirped. "Just the sympathy thing."

Wendy shook her head in mock exasperation, then growled as the extender twinged her knee. "Just be ready to step in and take my place when this stupid knee inevitably gets me killed," she grumbled.

Johns snorted. "I tell you what," he bargained, "if somehow you manage to get bested by a teeny-tiny joint, I'll take over, no questions asked," he promised. "But somehow I doubt you'll let that happen." He flicked the large scarred divot in her knee, then danced out of the way as Wendy reached to slug him. Johns let out a mirthful laugh before his expression sobered and he met her with a serious gaze. "But seriously, Darling. You're tougher than this thing. You'll beat it, it just might take some time."

He squeezed her shoulder reassuringly, then draped his towel over his shoulder and stretched. His muscles rippled as he peacocked a dramatic flex.

"Now, if you'll excuse me, there is a medic dying to tend to my boo-boos." He winked.

Wendy laughed and shook her head. "Just make sure you put a shirt on, first," she teased. "The last time SMEE saw your chest, he wrote a three-page report detailing his concerns about your condition."

"No condition except swole-itis," Johns proclaimed with another exaggerated flex.

"Whatever. Just don't stress out the cybernet!" she called after the retreating lieutenant-commander with a final laugh before returning her attention to the pulses thrumming through her leg. She pressed her hands over the joint to force her knee flat, then jumped at Johns' boisterous call.

"That's cheating, Darling."

Wendy's cheeks flamed as she snaked her hands back, guilty. "I thought you were leaving," she accused. Her only response was Johns' laughter as he disappeared behind the closing bay doors.

Alone with the machine, Wendy sighed and leaned against the chair, letting her mind wander as the rehab machine finished its program. Finally, it released a low beep, signaling the end of the session. The sensors released and slithered off her knee, reverting to their liquid-metal state. Wendy deposited them in the compartment and the machine hummed as it sent them to the processor for sterilization.

With a groan, she stood and stretched, ignoring the loud pop that erupted from her knee as she glanced around the room. She was about to begin a quick expedition on the synTrack, when a loud crash echoed from the corridor outside. Worried, Wendy grabbed her coat and hurriedly shrugged into it as she rushed from the physio deck. A shout sounded down the hall, and Wendy picked up her pace, recognizing Boyce's frustrated growl. She rushed through the hallway, appreciating the cool breeze from the *Roger's* regulated circulation as she left the stuffy physio room behind her. Her footsteps pounded against the ship's grated panels, chasing her with metallic echoes until she reached the bend that opened to the Main Bay.

Wendy slowed and was hit by the memory of the large room, empty save for a large, stone dais leaking thick, black fog. A shrill scream rang in her ears, and she shivered to clear the sudden chill that slithered through her body. The memory faded and through the hazy fog, Nibs hurtled toward her, his face split in a gleeful smile as he careened through the bay with a tattered bundle tucked under his shoulder. He saw Wendy, and his grin faltered as he skidded to a stop and shifted the parcel behind his back, guilt etched into his face.

"I sincerely hope that's not heavy artillery, Nibs," Wendy chided. "Our ship's got enough problems without having to worry about exploding."

Nibs dipped his shaggy head and he kicked a heavy-booted foot. "No, Captain," he confessed.

She held out her hand, and the boy dropped the grease-stained bundle into her palm. A small item was wrapped tightly in the dirty cloth, and Wendy picked carefully at the edges to loosen the knotted top. With her coaxing, the corners opened, revealing one of Boyce's brightly shined breast badges. Under the Brigade's intricate insignia, the commander's name was etched in delicate, rounded print. Wendy's face pulled in a stern glare.

"I will not tolerate theft on my ship, Airman," she reprimanded. Nibs' tawny eyes blinked worriedly. His lip quivered, and Wendy softened her stare. "Even if the lieutenant-commander finds it highly entertaining," she added. A mischievous smirk crept over Nibs' face, and Wendy made a mental note to talk to Johns about his influence on the Boys. She pocketed the badge and arranged her features in a hard-nosed stare before handing Nibs the greasy rag. "I intend to not have to speak to you about this again."

"Yes, Captain." Nibs raised his hand in a stiff salute, trailing the stained handkerchief down the side of his face.

"Very well," Wendy nodded, suppressing her smile. "You are dismissed. If you see Commander Boyce before I do, you can inform him his badge is with me."

Nibs paled, but nodded before turning to bound down the opposite corridor. Wendy shook her head as she watched him go, unsure if she was more amused or exasperated by the Boys' favorite game of teasing the stoic commander. She sighed and continued her trek through the *Roger* and rounded the bend to the kitchen. The shrill clang of pots and pans rang through the door's heavy paneling, and Wendy peeked inside to investigate the noise.

Inside, the kitchen was a mess. Pots and pans scattered across the narrow counters, and smoke billowed from a large pot simmering on the heating vector near the sink. The Twins rushed about happily, calling jokes back at one another as they zoomed around the room.

"Afternoon Captain," one Twin called as he raced past Wendy to the pantry. He whizzed past so quickly, the heat from the pan he carried zipped past her face.

"Or is it?" the other Twin countered as he stirred the smoky pot. "Do you really ever know in space?"

"Are we really in space at all," his brother challenged. He raced from the pantry, freshly equipped with a small shaker that he sprinkled over the contents of his pan. "Or has our disruption in the space-time continuum caused a ripple from which we might never know the effects?"

Both boys froze in their steps as they looked at each other, considering the implications of the suggestion before they split into synchronized grins.

"Nah, we're probably ok," the first Twin announced, then resumed his stirring. "What do you think Captain?" he inquired.

Wendy paused to consider. "Well, the systems suggest that we lost approximately a year in Neverland, but outside of the relatively brief time-lapse, all scans indicate that our stay in the Nebula hasn't generated any damage to the well-being of the universe."

"That you *know*," the second Twin chimed, setting his pan on the oversized island as he ripped open a bag of cryogenically-sealed potatoes.

"That I hope," Wendy agreed. She breathed in the savory scents wafting from the heat-vector. "Dinner smells good," she said. "What have you guys magicked tonight?"

"Jerky stew with dehydrated biscuits and freeze-dried mashed potatoes," Twin One announced over his peeling potatoes.

"It smells better than it sounds," his brother promised.

Wendy laughed. "That it does." She peeked at the open pantry, thinking of Michaels. Even with the temptation of food, she doubted she'd be able to coax him from the maintenance bay. "Do you guys have anything I could take to-go?" she asked, looking curiously at the assortment of liquid-filled containers. "Preferably something that won't leak and destroy my ship."

"Sure," the second Twin said. He disappeared into the pantry, then returned with a flat brown pack. "Hold this over the pawl heater for a few minutes and it'll be good to go."

Wendy accepted the bag and looked at the label claiming the contents contained powdered shrimp tacos. "Thanks," she said as she retreated from the kitchen. Behind her, the Twins' laughter resumed as they continued their easy banter.

Wendy proceeded down the hall on her way to the maintenance bay. She had nearly reached the access chute when the ship's overhead lights flickered and the *Roger* released another anguished groan. The ship rocked and Wendy tumbled as sparks cascaded from the surging lights above her. She covered her head as the shower fizzled and the barge evened its course. She crouched for a moment, awaiting another jolt. When nothing came, she scooped up Michael's packaged dinner and hurried down the hall to discuss with her technician the status of her ship.

4

A loud clang sounded from the belly of the *Roger* as Wendy opened the large metal hatch sealing the access chute from the rest of the ship. She leaned back, recoiling from the wave of heat that swept over her to escape the sealed room. Small tendrils of smoke danced around her face, tickling her with the *Roger's* hot breath. She coughed and brushed away the wisps before steeling herself and descending to the maintenance bay.

Wendy climbed down the chute, her feet slowly testing the rickety metal ladder that creaked with every step as she dipped further into the *Roger*. Burning red coils surrounded her, revealing the ship's internal heating system before the searing lines snaked and disappeared into the walls. The heat was stifling, but as she crawled further into the bay, the temperature began to drop as the *Roger's* cooling mechanisms swathed its integral machinery in a stabilizing blanket of temperate air.

Swiping the last beads of sweat from her forehead, Wendy dropped to the floor as a series of crackling pops erupted from a stationary mechrig and Michaels rushed over with a large wrench. His mousy brown hair dipped over his glasses as he peered at his pale fingers and prodded the complex tech. He rolled back his sleeves, revealing dark streaks of grease staining his skin. Based on the patches of soot dotting his cheeks and neck, Wendy was certain that his uniform's dark hues camouflaged several oily stains of their own. Oblivious to the mess and Wendy's presence, Michaels fixated on his work and coaxing the machine.

"Now listen up," he muttered, more commanding with the tech board than he would be any human, "you need to cut this shyte out or things are going to get hairy down here."

"Define hairy," Wendy said, as she moved to stand beside him.

Michaels glanced over at her with a sheepish shrug. "Oh God, oh God, we're all gonna die?"

Wendy's lips pressed in an unamused grimace. The tech coughed and rubbed his thumbs over his glasses to remove the cloud of fog that had condensed over the lenses. He peered at the rig, examining the parts and listening to the *Roger's* whirring heart. Wendy watched for a moment, but soon found her eyes wandering around the bay. She had only been in the ship's belly once before, when she said goodbye to Peter. Her heart lurched as she scanned the complex machinery and her gaze landed on the dusty Pix.E. The device whirred as it moved, spinning energy to the core of the ship, powering the enormous vessel with its tiny golden sparks.

She gnawed her lip as remembered her conversation with Peter deep inside the ship before he volunteered to stay on Neverland so they could return home. She licked her lips, remembering how Peter's mouth crashed against hers in their final, desperate kiss. A soft flush crept up the back of her neck then flamed to her cheeks as she remembered the way his fingers traced her skin and bunched in her hair. The kiss was reckless and wild, just like Peter, and even if she had stayed on Neverland for a thousand years, she would never have forgotten a single moment of it.

"Captain?" The lieutenant's probing call pulled Wendy from her reverie and back to the groaning maintenance bay. His shrewd gaze made her cheeks flame even hotter, and she was thankful for the burning heat blazing from the engine.

"Yes?" Wendy followed Michaels' buried hands to a gaping shaft revealing a tangled bunch of wires. His brow quirked in a silent question, but his gaze soon returned to the tech.

"The problem is internal," Michaels diagnosed, cool and detached. "The wires are so old, they're disintegrating from the inside. I've been able to patch them so far, but if the deterioration continues, we're going to have a serious problem on our hands."

"How serious?" Wendy asked, trying to calculate the severity of his revelation.

"Can we revisit the '*we're all gonna die*' thing?"

Wendy grimaced. "So that's what's causing all the turbulence. Or do you have more good news for me?"

Michaels smirked and withdrew his hands from the panel, then crossed the room to a large standing computer. His fingers blurred as he entered a series of commands and the *Roger* hummed its response. Electric green coding dashed across the screen, covering the monitor in an alien language. Though Wendy had passed all of her coding classes, she had never quite gotten the hang of it, and she was thankful she had her tech wizard to rely on. She peered at the symbols until the neon print blurred her eyes, and she had to look away to refocus the swimming text. As she did, her gaze landed on a makeshift hammock draping from the bay's beams adorned with a dated space blanket and a lumpy pillow. Beside the cot, a tangle of wires had been strung together to cobble a makeshift bed just big enough for a nanobot. Her breath caught, and she glanced around the room, slowly taking in the footprints Peter had left in his former home. Tears sprang to her eyes, but she brushed them away and refocused on the tech's racing hands. He tapped the keys with authority as he issued a few final commands and the *Roger* spit back her response in encrypted text. Michaels read over it, his glasses glinting in the ship's dim red lights before he turned to Wendy.

"As long as everything holds, we should be fine. The ship's not going to be voted best cruise liner anytime soon, but Fleet-willing, we'll make it home."

"That's all I ask," Wendy coughed away the lingering lump in her throat and forced a smile. Michaels blinked at her behind his glasses and a genuine laugh bubbled from her throat as she brushed a thick black smudge from the tip of his nose. "When was the last time you bathed, Michaels? You look like you've just finished a tour in the Nyxus sector."

He shrugged. "Not more than a day or two. Every time I try and leave, the ship gets jumpy. I think she's lonely."

"You do know you're talking about a machine, right?"

Michaels patted the panel lovingly. "Ships may not breathe like the rest of us, but they've got lives and stories of their own. And this girl? She's been through some things. Don't forget—the Lost Boys weren't the only ones trapped on Neverland."

Wendy looked around the room at all of the personal touches Peter had left, now mingled with the marks of Michaels' residence. The *Roger* thrummed around her, dutifully completing her mission even as her steel insides slowly rotted. Wendy nodded her acceptance, then reached for the meal the Twins had given her.

"Fair enough," she agreed, "but don't forget to come up for air every now and again," she chided, "I don't need you turning into a space-mole."

Michaels took the pack. "Deal." He ripped it open with his teeth, then paused, his brow furrowed as he searched Wendy's troubled gaze. "How are you, Captain?"

"I'm fine, Lieutenant. Now eat. It's my job to worry about you, not the other way around."

Michaels met her with a shrewd look. "Not asking for duty, Captain." He allowed his words to sink in as he probed her stoic stare. "I'm asking for you."

Wendy conjured an unconvincing half-smile. "I'll be better when we hit ground," she admitted. "Ten months is a long time to fly in a broken bird."

"But it's plenty of time for you to get some rest."

A harsh laugh escaped Wendy's throat. "I'll sleep when I'm dead Michaels, which, if we can't keep our girl in the air, might happen a lot sooner than later." She glanced warily around the hull, scanning the tech cocooning the walls.

Michaels patted the mechRig. "She'll make it home, Captain. Don't worry."

Wendy nodded. "If that was coming from anyone else but you, I wouldn't believe it," she admitted, then pointed to the mealpack. "The Twins said you need to heat that up first—I imagine it's not great cold."

Michaels twisted the pouch to examine the label. He scrunched his nose, bumping his glasses against his brow as examined the contents, then shrugged. "You're probably right." He raised it in a mock toast. "Thanks."

"Anytime," Wendy said, She began the steep trek up the access hatch, but paused to fix Michaels with a final stern stare. "Remember, I don't want any mole-people!"

Michaels' soft laughter mixed with the hum of the *Roger's* underbelly, and drew a small smile to her lips. Hoisting herself up the remainder of the ladder, she scurried through the miserable heat between the sweltering coils, then pushed through the hatch to crawl from the maintenance bay. She smashed the door shut behind her, sealing in the heat as she gulped in the climatized air.

Standing in the hall, Wendy smoothed the loose curls clinging to the sweat dotting her temple, then inspected her uniform to ensure it was free of residue from the *Roger's* intestines. When the dark fabric betrayed no stains, Wendy straightened her coat and continued down the hall. She had been gone for quite a while, she should at least check in with Dawes.

She walked through the corridors, listening carefully to the *Roger* as she walked. Outside of the maintenance bay, the ship soared silently through the sky, her stalking gait concealing the massive effort she gave to stay afloat. Wendy had crossed nearly the whole length of the ship when she came upon a small mop of bright blonde curls bent studiously over a torn slip of paper. Under the curls, a slew of charcoaled lines peeked up at Wendy.

"Hey Tootles, what are you looking at?"

Tootles glanced up from the delicate lines he had traced and fixed her with a soft smile. The youthful features of his face were betrayed by the depth of his gaze, something that always startled her when she looked at the young boy. Although *young* was relative. Wendy had to remind herself that even though Tootles looked no more than eleven years old, like all the other Lost Boys, he had decades of life experience on every member of her team. It was unsettling, especially since none of the Boys had aged a day under the Neverland's green glow, but in her short time there, she felt as though she had aged a hundred years.

"S-star charts." Tootles raised the page so she could see the rubbed marks tattooing the page. "S-see?"

Wendy's forehead wrinkled as she attempted to translate the foreign markings. "Impressive. How did you learn that?"

Tootles shrugged. "L-lots of t-time when t-time doesn't w-work." He returned the paper to his lap, his eyes smoldering like charred embers in molten lava. He considered her stoically for a moment before blinking his heavy lashes. "D-do you th-think Peter will be o-ok?"

Wendy gazed at the youngest Lost Boy, unsure what to say. They were only a few weeks gone from the ageless planet, yet time had already begun to leave its mark. Tootles' rounded cheeks had started to lengthen and define, stealing his baby face as time started to reclaim what it had lost.

"I do," she assured, forcing a braver expression than she felt.

"Do you th-think he'll remember m-me?" Tootles' lashes fluttered over the tears welling in his eyes. "I didn't c-care about going h-home, because I knew n-n-nobody there would r-remember us. We left behind the only p-person who ever took care of me."

Wendy's chest constricted, smashing her heart into a million pieces. She knelt to place her hand on Tootles' shoulder and his chin quivered. He dropped his face, but not fast enough to hide the crocodile tear that splashed onto the etching of his star chart.

"Of course he will. We're bringing him back as soon as we can." Wendy promised with a squeeze of his shoulder. "And even if it took a million years, Peter would never forget you." She wondered how it was so easy to reassure Tootles when she failed miserably to do the same with herself.

Tootles sniffled and wiped his tears with the back of his hand. "Y-you really th-think so?"

"Well, I know it would take *me* at least that long, so for Peter, probably even longer." She grinned and brushed a golden curl from his eyes.

Tootles loosed a trembling laugh and glanced back at the chart. Wendy followed his gaze to the tear stain blotting an intricate sketch. Her brow furrowed as she studied the clustered drawings surrounding the blurred image, and she leaned in, noting the familiar pattern.

"Tootles," she asked, pressing her finger to the image. "Is that the Second Star?"

Tootles nodded.

Wendy blinked. "And what are these?" she pointed to the surrounding sketches.

"Not s-sure," Tootles shrugged. "I've n-never been there, I've only ch-charted their moves."

"They aren't stationary?"

Tootles shook his head. "No. They only show up s-sometimes. They f-fade in and out— l-like a pulse."

Wendy hummed, then reached for the page. "Can I borrow this? I'd like to take a closer look at your charting skills. We might be able to use them."

Tootles beamed and handed her the page. "Yeah! I can d-do others too, if you'd like."

"This is enough for now," Wendy said. "But, in the meantime, I do have another job if you'd be interested?"

Tootles' shoulders perked as he nodded eagerly. Wendy leaned closer and glanced over her shoulders before lowering her voice conspiratorially.

"I need your help with the other Boys," she whispered. "I think they're having a hard time without Peter, too. I need someone to take charge and lead by example." She waited as Tootles considered her words. He nibbled on his lower lip, and Wendy gave him an encouraging smile. "If Peter were here, I know he'd pick you."

"I'll do it!" Tootles jumped to his feet and snapped his heels together in an elaborate salute. His chest puffed proudly, and Wendy stifled a charmed giggle.

"At ease, Recruit," she schooled her features into a solemn stare. "The Boys already have their assignments, but we're having some trouble with pranks," she explained. "Perhaps we could help them channel their energy into something more constructive?"

Tootles' curls glinted as he nodded eagerly, then bounded down the hall shouting for Curly. When the last of his shouts dissipated to echoes, Wendy looked back at the star chart. She studied the strange markings, noting the symbols Tootles had etched in the bottom. The jagged, slashing marks looked familiar, but she couldn't place the gnawing sense of familiarity. Nana buzzed on her wrist, and she glanced at the band, realizing she had been away from her post for nearly two hours. Wendy swore and hurried down the narrow halls, planning her apology to Dawes.

She reached her quarters and hurried inside, glancing anxiously around the cabin to ensure everything was safe. Dawes waited inside, calmly manning the helm while mellow beats washed over the cabin. Wendy sighed and shook her head. Her worry had been unwarranted. She stepped inside, and the door whooshed shut behind her, alerting the pilot to her presence.

"Hey, Captain," Dawes' fishtail dripped over her shoulder as she gave Wendy a small salute. "I was wondering where you were. I was about to send out a search party," she grinned at her joke, then returned her attention to the screen.

"All's well," Wendy promised. "Just had a few things to tend to outside of the 'king's quarters.'" she flapped Hooke's heavy crimson drapes. "Seriously, it's like he didn't even want it to look like a ship."

"Captain, is that *disdain* I'm hearing?" Dawes gasped dramatically. "I was sure you and Hooke would be so happy together. Whatever will I do with his file now?" She waved the tattered paperwork teasingly. Wendy stalked across the room to snatch the document from the laughing pilot.

"Watch it Dawes," Wendy threatened, though it was minimized by the laugh in her voice, "or I'll have Boyce man the helm and reassign you to the kitchens."

Dawes giggled. "I'll believe it when I see it," she scoffed. "You know full well I'd be lost in a devastating potato peeling incident—but not until after you had strangled the commander. Besides, you know you'd miss me."

Wendy laughed at Dawes' accuracy. "Boyce's sense of humor does leave something to be desired," she admitted while plopping into her seat. She flipped through the file, recalling the countless hours she spent fantasizing her mission to Neverland. Not one thing had turned out how she imagined. It had been so much better—and so much worse.

A pair of emerald eyes flashed through Wendy's mind as she pictured Peter's mischievous smile and how it melted to desire after their kiss. It made her heart beat unsteadily to think of the way his strong arms cradled her, so gentle in contrast to the crushing need of his mouth against hers. She pressed her hand to her lips, trying to stall the lingering feeling as the warm memory faded into the familiar ache that enveloped her chest whenever she thought of him.

Her eyes clouded and she exhaled a sharp breath, refusing her tears. There was no use in getting emotional. Emotions were not practical. But, even with her feelings out of the equation, Peter's absence was noticeable. It was just another way that she had failed. Her mission had been to retrieve and rescue the *Roger's* crew. Unfortunately, what was supposed to be a simple retrieval became infinitely more complicated when Captain Hooke revealed his loyalty to the Shadow and the dark entity possessed the decorated Captain as it tried to escape. With the *Roger's* crew divided, Wendy had to fight to defeat the defectors and to defend those loyal to the Fleet. With Peter's help, she managed to ward off the Shadow and save the crew. And then, he saved them again.

Now he was the only Lost Boy.

Wendy looked out the ship's visor toward the quickly vanishing Krawk Nebula. Even the bright green cast of the Second Star had long since disappeared from their sight. With a soft sigh, Wendy slowly turned back to her charts. She would make it back, she vowed.

She just hoped Peter wouldn't forget her by then.

5

FIDUCIA II (GROUNDED)

LEAD MECHANIC PETER PAN

"Hurry up, Tinc. I've seen enough Starsets to last a lifetime. There's no reason to stay for another one. Wendy's waiting."

Tinc jangled a snarky reply, eliciting an amused smirk from Peter.

"And to think after all these years, I still haven't managed to reconfigure that potty mouth," he laughed, then covered his head from the shower of angry orange sparks cascading from Tinc's buzzing processor. Flashing the bot a sideways grin, he stretched out his hand. His palm prickled as Tinc hummed and settled on his offered landing pad.

"I think that's everything." Peter stepped back and studied the pod with a shrewd eye. "We've checked the core adapter cable and the last run fixed the glitch in the orbital processor. The *Fiducia II* is ready."

Tinc shot in the air, buzzing happily as she released a torrent of golden sparks. It had taken what Peter guessed had been about a week to build the ship from the parts he'd harvested from the *Fede Fiducia* and the *Roger's* discards, and then a few days to make sure she was fully operational after a dismal test run. It took some serious modifications, but after several sleepless nights and a lot of swearing, he had gotten to a point where he was ninety-five percent sure it wouldn't explode on take-off. He cast his gaze to the soft haze of Neverland's atmosphere and envisioned Wendy's tear-stained face as she waved goodbye.

The odds were good enough. He had to find her.

"Come on. Let's make sure we've got everything." Peter stopped and looked inside the pilot's hatch. Curled behind his seat, in a compact ball of silvery fur, a small creature snored loudly. "Stay, Seven. We'll be right back."

The tiny ball shifted as the Neverfox untucked her triangular snout from where it nestled against her belly. She blinked her black, beady eyes and released a garbled chirp as her bushy tail thumped lazily against the floor.

"Good girl," Peter crooned, then sealed the hatch and turned to Tinc. "Let's go, Tinc. We're almost home free."

Tinc hummed and shot off, leaving a trail of sparks for Peter to chase through the overgrown jungles of the forgotten planet. They hurried through the underbrush, slowing only to skirt past the mermaid's lagoon. They darted past the tranquil water, ignoring the beautiful creatures laughing and splashing in the pool. Peter knew the true danger hidden beneath their lovely smiles and enchanting songs.

"Just a few more hours, and we're out of here. We'll be skyboard, flying free, on our way back ho—," Peter's steps slowed as he stumbled over his words. He had almost said home, but he wasn't sure that was true. Earth was where he was from, but home—that was a powerful word. He didn't know if he would ever have a place he could really call home, but his family—Tootles and the other Boys—they could be. He nodded to himself, and a small smile pulled his lips. "Back where we belong."

Tinc's buzz crackled in his ear as she swooped around his shoulders and flitted off through dim glow of the jungle, bobbing and weaving until they reached their old hollow tree.

Slowing to meet her, Peter's breaths came in steady rasps as he scanned the abandoned treehouse. It had always been quiet surrounding the secret fort, but now the looming forest seemed empty—as if even the air knew it was too still. He thumped the gnarled knot on the side of the tree, activating the hidden steps nestled in the base of the roots. A trap door slid open, pulling the tangled vines to reveal a steep, twisty staircase. Following Tinc's sparking trail, he slipped down the stairs into the empty hideout.

"I'm gonna miss this old place," Peter murmured as he glanced around the quiet room. The vaulted common area had been where the Boys spent most of their days, goofing off, plotting against the pirates, and dreaming about the day they'd get to go home. The Boys' belongings dotted the room, covered in settling dust as time lingered, preserving their past in an endless present.

Peter glanced at the forgotten mementos, the only remnants of his family. In the far corner, a large crate rested, filled with a dusty collection of odds and ends. Frayed wires stuck out of the top, and the words DO NOT

TOUCH were scratched across the fading bleached wood.

Next to the overstuffed crate, a silver tinderbox sat abandoned. Peter picked it up and smiled at Curly's tiny Fleet identifier taped to the top. The young boy smiled up under rich brown eyes that matched the deep tone of his skin. Peter twisted the box, revealing the spinner lock the cautious boy had rigged to protect his belongings. Smiling, he pressed his ear to the box to listen for the latch as he twisted the dial. There was a tiny click as the gears aligned and the door popped open, unveiling a thin beamlight nestled alongside a tattered blue blanket and a ragged teddy bear that sat, waiting for their Boy to return. Peter left the rusty light, but freed the bear and the blanket. Curly hadn't used the bear for a very long time, but he remembered their first days on Neverland when the boy forced himself awake until everyone else had fallen asleep so he could clutch the weathered items to his chest and finally sleep himself. They deserved to go home too.

Peter scanned the room again, noting how the thick roots of the hollow tree dangled sleepily in the quiet Neverland afternoon. The tree creaked and swayed in the gentle breeze, rocking the Boys' empty hammocks. A faded sleeve dangled from Slightly's red sling bed, and Peter tugged the fabric to free his wrinkled deck hand jacket. Peter poked his finger through a small hole in the elbow, then held out the coat to examine the rest. The tag on the inseam stuck up from the collar, pulling his attention to the written name scrawled in messy handwriting. Peter smiled, remembering the day Slightly dashed around the house meticulously labeling everyone's belongings after Nibs had eaten his last chocolate bar. He had done pretty well until he got to the Twins, who sniggered together and refused to help, so he ended up just labeling all their items 'Twins.'

Peter snorted at the memory. After a few months on Neverland, the Twins finally opened up to everyone, and had even revealed their names— Caleb and Noah. Truthfully though, the lanky boys were happy to go by 'the Twins' and only Peter had ever discovered how to discern between the two. It was in their hands—Caleb's were boxy with squared blocks for fingers, while Noah's quick and nimble paws were more slender. Peter had figured it out early on, but never told the others. It was too much fun keeping the secret and the Twins' restless energy kept them from sitting still long enough for anyone else to notice. Though they mostly kept to themselves, the Twins had a mischievous side and were often the anonymous puppeteers of many ill-received pranks. Unfortunately for Nibs, they were also quite clever, and liked to use him as a scapegoat. Peter couldn't count the times he'd found the stocky boy coming to blows in a terrible row while the Twins snickered in a corner.

Memories flooded Peter's mind as he regarded the unkempt room— every corner held a story. His reminiscing was interrupted by an impatient buzz when Tinc shot around the corner and scolded him for dawdling. She jangled loudly in his ear, then swooped around his head urging him to hurry.

"Alright, I'm coming," Peter swatted at her buzzing wings. He studied the room, etching the scene in his mind. "I just don't want to forget anything."

He carefully folded Slightly's jacket and laid it on the table beside Curly's things. He cast one final glance around the space and grinned when he saw Tootles' crooked bookshelf. The youngest boy had painstakingly measured and planned its exact location for 'optimum capacity.' Peter remembered the boy's dogged pout as he repeatedly denied the others' offers to help and his more stubborn scowl when he realized it hung skewed. Nearly in tears, he stubbornly positioned his books and watched them slowly slide off the edge before hanging his head and going to bed. Peter spent the better part of that night installing a concealed rod to secure the base of the shelf, then threatened the Boys within an inch of their lives if anyone told. Tootles' cry of delight when he discovered his neatly stacked books the next morning was worth the lack of sleep.

Peter paused to inspect his handiwork and his gaze landed on a weathered leather book with no title. He flipped through the pages, where Tootle's neat print formed hundreds of strange words. Next to each word was a familiar one, and Peter realized they were all translations. Intrigued, he turned to the first page, where *Tootles' Guide to Neverland* was painstakingly penned in clumsy script. On the next page, a handwritten table of contents separated the book into four main sections—Plants, Animals, Stjarnin, and Pirates.

"Look at this Tinc," Peter murmured, flipping through the brittle pages. Tinc hummed curiously and flitted to peek over his shoulder. "Did you know about this?"

Tinc's processor sparked as she zig-zagged a no.

"Me either," Peter said. "He pocketed the book, then gathered the last of the Boys' belongings. "Anything else before we go? I'm not turning around after we leave."

Tinc buzzed at his lame joke, then sparked toward the door. Peter inhaled a deep breath, appreciating the familiar smell. The gnarled treehouse had given them a lot over the years, it felt strange to think this was the last time he would ever see it. An odd pull tugged his gut, but he laughed and brushed the feeling away.

"It'll be nice to sleep without having to worry about dirt clods dusting your face, won't it Tinc?"

The nanobot hummed her agreement before buzzing around his head in an agitated circle.

"Yeah yeah." Peter ignored her snarky jab and stepped up the stairs. The hollow tree called to him, but he set his gaze forward. He had never been one to look back, and he didn't intend to start now.

The Stars met in a soft kiss as Peter and Tinc arrived back at the beach. The brisk air carried cool droplets of the Neversea on the wind, spraying them with a chilly mist. Peter shivered as the moisture tickled his skin while the clean scent of the sea mingled with the earthy jungle. He gazed at the Starset, noting the soft haze haloing the Second Star. Just a few more hours until Starfall. They needed to be gone before then.

He hurried to the *Fiducia II* and dropped his belongings next to where Seven sprawled at the foot of his chair, her tail twitching as she kicked her legs, caught in a dream. Peter scratched the creature behind her ear, earning a contented purr. A begrudging smile crept to his lips. Wendy was right—the blasted thing was cute, and almost disappointingly tame. At least if she had bitten off one of his fingers, he could have said 'I told you so.'

His smile widened as he remembered the joy on the captain's face when she discovered Seven and the friendly Neverfox burrowed deep in her dark chestnut curls. Wendy's happiness radiated in waves, and for the first time, he saw past her defenses. He saw her.

She was beautiful.

Peter reached in his pocket for the thimble Wendy had given him. His fingers brushed the rough edges, prodding the divots in their inlaid pattern. Wendy's captivating gaze swept through his thoughts and he gripped her gift, clutching it in resolve.

"I'm not waiting another hundred years to see you, Cap," he vowed, pocketing the thimble as he glanced around the deck. Everything was in place. Just one last check on the exterior hull and the processor cylinders, and they were ready.

He rushed from the *Fiducia* with Tinc close behind. His hurried steps kicked up the glistening sand as he scanned the vessel in a final systems check. Tinc jangled in his ear while they worked, her glowing central processor illuminating his nimble fingers as they inspected the smaller, more delicate systems.

"Looks good Tinc," Peter announced when they completed their final circuit. He clapped the soot from his hands as he appreciated his handiwork. "I think we're ready."

Tinc shot over the ship, showering him in a cascade of delighted pink sparks. Peter loosed a crowing laugh, then turned to hoist himself onto the loading pad. He had just released the edges of the rounded frame when a husky voice called from the shadowed the Nevertrees.

"Peter Pan. Wait."

6

Peter froze at the commanding timbre of the rasping voice. Slowly, he turned toward the quiet sound. Before him, a dozen Sjarnin warriors stood, decorated in war dress. They watched him intently, the onyx chambers of their eyes glinting brightly against their mossy green skin. Their clay-brown hair was bound from their faces with decorative ivory beads that matched the styled scars etched into their muted skin. Each one clung protectively to a finely carved weapon—long sticks carved from bone with a deadly clubbed base that elongated and ended in a needle-sharp top. Paired with the Stjarnin's extraordinary speed and agility, those weapons were more dangerous than most szikra.

Peter swallowed, but puffed his chest to meet the collection of warriors. He cast his stare determinedly over each one, ending with the Stjarnin whose long, ivory hair fluttered gently in the Neverbreeze.

Princess Tiger Lily.

"Haven't seen you guys since the party," Peter smirked, forcing his bravado. "I was wondering if you were going to say goodbye."

The princess' eyes flashed. "Not goodbye."

Peter's brow furrowed. His heart thumped in his chest, but he flashed a roguish smile. He tipped his hand in a jaunty salute, then stepped back, carefully noting his distance from the Stjarnins' wicked blades.

"Fair point. I hate goodbyes too," he quipped, then whirled to leap inside the *Fiducia*. A cry rang out, followed by the scuffle of feet and Tinc's furious jangles as a dozen spear points prodded his back.

Peter yelped, and Tiger Lily issued a slow, foreign command. The needled points edged away from his torso, and Peter glanced down, relieved there were no bloodstains dotting his suit. He looked at the princess, then let out a cavalier laugh.

"Alright, I guess I can make an exception this time." Peter poked his finger through a new hole in his shirt. He grinned at the Stjarnin, and his easy smile dipped. The warriors' stares narrowed into dangerous black slits, and though their weapons no longer prodded his flesh, they were still dangerously poised, ready to attack. Their sleek muscles tautened as they gripped their blades, prepped for a quick and deadly strike. Peter massaged the back of his neck and turned to the princess, who watched him from a mask of stone.

"Not goodbye," she repeated more firmly.

Peter's eyes narrowed as his face hardened into a mask of its own. "What do you mean not goodbye?"

Tiger Lily stepped closer and her warriors followed, tightening their circle. "Itzala cannot go," she said. "No one can go."

Sirens blared in Peter's mind as he looked from the princess to her coiled warriors, but snark won over self-preservation and he released a cocky grin.

"Well, that's not good," he scoffed, "because you missed the other ship."

A low murmur rustled through the warriors as Tiger Lily's large eyes rounded even wider. Pulsating energy rippled from the princess's stern posture as she leaned toward Peter, leveling her slender frame with his.

"Meaning?"

Peter met her steady stare with stunned silence. Up close, what he once thought was smooth, mossy skin was actually flesh covered in millions of tiny bumps packed so tightly that they formed an imperceptible armor of their own. He blinked dumbly at the princess, not unaware of the barrier she formed between him and her seething warriors. Tinc worried in his ear, and he brushed his shoulder, his silent signal for her to make herself scarce. Nervous blue sparks cascaded from her processor, but she zipped to hover over the *Fiducia II*, where she could observe from a safe distance.

Peter waited for Tinc to land, then crossed his arms. "They left. Weeks ago." He forced his lips into a tight line, so they wouldn't betray the worry pounding in his chest.

Translucent eyelids slithered over the princess' eyes in a slow blink as she sucked a steady breath through her gills. His body itched with nerves, but Tiger Lily only nodded and stepped away. He nearly let out a sigh of relief until the princess issued a sharp command. The warriors surged forward and Peter danced out of the way, making a desperate lunge for the *Fiducia*

II. He kicked the nearest guard, toppling her into the stocky warrior behind her, then thrust his fist into the stomach of another. While he struggled, Tinc zipped around the others' heads, disorienting them with her shower of sparks.

Darting away, Peter leapt into the hatch of the *Fiducia II.* He crowed at the chaos below, then turned to the safety of his pilot's seat and his boots skidded to a screeching stop. Waiting in the hull, the Stjarnin Prince stood, his spear drawn menacingly before him. Peter staggered back and bumped into Tiger Lily, whose looming figure towered proudly over him.

"The Shadow cannot escape." She reiterated, placing her hand on Peter's shoulder and sending thousands of memories careening through his mind. His eyes widened as a piercing pain lanced through his head and he fell, leaving the terrifying, imprinted images to be swallowed in black.

7

Peter woke with a throbbing headache and a large knot on the back of his head. A soft buzz whispered beside him as he stirred and sat, bracing his temple to keep the earth from spinning.

"Tinc? What's going on?"

Tinc hummed again, and he peeked up, relieved to see her fluttering freely beside him. He forced both eyes open and was less relieved to find he was back in the center of the Stjarnin camp where he and Tootles had been paraded in their first visit to the alien base. Several guards were posted around him, but they paid no mind as they stood, their backs to him while the Stjarnin chief approached, trailed by the prince and his bride.

The stooped alien shuffled slowly toward them, his dark eyes glazed with gray, but still sharp. The villagers watched his procession while their children ran through the camp, laughing and shouting in their native tongue. Peter was struck by how much they reminded him of his Boys.

"Peter Pan."

Tiger Lily's gravelly voice pulled his attention from a Stjarnin child tottering on lanky legs. His clay-colored hair was gathered in a low ponytail bound with vines. Peter turned from the child and glanced at the princess.

"I might have been before I got the sense knocked out of me," he groused, pressing his head where dull pain still throbbed in his skull. Though it was tender to touch, his fingers came away clear of blood. "Now I'm not so sure."

The princess' lips turned in a stacked frown. Beside her, the Prince gripped his staff menacingly. Peter looked at the large club at the base of the shaft, glowering as he realized what had knocked him out. The heavy staffs were no joke.

"Peter Pan."

Annoyed, Peter met her gaze. "If I say yes, is he going to hit me again?" Beside him, Tinc buzzed indignantly. Peter was pleased to note the wary way the warriors eyed the fuming bot. Not bad for a tiny mech with a sailor's mouth. He grinned and tapped the top of his shoulder. "It's alright Tinc, I've got it from here."

Tinc jangled a snarky remark that made Peter glad only he understood the cheeky bot. He tossed her a withering look, then returned his attention to the Stjarnin leaders. They stood, watching expectantly until the chief shuffled forward and brushed his slender fingers over the bridge of Peter's brow. He spoke in a rumbling wheeze that harmonized around his foreign words. Peter struggled to decipher the words, but he only recognized the one that ended the chief's speech: *Itzala.*

Peter glanced at Tiger Lily, whose face remained carefully neutral until the Shadow's name slipped her mask in a brief flash of fear. Peter didn't blame her. His nights were still plagued by haunting memories of the Shadow slithering from the dais to form the writhing mass that tried to encase his soul. Even during the day, when it got too quiet he could almost hear the Shadow whispering for him. Summoning him.

Chasing the shrouded thought away, Peter focused on the chief. He had removed his hand and now spoke as he painted invisible glyphs in the sky. Peter had no idea what they meant, but the chief's fixated gaze indicated they were very important.

The chief finished his speech, allowing silence to hang in the air as he stared intently at Peter. Slowly, Peter rose, spurring the surrounding warriors to inch closer in warning. Peter eyed them warily, then turned to the princess, his voice laced with frustration.

"That's all very interesting, but seeing as how I have no idea what he just said, can I go now?"

Tiger Lily's response was interrupted by a whirlwind of harsh syllables and flailing movements from the prince. His features pulled in a furious scowl as he motioned to the chief and then the princess, who waited calmly for him to finish. When he settled, Tiger Lily looked from the chief to her betrothed, then smoothly responded in a low, clear rumble. She brushed her fingertips against the prince's long, angular cheek as her lips pulled in a distorted smile. The prince softened, then turned to the chief, who watched the exchange through his milky gray orbs before bestowing upon them a silent, stooped nod.

Tiger Lily's slitted lips buttoned as she fixed Peter in her drowning stare and took a slow, deliberate step toward him. Garbled words tumbled from her lips in a continuous whisper until her hand darted out to clamp over Peter's forehead. Peter jerked back, but he was immobilized as the princess' deep voice rumbled through his thoughts.

The galaxies have been protected from the Stjarnin's shame for millions of years. Now it is time to share our secrets. To fight the Darkness, we must unite as one or altogether we will fall.

Peter gasped and staggered back, blinking as their telepathic connection severed. Tinc flitted around his head, her buzzes sharp and agitated as he gasped in deep, whooping breaths. Tiger Lily watched patiently, her hands clasped tightly while she trapped him in her bottomless gaze.

"What just happened? What do you mean we've been protected?" Peter demanded. The words tumbled from his lips as he scanned his surroundings, eyeing the warriors as he searched for an exit. He had escaped the Stjarnin once before, he was certain they would not allow him to do the same again.

Tiger Lily blinked slowly, then spoke again. This time, though it didn't match the movements of her mouth, her voice formed clear words inside his mind.

We were connected the moment Itzala chose you, Pan. You are one of few mortals who have experienced the Darkness, and even more rare, survived its touch. Itzala hangs over us all. Once his shadow covers the universe, there will be nothing left for anyone. We must not let the Darkness win.

Peter paused as the princess' voice faded, leaving only his thoughts. They warred with one another, marveling at her communication and worrying over the message shared. His head throbbed as he compartmentalized the information and tried to make sense of it all. Drowning in roiling thoughts, he remembered when the Shadow tried to claim him as its own. Uneven gasps stole his breath as fear threatened to overtake him, then angrily dropped his eyes.

"I never asked for this," Peter countered. "Hooke is the one who called the Shadow—and you saw what happened to him. He's the one Itzala wanted. Not me. Not my Boys. All we've ever wanted was to go home." His hands tugged through his knotted red tangles while Tinc hummed reassurances in his ear. The Stjarnin didn't speak, but Tiger Lily gently gripped his shoulder.

"*You understand the importance of keeping the Shadow bound.*"

Peter gritted his teeth. He had seen firsthand what happened to those caught in Itzala's grasp. He searched the depths of the princess' gaze and nodded.

"I do. But I can't help you."

"*I do not understand.*"

A frustrated laugh escaped Peter's constricting chest. "You've only stopped me. There's a ship full of others that have already gone. What if the all-powerful death-being caught a ride with one of them?"

"*Then we are all doomed.*"

Peter balked at the certainty in her voice. He glanced at the others, but their expressionless faces mirrored their princess' severity. His cocky grin quavered, but he scoffed.

"Doomed? That seems a bit dramatic, don't you think?"

"*You've experienced the Shadow,*" Tiger Lily spoke calmly. "*Do you?*"

She stepped back to rejoin the Stjarnin royalty as the prince and chief fixed Peter with their unending stares.

"If the Shadow is not contained, the entire world will be his. And we will all be consumed."

Peter forced a disdainful laugh, clinging stubbornly to his arrogant facade. "Not to downplay your worry, but I fought that thing. And won." His smirk quelled under Tiger Lily's piercing gaze.

"Did you?" She asked. *"Are you truly free? Or does Itzala still cling to the edges of your mind?"*

Peter frowned as he thought of the nightmares that plagued him. Vicious, gripping terrors where he was bound by inky tendrils suffocating him, forcing him to watch helplessly while Itzala consumed everything he loved. Though the dream had faded in intensity, there were nights where he still woke screaming. It was not a future he was willing to see foretold, even if it meant trusting the Stjarnin.

He released a heavy sigh. "How do we beat it?"

Tiger Lily exchanged a long look with the chief, who returned her gaze with a deep nod. The princess smiled and extended her moss green palm.

"We will show you."

The warriors looked nervously from the princess to her betrothed, but the chief gave a sage nod and they tentatively lowered their weapons. Peter allowed the princess to guide him toward the largest tent in the village. As they approached, the princess pulled back the canvas flap, revealing a large, cozy room with a hole cut deep inside the floor.

Peter's face clouded in confusion as he studied the gaping opening. An amused smile laced the princess' lips as she led him toward the gap, which was lined by a stepped ledge that created a spiral staircase leading deep underground.

"*There is much you don't know about my people,*" the princess said. "*Much you need to know to survive.*"

Peter bristled at the unspoken challenge. "Show me."

Taking Peter's hand, the princess led him quietly down the stairs. The surrounding air began to cool as they descended deep inside the mountain. Peter's breath hitched as he felt the ground compressing on him until they rounded a darkened bend and he was nipped by a gentle breeze.

Peter stuttered to a stop as the winding staircase opened to a sprawling, underground cavern. Stunned, he departed the narrow passage, gaping at the shimmering underground. Buried deep below the village surface, dozens of identical tunnels opened to a glittering city. Pillared walls were carved into the stony mountain, supporting the structure with their elaborate patterns. They lit like beacons, glowing in a brilliant turquoise hue that emanated deep within the rock, matching the scattered pools dotting the hidden landscape. Soft tendrils of steam wisped from the glassy liquid, hovering delicately over the luminescent surface to dance in the faint blue cast that lit the underground village.

"*It seems your impression of my people has changed,*" Tiger Lily's amused tenor lilted through his mind. Peter turned to the Stjarnin princess in shock. Under the dazzling village light, Tiger Lily's skin glimmered, matching her comrades as they were wrapped in the faint glow illuminating from the ivory patterns etched into their mossy skin.

"Who are you?" he breathed, still reeling over the world hidden beneath Neverland's surface. Tiger Lily motioned forward, propelling him through the city as she explained.

"We are an ancient people. A proud race that have outlasted most galaxies. Our years are marked by the birth of constellations. All that outlives us is the Star Emerald."

"The Star Emerald? You mean the Second Star?"

Tiger Lily nodded. Her ivory hair draped over her shoulder, nearly touching the earth with her deep bow. *"The Stjarnin have worshipped the Star Emerald since the dawn of our time. We were birthed from it, bathed in it, and raised in its light."*

She traced one of the glowing lines on her arm. The swirling pattern flared under her touch, then burrowed into her skin, pulsating under her mossy flesh with a dull glow.

"It is who we are, and what we will become. We have been protected by its guiding light for millennia. It led us in peace and prosperity—until the Darkness found us."

"The Darkness as in, the Shadow," Peter guessed. A soft flare of sadness burned through the back of his mind. He glanced at the princess' drawn features and realized that not only did he have access to the princess' words, he could reach her emotions as well.

"We have fought the Darkness long before your Earth came to be. Itzala has plagued the Stjarnin's history since before most of us can remember."

Tiger Lily watched the villagers walking through their underground home. Small children laughed and jumped over the wispy pools while their parents looked on from their daily tasks. Clustered groups of men and women worked together to prepare food and to create beautiful crafts. Peter's attention pulled to a pair of Stjarnin women hovering over a large, illuminated panel. He couldn't tell from where he stood, but it resembled a centrifugal calibration core. From the looks of it, an advanced one. He glanced at the Princess, wondering how many secrets the Stjarnin had to share.

Ignoring his piercing gaze, Tiger Lily led Peter to the edge of the buried city where the tunnel sloped into a dark, looming cave.

"This is where we keep our knowledge. The past lives and wisdom of all the Stjarnin can be found here. Our ancestors knew the true evil hidden within Itzala, and left a piece of themselves to help us remember. There are many things my people have done to protect against the Shadow's evil. Many of which have brought great heartache. Many which we would choose to forget. Our ancestors linger to remind us of their sacrifice and the importance of ours. We remembered our darkest moments so the darkness wouldn't escape."

A chill crept through Peter as he gazed into the gaping cave. Though the mountain air was thick and still, a cold breeze rushed from the mouth of the cavern, carrying on its wings an ancient, earthy scent. Peter's flesh prickled as it swept over him, wrapping him in a primal power. Tinc jangled nervously and hovered closer to his shoulder, but he turned to the princess.

"What do you want me to do?" he asked, afraid he already knew the answer.

"Go to them," Tiger Lily commanded, confirming his fears. *"They will tell you what they can. Perhaps you truly are what we need to defeat the Darkness."*

Peter swallowed his suddenly parched throat as warring thoughts competed in his mind. He wanted to believe the Shadow was gone, but part of him knew that was wishful thinking. He gave Tinc a stiff nod and forced a jaunty smile to his lips.

"Ready for another adventure, Tinc?"

Tinc's enthusiastic jangle was interrupted by Tiger Lily's halting hand. Angry red sparks erupted from the bot's processor as she rammed the wall of staffs blocking her path.

"Only you may enter. Your companion must remain."

Peter glanced from Tiger Lily to Tinc, whose stream of foul language was still translating into his cochlear implant. He stared at the Stjarnin's impassive glares, then looked at the village behind him. He didn't understand their ways, but his regard for the race had been highly raised. And his curiosity was burning to discover what laid deep within the cave.

Maybe it would help him find Wendy.

"Looks like you're gonna have to stay here, Tinc," he said. Tiny blue sparks bounced across his palm. "I know," he assured, "I want you to come too. But now, you can make sure I come back." He released the bot and she flitted to hover over Tiger Lily while the Stjarnin warriors untangled their barricade.

His path clear, Peter took in a quick breath, mentally preparing himself for whatever he might find on the other side. He had nearly reached the cave's beckoning mouth when the princess' smooth voice rustled through his thoughts.

"We have never allowed anyone outside our brothers to enter our memories, Pan. Do not take this honor lightly." Her words chased him as he crossed the darkened threshold and the pitch maw enveloped him, sealing him in black.

"Our ancestors may be sleeping, but they still have power of their own."

8

THE JOLLY ROGER

CAPTAIN WENDY DARLING

Wendy woke in the middle of the night to a sharp pain lancing through her knee. Gingerly, she rolled to sit in the elaborate bed. Hooke's heavy feather blanket still covered the plush mattress nestled in the carved mahogany frame. The fabric rustled beneath her as she shifted her weight—she preferred to sleep on top of the thick blankets rather than buried underneath them; their bulk restricted her movements and made her feel trapped.

She exhaled as she straightened her stiff leg, and was surprised by the soft puff of air that flared in front of her nose. The climate-controlled cabins sometimes got a little chilly due to fluctuating basal temperatures, but they had never been so cold that she could see her breath.

Wendy huffed out another long breath, forming a cloud of condensation.

Fascinated, she clapped her hands around the tiny puff to capture its writhing wisps. They tickled her slender fingers, betraying the cold that seeped into her skin. She blew a few warm breaths into her palms, then moved them to gingerly massage the ache wrapping her joints before she flexed her leg again. Her kneecap creaked in protest then extended with a loud pop that echoed into the silent chamber. Wendy glanced around the room, but could only see the soft blinking lights of the Starboard flashing into the dark. Dawes was still sleeping, then.

Wendy yawned and twisted to check the time. She cursed under her breath at the ungodly hour Nana's flash revealed, then flopped back on the bed to force herself to sleep. She stared blindly at the black space above her until another stabbing pain ripped through her knee and she shot to the edge of the bed, clamping her hands tightly around the bones as if her grip alone could somehow mitigate the pain.

Grinding her teeth, Wendy peeked through her wince at the offending appendage. Her vision blurred until her eyes adjusted, allowing her to trace the shape of her laced hands over her leg. A cold chill swept through her stomach to lodge in her throat as she peered closer and saw gnarled knuckles covered in darkened age spots clutching her withered skin.

Wendy released her hold and whipped her hands up to examine them. She hit the light beside her bed and the lamp clicked on, flaring a beacon over the darkened room until only the corners remained shrouded in dingy gray. Her hands shook as the fluorescent light washed over her, illuminating once smooth, slender hands that had knotted in ancient claws. Spidering veins dotted her flesh, traveling from the back of her hands all the way to her biceps. With a shudder, Wendy tugged her sleeve to reveal a collection of spots sprinkling her shoulders too.

Panicked, Wendy quickly lifted the bottom of her shirt to reveal her torso. Her stomach, which before had been taut and smooth, was now fleshy and loose with sagging skin drooping lazily over the lining of her spandex. She twisted to check her back, but her knee buckled, sending her tumbling to the floor. Her shoulder crunched against the paneling, and she yelped as her head slammed against the ground.

Disoriented, Wendy's eyelids fluttered lazily as she pulled herself to Hooke's wardrobe. Her arms trembled with every movement, but finally, she reached the ornate fixture and pried open the door, revealing the gilded mirror hanging inside. Using all of her strength, Wendy propped herself onto her elbows to peer in the base of the mirror.

A terrified howl caught in her throat as she stared into the abandoned mirror. The dark blemishes that covered her hands traveled up her neck and face, coating her cheeks and forehead in the uneven, browning spots. The rest of her flesh had been ravaged by wrinkles, pulling the skin from her bones to hang loosely toward the ground. Her hair, once dark and full, had thinned and grayed to pale wisps that clung to her sweat-damp skin. She raised a trembling hand to her face and paled as the wizened crone mimicked her movement. Her chin trembled as her gnarled fingers pressed against her gaunt cheek, repulsing her with their paper-thin feel. A single tear coursed down her cheek as she gazed at her age-wrecked reflection.

A sudden movement at the edge of the mirror caught Wendy's attention, and her eyes darted to the motion. The cabin rippled with the echoes of a husky laugh as her tired gaze landed on Peter. He stood behind her, his head cocked as he studied her haggard appearance. Lazy strands of shaggy red hair fell in his face, a stark contrast against his pale skin and shocking green eyes.

"Wait," Wendy croaked, then clamped her hand around her hoarse throat. "Peter. It's me."

She turned from the mirror, grateful to no longer see her gruesome appearance, until the revulsion on Peter's face hit her like a physical blow. She gasped a ragged breath as he stepped away, shaking his head and slinking toward the darkened corners of the room. His lips twisted in a hushed murmur, but though words formed on his lips, no sound reached her ears.

"No, Peter. It's me, I just—"burning tears trickled down Wendy's cragged cheeks as she reached her wraithlike arm toward Peter's strong, solid bicep. He jerked back, but not before her spotted hand knotted in the edge of his shirt sleeve. Clinging to him, she pulled her hobbled body forward, and with all the strength she could muster, cupped her hand to his perfect face. His lips curled in a disgusted sneer and he spoke again, leaving her sobbing as she tried to comprehend him through the silence. His green eyes sparked as he flashed a final mischievous smile then disappeared from the lamp's dim glow into the cabins shadowed edge.

With Peter gone, Wendy once again plunged into the cold. She moved to follow him, but when her outstretched palm met the dark, her feathery skin began to crumble and flake before riding on the chilly air to disappear into the gloom. She shrank back, but it was too late. Tiny cracks spidered from her dissolving fingers to the rest of her arm, then shot up her body, splintering her into a thousand moaning shards until Wendy released an agonized wail and they exploded, turning her into a cloud of dust.

"No!" Wendy bolted upright in bed. Frantic, she batted away the sweat-drenched curls clinging to her neck and forehead then gulped ragged gasps of air as she tried to steady the erratic cadence of her pounding heart.

"Is everything alright Captain?" SMEE's artificial tenor cut through the dark, sending a fresh wave of adrenaline rippling through her chest. Startled, Wendy let out an unladylike yelp as panic lanced physically through her chest.

"For the love of the Fleet, SMEE, how long have you been standing there?" Wendy gasped, trying to steady her shattered nerves.

SMEE's cybernetic eyes blinked gold in the dim light. "Only a moment Captain. I was monitoring the route, but you started to stir. I ran your biometrics and your adrenaline levels were startlingly high. Are you feeling unwell?"

"Something like that," Wendy grumbled. She motioned for the first mate to activate the lights and squinted as the fluorescent glow filled the room, banishing her night-terror with a haunted whisper. Wendy jerked toward the slithering sound and a curling shadow dissipated with a hiss. She blinked, searching for the remnants of the wraith, but only found empty space. Sighing, she scrubbed her face until her eyes adjusted to the fabricated luminescence, then peeked them open to peer at her unblemished skin. Though her breath had calmed, her hands still trembled as she brushed them up her arms and shoulders before finally resting on her heat-flushed cheeks. No wrinkles, only damp traces of sweat left from her nightmare. Relieved, Wendy exhaled and drew her knees to her chest to curl into a ball. She buried her head in her knees, grounding herself until her heart beat without skipping, then straightened her spine into a long, straight line.

"Are you sure you're alright, Captain? Shall I fetch you some tea?" The synth's fabricated brow creased as he worried over her. "Your metrics still haven't regulated."

Wendy sighed. "I'm fine, SMEE. Just a bad dream. Nothing to worry about." She sighed, frustrated at the panicky feeling slowly seeping from her bones. She'd had nightmares in the past, but they had never gripped her the way this one had. It had seemed so real. Her gaze darted back to where the shadowed figure had spidered away, but the illuminated corner was only filled with empty air. A shiver rippled down her spine and she quashed it with an irritated sigh. Nothing there. Just her mind playing tricks.

Her eyes narrowed to focus on her wrist display. 04:45. Earlier than she cared to wake up, but with her adrenaline coursing freely through her veins, sleep was a lost cause. With a resolved sigh, she scrubbed the final crumbs of sleep from her eyes and hoisted herself to stand. She glanced around the still room, half expecting to find Peter in the shrouded corner. Her only response was from the flickering lights of the navigation panel blipping innocently in the silent room. When no new nightmare manifested, she slowly stretched, wincing at the discomfort in her knee. She flexed it a few times to loosen the stiffness in her muscles, then crossed the room to her oversized wardrobe. She stepped inside, leaving SMEE waiting quietly by her bed while she shrugged into her uniform.

"What's our status SMEE? Do we have any updates?" she asked as she secured her last coat button, then tackled the task of taming her hair. Her hazel eyes flashed as she frowned at herself in the mirror. Her already unruly locks had kicked up to wild as she tossed in her sleep, surrounding her in a halo of tangled, chestnut curls. She smoothed them as best as she could, then tethered them in a low bun at the nape of her neck. A few loose curls pulled free and she swept them from her face, too tired to care. Right now, she had more important things to tend to.

SMEE shook his head. "No, Captain. Lieutenant Dawes' charted course stayed true. We experienced minor turbulence at 01:26, but it resolved quickly. Just the Shakes."

Wendy's lips pulled in a grim line at the Crew's coined term for the ship's growing malfunctions. While minor turbulence was a relief compared to the alternative, the *Roger's* current state still weighed heavily on her. Michaels was doing his best to hold her together, but the vessel was old, and half the bird she used to be.

"Aside from the turbulence, there were no other problems?" Wendy asked. She stalked to the StarBoard to access the automated systems report. "If not, I'll let Michaels sleep a bit longer."

SMEE's gears whirred as he moved to stand beside her. "No, Captain. Nothing abnormal. However, if history is any indicator, Lieutenant Michaels is probably already awake."

Wendy let out a begrudging hum of agreement. The first mate was likely right. Michaels was probably up and working from the moment the *Roger* trembled. Wendy was ninety-nine percent sure he was the only reason they hadn't already fallen out of the sky.

"Agreed," she said, then frowned. Now that she thought about it, it had been a few days since Michaels had emerged from the maintenance bay. "Would you please check on the Lieutenant to make sure he doesn't need any assistance? And bring him something to eat. I think sometimes he forgets he's not a robot—er, I mean …"Wendy blushed at SMEE's unblinking stare.

An automated laugh rumbled from the synth's chest. "It's quite alright, Captain." He chuckled. "Not having to rely on daily sustenance is one of the perks of my existence. Although I would quite like to try macarons. I hear they are delightful."

Wendy grinned. "I don't know about macarons, but I'd be lying if I said you weren't missing out on coffee."

"Shall I get you some before I tend to the lieutenant?"

"No," she waved her hand. "Check on Michaels first. He's more valuable than I am, whether he'll admit it or not. If he needs anything, make sure he gets it."

SMEE nodded then turned to leave. "Yes, Captain."

"Thank you, SMEE." She waited for the sliding door to whir shut, then finished her scan of the grid. The lazy lights indicated everything was in working order, so she moved to a cursory check of the charted course. Again, everything checked out. Not that Wendy was surprised, Dawes' piloting was impeccable. Between her and Michaels, Wendy had never been more grateful for the crew the Admiral had assembled. If she'd been paired with anyone less skilled their return trip would have been exponentially more stressful.

And that was nothing she needed.

Satisfied with the *Roger's* progress, Wendy accessed the comms log. SMEE would have informed her if there had been any communications attempts, but at this point, it was habit. She found herself compulsively checking the log throughout the day, hoping for a new transmission.

It never happened.

Wendy scrolled the records aimlessly, noting all her outgoing messages that had yet to be hailed. Even with her Spartan usage of the system, it had accumulated quite the roster. She hoped for an incoming message soon, but knew if she held her breath, she'd suffocate long before she ever saw through to the end. She was about to scroll through one last time to make sure she didn't miss anything when Dawes breezed in, carrying two steaming cups of coffee.

"Morning, Captain," she chirped, handing Wendy a cup before settling into her pilot's chair. "Sleep well?"

"Not exactly," Wendy deadpanned. A slight shudder rippled through her. "Did you get some rest?"

Dawes shrugged. "As much as one can on a rickety boat filled with miscreants."

Wendy grinned. "The Boys aren't that bad, are they? I thought they preferred to terrorize Boyce."

Dawes laughed. "Oh, the boys are fine. Aside from the fact that the Twins won't even look at me when I walk in the kitchen, they've all been perfect gentlemen. I was talking about Johns."

Wendy snorted into her coffee. "Touché."

A smirk settled over Dawes' lips as her fingers danced across the navigation grid. She summoned a chorus of beeps and whirs as she entered a series of complex commands to override the autopilot she enabled for SMEE. With a flick of her wrist, Dawes activated the speaker system and the slow cadence of steel drums filled the cabin while she hummed softly along. Wendy sipped her coffee, enjoying the comfortable quiet, thankful for the pilot's easy presence. Soothed by the caffeine coursing through her veins, Wendy collected their empty cups and moved to review their course.

"Captain, no matter how many times you check those charts, they're going to stay the same," Dawes tossed Wendy a sideways glance. "Unless someone is changing them while we sleep, and then we've got bigger problems."

Wendy shook her head. "Same as always," she confirmed, but her gaze fixed on the charts until she completed her scan. Satisfied that everything was in place, she met the pilot with a shrug. "I just hate waiting around. Even though we're moving, I feel like we're dead in the water."

Dawes nodded. "I get it, but you're going to give yourself an ulcer if you keep worrying so much. You might even give me one from being stuck watching you."

Wendy rolled her eyes, but abandoned the charts and walked to the bookshelves to busy herself with searching the titles. Thick tomes covered the shelves, each hosting a healthy collection of dust. She scanned the row before her, then paused when she realized a book was missing. A streak of dust pulled to the edge of the shelf, showing it had been recently moved.

Wendy frowned. "Dawes, did you take one of Hooke's books?"

Dawes quirked her brow. "For a little light reading?" She laughed and shook her head. "No thanks. That's not really my style. I like my books to be a little more not awful to read."

Wendy chuckled. She couldn't deny Dawes' claims, because she had no idea which book had gone missing. Looking through Hooke's collection, the majority were informational texts about ship systems, navigations, and the outer reaches of space. She swept over the shelf once more to see if it had been moved, then shrugged. It wasn't as if Hooke would miss the tome. It worried her that someone had entered her quarters though.

Dawes shook her head with a small laugh. "You know, Captain, it might be easier to just paint worry lines on your face—they're going to be etched there before long."

Wendy scowled, but Dawes only grinned.

"You know I'm right."

Wendy's lips screwed together to fight her admissive smile. "I might be known to be overzealous in planning and preparation. That's all."

"Captain, I love you, but you're a hot ball of nerves," Dawes laughed. "I'm not complaining. It's served you well. There's absolutely no one else I'd rather have commanding this ship, but sometimes I wonder how all your hair hasn't gone gray."

A self-conscious hand slicked over Wendy's bun as Dawes' casual comment conjured a memory of the withered crone from her dream. The pilot noticed the motion, and her accusatory look softened.

"Really, Captain. Of all the people in the 'verse, you're the one I trust more than anyone to get us home. You just need to relax and see what everyone else sees."

"Be careful, you're starting to sound like Johns," Wendy teased.

"Eh, even miscreants can be right about some things," Dawes winked, earning a begrudging laugh from Wendy.

"I'll try and ease up a bit."

"Try and ease up a *lot*," Dawes interjected. "Maybe try some meditation. You know, balance your chi and all that."

Wendy's brow quirked. "I let you play reggae on repeat," she countered, then leveled a shrewd glance at the pilot. "Let's not get carried away," she said, then raised the empty mugs. "I'm going to take these back to the kitchen. You need anything?"

Dawes shook her head and refocused on the open visor before waving Wendy out of the room. "All good here. Me and my chi are all sorts of centered."

"I'm very happy for you both," Wendy quipped. She chuckled and turned to leave, smiling at the pilot's lovely voice singing softly along to the lilting beat.

9

Mugs in hand, Wendy slowly made her way down the metallic corridor. She scanned the dark edges of distant halls, straining to make out shapes in the darkness. When nothing formed from the shadows, she exhaled, releasing the breath she hadn't realized she'd been holding.

"You're being ridiculous," she scolded herself. "It was just a dream. And a silly one at that. You got old—everyone gets old. You're acting worse than your mother." At this, a wry smile pulled the corners of her lips. She could only imagine the condition her mother would be in after a dream like that. No amount of vapors would resuscitate her—she'd go completely catatonic.

The image played in her mind, leaving a grim smile on her face. She'd never cared about aging before. For all of the times her mother told her about special ointments and cure-alls to preserve the youthfulness of her features,

Wendy had only scoffed. So why had the dream bothered her so much?

Wendy gritted her teeth and picked up her pace. Dawes was right. She worried too much. But it wasn't for lack of trying. She wished more than anyone that her brain would calm down. Unfortunately, her anxiety was a shadowed opponent. How could she fight something hidden in her mind?

Restless thoughts continued to barrage her as she hurried through the halls. She batted them away, but each time, they returned with a vengeance. It was almost a welcome distraction when the *Roger* shuddered and the running lights flickered, washing the corridor in darkness. Wendy froze as the ship groaned, then with a heavy wheeze, kicked the lights back on.

She glanced around, listening carefully. The *Roger's* soft hums surrounded her, revealing no sign of her earlier strain. Added to SMEE's reported malfunction, that was two separate incidents already today. The frequency was alarming. It had only been a few hours. Pressure mounted in her head and Wendy massaged her temples to combat the building migraine.

They needed to contact the Fleet.

Expelling her tension with a breath, Wendy twisted her neck to loosen the strain in her shoulders then hurried to the kitchen to deposit the mugs. The large space was unusually quiet without the Twins bustling about, clanging pots and pans. She checked the time. 06:15. The crew would be waking soon.

Wendy hovered in place, feeling strangely listless. She wasn't ready to return to Navs, but she didn't know what else to do either. Slowly, she rinsed the remains in the mugs and wiped them down before placing them on the shelf. Overhead, the hanging pots swayed gently, casting shadows on the steel island in the center of the room.

She watched their lazy movements, noting the *Roger's* smooth trajectory over the dull ache lingering in her knee. She needed to visit physio. It had been a few days since her last session, and DeLaCruz was a pit bull. If the medic didn't see her soon, she would never hear the end of it.

Turning to leave, her gaze caught the mounted knife rack and she frowned. A large gap had been left in the Twins' pristinely arranged equipment--they were missing a large chef's knife. She scanned the countertops to see if it had been left out, but the workspace was clear, save a few spices arranged in the corner. A loud buzz sounded behind her and Wendy whirled to face the sterilization cabinet, blinking through a cycle. She exhaled, releasing the nervous energy ballooning in her chest.

"Seriously, Darling. You *have to* calm down," she hissed, repeating Dawes' words angrily. She slapped the cabinet and shook her head, grumbling as she made her way toward the bay.

By the time Wendy reached the hall, the *Roger's* automated lighting was gradually illuminating the inner corridors. To preserve energy, Michaels had set the system for peak operational hours. It maximized capacity and gave the added bonus of a built-in alarm system. Lights on, everyone reported to their stations. If the stirrings Wendy heard in the crew's quarters were any indication, the system was working quite nicely.

Meandering through the *Roger,* Wendy passed the ship's early risers as they trekked to their respective stations. The Twins nodded at her in unison before shuffling sleepily to the kitchen, then she turned the corner and nearly ran into Nibs, who bounded through the hall with an impish grin.

He stuttered to a stop and swept a rigid salute before breaking free to tear through the ship.

Wendy watched him go, then returned to her rounds. Pleased to note that everything seemed in place, she re-routed her path back to physio. Reaching the deck, Wendy keyed the code to activate the access panel. The sleek panel whirred as it swept open, revealing the vacant therapy machines. Well, mostly vacant.

"Holy—Johns!" Wendy covered her face and turned from where her medic and ammunitions officer were tangled on the physiokinesis machine. "I have therapy on that!"

She scowled when she heard Johns snicker before he bounded over and planted a loud kiss on her forehead.

"All clear Darling. You can open your eyes." He chuckled, slinging his arm over her shoulder and ignoring her scowl. "Not that you needed to close them in the first place."

Johns grinned as Wendy peeked through her fingers at his tight black undershirt. To her immense relief, she noted the rest of his uniform was firmly in place, albeit a bit wrinkled. DeLaCruz hovered next to him in her own disheveled suit before looking properly mortified, she scurried into her office.

"I'm not going to micromanage your free-time Johns, but there is to be *no* fraternizing on the physio equipment!" She turned her nose at the vacant machine. "Particularly mine."

"But you never use i—" Johns' rebuttal dissipated under Wendy's furious glower. He loosed another hearty laugh, but this time, tempered it with a sheepish grin. "Affirmative." He schooled his features into an apologetic mask and swept a quick salute. "Sorry about that, Darling. Just going a little stir crazy on this tin can."

"I get it," Wendy sighed, "but let's keep the common areas PG, please."

"You got it, Captain," Johns grinned. "I'll tell 'Rissa she's gotta keep her hands to herself. Not that I can blame her," he paired his flex with a wink. "It takes a lot of self-control to say no to this."

Wendy rolled her eyes. "I'm sure she'll figure it out." She turned to the soft whir from the office door's track. "Isn't that right DeLaCruz?"

"Absolutely Captain," the medic assured, moving sheepishly to stand beside Johns. "What did I just agree to?"

"Captain just swore you to a life of celibacy," Johns chirped and wrapped his arm around the Medic. "No more swoony man time for you." He wiggled his hips in a ridiculous tease.

DeLaCruz scoffed then tapped him on the nose, laughing at his dumbfounded expression. "Which also means none for you."

Johns feigned a dramatic gasp. "But without my swoony man time, whatever will I do?"

"How about your job," Wendy suggested smartly. "I like Nibs, but I'm not sure I trust him in Ammunitions alone."

Johns groaned, then nodded with a sigh. He squeezed DeLaCruz' shoulders before planting a theatrical kiss on her temple. "Duty calls. I'll catch you for not-swoony time later." He winked, then grabbed his coat as he hurried out the deck.

Wendy watched him go, then reached to stop him as a stray thought struck her. "Johns, on your way, could you check something with the Boys for me?"

The crease in Johns' forehead deepened. "Sure thing, Darling. But, why?"

"It seems things are going missing. I don't think they're to blame, but I know how they like to play—especially with Boyce. For whatever reason, they seem to like you. Maybe you could feel it out without causing a stir?"

"Consider it done," Johns saluted. "You need anything else? An ammsTest? Help moving some furniture? Swoony man-time?" He waggled his brows before casting a teasing grin at DeLaCruz.

Wendy snorted. "All good here. Talking to the Boys will be more than enough."

"You got it, Captain." Johns affirmed. With a jaunty wave, he was gone, leaving Wendy exchanging an exasperated glance with DeLaCruz.

"You really find that charming?" Wendy thumbed over her shoulder after his departure.

"You tell me," DeLaCruz grinned. "He's been yours longer."

Wendy laughed, but she couldn't argue. "Elias always did have a knack for being obnoxiously endearing."

"Pretty sure that's the definition of charm," DeLaCruz shrugged, then opened her charts. "What can I do for you Captain? It's been a few days. How's the knee?"

Wendy grimaced, but flexed her leg to give the medic an accurate gauge. "It's alright. A six, maybe? It bothers me sometimes, but for the most part it's fine."

"And your range of motion?" DeLaCruz crouched to prod the cartilage around Wendy's knee.

"Fine. It doesn't stretch as far as it used to, but it's functional."

DeLaCruz side-eyed Wendy before she stood. "Functional is not the same as fine, Captain. We've talked about this." She gestured to the physiokinesis machine. "Sit."

Wendy groaned, but obeyed. She leaned against the recliner allowing DeLaCruz to maneuver her leg, contorting it in all sorts of awkward angles until a quick twist provoked a surprised wince.

The medic halted her prodding and glanced up. "That hurt?" she asked. "How much? *Honestly.*"

"It's fine. I just wasn't ready for it."

"You're never going to be ready for it. How much did it hurt?"

Wendy guessed, then subtracted a couple numbers. No need to worry the medic. "A four?"

DeLaCruz' brows shot behind her jagged bangs in disbelief. She held Wendy's stare, but when Wendy didn't break, she nodded, appeased.

"A four isn't terrible, but if it gets worse, you really need to let me know. If not, it won't heal properly. I'm already not thrilled about the equipment we have to use. It means you're going to have to be twice as disciplined in taking care of yourself." She fixed Wendy with a stern look. "Which, normally with you, I wouldn't say would be a problem; but for whatever reason, you're shyte at self-preservation. I've half a mind to request a psych-eval when we get home."

Wendy's eyes rounded, and the medic waved her hand.

"I'm kidding. But honestly, Captain? If you don't take it easy, you could cause permanent damage. Knees are tough, but once they're busted, they take *a lot* to heal, and an injury like yours? It may never be a hundred percent again. I'll do everything I can to get it to full capacity, but you're gonna have to give a little too."

DeLaCruz pulled out a small pack and handed it to Wendy.

"Take this. Ice it, then come back for a full session. I want to see you in three hours or I'll send Johns after you." DeLaCruz' friendly smile fell flat against Wendy's grimace. Seeing the hurt in the medic's eyes, she bolstered her grin.

"I'll come back," she assured. "I just have a few things to check first."

DeLaCruz nodded. "I have some meditech inventories slated as well," she admitted, but pointed at Wendy with a stern glare. "*Three hours.*"

"It's a date," Wendy promised before the Medic retreated to her office.

Wendy waited until DeLaCruz was out of sight before glaring at her knee. It responded with a defiant twinge that elicited an unbidden curse. Biting her tongue, Wendy hurried from the room before DeLaCruz came back to check on her. Outside the physio room, soothing air breezed against her cheeks as she leaned against the panel. Angry tears collected in her eyes, and she slammed her eyelids to chase them away.

Helpless.

The feeling she hated more than anything, and yet, here she was. Trapped in her own personal hell. She buried her face in her palms, crumpling in on herself as misery overtook her. Maybe she hadn't survived the Shadow. Maybe she had died and was condemned to spend eternity on a broken ship with a broken body trying to maintain a broken crew when really, there was nothing she could do…

"Captain?" Humiliated, Wendy's eyes flew open as she shoved off the wall and adjusted her jacket before turning to address the commander.

"Yes Boyce?" she inquired, not oblivious to the edge in her tone.

Her abrasiveness earned a puzzled look, but Boyce's stance held firm. He stepped closer, shrinking the distance between them. "Are you alright? You seem upset."

The concern in his voice deflated Wendy's aggression. The fight seeped out of her, leaving her with only exhaustion. "I'm fine, Commander. Just tired. I didn't sleep well."

Boyce reached for her shoulder, but paused halfway. His hand hung awkwardly in the air before it lowered to clench against his hip. "Sleep seems to evade the best of us these days."

Wendy nodded, then glanced at the commander. His normally flush skin had an ashy pallor and his normally immaculate hair poked in disarray. Only his eyes remained bright and alert, and even they seemed restless as they darted around the hall before landing anxiously on her.

"It will be good to get home," she admitted earnestly. "It's not just the *Roger* that needs to rest."

"Yes. Home," Boyce agreed, his gaze distant. He let out a raspy cough and scratched absently at his wrist before refocusing his attention on Wendy. "I'm sure your parents will be glad to see you."

Wendy scoffed. "You know better than that, Commander," she teased. "In fact, you might be the only one in all the galaxies who knows their concern is about as real as my mother's friends."

A barking laugh escaped Boyce's lips. "At least your parents are content to leave you alone," he countered. "The best thing about enlisting in this blasted mission was being free from my father's incessant briefings." He grinned at Wendy's pulled face and nodded. "Trust me, they're as awful as they sound."

Wendy winced in exaggerated sympathy. Born into the same social circle as Boyce, she had met his father on several occasions. He exemplified every bit of the expected celebrated militaryman—and not in a good way. General Boyce was loud, brash, and commandeering on his best day, and as much as she resented the way her parents dismissed her, Boyce was right—she'd much prefer to deal with the Darlings from afar.

"I believe it," Wendy agreed. "I guess that's one positive we can add to this shytestorm of a mission." Boyce smiled, easing the sharp angles in his jaw as warmth seemed to finally seep back into his cheeks.

"Only one?" He queried in a husky tenor. His gaze darted shyly over her features and Wendy dipped her head, flustered by his suggestion until her mind turned to the other positive his remark conjured.

Peter.

Peter, still on Neverland, while she was here. With Boyce. Reminiscing. Her head spun until Boyce coughed politely, pulling her from her conflicted thoughts. Combing her mind for an excuse to leave, she met the commander's stare. Seeing her hesitation, Boyce pulled away, his gaze storming.

"I apologize Captain, that was out of line." The sentiment tumbled from his lips as he feverishly scratched his wrist. "I should go."

"No, Boyce that's not—" Wendy moved to stop his hasty retreat, then paused. She cleared her throat and drew back to stand at attention. "There was no harm in your inquiry, I simply realized I need to report to Navs. It slipped my mind and now I'm afraid I'm late."

"Late." Boyce drawled as he continued to scratch his cuff. His gaze hovered over her shoulder as he spoke, refusing eye contact. "We can't be late," he murmured before a quick shake of his head sharpened his distant stare. He frowned, replacing the smooth lines in his jaw with his familiar scowl. "That would be devastating."

With a curt nod, Boyce brushed past her to escape down the hall, his shoulders tense as he fumed. Wendy watched as he left, her stomach coiling in knots.

Her life had been so much easier when he hated her.

She stood in the hallway, battling her sudden onset of nausea. A heavy groan escaped her as she added another mental tic to her list of problems that she wasn't equipped to handle. She stalked through the halls, retreating to the safety of her quarters. *Your list is getting pretty long, Darling*, she chided mentally. *You're slipping.*

Her pessimistic reprimand darkened her mood, but she had no way to refute it. Her inner monologue may have been a bitch, but it was right. She *was* slipping. Things were spiraling out of control and she had no idea how to rein them in.

Angry thoughts chased her to her quarters. She slapped the access panel, and the screen flashed in protest against her abuse. Wendy lightened her touch, allowing the screen to recalibrate and release the latch, granting her passage. Dawes' chipper greeting was lost in her roiling emotions as she stormed in, caught in her thoughts until Nana let out a worried beep, signaling her elevated stress levels. Wendy gave the band a surly glare, but the reminder was enough to pull her from her tumultuous headspace.

"Is everything ok?" Dawes asked, grounding her in the present.

"Hmm?" Wendy responded absently before her mind processed the question. "Oh. Yes, Dawes. I'm fine." She straightened her shoulders and diverted her gaze, pointedly ignoring the pilot's scrutiny.

Dawes' features tightened. "Of course, Captain," she twisted to her charts before pausing and swinging back around, her brows drawn in a worry. "Are you sure you're alright?"

"Yes," Wendy retorted in an explosive huff. Her pent anger rushed from her lips, streaming out on her words. "I'm broken, so is my ship, and the only people that can help us are unreachable. My life is the definition of alright."

The pilot flinched at Wendy's verbal eruption, her face pulled in hurt. Wendy groaned, frustrated her emotions had gotten the best of her.

"I'm sorry Dawes, that wasn't fair." She scrubbed her face and released a tired groan. "You must be thrilled you get to spend every day with me."

Dawes flashed a wry grin. "Well, someone's gotta do it."

Wendy let out a weak laugh. "Very true," she said. "But that doesn't mean I appreciate it any less."

"Aww I love you too, Captain." Dawes chirped, then returned to her charts with a musical giggle. Wrapped in her work, the pilot's happy humming lilted through the room mixing with the breezy melody.

Wendy stood a moment, allowing her thoughts to drift with the music. The soft sounds faded into the quiet crash of waves rolling from a shallow cove. She lay on the sand, the tiny granules digging into her flesh as she looked up at Peter, his chest heaving in tired gasps while his emerald eyes scoured her face. Meeting her gaze, his worried features loosened into a mischievous grin before the brilliant glow of the Second Star washed over him, stealing him away and leaving her alone. Wendy looked around as the ocean's spray whipped her skin in a cool mist as the turquoise water washing over the shore rippled and darkened to an inky blot that clawed for her legs. It reached for her, the waves transitioning into wispy black tendrils over the crashing whisper's hiss.

Come to me...

Wendy jumped, dashing the image in her mind into a thousand scattered images. Her heart pounded against her chest, but the cabin remained unchanged. Dawes sat in her chair, oblivious to her distress as she consulted the StarBoard. Wendy glanced around, allowing the familiar scene to anchor her distressed thoughts. She brought her hand to her chest, and felt the thin necklace resting under the collar of her uniform. Her fingers clasped the charm dangling from the slender chain. The ridges of the small mechanic acorn pressed into her skin, its cool metal warming under her touch.

She gripped the charm until the erratic rhythm of her heart slowed, then let out a quiet exhale as the paneled doors behind her hummed open. Tucking the acorn inside her uniform, she patted her collar to ensure it was secure before addressing their visitor. Her features twisted in surprise at the grease-stained officer crossing the room.

"Michaels? Is something wrong?"

"Always," Michaels' joke was terse. He scanned the cabin, his eyes darting over the tech before landing on Dawes. His gaze lingered on the pilot before he returned his grim stare to Wendy.

"There's something I need to show you."

10

Wendy followed Michaels through the halls toward the wheezing groans of the *Roger's* maintenance bay. The distant rumble swelled as they approached until Michaels unsealed the access hatch and the muffled sounds of the engine's strain escaped from deep within the barge. It clattered in her ears, nearly cancelling out the swishing whisper that breezed past her.

"What?" Wendy yelled after Michaels' purposeful stride. He paused and turned to her with a quizzical stare before gesturing to his ear.

"We're almost there," he yelled. "You won't be able to hear anything until we get below deck under the sound insulators."

He waited for Wendy's understanding nod, then opened the hatch to belly of the barge. Wendy watched him descend, then moved to follow as another subtle breeze whispered past her to echo above the surface. A chill swept down her spine, but she quashed it with a scoff. Strange sounds weren't unusual on aged vessels, and the *Roger* was a certified antique. Old things creaked and groaned—it was the Shakes she was worried about.

She hurried after Michaels, quickly dropping down the ladder to meet him below deck. He steered her toward a large panel, and Wendy recognized the Pix.E device neatly nestled into the tech. The machine whirred as it worked, but she couldn't help but notice the tired whine it emitted while it spun.

Michaels inspected the panel, his shrewd gaze darting over each piece and lingering in a few poignant pauses before he turned to Wendy, his face pulled in a grim line.

"Our malfunction ratio is increasing drastically, Captain," he disclosed. "In the past three days alone we have experienced eight significant Shakes, which is up three recordable incidents from last week. Not only that, but the events are longer and more pronounced. We are deteriorating at an alarming rate."

Wendy bit her lip as she scanned the tech before her, searching the foreign pieces for a hidden answer. Hard surfaces and glinting edges were her only response, giving nothing more than an indecipherable code.

"Where is the malfunction originating?" she asked. "Can you pinpoint the source of the problem."

Michaels repositioned his glasses with a sigh. "No. We're hemorrhaging energy, but I can't figure out where from. I keep thinking I've pinpointed the issue, only to have another turn up in the next day or so." He scanned the panel in front of him and his glasses glowed lime green with the reflection of a dozen indicator lights. "She's flying stable for now, but that's about all I can promise."

He crossed the room to monitor another switchboard. His fingers flew over the keys as he entered a series of commands and the *Roger* hummed in response.

"I've been able to redirect the unused power to siphon it to an emergency reserve. If we can get the crew on board to be as conservative with the power as they can be on their own, I think I can make do with what I've got. But if anything changes..."

"Let me know immediately." Wendy asserted as she turned to leave, her mind whirring to calculate the ramifications of Michaels' revelation. She paused at the base of the hatch, then turned to the tech, raising her voice to register over the *Roger's* dull roar. "Whatever it takes Michaels, handle the ship."

Michaels nodded and waved after her as she hoisted herself up to the main floor. Her feet hit steel with a loud clang and she closed the hatch, burying the *Roger's* sweltering underbelly beneath the heavy metal. She stood in the corridor until the ringing echo of the closing door finally faded, leaving her in calm silence. Sweat beaded on her neck and forehead, cooling as the ship's climatized air brushed against her skin.

Glancing around, Wendy scanned the dim hallway lighting as she considered Michaels' grim prognosis. While the corridor beams had never been set to full illumination, they had always been bright enough to clearly light the reaches of the rounded roof. Now, shadows danced overhead, crouching in the arches where the light no longer touched.

Wendy shuddered, debating whether she made the best decision. It was her directive to decrease the lighting output in the corridors and lesser-used rooms to preserve power. Michaels had suggested that diverting energy from non-essentials would increase the *Roger's* overall functionality. There was no hard evidence to support his theory, but the mechanic had never steered her wrong before. She just wondered how long it would work. Even Michaels admitted it wasn't a permanent fix, but rather a precautionary measure that would need to be revisited if the ship continued deteriorating.

Her chest squeezed as she looked up at the rafters. Watching the shadows shift and move to follow the movements of her head, Wendy had to admit that though she had never been afraid of the dark, she would be lying if she said she didn't find it *unsettling*.

Scanning the ship's walls as she made her way through the dingy corridors, she noted that nothing looked out of place. Aside from normal wear and tear—and some expertly applied graffiti— the *Roger* looked like any other Fleet vessel, albeit much more dated.

"You can make it, girl," Wendy murmured. She reached to pet the *Roger's* walls reassuringly. "I know you're tired, but you can do it. We need you."

A soft shiver ran up her fingertips from the panel beneath them, pulling Wendy's lips in a tight smile. She continued on in quiet consideration until she heard an alarming clang.

Wendy slowed, her brows furrowed as she strained to identify the strange sound. She focused so intently on the noise that a soft tap against her shoulder sent her jumping from her skin.

"Johns!" Wendy staggered, glaring accusingly at the lieutenant-commander as she clutched her unsteady heart. "I thought you were talking to the Boys!"

"Huh?" Johns frowned before his lips split into an easy grin. "Oh, right. All squared, Darling. But—" he paused to scratch his head, "none of the Boys have nicked anything. Well, not since you let Nibs have it. Apparently you scared the poor kid straight."

Wendy snickered. "I highly doubt that, but I'll take it." She said, pausing
to follow Johns' darting glance. "Is everything alright, Johns? You're acting
jumpier than the day Commandant Velasquez found you in her Skyball
team's dorm."

Johns' laugh boomed through the open corridor.

"Oh, Velasquez. I thought she was gonna *kill* me that night," he chuckled,
caught in the memory. "Did I ever thank you for saving my ass that day?"

"Not nearly enough," Wendy grumbled, remembering the week she spent
hiding him in her dorm. She'd never been so worried about expulsion—or
starvation before in her life. Johns hadn't been in her room nearly two hours
and he'd cleaned out her pantry. She was pretty sure she hadn't gone to the
commissary as much in her entire duration at the Academy as she had that
week. She huffed an exasperated laugh. "So, for what non-life threatening,
completely normal reason are you looking for me?"

Johns opened his mouth to respond, then dropped his jaw as his finger
raised proudly in the air. "I forgot?"

Wendy scoffed. "Seriously, Johns? You were looking everywhere and you
forgot? I know I said the ship was big, but that's ridiculous."

"No! I mean, I didn't forget," Johns argued, "I just ..." He trailed off to
glance around the corridor.

An agitated growl escaped Wendy's chest. "If this is some sort of weird
game, I really don't have time, Elias," she emphasized her irritation with his first
name. "Remember all those catastrophic situations I was telling you about?"

"You do keep mentioning those," Johns smirked and glanced at his watch. "I tell you what, I'll escort you back to your cabin where you deal with allllll those life-threatening situations, and that way, if I remember, I can tell you."

"Fine," Wendy frowned at his exuberance. "But if you don't remember by the time we make it back, you're out of luck."

"And I thought what we had was special."

Johns' dramatic sigh pulled a begrudging smile from Wendy. She shook her head and started down the corridor, biting back the legion of comebacks his remark summoned. Johns followed, humming badly off tune while he juggled a set of three bandage rolls.

"I see our medical equipment is being put to excellent use," Wendy groused.

"Half the battle is in your mind, Darling," Johns retorted, his focus on the tumbling rolls. "Gotta stay sharp." He winked at her, and the bandages scattered to the ground.

Wendy laughed. "Speaking of sharp, have you remembered why you were looking for me yet?"

"Nope." Johns shrugged, his attention back on his juggling. Wendy sighed. She was about to respond when they rounded the corner to her cabin doors, stretched wide open, revealing darkened quarters behind them.

"Hold on Johns," her arm whipped out, blocking the lieutenant-commander' path. Three soft thuds hit the ground as he followed her gaze.

"I'm guessing you don't leave your room like that often?"

Wendy shook her head, her lips pressed firmly together as she assessed the situation.

"No," she said. "Not ever. Something's wrong."

11

Wendy tensed as she crept toward the darkened room. Johns followed suit, mimicking her ready stance. The hairs pricked on the back of her neck, but she snuck her hand to the light panel. After a moment of blind fumbling, she located the switch to illuminate the darkened room. Wendy slithered back, preparing to strike as the cabin lights flickered wearily to life.

"SURPRISE!"

A pack of cheering figures jumped from the shadows, blind to Wendy's defensive stance. She met the intruders with raised fists until her crew's happy laughter registered in her ears.

"What the hell—"

"Calm down Darling," Johns' booming laugh erupted behind her. "We know you don't like your birthday but there's no reason to assault people."

Wendy dropped her arms, flabbergasted by the crowd filling her brightly decorated cabin.

"But, it's April," Wendy protested dumbly. "My birthday was over a month ago. We missed it."

Johns laughed again, drowning the happy chatter that filled the room. "I'm sure that's what you were hoping," he grinned.

"I was not," Wendy grumbled. Johns was only partly right. She didn't like to celebrate her birthday, but she hadn't hoped they'd forgotten. She had forgotten on her own. "I just didn't remember," she admitted.

Johns feigned a scandalized gasp. "You *forgot*? How could you forget the birth of the most celebrated captain in all of Brigade history?"

Wendy flushed, embarrassed by his theatrics, but no one seemed to notice. The others milled around the room, chatting lazily while Dawes' reggae mix warbled in the background. Satisfied there wasn't an audience to Johns' antics, Wendy relaxed and rolled her eyes.

"Taking a little liberty with the term *most* there, aren't you Johns?"

Johns shrugged. "I can think of a few people that would second my statement."

"Michaels doesn't count."

"Semantics," Johns dismissed her with a wave of his hand. "But seriously, how does one forget their birthday?"

"*One* doesn't know," Wendy needled before she shrugged. "There were more important things happening."

"Like what," Johns challenged.

"Oh, I don't know," she quipped breezily. "Lots of things; like trying not to get eaten by demon mermaids, or discovering our childhood hero was actually a villain. Oh, and fighting an evil entity that wanted to destroy the planet." She quirked her brow. "But you know, *those*, and also my birthday. How could I have forgotten?"

"Exactly." Johns persisted, then laughed good-naturedly. "Either way, you should know we'd never miss your birthday! Especially if it gives us a chance to liven up this busted-ass cruise ship." He glanced around the bustling room. "She cleans up alright with a bit of work though."

Wendy followed his gaze. She had to give it to Johns, he was right. Bright streamers hung from the vaulted ceilings adding splashes of color to the monochromatic walls while shiny space blankets formed makeshift tablecloths that protected the antiquated fixtures from the surprising spread of food arranged over them. If Wendy hadn't known better, she'd never have guessed the offerings were cobbled from dehydrated meal-packs.

"How did you do all this?" Wendy asked, appreciatively. A large space was cleared in the center of the room, giving the crew space to mingle. To add to the ambiance, someone—most likely Dawes based on the imagery—had rigged a hologram to project on closed visor screen, submerging the cabin in rocking ocean waves. The shimmering backdrop transformed the space into a picturesque beach escape. "*When* did you do this?"

Johns smirked. "A good magician never reveals his tricks," he preened. Wendy was about to protest when she was nearly tackled from behind.

"Do you like it?" Dawes squealed, bouncing on her toes. "Were you surprised?"

"Surprised is an understatement," Wendy admitted before narrowing her eyes suspiciously. "How many of you were in on this?"

Dawes beamed. "All of us, of course."

Wendy's jaw dropped. "You *all* were in on this and you didn't tell me?" She whirled to the lieutenant-commander with an accusing glare. "Johns!"

"I really think you're missing the concept of a surprise party," Johns mumbled, handing her a cup filled with a sparkling pink liquid. "Now take this, shut up, and enjoy the attention for once."

Wendy scowled, but accepted the drink. Taking a sip, she was pleasantly surprised to discover that it was tart, but not terrible. She raised her glass to the surrounding crew. "This is all wonderful," she said. "Thank you."

Dawes let out a delighted giggle, then bounded off to change the track while Johns gave Wendy a tight squeeze. "Now, Captain, if you don't mind, I have other guests to attend to." He raised his glass and waggled his brows at DeLaCruz, who blushed from across the room. Wendy let out an amused sigh.

"At ease, Soldier," she waved him off and smiled. "Take the night off, you've earned it."

Johns whooped and barreled off, but not before wrapping her in a giant hug.

"Happy birthday, Darling," he whispered, holding her tight. "Thanks for another fantastic year. Let's keep 'em coming, eh?"

Wendy sank into his embrace. "I'll do my best," she murmured.

"See to it that you do," he lectured, his voice tight. "I thought we lost you once. I don't plan on living through that again." His voice caught, and there was a pause before he continued. "Michaels was a wreck."

"Noted," Wendy buried her smile in Johns' shoulder and allowed his arms to tighten in one last squeeze before he released her. She stepped away, then slugged his shoulder and tipped her head toward DeLaCruz. "Now get outta here. You have other people waiting for you."

Johns laughed as his gaze flicked behind her. "I'm not the only one," he winked, then bounded across the room, wiggling his hips to the cadence of steel drums.

Wendy shook her head as she watched him go until a throat cleared softly behind her. Startled, she turned to where Boyce waited uncomfortably. His muscles flexed against his fitted jacket as his arms clasped at attention.

"Captain," he dipped his head in greeting. His tired eyes darted over the bright decorations and laughing crew. "Happy birthday."

He handed her a small box wrapped in shiny fabric. Wendy's eyes widened in surprise.

"Dawes said she didn't need all the space blankets, and that we could use what she didn't," he explained sheepishly. "I figured it didn't count as a birthday present if it wasn't wrapped."

Wendy accepted the gift and looked up at him. "You didn't have to do that," she murmured. Boyce's tremulous smile wavered. "But I appreciate it," she added hastily, "Thank you."

"Well, you've managed to get this far without killing us all," Boyce needled. "I figured it was the least I could do."

"Commander, is that a joke?"

Boyce's scowl drifted into a smile. "A birthday miracle," he grumbled, before nodding to the gift. "Now open it before I change my mind."

Intrigued, Wendy glanced at the package. It was beautiful, with the shiny wrapping bound by thin strips of black fabric that had been painstakingly cut into ribbons. She worked slowly to preserve the handiwork until Boyce let out an impatient sigh, then she stripped the paper to reveal a small metal box with a thin seam slit down the middle. Wendy pried it open to reveal its contents and let out a surprised gasp when she discovered a delicate linked charm bracelet inside. Only one charm dangled from a tiny loop. A small metal replica of the *Fede Fiducia*.

Wendy glanced at Boyce, who worried at his lip while he studied her reaction. "Where did you get this?"

A flush of color tinged the commander's pallid skin, making him look healthier than he had in weeks. "I made it," he admitted, before hastily adding, "It's from the extra scrap we had lying around, so don't get too excited."

Wendy lifted the bracelet to examine it better. The charm was rusted and tinged with aged metal. "My mother would *never* approve," she exclaimed.

"So, you like it?"

"I love it," Wendy declared. "Thank you."

Boyce released a heavy breath. Wendy almost felt the tension leave his body, and was hit with a soft twinge of guilt. Over the past few weeks the commander had been looking more harried each time she saw him. If it had been anyone besides Boyce, she might have described his appearance as haggard, but his impeccable uniform prevented that descriptor—if only barely. She studied him in silent appraisal. Though his jacket still wrapped tight across the broad muscles of his chest and arms, she could see where the tapered material rested loosely against his torso. That, and the prominent lines in his already sharp cheekbones indicated he had lost weight. His skin had lost its golden tint and paled under the ship's fluorescent lights, which wouldn't have been too concerning, given the situation—there wasn't a whole lot of Sun exposure happening inside the sealed vessel—but with the dark circles forming under his eyes, it made him look gaunt and sickly.

"How are you feeling Commander," Wendy asked as she tucked the bracelet safely in its box.

"As well as anyone else on board, I imagine," Boyce answered, his tone curt. His gaze landed on the Lost Boys laughing in the corner and his nose turned in a haughty sneer. "Better I suppose, if it weren't for the refuse we picked up on the way."

Wendy followed his stare to where Nibs and the Twins whooped loudly as they played hackeyball with a wadded blue napkin. She opened her mouth to protest, when she was accosted by small arms wrapping her waist in a tight squeeze.

"Happy b-birthday, C-captain!" Tootles exclaimed with a bright smile.

"Thank you, Tootles," she acknowledged, freeing herself from his grip. "I don't suppose you had any part in this," she indicated to the buzzing room. Tootles gave a shy nod.

"We all h-helped," he said proudly, then pointed at the streamers. "C-Curly, Nibs, and I m-made the decorations," he beckoned Wendy closer. She leaned in, and he pushed on his toes to whisper in his ear. "The T-Twins even made a c-cake," he whispered conspiratorially.

"Well, I love it," she said, glancing over the boy to the commander. He stood, watching impatiently from where he had been shoved to the side. Wendy shrugged apologetically, then returned her attention to Tootles. "It's all perfect."

Tootles' smile faltered. "Well, a-almost," he said sadly. "It w-would be p-perfect if P-peter was h-here."

Wendy's stomach twisted, but she brushed the boy's blonde hair. "You're right," she nodded, then tucked his chin. "But Peter would still want you to have a good time," she asserted. "So get to it." She issued the command with a stern face. Tootles' eyes sparked and he snapped a tight salute.

"Yes, C-captain," he said, before running off in the other direction.

Wendy watched him go, then turned to where Boyce had been relegated. Her face fell as she realized the commander's space was empty. She glanced around the room, but Boyce had disappeared. With a heavy sigh, she gripped at the small box in her hand and shoved it in her pocket, forcing the mixed emotions it conjured with it.

"I told Johns you hated surprises," a familiar voice mumbled, freeing Wendy from her churning thoughts. "Shocking he didn't listen."

"Very uncharacteristic of Johns," Wendy agreed with a smirk. She turned to Michaels. His mousy brown hair dipped over his eyes as he monitored the comm he gripped in his hand, securing it from the glass of punch he held in the other. "Honestly, I'm surprised he hasn't come up with an excuse to throw a basher before this. They were a weekend staple at the Academy."

"Well, it got you out of the maintenance bay, so it can't be all bad." Wendy grinned and brushed the soot from Michaels' split ends. "I was worried you were turning into a mole-person."

"Mole people live in the ground," Michaels pointed out as he scanned the cabin's rafters. His brown eyes darted over the metallic fixtures. "I needed to come up anyway. It's been a while since I did a visual inspection."

"Stop that right now," Wendy chided. "If the ship hasn't already capsized, it's not going to today. Take the night off. That's an order."

Michaels pursed his lips, but nodded. Begrudgingly, he tucked the comm in his pocket, leaving his hand strangely empty.

"Don't look so upset," Wendy teased. "The issues will still be here tomorrow."

Michaels' smile didn't quite meet his eyes.

"Along with about twenty new ones," he muttered and scrubbed his eyes. "I just can't keep up with them all. Most are surface-level," he reached into his pocket and absently retrieved his comm to tap the screen. Wendy was about to make a smart comment, but the furrow in his brow stopped her. He continued scrolling before issuing a sigh. "But I still can't locate the underlying problem. Until I do, everything is just a band aid. We're hemorrhaging, and there's nothing I can do to stop it."

Wendy placed her hand over the screen. "Give it a break. Focus on something else for a bit. Clear your head." She met his dubious look with an authoritative stare. "You're too close to it. Take the night off, and come back fresh tomorrow."

Michaels sighed, but nodded as he tucked the comm away. He observed the party, scrutinizing the scene. "I never much cared for reggae," he grumbled, though his brown eyes drifted to Dawes. "But techno, *that* I can get behind."

"I'm not surprised." Wendy laughed. "So, aside from telling Johns it was a terrible idea, did you have any part in this shindig?"

Michaels nodded at the holograph displayed on the visor. "Dawes made me help. I told her it was frivolous, but she threatened to figure it out on her own. She's almost as stubborn as you are." He grumbled, but Wendy noticed the way his attention lingered on the pretty pilot. "I think you two are spending too much time together."

Wendy snorted. "Well, my best friend has been buried in the bottom of a spaceship," she countered. "I had to find someone to talk to."

Michaels studied her quietly. "You miss him a lot, don't you?"

Wendy's brow furrowed. "Of course I miss you, Michaels, I just told you that."

"Not me. *Him.*"

Wendy's stomach writhed. A sudden burst of energy keyed through her, screaming for her to run. Instead, she dropped her gaze. "Is it that obvious?" she laughed bitterly. "Here I was thinking I was doing a good job."

Michaels matched her weak smile. "I doubt anyone else knows," he said. "They aren't as observant," he confided. "For all they know, you're just broody and angsty. Very apropos for the suffering captain vibe you've got going on."

"Wonderful." Wendy scoffed. "Broody and angsty was exactly what I was going for." She cast the room for a topic change. "Did you try any of the food? I heard there was a cake—but I you didn't hear it from me."

"Not yet," Michaels glanced at the shiny table and shrugged. "But that reminds me. Watch out for SMEE's gift. He asked me to help rig it, but," He cast a surreptitious glance at the robot. "Don't ever let that synth near my maintenance bay."

A surprised laugh gurgled from Wendy's chest. "What do you mean?"

"Let's just say, I never thought I'd meet a synth who could actually *damage* tech," Michaels grimaced. "The day I ask for his help with repairs is the day we're all doomed." He shuddered. "I seriously wonder what exactly he's done all these years."

"The world may never know," Wendy consoled, then gave him a small shove. "Now, go be social. Or at least talk to someone besides your comm," she fixed the tech with a knowing stare. "Captain's orders."

Michaels gave a withered scowl. "Aye, aye Captain." He pocketed his comm as he shuffled off, grumbling under his breath.

"I mean it Michaels," Wendy called, watching him go. "No tech, or I'll have SMEE shadow you tomorrow."

She ignored Michaels' panicked expression and pointed meaningfully where Dawes danced in front of the visor. He followed her gesture, dragging his heels as he trudged toward the dancing pilot, his face contorting like he was considering the lesser of two evils. Wendy snorted at the tech's pained look, but her amusement was interrupted by a mechanical hum.

"You would like me to work in the maintenance bay tomorrow, Captain?"

"What?" Wendy spun guiltily to face her adopted first mate, fumbling for an excuse under the synth's eager stare. "Oh. No, SMEE. Michaels was saying he might need assistance, but I told him your help was required elsewhere."

SMEE nodded. "I am happy to help the lieutenant as well," he pointed out. "Sleep is not a necessity."

Wendy shook her head, certain Michaels would strangle her—or at least infect every piece of tech she owned—if the cybernet even approached his station. "That's very kind, but I don't think it's necessary. I'll let you know if needs change."

"Very well." SMEE's gears whirred as he reached for his pocket. "While I have you, Captain, happy birthday." He beamed and offered her a small, misshapen package. "I must admit, I don't understand the ideology of the tradition, but I can appreciate the sentiment. I was told in celebrating the anniversary of one's human birth, it is proper etiquette to exchange gifts." He dropped the package in her hands. "I do hope you like it."

Remembering Michaels warning, Wendy eyeballed the lump. "Thank you, SMEE. I'm sure I'll love it."

A fabricated blush tinged the first mate's ears as he chuckled with delight. "You're welcome Captain." His gaze trailed from the gift to Wendy's anxious stare. "I believe the next step in the exchange is for you to open it."

Now it was Wendy's turn to flush. She studied the package, pretending to pick at the wrapping while she discreetly tried to determine what was inside. Her fingers caught an edge and she peeked at SMEE, whose manufactured features twisted in excitement. His lips pulled in an eager smile, and she dropped her gaze, preparing her reaction. She tugged the corner, but the soft rip of the decorative paper was drowned in a deafening crash as the *Roger* rocked wildly, filling the room with a chorus of surprised yelps as the crew tumbled in the turbulence.

Wendy's knee buckled and she stumbled forward, her palms stinging as she righted herself and hurried to assess the situation.

"Is everyone alright?" she yelled. Her team grumbled in response, but when they all appeared unharmed, Wendy snapped to business. "Good. Man your stations. We need to figure out what just happened." She commanded, scanning the room. "Michaels, downstairs. Take Tootles with you. He can help you run inventory. Do you need anyone else?"

Michaels studied Tootles before considering his other options. "He'll do."

Wendy nodded. "You're dismissed. I want to know *exactly* what the problem is."

"Uh, Captain?" Johns interrupted, "I don't think that's going to be necessary."

"Of course it's necessary," Wendy barked, but her words faltered as she spun toward the lieutenant-commander and saw his face pale as he gaped at the visor. The lens had jarred open, replacing the hologram's gentle, lapping waves with the open sky before them. A startled gasp slipped from Wendy's lips as she stepped forward to peer at the screen. The once vast expanse of space had been replaced, filled with a tangle of dense, floating objects. They spun lazily as they passed through the screen, bumping together in a slow, muddled dance.

"Is it an asteroid belt?" Curly's thinly veiled panic bubbled through the cabin.

"No," Wendy whispered. "It's a graveyard."

THE
FLIGHT

12

FIDUCIA II (GROUNDED)

LEAD MECHANIC PETER PAN

Tiger Lily's husky timbre followed Peter long after he crept inside the maw of the cave. But once he crossed the threshold of the crevice's gaping mouth, the underground city's bioluminous lighting was snuffed like a match.

A soft tremor rushed through Peter as the darkness encased him. He missed Tinc's orienting glow, and in the stifling silence, felt acutely alone without her buzzing snark. The dark pressed down on him, thrusting his mind back to the Shadow. Suffocating in the black, he was seized by tangible certainty that this would be what the world was reduced to if Itzala truly won.

Peter closed his eyes to blot the invasive gloom and took a steadying breath to alleviate his fears. When his breathing slowed, he peeked into the dark and was surprised by a faint glow burning in the depths of the cave. It flickered softly in the distance—casting a beautiful turquoise shine against the endless black pitch. Curious, he glanced back, but the cave's opening had disappeared, like him, swallowed by the dark. Trembling, he turned toward the pulsing light, which beckoned patiently with its azure glow.

Peter's steps echoed faintly behind him as he pushed onward, his fear quelled by intrigue as he drew toward the throbbing beacon. A mysterious breeze whipped through the rocky fixture, mixing the heady smell of must and earth the farther he descended. The light intensified as Peter approached, and he soon discovered it pulsated in waves of alternating blue and white. Peter walked in breathless silence, caught in its beauty, ignoring the tiny splashes under his feet until they turned into the crunch of crumbling ice. He glanced down, surprised to find the light now illuminated the area around him, revealing a sparkling layer of ice crystallized across the cavern walls. His breath puffed into the frigid air as he slowly reached for the shimmering stone. Surprising warmth seeped into his skin revealing the chill in the surrounding air was as the cave thrummed, filling him with a resonating hum that sank to the core of his bones. He withdrew his hand, marveling at the reverberations that flooded his palm long after he broke contact with the glistening wall.

Peter flexed his hand in wonder before returning his gaze to the ghostly light. He continued his path, squinting as he neared the beacon. At the end of the cave, an ancient dais waited, similar to the one Hooke used to summon the Shadow. Like the other, this altar was also formed from heavy stone, but instead of cracked ebony edging, it was a beautiful ivory with turquoise gilding tracking the surface. From every thinly carved line, soft light shimmered, pouring from the heart of the dais to illuminate the surrounding cave in a stunning constellation that rivaled the stars.

Peter sucked in a breath, then took a wary step forward to peer into the dais, remembering the onyx pitch that writhed from the dark altar. He peeked over the shallow bowl and was surprised when he looked deep into his own reflection. His green eyes shined against the glowing light, matching his other features washed in the shimmering cast. Awestruck, he reached for the clear liquid, but before he touched the glistening surface, another face appeared in the reflection.

Surprised, Peter glanced up at an ancient Stjarnin, stooped with age. Her muted skin was far from the rich, mossy green of the Stjarnin in the village and had paled to a soft cream. She had the same scars etched into her flesh, but unlike the others, they were the dark color of verdant earth. Her onyx stare gripped Peter, unblinking as he studied her. An elaborate braided crown of circled her head, then trailed down her back, ending in a cluster of smooth stone beads. Peter gaped at the Stjarnin, who waited patiently for him to speak. Finally, he broke her gaze by dipping in a long, low bow. When he straightened, the Stjarnin had circled the dais to stand before him.

You are not a Stjarnin warrior, the Stjarnin's raspy voice had a musical quality to it, like Neverbreeze whipping through the trees. *Only the most worthy can commune with the spirits of the ancient, and you are not our kind. Why are you here?* Her lips drew in a pinched trio as she stared, waiting imperiously for his response.

"I don't know." The rough edges of Peter's voice bounced around the hollow tunnel. "I was hoping you could tell me."

The Stjarnin hummed then struck the collar of Peter's shirt. She yanked the fabric, revealing his chest and the dark mark throbbing under the surface of his skin. Her eyes widened as she loosened her grip and staggered back, her features contorting into an accusatory glare.

You bear the mark of the Shadow, she murmured. The timbre of her voice shook the walls with rage.

"No, I..." Peter clamped his hand over the marred spot, his words failing as he rubbed the blemish. The mark had appeared during his first encounter with the Shadow, and after it had been defeated, had slowly begun to fade. It had been days since he had seen the stain's trace, and he thought it had disappeared. It shook him to the core that the mark still remained. He stared at the ancient alien—even with her foreign features he could read her anger and fear. He dropped his hands and faced her directly, addressing her with as much authority as he could muster.

"I have come to fight it."

The Stjarnin held his stare for an unending moment, then stepped forward, her outstretched hand trembling with age or fear, Peter couldn't tell. After a brief hesitation, her palm pressed against Peter's forehead, summoning all his memories in a raw, flooding wave.

Peter rooted to the spot as visions of his past spiraled to the forefront of his mind, creating a spooling reel of images that danced across the dais' quicksilver liquid, playing his life in a blinding flash. *Waking in a tattered bed and walking out to a broken table with no food for the fourth day in a row... hiding under a filthy blanket while a man screamed at his mother before a shuddering door slammed, leaving the house silent except for wracking sobs streaming through the kitchen… holding his mother's hand as they walked through the dirtiest of the New London streets… her instructions to wait for her on the corner before never coming back…*

Peter gasped as his eyes flung open to meet the Stjarnin, who observed with an expressionless stare before she dipped her head and plunged Peter back into his past. Memories continued to wash over him, reflected by the pooling liquid that churned and stirred as his life-show played, changing colors with each and every scene. He blinked and the muted gray wisps faded to a dirty brown haze surrounding the dingy streets of New London.

He was older now. He had been on the streets a few years and discovered a penchant for mech and talking shyte. The stodgy doxie in the fancy red jacket looked like he had a stick up his ass and Peter took it upon himself to tell him. It was only when a sizzling blade was pressed against his throat that he realized James Hooke might not have been the best mark… quick talking and showing the captain his work… being offered a place on his boat… long, exhausting hours inside a sweltering rig, but falling asleep each night sailing the skies with Tinc humming softly beside him in her sleep…

The grip on Peter's forehead tightened as the Stjarnin's eyes narrowed and the remaining scenes whirred by blindingly fast.

…Hooke's journal entry didn't make sense. What did he mean he was leaving? Why would he abandon them for a star… sabotaging the Roger *and confronting Hooke for his treachery before the ship rumbled and fell from the sky… waking in Neverland with Tootles and the others… slowly forming a family… a deafening crash followed by a cloud of billowing smoke that led to a downed bird and the most beautiful girl he had ever seen…*

The wispy background transitioned to soft purple as Wendy charged to the front of his mind. She stood in all her glory, her hair cascading over her shoulders in wild chestnut curls as she leveled her challenging glare. A beautiful smile softened her serious features, then in a flash, she was all hard edges as she watched in fear as the Shadow swirled from Hooke's ancient dais.

Beneath his memories, the liquid churned, swirling from lilac to pitch as the flashback culminated in their final battle with Wendy at his side. Peter stared in awe as he watched her bravery. His hands itched to draw her to him and never let go, but when his arms stretched to cover the distance, the cloudy memories wiped away, leaving only the wizened alien standing before him.

Where is she now? The Stjarnin asked, piercing Peter with her endless gaze.

"She had to return," Peter answered, feeling the stabbing pain of her departure lance fresh through his heart.

That is why you have come. To save her.

"She doesn't need saving," Peter answered as a rueful smile crept to his face. "She'll tell you that herself."

The Stjarnin nodded politely, but quickly fixed her penetrating gaze on Peter.

Even the strongest warrior can fall to Itzala's dark embrace.

Peter frowned. He knew the Stjarnin's words were all too true. He had felt the Shadow's strength firsthand and the crushing power it used to wriggle inside and claim its victims. Wendy was the strongest person he knew, but her brilliant inner-light would be a beacon to the darkness' consuming greed. He looked at the Stjarnin, who watched him with her uncanny stare.

Even the greatest warrior can fall to the darkness.

"What do I do?"

The Stjarnin didn't speak, she only withdrew from Peter to shuffle to the opposite side of the altar. Her fingertips rested lightly on the edge of the ivory stone and the glyphs flashed in shivering anticipation.

Come, her voice echoed through the vaulted cave. *I will show you.*

She stretched her hand across the dais as the shimmering contents swirled below. Peter eyed the grooves in her palm then reached to slip his hand in hers. As soon as their grip met, the Stjarnin plunged his fist into the shimmering liquid.

Bubbling around Peter's hand, the surface roiled and churned, a living thing pulsing and undulating as it climbed his arm. It enveloped his sinewy muscles like a second skin, coating his freckled forearms in quicksilver. Surprised, Peter yelped and tried to pull free, but the liquid cinched tighter to encase his shoulders and slither across his face. The Stjarnin hummed as the writhing liquid shrouded Peter's body, filling the cavern with a low, droning hum.

"Don't do this!" Peter struggled to get away, but the ancient Stjarnin simply blinked her vacant eyes and continued her toneless hum. The liquid lapped Peter's cheeks before it arched like a snake and struck, covering Peter's eyes with a freezing quicksilver veil that blocked the cavern's dazzling glow.

Suddenly, the humming stopped and Peter froze, straining to hear through the cave's deathly silence. His icy mask began to warm and smooth until became a thin cloak that stretched to cover his whole body. Peter watched in wonder as the liquid surrounded him, then with a final deep hum, shimmered and absorbed into his skin. He gaped at his flesh, completely unscathed, then turned to the Stjarnin, fuming.

"What do you think you're—" he started, but before he could finish, the Stjarnin bowed, then shimmered and disappeared, sinking into the hollowed dais as her body transformed into the same substance. Peter watched the transformation, then, against his better judgement, reached into the Stjarnin's shimmering remains.

A million whispers washed over him as he was surrounded in light, revealing thousands of glyphs traced over his skin. He charted the marks, following the story they wove as the Stjarnin ancients droned in unison, offering their secrets.

Long before the earliest galaxies began, there was the Star and all its beauty. Its light stretched into the emptiness of space, fighting the darkness with its gentle glow. It burned so brightly that it sparked a great flare before almost fizzling out. But the Star was powerful, and closed itself to preserve its power. The great motion drew its neighboring stars and clusters of floating earth, and as the Star regenerated, its power was cast into the objects caught in its embrace. The Star healed, and soon unraveled to once again form a beacon in the dark. As it did, it left behind a small, newly formed planet that thrummed with the remnants of its power. The Star was fascinated by the tiny planet, and brushed it softly to examine its creation. Its brilliant light illuminated the darkened rock, and sent reservoirs of power bubbling across the landscape like rivers. The planet responded to its creator and lit from within to form lush, verdant lands from the sparking, winding lines. The Star delighted with its creation until it realized the land was still—there was nothing to enjoy its beauty. It caught a passing comet and trapped it in its grip. Once more the Star pushed its life force into the elements, and this time, the Stjarnin were formed. The Star lowered the rock to the planet, and with its final kiss, cracked the stone, revealing the first Stjarnin Chief Itenzo and his wife Joxtani. Under the light of their birthing Star, the Stjarnin lived a peaceful existence in the land they had been created for.

The Stjarnin's voice trailed to a stop, but the whispers behind it continued to grow as they painted the picture of their planet before him. It resembled Neverland, but the topography was different than the landscape above him. Peter watched in awe until the picture shifted and its twisting wisps formed the image of a tall Stjarnin warrior with gleaming silver eyes.

Itzala was the most powerful of our warriors. Even now—though the Stjarnin claim tribute to many valiant warriors—none compared to the sheer strength and cunning of Itzala. He did many great things for our people. Bringing down dangerous threats and helping to construct great monuments, and earning the adoration of all the Stjarnin. His only weakness was his pride. When the clamoring of his name was no longer enough to sate his arrogance, he turned his attention outward. It was no longer enough that he had the Stjarnin's respect, he wanted the power to command it.

Itzala knew he could not steal the throne from the reigning chief, who had been blessed with the Star's favor, and so he scoured the land, searching for another way. Deep in the heart of the planet, he found the soul of a demon, trapped during the Star's rebirth. It promised Itzala that if he freed it, it would exchange with him its power. Driven by greed, Itzala released the demon, freeing it from captivity. Once free, the demon was bound to its promise, but it was a wily spirit, and had a plan of its own. It took part of Itzala's soul, claiming it for his own. The demon replaced it with a piece of itself, tainting the great warrior's heart before he returned to its home in the galaxy's darkest depths.

Itzala, now corrupted with the demon's tainted soul, returned to the village, with destruction in his heart. Brazen, he approached Ijara, the third born-line of the great chief Itenzo and challenged him to atja, a great Sjarnin battle. The chief recognized the darkness in Itzala's heart and tried to deny him, but Itzala would not back down. He forced Ijara to battle in the heart of the city, for all the Stjarnin to see.

The ancient Stjarnin's voice faded into the glowing cavern as the picture her words conjured sprung to life. Peter watched as Itzala, bolstered by the demon's power, stalked into the peaceful Stjarnin village. The warrior's silver eyes blazed as he strode forward with wispy tendrils of darkness biting his heels as he issued his challenge. The chief's head shook in silent denial, but Itzala flung his spear across the opening to strike Ijara in the shoulder. Clasping his wound, the chief stared at the warrior in surprise, while the other Stjarnin rushed to his aide. Ijara raised his hand, his eyes wide as he glimpsed the darkness enshrouding Itzala. Slowly, he pulled the bloody spear from his flesh and rose to meet the looming warrior.

Cold dread gripped Peter as the rolling cloud surrounding Itzala began to grow, blossoming from behind him, revealing the same Darkness that had gripped him. Before he collapsed into paralyzing fear, Ijara's voice strengthened, wrapping Peter in its reedy tone to pull him back into the tale.

Ijara fought bravely, but he was no match for Itzala's newly acquired strength. When the chief fell, instead of releasing him to the Everworld, Itzala plunged his atja staff into Ijara's chest, destroying his heart to deny the good king's entrance to the Home of the Ancients. When the watching warriors saw what

Itzala had done, they moved to stop him, but it was too late. Consumed by the darkness, Itzala descended upon them all. The evil that the demon injected in his heart enveloped the once-great warrior, forming a cloud of devastation as he cut down the Stjarnin one by one. With every fallen warrior, the blackness inside Itzala grew, until his silver eyes spilled over crimson. It was in that moment, when the Stjarnin were certain all hope was lost, that the fallen chief's daughter stepped forward. Lareli approached the growing darkness and called upon the Star, who heard her daughter's piteous cry.

The Star gazed down, filled with sadness at what its beautiful creation had become reached out to Lareli. Her soft touch brushed the princess' cheek, and left a glowing green kiss. That left a delicate, carved star above the princess' cheek. Lareli stooped to pick up her father's atja staff and hefted it before moving to stand before Itzala.

Itzala sneered at Lareli, for though she was trained in battle, she was young and lacked the skill of the practiced warrior. He strode forward, then paused as the princess twirled her atja in the air, moving with unparalleled speed and grace. Itzala's face turned in fear for the first time since the demon left him, for he knew what the Star's blessing had given the princess. But his pride, a tangible, growing thing that had blossomed with the Darkness, spurred him onward, convinced of his invincibility. Their battle was fierce, with each warrior holding fast in the deathly dance, until, with a mighty cry, Lareli's atja flashed, striking the shrouded warrior with a beam of glowing energy. Itzala stumbled, and the princess, wracked with grief, advanced over the fallen warrior.

The Star warned Lareli against what she had planned, but the princess' pain was too great. Her atja crashed down, tearing Itzala's heart to desecrate it the way he had done to her father's, but the damage had already been done. Itzala's deal *with the demon had seen to that. Lareli pierced Itzala's chest, and thick, black evil spilled from the wound, encasing the warrior's strong body until his physical form dissipated, leaving only Shadow.*

The Shadow rose from Itzala's shriveled husk, reaching to claim the surrounding Stjarnin. Lareli, ashamed of what she had done, begged once more for the grace of the Star. The Star saw her genuine sorrow and bestowed upon her one final favor. The glowing kiss on the Princess' cheek snaked across Lareli's earthen skin. As the mark spread, the Star's power grew inside her. Lareli reached deep within, searching for the Star's guidance, then uttered the Star's whispered words as she faced Itzala. The Star's glowing light cut through the Darkness, scattering its power across the land. The Stjarnin moved to contain it, but the Shadow escaped, its seeping Darkness razed the ground as it retreated. Lareli sent a party of warriors to follow, but it was too late. Itzala had gone.

The Stjarnin's voice faded, leaving the glowing cavern in too-still silence. Spell broken, Peter blinked and glanced around, plunged once again into the eerie room. The dais before him spilled over with flowing tendrils of smoke that billowed to the floor in a cool mist. Behind it, the withered Stjarnin stood, watching with knowing eyes. She dipped her head in a slow nod, drawing Peter's gaze to a mark on her cheek he had not seen.

Eyes wide, he stepped forward, but as he approached, the Stjarnin shimmered and blurred until the stooped figure before him transformed into a tall, graceful queen.

"It was you," Peter marveled in a hushed whisper. "You made the Shadow."

The Stjarnin nodded, her lips pulled in shame. She waved her hand over the dais, scattering the mist to reveal a clear pool.

Itzala is the burden of the Stjarnin. He is of us, and without us, he would not be. This is why our people have chased him for so long. She glanced at the dais. Peter followed her gaze to the figure of the Stjarnin Itzala as it twisted into the Shadow he recognized. *It has been so long, many have forgotten his true origin. He must be stopped before we forget entirely. For if Itzala escapes, he will not rest until he consumes the world.* Lareli pressed her fingertips to her cheek, her silver gaze lost in a memory. *When I destroyed his heart, I took any chance he had at redemption. There is now only evil.* A ghostly tear trickled down her jaw.

"Why are you showing me this?"

Lareli swept away her tear. The sparkling drop hovered in the air before vanishing into the void.

My people have fought to vanquish the Darkness for years, but our efforts haven't been enough. She glanced at Peter, her dark eyes narrowing shrewdly as she searched his face. *Perhaps with your help, however...* Her words ended in a considering hum before she slowly turned away.

"But what can I possibly do that you haven't?" he asked, thinking about the terrible powers the Shadow harnessed. The Stjarnin did not respond, but continued her shuffle to the dais. Nearing the altar, Lareli's form began to shimmer and fade as its azure cast began to pulse.

"Wait," Peter stepped forward to stall the Stjarnin, his hand outstretched. "I still don't know what you want me to do."

Before he could reach her, a low throbbing sound bubbled from deep within the cave, flowing into Peter before paralyzing him in its powerful wave. Peter clapped his hands over his ears and squinted at the beacon, watching as the Stjarnin disappeared until it illuminated brighter than the

Star. Covering his face, staggered from the overpowering stimulus as the cave was encapsulated in an endless, droning roar.

When the sound finally dissipated, Peter looked up, his cheek dripping icy water from where he lay in a shallow pool in a large hollow opening. The cavern retained its soft glow, but as Peter glanced around, he found it came from the luminescent carvings etched into the mountain. The dais and the elder Stjarnin were gone, leaving him alone in the glimmering cave. Peter lifted his arm, but instead of the bright glyphs that had appeared on his skin minutes before, only darkened freckles dotted his flesh. There was no mark remaining that evidenced what happened with the ancient Stjarnin.

Groggy, Peter brushed the crystallized liquid from his trousers as he scanned the now empty cave. A ghost of a whisper echoed through his ears, but before he could catch it, it was gone, carried off on the soft howl of a light breeze through the distant tunnel.

Peter shot through the cave, his mind burning with the secrets seared inside. Reaching the opening, he burst through the darkened entry into the dazzling underground city. Outside the mouth, Tiger Lily waited, watching expectantly behind a wall of warriors. As soon as he stepped into the clearing, Tinc issued a relieved buzz and zipped over the Stjarnin's blades to flutter delightedly around his head.

"It's alright Tinc, I'm fine." He forced a smile to ease the nanobot's nervous hovering, then glanced back at the princess, his mouth pulling in a hard line. He stepped toward her, ignoring her warriors' staffed barricade.

"We need to leave," he said, shocked by the urgency in his voice. "Take me to Skull Rock."

13

"Why do you wish to visit the Skull?" Tiger Lily demanded.

"Because it's where we'll find our answers." Peter said, setting his jaw defiantly. The prince strode forward, towering over him with his blackened gaze before Tiger Lily interceded with a quiet rebuke. The prince stilled, his features twisting furiously as he let out a frustrated growl and stalked toward the princess. He grabbed Tiger Lily's hands in his, entwining their slender fingers as he pressed his forehead to hers and murmured to her with gentle urgency.

Tiger Lily listened to the prince, then brushed her fingers across his broad forehead before she responded in a smooth whisper.

"*The ancients spoke to him,*" she murmured, glancing inquisitively at Peter. "*Perhaps they have seen something we have not.*"

The prince turned, his lips drawn in a disbelieving stare. Finally, he returned his gaze to the princess and traced his fingers across her forehead before nodding and striding away. Tiger Lily watched until his stiff figure disappeared from sight, then turned to Peter with a thoughtful expression.

"*We will take you.*" She motioned to her guards and uttered a quick command. "Garinzte Iskolja," she said, then translated for Peter. "*Skull Rock.*"

The warrior's ochre eyes widened as they exchanged an uncertain glance. Their gilled lips pressed in clear displeasure before the tallest male reached into the folds of fabric resting on his hip. His slender fingers snaked inside the pocket, then returned, clasping a small cylinder.

Silently, he extended his hand, and motioned for Peter to do the same. Peter offered his palm and the Stjarnin released the cylinder, surprising Peter with its cool, heavy weight.

"Um, I know there's a slight language barrier here, Princess, but . . ." Peter's brow furrowed as he studied the alien object. He pinched the cylinder between his thumb and forefinger, then held it parallel to the warrior's spear. "I'm not following."

Tiger Lily nodded again to her warrior. His scowl deepened, and with an almost imperceptible motion, he spun the cylinder. It began to hum as tiny threadlike carvings etched in the stone illuminated the surface until it glowed and stretched into a replica of his own weapon.

Unbidden, a low whistle whooshed from Peter's lips. "Cool trick." He studied the impressive craftsmanship with a wry grin then swung the spear, noting how the smooth weapon sliced through the air. After a few practice thrusts, he turned to the silent Stjarnin.

"Well, what are we waiting for?"

Tiger Lily cast one last look to her accompanying warriors. "Stjantani henadi intento. Kesansa indadi ne irentzani alta."

The Stjarnin exchanged a glance before shaking their heads somberly at the princess. The princess nodded, then met the confused look on Peter's face.

"*I told them this was their final chance to stay,*" the princess explained. "*Once we leave, I cannot guarantee anyone will survive.*"

When no one balked, Tiger Lily led the group to the village surface. Peter squinted as they stepped into the open air and were washed in Starlight. They made their way through the cover of the hidden city, walking silently until they passed the last scattered huts to approach the looming mountain. Peter cast a questioning glance at the warrior beside him, but the Stjarnin averted his gaze and tromped to stand behind the princess. Focused on the wall, Tiger Lily raised her palm to a small rock protruding from the surface. It slid back, disappearing seamlessly into the cliff. Under Peter's feet, the ground began to tremble, scattering tiny pebbles over the stony floor as the air filled with the dull roar of scraping stone. Hairline cracks webbed across the smooth surface, then began to widen and stretch, spreading until they formed the frame of an oversized, arched door that cut into the heart of the mountain.

Tiger Lily smiled at Peter's dumbstruck pose. "*We know a quicker way.*"

"No kidding," Peter mumbled. He traced the uneven path until it rounded into a sloping bend. Tinc jangled excitedly in his ear and then shot off, shooting her tinkling echo down the narrow corridor.

"*It seems she approves,*" Tiger Lily hummed.

"It seems she does," Peter conceded. "After you," he swept his arm wide, allowing the Stjarnin to pass.

Tiger Lily stepped forward, confidently navigating the divoted stone. Her long, limber legs picked gracefully through the jagged path, landing nimbly with each step. Peter hurried after, matching her steps until they reached a slight outcropping that jutted over the forest, providing a clear view of the horizon.

Peter's breath caught as he gazed at the reach. The crystal waves stretched endlessly until they flattened to meet the sky. In the distance, the Stars hovered, sitting alongside each other as they surveyed their tranquil kingdom. Peter smiled at the beauty of their hazy glow, wondering briefly if he would miss it. The moment was lost, however, when he turned to the princess and followed her stony stare. Her features flattened into a grim expression as she stared at the rock formation jutting from the sea. The stone was dark and jagged, protruding from the splashing waves like a skeleton sprouting from the ground.

Skull Rock.

Seeping dread washed through Peter as he stared at the distorted formation. The Skull's gaping eyes stared out at him, two jagged holes washed into the sloping black rock. He shuddered and averted his gaze, trailing down the sharp, eerily formed teeth carved to dangling points over the Neversea's low tide. When the current came in, the mouth would disappear, hiding under the coursing waves, turning the rock into a living, moving thing that fed endlessly on the ebb and flow of the tide.

Peter turned to his companions and noted how the warriors watched the Skull with the same nervous apprehension. Their pause bolstered his confidence, and resumed his trek, chasing after the princess who continued on, unphased by the menacing landform.

"So tell me," he called, hurrying after the princess' long strides. "What has your people up in arms about our little journey?"

Tiger Lily continued her steady gait down the winding pathway, but slowed to allow him to walk beside her. She shortened her steps to match his pace as he clumsily picked his way through the mountain.

"I mean, I know why I don't like it," Peter jabbered breathlessly. "It gives me the heebie-jeebies. But you guys are supposed to be this big bad-ass ancient alien race that creates magical weapons from rocks. What's got you worried?"

"*The* heebie-jeebies," Tiger Lily tested the words on her tongue. "*I am guessing this is not a positive emotion.*"

Peter snorted. "You guessed right. The heebie-jeebies are like," he searched for words to explain, then gave up and shook his arms in an exaggerated shudder.

Tiger Lily nodded in understanding. "*Je adi,*" she declared. "*Heebie-jeebies mean fear. You are frightened.*"

Peter focused on navigating a narrow ledge. "Fear might be a strong word," he grumbled.

"*Fear is the right word.*"

They followed the path until the ledge widened into a platform near the base of the mountain. Under the protruding stone, the jungle canopy swayed peacefully in the air. Lush leaves formed a thick blanket that thinned and disappeared, leaving a perimeter of empty sand surrounding the Skull in an invisible barrier. The princess motioned to the trees. "*Even the jungle feels fear. The Skull is touched by Darkness.*"

Peter swallowed a thick lump. "You mean the Shadow?"

The princess nodded. "*It is where we bound Itzala. It was the home of the darkness, and darkness changed it.*"

"It looked different before?"

"*It was beautiful.*"

Peter considered the jagged, reaching rock. "I doubt that," he argued, then spluttered in surprise as Tiger Lily pressed her hand to his chest. Under her touch, his Shadowmark pulsed, emitting an eerie glow before fading into smooth skin.

"*The Darkness leaves its mark wherever it goes,*" the princess murmured. Peter staggered back, scrubbing his hand absently over the stain as she explained. "*The Shadow cannot hold a host without deteriorating it.*" She motioned to the Skull. "*You can always tell where Itzala lingers. You just have to know how to look.*"

Peter followed her stoic gaze to the curling mist rolling from the Skull while his fingers played nervously at the invisible spot on his chest. They stood in contemplative silence until Tiger Lily picked up her staff and stepped from the platform, gracefully turning toward a small, hidden divot in the cragged wall.

Behind, her warriors silently followed, their soft steps echoing after the princess. Peter watched as their tall frames disappeared into the carved gap, then turned to Tinc, who flitted to perch on his shoulder.

"Just remember, if we die, this was all your idea." Tinc's brusque reply hummed in his ear as the bot shot off, showering him in golden sparks. Peter grinned. "Here goes nothing," he muttered.

Continuing his descent, Peter marveled at the hidden passage. The mountain's hum surrounded him, ricocheting around the corridor until he dropped further into the heavy stone and the droning notes were overpowered by a stronger, more distinct sound. Curious, Peter rounded to the final bend, where the narrow stone opened to a large arched landing where two carved boats sat tethered to a crude dock.

Peter stepped toward the boats, still admiring the hidden alcove. "Which one is mine?"

Tiger Lily pointed to the one on the left. "*You will ride with Jaxtara, and I will accompany Tizari. Your* Tinc *can fit in either.*"

Tinc buzzed loudly before landed prominently on Peter's shoulder. Tiger Lily watched in mild amusement, then nodded to the bot. "*Very well. All is settled.*"

They boarded the boats and cast off, using the carved wooden oars to push through the choppy water. Dark liquid sloshed over their oars, filling the cavern with soft laps as they sliced through the mountain. Peter's sight adjusted to the dim, but he was grateful for the added light from Tinc's glowing processor and the Stjarnin's illuminated tattoos.

"You have to give me the name of your artist," Peter said as he examined Jaxtara's glowing shoulder. Jaxtara cast a scathing glare before Tiger Lily's calm voice whispered over the slapping waves.

"*It is better to hold your tongue than ransom your life,*" the princess admonished. Her dark eyes illuminated against the glowing tapestry of her skin. "*The water awakens.*"

Peter laughed and dipped his hand in a chopping wave. Jaxtara's charcoal gaze followed the motion in shock. Peter met his stare with a silent question until something slithered over his fingers and he jerked back, twisting his arm as though the water was a snake. He leaned over the boat's ledge to scan the surface, and a ghostly shimmer flashed deep below the waves.

"What was that?" Peter cried in surprise.

"Estjaski Damani." Jaxtara seethed. His glower deepened as he issued a quick command to Tizari. The boats stilled as the warriors laid down their oars and replaced them with raised staffs as they stared into the water, their bodies tensed and ready.

Peter glanced at the princess, who had slowly risen, her tattoos glowing as she stared into the water. Very slowly, she raised a warning hand to still Peter, who strained to hear the indiscernible sounds the Stjarnin were so attentive to. Only the coarse waves rocking the boats could be heard inside the cavern until a faint melody warbled from below, haunting and lilting as the tune bubbled from the deep.

"Mermaids?" Peter sprang to grip his own staff. "But their cove is on the other side of the island!"

Tiger Lily's head jerked an imperceptible shake. "*Etjaski Damani are connected to water throughout the island. They prefer calmer tides, but they are not bound to them.*"

Peter grimaced as he scanned the water. The siren song was growing louder and sweeter—the mermaids were getting closer. He looked back to see how far they were from shore, but in the faint lighting, the tiny landing was nowhere to be found. They were trapped in the mermaids' element. He listened to their song as it washed over the waves. The tune was so lovely, but it kept getting interrupted by the boat slapping against the choppy water. How he wished he could jump free from the vessel and dip his head under the surface to better hear...

"*Pan!*" Tiger Lily's harsh cry ripped him from the siren's song. Peter reeled, realizing he had thrown a leg over the side of the boat. Tinc swooped in his face, buzzing angrily as she forced him back, pushing him to the base of the boat. Lying flat, he blinked at the cavern roof, feeling the cove's icy water seep into his pants as the unsteady boat trembled with the shift of balance.

Peter shook his head, chasing away the remnants of the mermaids' song clinging to his conscience. As he did, the princess deftly unstrung a large silver disc from her necklace and cupped it in her palms. Inside her clasped hands, a soft light began to glow. It blossomed until the light seeped from the cracks in her grip and gathered to form an orb around her fists. The princess lifted it to her mouth, her eyes closed as she murmured a soft incantation to the glowing stone before she hurled it into the waves. The orb plunged under the water, its glow illuminating the dark until, with a furious screech, a mermaid lurched from the waves, her face contorted in a wicked snarl. Long blonde curls trailed behind her, streaming down her back to the tip of her fuchsia tail. As she drew closer, the scales on her tail faded as the illusion disappeared, revealing a skeleton attached to its wraith-thin body. Her bouncy yellow curls dissolved into stringy strands of ash that tangled around her bony face as she clawed greedily at the princess.

Tizari swung her spear, ramming it into the creature's belly. With an angry yowl, the mermaid fell, her clawed fingers grasping the edge of the boat. She clung to the side, fighting to reach the Stjarnin as the haunting melody amplified through the vaulted cavern. Tizari lunged, her quick, sharp attacks staving off the raging beast while Tiger Lily scoured the chopping waves.

Peter followed her worried stare to where she cast the glowing stone. It hovered deep under the surface, its blue light thrumming in time with the mermaids' unearthly soundtrack until it blazed silver and a muted pulse slammed through the water, rocking the boats with the sheer force of its energy.

A chorus of agonized howls erupted from the water's surface as the struggling mermaid retreated to her sisters. Their angry cries dissipated as they fled, replacing their sweet melody with pained sobs until the only sound left was gently churning waves.

Peter watched in stunned silence as Tiger Lily exhaled and slumped to the floor of her boat. Beside her, Tizari crouched next to the princess, worriedly examining her before issuing a quick command to Jaxtara.

The large warrior watched anxiously, then cast a furious glare at Peter before quickly replacing his staff with an oar. With a few strong, deliberate strokes he pulled alongside the other boat to find the princess fending of Tizari's worried inspection.

"Adona nie," she said kindly as she pushed the warrior's fidgeting hands from her face before turning to Peter with a labored smile. "*I'm fine.*"

"What the Neverhell was that?" Peter gestured wildly, his hands mimicking his best reenactment of the powerful light.

Tiger Lily smiled weakly. "*The water demons are vulnerable to sound. The olskjinza amplifies it underwater. It is very unpleasant for them.*"

"Knowing that would have made the last century a whole lot easier," Peter grumbled, remembering all the times he tiptoed around Mermaid Cove. Tiger Lily gave him a questioning glance, but before he could explain, a powerful blow cratered his stomach.

Staggering, Peter raised his fists to his face as Jaxtara advanced, his grating syllables exploding through the cave in a furious roar. Incensed by Tinc's thrumming obscenities, Peter prepared to strike back until a steely command burst through the ringing cave.

"*Kefani. Stop* now."

Peter stilled at the crackling authority behind her words. His chest heaved as he met Jaxtara's seething gaze, and the warrior lowered his staff. Slowly, Peter dropped his fists and turned to the princess.

"*Discord is what the Darkness wants,*" she cautioned. "*Jaxtara is not your enemy.*" Tiger Lily looked deliberately from him to her warrior, then returned to her seat, leaving Peter to his rage as the Stjarnin resumed their rowing.

"*You need to release your anger,*" the princess cut into his dark musings as light trickled over the damp walls of the cave. "*Rage, accusations, and distrust are all weapons the Darkness will use against you.*"

Peter scowled, but before he could respond, the cove wall opened, clearing his view to the looming form of Skull Rock. A gnawing tug pulled the pit of his stomach as he looked at the wicked fog writhing from the skull's leering grin.

"*The Darkness awaits,*" Tiger Lily prompted, interrupting his thoughts. "*It knows we are almost there.*"

14

A hush fell over the group as they neared the looming skull. Even the cawing of the swooping Neverbirds quieted as they inched toward the rock. A chilled mist swept over the waves, prickling Peter's flesh in a blanket of goosebumps. He looked around, noticing the keyed energy of his comrades. Tizari fidgeted with every stroke, and Jaxtara's shoulders coiled so tautly, Peter worried were the Stjarnin surprised, his neck might spring from his body.

Only the princess remained unnerved. There was tension in her angular jaw, but her expression was serene, even as the swirling mist enveloped them, drawing them toward the skull's gaping mouth. The wind howled past them, cutting like a knife, carrying on it the echo of a ghost.

You've come back to me.

Peter grimaced and shook his head, banishing the unwelcome voice.

He cast a furtive glance to his comrades, but the Stjarnin stared ahead, their stoic expressions hardening as they approached.

"Tell me Princess," Peter called boisterously over the water to lessen the dread billowing in his stomach. "Why here?"

Tiger Lily looked over the waves at Peter.

"*I only know the stories I was told as a young girl,*" the princess admitted after a contemplative silence. "*After the Shadow revealed itself, the Stjarnin vowed to stop the Darkness. We followed Itzala across the galaxies in our efforts to bind its evil.*" She paused for a breath. "*It was not the Stjarnin who chose Neverland, but the Shadow.*"

The princess gazed at Peter, her onyx eyes penetrating his across the water before she continued her recital.

"*This planet was different than the others Itzala inhabited. Its power was in the air, bestowed by the same Star that brought us life. It strengthened Itzala, but made him brazen, drunk on the heightened might. Our greatest chief Lareji recognized this weakness, and used it to exploit the Shadow. Together, our warriors attacked, and fought Itzala until it was only a fragment of its former self, and then Lareji cast a binding spell to tether it to the planet.*" Tiger Lily paused to cast a sorrowful look at the wasted rock. "*In its weakened state, Lareji banished the Shadow. So they took the withered entity and buried it deep inside the Iskolja, where Itzala's reach could not taint the rest of the land. Then, we built our new home in the mountain, to overlook the Shadow's doings, for the Lareji was wise, and knew the time would come when Itzala would rise again.*"

Peter shifted uncomfortably. He knew what the princess was insinuating, and she was right. The Stjarnin had fought for eons to keep the Darkness contained, then as soon as humans made their way to Neverland, it escaped. He scratched his hands through his hair, as if trying to claw the guilt from his mind.

Another cold spray splashed from the chopping waves, pulling Peter to the present. Skull Rock loomed before them, dwarfing their party in its sinister grin. Peter shuddered as they paddled toward its gaping maw, formed from jagged, dripping stalactites. He studied them as they passed, half afraid that once they entered, the skull would bite down, trapping them forever.

Passed through, he let out a tiny sigh of relief. But as he drew his next breath, icy air swirled through his chest, freezing his lungs. He gasped, billowing a plume of hot air into the gaping cave as his choking breaths ricocheted through the vaulted ceiling. The air felt thick around him, like a living thing. He strained to see in the dark, but aside from Tinc's tiny green orb and the faint lines of the Stjarnins' glowing tattoos, no light filtered through the cove. The space was claimed by shadows.

"Iksana estola stjarni ataxi. Ne jaadi irentza le ni je adi. Ge adi henazi le isjafani." Jaxtara's murmur was smothered in the stagnant air.

"What?" Peter asked, twisting in his seat.

"*It's a prayer to the Star,*" Tiger Lily explained. "*He is asking for its protection.*"

Another cold breath whooshed down Peter's lungs, chilling him to the bone. They passed a looming wall, and the sharp edges of the cavern's reflective walls glinted dangerously under Tinc's glow. Peter followed her light, seeing nothing except her tiny form mirrored in the shining rock. The oars' steady slaps droned in his ears as they ventured deeper into the formation, and Peter wondered if they would ever find an end to the void.

A faint cough whispered over the deafening quiet, and Peter's shoulders stiffened. He froze, casting his gaze into the pitch, searching for the source. Tinc released an excited hum and swooped toward the sound, illuminating a large gray mass huddled on a rocky ledge.

"Over there!" Peter cried, following her faint glow. "Something's moving!" He pointed to the figure, his eyes straining against the dark.

"Tinc! Fly closer, would you?"

Tinc bobbed and swooped low, trailing a shimmer of golden sparks that glistened on the water's surface before disappearing under the choppy waves.

"Follow her!" he demanded, then dipped his own hand into the chilling waves to paddle faster. Freezing water seeped into his sleeve as he dug furiously into the waves to spur the boat forward. He didn't know what they would find, he only knew that the gnawing feeling drawing him to the cursed rock screamed that the answer was there.

Moments stretched into an eternity until they reached where Tinc hovered. She bobbed anxiously over the water then swooped to Peter, bathing him in a flurry of agitated sparks. Peter peered over the ledge to a jagged slate of glassy rock formed over the waves.

"What is it, Tinc?"

Tinc's wings whirred in a huff before she shot further into the dark. Her tiny processor reflected in the onyx beneath her, following her in a glowing trail until she stopped and swooped in the air to flit furiously over a huddled figure. Peter followed her motion, then bounded from the boat across the uneven surface as the apprehensive shouts of the Stjarnin followed behind him. The damp rocks unsettled his footing, but his gaze fixed where Tinc hovered.

Chest heaving, he knelt to the huddled figure, shivering in a mass of sopping wet clothes. Peter prodded the figure and it started before slumping against the ground with a heavy clang.

Peter jerked back with a surprised yelp as Tinc swooped down, illuminating the form. Her dim glow settled over the body, lighting a mop of tangled gray hair draping across its sunken face. A ragged wheeze rattled through the cave as it exhaled a fading breath, expelling a sickly cloud of air over a heavy, metal hand.

Peter's face twisted in horror. It was worse than the Stjarnin feared. Captain James Hooke was alive.

And the Shadow was nowhere to be found.

15

THE JOLLY ROGER

CAPTAIN WENDY DARLING

"Everyone to your stations," Wendy commanded. Immediately, the crew sprang to life, moving to follow the captain's orders. "Michaels, I need you to assess the damage and what impact it has on our current situation. Tootles was going to go with you before, bring him too.

"Dawes, figure out where the hell we are. Johns, take Curly and Nibs to Ammunitions and see if you can blast a path for us. We've already been hit hard, I don't care to take any more.

"DeLaCruz—grab SMEE and run a visual. If there's *any* damage I want to know about it. Twins: I need you to perform a supply inventory. I want to know what we have on board and how much is left in case we've just run into an emergency. And Boyce—" she glanced around, pausing when she realized the commander was nowhere in sight. Her brows tied a knot. "If anyone sees Boyce tell him to report to me immediately. In the meantime, you have your assignments. *Anything* you see that's out of the ordinary; notify me immediately."

"You mean besides the terrifying space dump," Johns smarted.

"Not the time, Elias," Wendy admonished, then turned toward Dawes. She scanned the visor as she waited for the crew to clear out. When the last hurried footsteps disappeared behind her quarter doors, she rounded on the pilot.

"Dawes, what the hell is this?"

"I don't know Captain," Dawes' fingers blurred over the Navigation grid. Her forehead creased in fervent concentration as she scanned the slow-moving forms slinking across the visor. A grating scratch ripped through the cabin as a large chunk of shrapnel flew in front of them, scraping the ship's nose as it passed. Wendy flinched against the grating sound until the twisted metal cleared its path.

"You didn't see this on the reading?" Wendy interrogated, gaping at the tangled fixtures before them. Large sheets of metal sailed silently past the crumpled hulls of decimated boats, as their remains spilled across the skyline. Floating pieces of debris scattered, bouncing in and out of the massive mines like a twisted pinball machine.

"No," Dawes answered through brimming tears. "We did a scan before we put up the visor screen, but I swear the reading came up empty."

"Then what the hell happened?" Wendy erupted, staring at the web of shrapnel before her. "There's no way bogeys this size wouldn't have been seen. You must have looked in the wrong place."

"I swear, Captain, there was *nothing here*," Dawes protested.

"Clearly there is," Wendy bit. She slammed her hand against the StarBoard. "We should have seen it."

"Yes Captain," Dawes' voice was thin without its lilting laugh.

Wendy pinched the bridge of her nose. Lashing out wouldn't help. This was on her. If the visor hadn't been disabled for the damn hologram, they would have seen the metallic graveyard long before they hit. She let her guard down and put her crew in danger.

But she wouldn't let it cost her the ship.

Wendy initiated the transmitter. They hadn't been able to reach the Admiral, but she could still use the spooling pulse as a beacon. Maybe they could hail something within the floating debris. She activated her earpiece, then cast the dummy transmission. The moment the signal released, Wendy fell back in excruciating pain. A keening whine reeled through the speaker, assaulting her ears with a blizzard of white noise. She fumbled for the control, cursing as she silenced the scrambled signal. A throbbing headache blossomed in her temples, but Wendy grit her teeth and strained to make out a clear frequency through the inaudible shrill. Frustrated, Wendy switched the channel, only to receive the same angry keening. Again, she flipped the station, this time accessing a garbled monotone that she couldn't decipher into any coherent sounds.

Wendy activated her comm.

"Michaels. Come in." She flinched as she activated the transmitter, worried her ears might suffer another round of abuse, but there was only dead air. She waited, the lump in her throat hardening with every silent second, until it was too much to bear. Swallowing the growing stone, she gripped her comm again.

"Michaels. Report. What is your status?"

Her tender ears strained against the deafening silence. It wasn't until she tasted the bitter copper on her tongue that she realized she had gnawed a gash in her lip. She licked the metallic tang, then stoppered the blood with her finger, ignoring the pain as she awaited Michaels' response.

Finally, a needling whine emanated from the recesses of the set. It was so faint, Wendy thought she imagined the sound until the whine swelled and was replaced with a gravelly staccato.

"—'re down ... the bay. It looks . . . mess." Wendy's wave of relief dissipated as she tried to decipher the fractured message.

"Again, Michaels. Repeat. Your comm is fractured. Report not received."

Wendy cursed as another shrill keen screeched into her eardrum then faded to a low, crackling hum replaced by Michaels' reedy voice.

"Captain? Are you there?"

A relieved smile shattered through Wendy's troubled expression. "Yes Michaels, I'm reading." She spoke over the metal clangs crashing through the feed. "Can you repeat?"

The banging faded, and Michaels returned, sounding winded. "Sorry Captain. We found some surprises down here, and not good ones," he said grimly. "I'm attempting a diagnostic, but the system's a wreck. I can't make it through a full read without finding something else that's about to fall apart. It doesn't look like anything is critical *yet*," he intoned, "but that could change any second."

Michaels paused to bark a quick command at Tootles. Wendy heard their muffled voices, but couldn't make out the message. He must have palmed the mic. She tapped her fingers anxiously, waiting for his return. The murmurs stopped and there was a loud rustle before he dropped back in.

"We located where the ship was breached," he said. "Looks like the rear thruster took a pretty good knock. It's not completely down, but we've lost a large range of functionality. Hopefully we don't need to get anywhere quick," he ended with a bitter laugh.

Wendy scrubbed her face, glad Michaels couldn't see. "Can it be fixed?"

There was a brief pause. "Maybe?" he offered. "If I had the right parts. And if nothing bigger gets in the way."

Wendy's lips pressed in a thin line. "Then I don't suppose this is a good time to tell you our transmitters are down," she sighed.

"I could think of a better time," Michaels admitted. His sharp exhale washed Wendy's earpiece in static. "I can try and repair it, but right now the system analysis takes priority. If something pulls up and I'm gone… I don't even want to think worst case," he disclosed.

"No," Wendy agreed. "Determine our status. Dawes and I can handle things up here. But if you find out anything, Michaels—"

"I'll let you know," he finished in a rush over his furious typing. "Way ahead of you, Captain."

"Let's keep it that way," Wendy said, then disconnected the comm. Silence hovered in her ear, and she exhaled loudly as she twisted to stretch her back. Everything was so tight. She wondered when her muscles had turned to coils. She glanced at Dawes, who watched quietly from her peripheral while she continued to scour the path before them. Wendy followed her gaze to the tangled mess of parts and her expression darkened. Slowly, she reached for the transmitter to attempt another cast.

Bracing herself, she activated the device, prepared for another static explosion. The sharp wailing didn't sound, but garbled audio washed from the receiver.

"Listen to this," she turned to Dawes, still straining to make sense of the unintelligible noise. "I caught a signal, but it doesn't make any sense."

Dawes' troubled expression turned to confusion as she stopped to listen to the transmission Wendy broadcasted through the cabin. Jumbled audio tones crashed through the speakers, tumbling together in a jarring, inaudible roar.

"Do you hear anything?" Wendy yelled over the din.

Dawes shook her head. "Is it just one cast?" She angled her ear toward the speaker, as if it would help her pick out the sounds. "Can we isolate them?"

Wendy strained to listen. "Maybe," she nodded, "But how?"

She glanced at the board in front of her. Although she had learned enough to operate the *Roger*, troubleshooting was another issue entirely. She had just started exploring the settings when her door whirred open and Boyce strode through, his face pulled in a tight frown at the static accosting the room.

"I felt the turbulence below deck." He glanced at the visor over Wendy's shoulder, and his troubled gaze darkened. "What happened?"

"That's what we're trying to find out," Wendy yelled over the garbled recording still streaming through the room. Quickly, she redirected the transmission to her earpiece to quiet the cabin, leaving only the lingering ringing tinning in her ears. She turned back to the commander, who studied the mess of metal on the visor before him.

"Where are we?" he demanded. His jaw clenched as a passing rocket booster sparked and shot a blast of sparks across the screen.

"We don't know," Wendy retorted. "That's what we need to find out." She returned her attention to the screen. "I'm guessing you don't have any ideas?"

Boyce stepped closer to the visor screen. His body was rigid, in proper soldier's pose, but Wendy noticed the tremble in his hands as he studied the scene. After a heavy pause, he pointed at the transmitter.

"Can you play the scramble again?"

Wendy nodded and reached forward, her shoulders tensing as she braced for the impending ruckus. A sea of jumbled voices rushed from the speaker to drown out the room, in a wave of flooding noise.

"Turn it down!" Boyce screamed. Obediently, Dawes lowered the audio to a low roar. Without the deafening sound of clamoring voices accosting her ears, Wendy could identify clips of individual feeds. Similar vocals and speech patterns emerged, exposing unique messages among the pack. Interwoven to the feed, a familiar voice played, its determined tenor, soft but fierce.

"Wait." Boyce paused the audio to fiddle with transmitter. His brow dipped in concentration before he motioned for Dawes to resume the feed. The audio crackled to life, but this time the scattered conversations were a backdrop to the lone female voice. It streamed over the cabin, while its listeners fell in hushed silence.

...*Captain Darling of the* Fede Fiducia—*but if you're listening Peter, it's just me, Wendy. It always feels so strange to begin these transmissions. Formal seems more appropriate, but then—these are intended solely for you, so—*

The transmission clicked off as Wendy reached to still the recording. Silence hung in the air as the echoes of her message ricocheted through her ears. Her shoulders tensed as she slowly lowered her hand and turned to face the others. Dawes dipped her head, shying away to offer privacy while Boyce gaped at her in utter betrayal. Wendy started to explain, but her protest jarred the stunned commander. A defensive scowl slammed over his features, replacing the hurt in his gaze with a mask of rage.

"It seems everything is in working order," he announced curtly. "If there is nothing else Captain, I'm sure there are other issues I can tend to." He executed a stiff salute and strode from the room, tension rolling from his shoulders in thick waves. He slowed as he neared the door, then shoved past Tootles, who hovered in the frame, his expression married in grief and hope.

"Y-you m-messaged Peter?" he asked, his voice full of hope.

Wendy dropped her eyes, unable to meet his longing gaze.

"Yes. But I've been unable to reach him. It sounds like the spool was intercepted." She scrubbed her face before turning to the floating debris. "I'd be willing to bet all our other transmissions were, too."

"So none of our messages have gotten out," Dawes reiterated, her face grim.

Wendy shook her head. She glanced at the receiver and slowly reached to replay the thread. After a short crackle, her message resumed until she twisted the dial and another voice slowly needled in.

"Mayday! Mayday! We've been hit by a ro—" The message faded into static, and there was another flurry as Wendy flipped channels.

" ...caught in some sort of..."

" ...our backup boosters dried out and we're running out of power..."

"...tell Lena daddy's sorry he didn't come home."

"I don't think we'll make it."

Wendy clicked through each station, creating a looping web of voices in the mess of lost communications. Her chest squeezed as she killed the transmitter and turned to the others.

"I trust there's a good reason you're here and not down in the bay, Tootles?"

Tootles' gaze lingered on the visor a moment too long before he jumped to attention.

"Y-yes Captain." He snapped his heels, miming an exaggerated salute. "L-lieutenant Michaels has identified th-the problem. He said our s-something corollary s-sling is damaged. It's s-stalled our system a-and," his brow furrowed as he struggled to recall the message. "It b-basically put us i-in lockdown. He s-said if w-we can't f-fix it, we're dead in th-the water."

"And the sharks are closing in."

Wendy grimaced at the sharp protrusions and sparking wires spinning ominously across the visor screen. Her head reeled as she considered all of the information, but she forced a tight smile as she looked at Tootles.

"Thank-you," she said. "You're dismissed. Go help Michaels. If he needs anything, you get it for him. No questions asked." She waved him off and he dashed out the door, his little feet slapping the grating as he hurried to obey. Wendy watched as the door hummed open and shut, then turned grimly to face Dawes. The pilot watched her expectantly, her features arranged in an unfamiliar frown.

"Captain?" Dawes ventured, her voice thin.

Wendy's gaze roved over the foreign objects orbiting across the screen, their metal hulls gleaming as their scrambled messages spiraled into the abyss.

"We're not going to get out any communications until we clear this electroacoustic barrier," she muttered. "And until we fix the ship, we aren't moving anywhere."

"What does that mean, Captain?"

She ground her palms against her eyes as she weighed their options. They hung heavy on her shoulders until an impossible idea sprang to mind. She glanced at the visor, hope flaring as she steeled her resolve against the universe.

"It means we're going out."

16

"**O**ut?" Dawes boggled at the mess of metal floating across the visor. "Captain, you don't mean out *there*! It's a death trap! If the debris doesn't skewer you, the wires'll roast you. You'll get shredded."

Wendy shrugged. "We don't have another choice. Either we sit here sending useless messages from our ready-made tomb, or we take a risk and maybe make it home. Personally, I'll take my chances with the shrapnel."

Dawes' frown deepened. "I don't like it."

"I'm not exactly thrilled with the idea either," Wendy quipped, "but I don't see any other way. Besides, you aren't coming. I need your eyes inside." She ignored Dawes' spluttering protest to activate her comm. "Johns, grab Nibs and Curly and meet me up here. We've got a job."

She disconnected, then initiated a new stream to the maintenance bay, pointedly avoiding Dawes' furious glare. "Michaels. Sorry to interrupt, but I need Tootles. That is, if you can manage without him for a bit."

Michaels reedy voice whistled through her earpiece. "Considering I've kept the boat functional for months without the small child, I think I'll survive."

"Fair point," Wendy ceded. "In that case, send him up. I need his help with something. Also," her nose wrinkled at the imposing request, "While you're working, I want you to keep an ear out for Dawes. She's going to man the helm solo for a minute."

The clatters behind Michaels stilled. Wendy thought the connection went dead until the tech needled through the line.

"What are you planning, Captain?"

"Nothing sane," Wendy admitted.

Michaels swore. "Keep your ear in," he ordered, his voice surprisingly sharp. "If I lose you for a millisecond, I'll wire a dozen mechghosts to haunt you for eternity."

"Deal," Wendy promised. "Keep an eye out for Dawes. I'm counting on you two to keep us all alive."

"Heard." Michaels ended the comm and Wendy slowly turned to the pilot, who leveled her with a steely glare. A wry smile pulled her lips as she met the girl's furious expression.

"Alright, Dawes, spit it out."

The pilot huffed. "I would just like to go on record saying this is a *terrible* idea, and that you're probably going to get yourself killed. I would also like the transcripts to note that your highly intelligent pilot strongly advised against it and was quite rudely disregarded."

Wendy laughed and clapped a reassuring hand on Dawes' shoulder. "We'll be fine. I'm bringing Johns topside and I've got you and Michaels at the helm. It's the safest I could possibly be," she fixed her friend with a teasing wink. "Just don't let Boyce get too comfortable as acting captain."

Dawes groaned. "There's another reason to be mad at you."

"They're adding up quick," Wendy remarked. With a huff, Dawes flopped in her pilot's chair to issued a few quick commands to the StarBoard before activating her comm. After a brief pause, Michaels' dry voice burst through the muffled speaker.

"You know, it's easier to keep everyone alive when I'm not getting interrupted every three seconds."

Dawes smirked. "Has anyone ever told you you're a real charmer, Michaels?"

"Dawes?"

Wendy covered her laugh over Michaels' choked splutters.

"The one and only," the pilot trilled as she swiveled in her chair. "Captain's heading out, so it's you and me keeping tabs, wizard. Think you can handle that?" Her confident smile vanished as Michaels' audio silenced. She cast a troubled glanc at Wendy before her nav screen flickered and a small video feed appeared in the upper corner. Inside the feed, the red cast of the maintenance bay tinged Michaels' features pink. He observed Wendy and Dawes with a satisfied smirk.

"If we're gonna do this, we're gonna do it right," he said.

Wendy grinned at the pair before her. "Good," she declared as Johns sauntered through the cabin door with Nibs and Curly close on his heels. Wendy acknowledged the men, then turned back to Michaels. "I'm going to need you to inform Mr. SMEE when he returns and have him pass the message to Commander Boyce. I'd debrief them myself, but I think it's more important to move swiftly than to personalize notes," she explained before adding, "But break the news to SMEE gently Dawes, you know how he gets."

Dawes laughed. "You got it, Captain. Take it easy on the cyborg," she teased, earning a scathing look from Michaels.

Wendy smirked. "You're going to regret saying that," she warned, nodding toward the scandalized tech. "You just earned yourself an extensive lecture on the variations of automatons and their capabilities."

Dawes' wince turned her grin to a full-blown laugh. She shook her head, then turned back to Johns, who waited in interest.

"You rang, Captain?" His quick eyes darted around the crowded room, ending on Michaels' image in the nav screen. "You didn't restart the party without us, did you?"

Wendy snorted. "Unfortunately not. But there's about to be another one, and *you're* invited." Johns puzzled at her cryptic words, but a keen smile played on his lips.

He rubbed his hands together eagerly. "Just need a time and place, and I'm in," he said. "When's this shindig starting?"

"Right now," Wendy replied. Her gaze flitted to each crew member. Tootles stiffened to attention while Nibs' eyes lit with excitement, and Curly shrank in worry. "The *Roger* is dead in the water and we need parts for repairs." She indicated the looming ships hovering across the visor. "It just so happens, we have them. All we need to do is grab them. Michaels and Dawes are our spotters. With their help, we'll harvest the parts we need and bring them home. Quick and easy."

She met the awed faces lined before her.

"Any questions?"

Johns raised his hand, a mischievous look on his face. Wendy suppressed a grin.

"Yes, Commander?"

"What about the part where we try not to get crushed by floating space junk?"

Wendy's sigh was drowned by Nibs and Curly's hushed snickers. She shook her head in an exasperated smile. "You'll just have to be smarter than the scraps."

The Boys' snickers erupted into full-on hoots as Johns scratched the back of his head. Wendy tightened her grin.

"If there are no other questions," she prompted, waiting for her team's final remarks. Johns and Tootles swept a united salute followed by a delayed movement from Curly, who kicked Nibs to attention. Wendy nodded at the ragtag group. "Let's go."

The walk to the loading deck was filled with a strange mix of tension and excitement. Curly, of course, was a ball of nerves. He clenched and unclenched his fists as he walked, silently working his fears. Wendy nearly offered to let him stay, but she knew his caution would be an asset in the field. It would temper Nibs' recklessness, which interestingly enough, was the reason she chose the brazen Lost Boy. She had no idea what to expect outside, and an uninhibited team member was exactly what she needed. Together, Nibs and Curly were the perfect yin and yang for the unknown—

Wendy just hoped they worked that way.

She cast a worried glance at Tootles, who beamed at her as he continued his proud march down the hall. If the youngest Lost Boy was nervous, he didn't show it. No wonder Peter had a soft spot for the golden-haired boy—he was starting to carve a place in her heart as well. She hoped the mission wasn't too much for him. Beside him Johns strode along, bouncing on his heels. Though he kept a formal appearance for the boys, she could tell simply by the way he carried himself that he could barely contain his excitement.

Wendy wasn't sure she could blame him. Although her stomach was in tangles, she had to admit, she was glad to be free from the *Roger*—if only for a short while.

They neared the dock and turned down the thin corridor that led to the exterior hatch. Though the small door was only intended for singular maintenance access, the smaller entrance would use only a fraction of the energy it would take to open and reseal the loading dock. Outside the entry, Wendy paused to activate the storage panel.

"Suit up, men," she pointed to the atmosuits hanging in the compartment before helping Tootles shrug into his.

"None for me?" Johns asked. Wendy grinned and reached for his Fleet issued utility belt. She triggered a small button on the side of the sleek buckle and a thin electric blue wave of spooled from the belt to wrap around the commander like a second skin. She did the same to her suit, and stood straight, allowing the nanosynthetic fabric to weave around her body. It tickled as it crept over her, but when it was done, she could move freely though she felt the suit's protective pressure wrapped tight around her.

"Now your mask," she instructed, handing Johns a sleek visor. She pressed hers to her brow and it clamped in place, fastening it over her suit to seal her face in a comfortable cocoon. Over her eyes, the visor screen adjusted to its default setting, displaying her biometrics in the upper corner as she scanned the room and her crew. Johns stood beside her, studying the three Boys wrapped in their antiquated gear.

"You sure this is a good idea Darling?" he murmured under his breath.

"Not at all," Wendy disclosed, "but it's the only option we have. I need Michaels and Dawes on hand and DeLaCruz needs to be ready for us if anything happens outside," she motioned to the three young men before her. "They're our best chance."

"What about Boyce?" Johns asked.

Wendy's gut wrenched. *What about Boyce?* Her conscience repeated accusingly. Boyce was a good soldier, but he made things muddled. She thought to the pallor of the commander's skin and the dark bags under his eyes that deepened every day.

"Boyce hasn't been feeling well." The half-truth slithered off her tongue. "We need everyone at one hundred percent. We can't afford mistakes."

Johns accepted her logic with a shrug. "Boyce has looked like a garbage-fire recently," he agreed with a chuckle. "I've never seen him so sloppy. I almost asked him if he lost his mirror, but I was afraid it might set him over the edge. Do you think he's dying?"

The joke was light on Johns' tongue, but his words weighed heavily on Wendy. "No," she sighed. "I don't think so." She finished shrugging into her skintight suit, then looked at her team. Tootles blinked under his too-large suit, but the small boy stood tall, awaiting her command. Wendy leaned forward and adjusted his visor.

"Alright, Tootles?"

"J-just a little extra r-room, Captain," he said, executing a neat salute. "More s-space for air," he announced with a shout. Wendy smiled, then turned to stare proudly at the rest of her team.

"Alright men. Our mission is two-fold. Our primary focus is to recover parts for the *Roger*, and while we're working, to clear as much of a path through the rubble as we can. If we succeed, we should be able to activate our transmissions *and* give Michaels what he needs to get the ship moving. We'll work in teams. Johns, you'll take Curly and Nibs and work on clearing debris. I want you on your comm listening for directions from Dawes. She'll tell you what she needs moved. Tootles, you're with me. There are some big birds out there—we're going to see what treasure we can find inside."

She tipped her head in a proud nod before opening the evacuation hatch. "The ship is counting on us, men," she declared fiercely. "Let's bring her home."

17

Wendy's words were drowned out as the hatch opened and the compact cabin met the vortex of space. The heavy panel groaned at the change in pressure, then quieted as the world equalized and Wendy was immersed in the stars. She didn't realize she was holding her breath until her ears started ringing, and then she exhaled, still staring in wonder.

The graveyard waited before her, spinning lazily in its orbit. Massive pieces of machinery bobbed through the canvassed scraps, weaving a slow cadence across the endless backdrop of the sky. Wendy had never felt more insignificant in her life. Or more alive.

"Has a certain beauty, doesn't it?" Johns murmured over the comm. "You know, in a terrifying, life-threatening sort of way."

"Just be careful," Wendy snickered, "the Academy spent a lot of time and money training you to be useful—let's try and put their efforts to good use and stay alive."

"Yeah Johns," Dawes crackled over the intercom. "I just got offline with DeLaCruz. She said to tell you if you break yourself pulling some stupid stunt she won't be the one taking care of you."

"Hey!" Johns exclaimed. "What about her hippopotamus oath, or whatever?"

Wendy stifled an eyeroll. "It's *hippocratic,* you meathead. Seriously, I worry that your muscle cells are invading your brain."

Johns grinned good-naturedly. "Well Darling, lucky for me, I've got you here to do all that pesky thinking."

"Just don't get yourself killed," Wendy directed. "We'll discuss your mental facilities later—providing you last that long."

"I aim to please," Johns swept a mock bow then flourished an exaggerated wave, motioning to the vast expanse before them. "After you milady."

An exhilarated smile crept to Wendy's lips as the excitement playing in her chest was overpowered by a fresh wave of air rushing through her suit. Giddy from the heady concoction of adrenaline mixed with pure oxygen, she stepped off the *Roger's* dock into the glorious abyss.

Her stomach dropped as she plummeted into the void then let out an elated laugh when she caught in antigravity. She pirouetted a small spin, the universe's most awkward ballerina. When she saw the others watching, she gave a large smile and motioned for them to join.

"Come on in boys, the water's fine!"

With a bellowing whoop, Johns front flipped off the hatch. He overdid his jump and spun in a neat three-sixty then turned a slow somersault before anti-gravity caught him, leaving him head down and flailing to right himself. After a moment's struggle, he let out a defeated cry. "A little help here?"

"And interfere with the intrepid explorer?"

"Blood rushing to brain. Losing ability to form sentences," Johns spluttered.

Wendy rolled her eyes, but tugged the commander upright. He slowly spun to standing position, then reached out to pat her shoulder. "Good looking out, Darling."

"I aim to please," Wendy teased, mimicking his earlier bow.

Johns laughed, then glanced back at the Boys. "You cowards coming, or what?"

Nibs glanced at Curly. "He's talking about you, not me!" he whooped, then cannonballed off the deck. Behind him, Tootles let out a delighted giggle and did the same. Curly watched them nervously until Nibs, bobbing up and down, turned and hollered at him. "Are you coming, or are we telling the Twins to serve you space-dried codfish?"

"I ain't eating no codfish!" Curly cried. He screwed his face then released a warrior cry and flung himself into the stars. Wendy watched as he sailed over the rest of the crew then finally came to a slow stop. He twisted to face the others with a fresh look of panic. "Guys?"

"Hold on Curly, we're coming," Wendy called, then motioned to the others. "Come on guys, let's get to him before his anxiety does."

"Not a chance of that," Nibs muttered under his breath, but he followed obediently as Wendy initiated her StreamPak to steer toward Curly. She sliced through the open air, awed by the sheer vastness around her.

"Are you alright, Curly?"

"I'm fine," Curly squeaked through the tremor in his voice. "It's not like we're hovering in open space surrounded by a million floating death-bombs or anything."

Nibs snickered. "Yeah, he's not panicked at all."

Curly pounded his fists at Nibs and made a rude face. Wendy ignored the gesture as she maneuvered around a sparking shuttle fin. Broken wires dangled from where the piece had disconnected from its ship. She glanced around, hoping the rest of its body wasn't following behind. There was no sign of the ship, but she was hit by the bouncing broadcasts ricocheting through the abandoned machinery. She almost reached for her earpiece to silence the noise when she realized it was coming from outside her suit. Trapped in the field, the frequencies had formed their own vortex, a massive collection of static and the occasional clear soundbyte from a panicked captain.

Batting bits of obliterated vessels from her path ranging in size from smaller than a bitCard to pieces as large as home simulators, Wendy did her best to quash the unsettling frequencies from her mind to focus on reaching Curly. The others followed behind, shadowing her cleared path through polluted space. They finished their glide, and hovered in a small circle.

Wendy scanned the space surrounding them. Most of the debris was fragmented pieces of larger vessels that waited at the outskirts of the pack, a floating barricade to the smaller pieces that scraped past in their never-ending path. Another ship hovered in the center of the vortex, its outside charred and black—clearly the remains of a shuttle fire. Nothing on that ship would be salvageable—at least not enough that it was worth risking her men for. Their best option was a mid-sized star vessel positioned near the middle of the graveyard. It was dented and badly pocked, scarred from the brunt of debris littering the sky, but aside from a missing left wing, its structuring remained mostly intact. Wendy peered closer at the ship. Most of the paint had been scraped off the side, but some remained, leaving traces of the ship's name on the tail end near the thrusters. The *Lucky Day*.

Wendy activated her comm. "Dawes, we're outside and getting ready to move. Do you read?"

"Yes, Captain. You're coming in loud and clear," Dawes answered. "Michaels says he hears you too. He—what?" The feed muffled as Dawes shifted and muttered something to Michaels. Wendy's brow quirked at their bickering exchange before Dawes returned with a huff. "He wants you to hold on one second."

"Alright?" Wendy said curiously. She was about to ask what Michaels was up to when a whine keened in her ear then cleared into Michaels' voice.

"Captain?" Michaels cut into the feed, interlacing his audio to her connection.

"Of course, who else would it be," Dawes jabbed, but her voice tinged with pride. "The wizard worked some magic. Now you can talk to both of us."

"You're a genius, Michaels," Wendy commended.

"Thanks," he granted, then hurried to business. "I'm not sure how long the rig will last, so you need to get moving. Dawes and I have eyes on. We think your plan is solid, but we have a few suggestions," he explained before his thin voice was overpowered by Dawes' chipper instructions.

"Johns needs to take the boys to the front of the *Roger*," she directed.

"We're still getting hit by lots of scraps, and we want to get cleared as soon as possible."

Wendy nodded and motioned to the lieutenant-commander. "Johns, take the boys and head around front. You're going to clear a path." She paused and held her hand up for Johns to wait as a thought struck her. "Michaels, can you splice our feed into Johns' headset too? It would be good to have all eyes on one channel."

There line was quiet save for the sound of muffled tapping. "It's possible," Michaels offered. "Give me a few minutes to look into—actually, wait. I got it! Johns are you there?"

"Heyyyy Michaels!" Johns boomed into the conversation. "What's up bro?"

"Living the dream," Michaels grumbled. "Did you hear the plan?"

"Do you really think our captain would ever delay in sharing logistics? Those are the things our dear sister lives for."

Dawes snorted on the end of the line.

"Everyone has their assignments," Wendy deadpanned. "Elias was just leaving." She waved to Johns, who laughed and motioned for the older boys to follow. Nibs let out an excited hoot while Curly gave a nervous wave before streaming toward the nose of the ship. Wendy watched them go, knocking aside pieces of debris as they went, and rolled her eyes as Johns roundhoused a large piece of side-paneling.

"That door didn't stand a chance," Dawes teased.

Wendy groaned. "Don't encourage him or you'll get your own personal reenactment of Kung Fu Hustle."

"Oh, come on," Dawes prodded. "It could be fun. Michaels and I could dub a bad lip reading. Too bad we don't have popcorn; it could be a date."

Wendy laughed at Michaels' garbled choke.

"Careful Dawes," Johns warned. "You're gonna kill the boy."

"And we need our mechanic," Wendy noted.

"How about we all get back to work," Michaels grumbled, then quickly changed the subject. "I'd really like to get inside that X14 Tri-Wing, but I think that's probably too ambitious. If you can get to the Nautilus 6-Sweeper over there I bet we can find some parts to work with."

Wendy nodded. "That's where Tootles and I are headed. Do you have a visual of our end, or can we just hear each other?"

"I only have audio coming in. But, if you…" Michaels trailed off as he resumed his furious typing. "Feel alongside the top of your visor by your right temple," he instructed. "It might—"

Wendy swiped her finger across the sleek screenguard. A small circular ring of light flashed across the visor before pulsing to a tiny dot. The dot disappeared and her whole cover flared green before Michaels triumphed in her ear.

"Got it," he announced. "Now we'll have a running track of everything you see. Do me a favor and spin around a few times. I want to see the timing of the transmitter."

"Ok?" Wendy spun a smooth one-eighty before stopping to wink at Tootles, who waited patiently beside her.

"Thanks." Michaels said over more tapping. "We've got a bit of lag, but all things considered, I'll take it," he said. "Again, I'm not sure how long the feed will last, but we'll use it while we can. If you move quick enough, we should be fine."

"That's our cue, Tootles," Wendy motioned to the small boy beside her. "Sounds like we're on a time crunch."

"*Maybe*," Michaels corrected.

"Let's just say yes, then be pleasantly surprised if it turns out otherwise," Wendy countered. She turned to Tootles. "You ready?"

"Let's d-do this." Tootles' expression screwed in determination and Wendy grinned. She nodded, and activated her StreamPak to glide through the orbital debris. Tootles streamed alongside her, boggling at the carnage.

"Do you see anything you need, Michaels?" Wendy asked as she slid past a large, oblong panel. Its lights were still activated, and it blipped feebly in the dark.

"Nothing worth carrying," Michaels answered, his voice pinched as he followed her view. They were approaching the Sweeper, abandoned and battered in the crowded orbital stream. It loomed over them, its once shiny hull now dilapidated and uninviting.

"What we want is inside."

18

Wendy gaped at the looming ship as they approached. Up close, she realized it was much larger than she had originally anticipated. Sweepers were a popular model about fifty years ago, but had been discontinued long before Wendy's military career began. She scanned the rig, searching for its insignia. The markings were emblazoned on the side, faded and chipped with age, but clearly not Brigade.

"This isn't a Fleet ship," Wendy declared, studying the call signs decorating the battered vessel.

"No," Michaels said, his voice grim. "That's not regulation. Look at the wing. Do you see that sensor? By its belly?"

Wendy peered where Michaels described, and saw a thin rectangular panel plastered discreetly to its underside. "Yeah?"

"That's a scrambler. Whoever put it on didn't want this ship tracked.

Either the people who ran the boat were doing something very bad—"

"Or someone didn't want it to leave." Wendy finished.

"Hopefully it's the latter," Dawes' chirp rang out after a pregnant pause. Wendy cleared her throat.

"We'll be careful either way," she assured, then glanced at her comrade. "Right Tootles?"

"Y-yes Captain," the Boy's head bobbed in an aggressive nod.

"Good." Wendy's gaze pulled to the ship as she tried to visualize the blueprints of this particular model. Sweepers docked heavy, which meant their access points were positioned low on the vessel's side. She followed its belly to the base of the angled wing, then slid up the steel siding.

"The entrance should be right in front of you," Michaels instructed in her ear. "Hopefully the latching system is down. Otherwise we'll have to crack the sequencing."

"I see it," Wendy verified, locating a gaping hole where the access hatch should be. Rough edges and protruding wires jutted from the singed blast, marking the outline of a large explosion. "At least, what's left of it."

The image registered in Wendy's cam, and Dawes gasped. "What the hell happened?" she asked. "Sweepers are notorious for their structural integrity. There's no way the seal would have defected like that."

"She's right," Michaels confirmed. "That's the Andromeda models— shyte rigging. Sweepers are solid. That was done by something else."

"Maybe you should just come back, Captain," Dawes suggested. Though she tried to hide it, Wendy could hear the edge of fear in her voice.

Wendy peered at the damage. Charred marks ringed the hole, evidence of a fire. She swept her hand along the metal.

"Whatever it was, it happened a while ago," she said, raising her hand. "See? No residue. That stain is old. Whatever was here is long gone by now."

She streamed to the door and peered inside. "The interior has definitely been compromised, but if you think it has what we need, I'm not turning back now."

Michaels expelled a heavy sigh. "I'm not thrilled, but yes. We need the parts," he admitted. "I didn't want to say anything, but our calefaction system has failed. The radioisotopes are junked. If we don't get it up and running, it won't matter what state our thrusters are in, they'll be frozen solid."

"Then I guess we don't have any other options," Wendy grimaced. She looked at Tootles, who followed her with his pensive stare. "When we go in, I want you to stay behind me." She pulled a vintage blaster from his side pocket and aimed it at a long piece of scrap before clapping her grip over the energy chamber and pulling the trigger. "That's how you shoot," she said. "If anything tries to get you, you get it first. Understand?"

Tootles nodded, and Wendy gave him a grim grin.

"Hands off the trigger. It's only a last resort," she instructed. "We don't need to punch any more holes in the ship." She surveyed the charred staircase. Everything visible was stained black. "Here goes nothing," she muttered.

If Michaels or Dawes heard, they didn't say. The roar of the trapped recordings dulled as Wendy slipped inside the abandoned vessel, enveloping herself in the silent, metallic hull. Her magboots gripped the floor, suctioning her to the stairs. She moved slowly, allowing her body to readjust to her forced gravity as she crept up the stairs. Behind her, Tootles' footsteps thudded dully, revealing his proximity. True to his word, the boy stayed right behind her, echoing her every step.

Near the top, Wendy paused. In Sweepers, the staircase built into the ship, opening the steps to the base of the main floor. She held out her hand to stall Tootles and peeked into the ship, only her visor visible as she strained for a full scan of the interior. To her relief, most of the fire damage had been contained to the staircase itself. There was minor charring on the steel panels leading down the hall, but it faded and disappeared, leaving the corridor clear of residual soot.

Still blocking Tootles, Wendy took another step up. The passage was dim, with only red emergency lights granting any visibility. They cast the hall in a severe sheen, coating the walls in what looked like a thin layer of ebbing blood. Deafened by the silence echoing through the chamber, Wendy hoisted herself from the final stair and drew her own weapon, completing her sweep before finally indicating for Tootles to follow.

"If I tell you to run, you get the hell out of here and don't look back," she commanded.

"H-heard." Tootles said.

Wendy curled a half smile then continued down, out of the red cast from the main floor into the ship's darkened interior. As the last traces of light faded, she activated her magbeam. It flickered on, bathing the space in a soft, yellow glow.

"You're getting close to the heart," Michaels rasped over the silence. "Follow the hall until you reach the emergency access ladder. Then, you get to climb."

"Sounds delightful," Wendy murmured, straining her eyes against the dark. The dimmed edges of her beam's cast illuminated a small depression in the wall. Heart pounding, she crept closer and found a metal ladder dipping deep into the belly of the ship.

She gripped the rungs and with a final glance at Tootles, began her descent. The steel bars clanged under her feet, stirring ghostly echoes with every step she took. She reached the end of the ladder, which hovered high above the Sweeper's floor. Bracing herself, she released her grip and jumped, landing with a muted thud. Tinny peals rippled through the paneling, cutting the silence with their ringing whine.

Wendy froze, gun raised as she searched for signs of life. She took a tentative step, twisting to illuminate the room as she scanned the abandoned space. The hull was similar to the bay of the *Roger*, but unlike the sweltering, living belly of their ship, the Sweeper's rig was desolate. Wendy shivered, and realized how cold it was deep inside the vessel. Without active heating, the ship had adopted its environmental temperature. She glanced around, awed by small patches of frost that collected over ancient condensation, covering the walls in glistening swathes of white. Gooseflesh tickled over her skin, and Wendy rubbed her arms to chase away the prickling sensation. If she was cold in her reinforced space suit, she didn't want to know what it felt like outside.

"Ok Michaels, I'm in," she whispered.

"You're almost home free," Michaels encouraged. "There's just a couple parts I need to repair the aperture. I'd like to bring more, but obviously we've got a limited capacity on what we can carry, so for now it looks like just the essentials."

"Just the essentials," Wendy repeated. "Sounds good. What are the essentials?"

"I need an oxidizer valve and a calefaction aperture. And if you can find one in decent condition, I wouldn't say no to a trajectory stabilizer grid."

"English, Michaels. Give me English."

Dawes' snort shadowed Michaels' soft snicker. "You're looking for a part that looks like a magRing connected to a blue adapter and a small cylindrical capsule with three tight bands etched in the middle. The stabilizer grid isn't as important, but it looks like a miniature version of the switchboard on your Navs system."

"Alright," Wendy confirmed, studying the unfamiliar tech. "Where exactly will those be?"

"Near the kinetic propulsion terminal. You're going to have to go to the far wall. There's a large reactor port that houses the thermonetics. You're going to have to sift through some wires and gears, but they should be there."

"Reactor port. Got it," Wendy issued a steadying breath. Her scanband pulsed again, as it had every other minute or so since they arrived at the abandoned ship. Apparently, Nana did not appreciate the extended output of adrenaline coursing her veins. She shook her arm to banish the annoying buzz, then crept further into the cavernous pitch, illuminating the walls before her while the space behind slipped silently back into darkness.

Cold pressed down on her as she inched further and inspected the panels, noting the spread of the frosty patches. The farther she walked, the larger they grew, until the icy cobwebs transformed into sheets of ice blanketing the metal hull. Wendy paused as she passed a large panel and discovered a gaping gash cut into the side. Trembling, she reached for the cut to examine the damage.

Icy frost crystals clung to her sleek gloves as she stroked the frozen wall. Pushing her hand further, Wendy prodded at the gap. It was large enough for her to slip her whole hand through. She reached in and as her hand disappeared into the void, she imagined a clawing darkness gripping her and refusing to let go. Quickly, she shrank back, placing a safe distance between herself and the jagged hole.

"Michaels," she whispered, her mouth suddenly parched. "The frost was displaced before I touched it," she said. "That cut is new."

"Captain, you need to get out of there," Dawes asserted, her panic no longer contained. "Michaels. Tell her. She needs to leave."

The line went quiet before Johns' worried voice patched in, reminding Wendy of the others waiting. "Michaels?"

"I'm sorry, but no." Michaels voice was strained. "As much as I want her out, we need those parts. I don't think you understand how cold space gets."

"-270.45 degrees Celsius," Dawes clipped. "But we have the synthetic radioisotopes and individual thermosuits. As long as we can clear enough of the junk to radio you said we could call for help. We'll manage," the pilot said emphatically, "but she can't stay there!"

"It won't work," Wendy contended. "Michaels is right. Saying a number is different than feeling it. I'm freezing down here and I've got fully regulated stabilizer gear. If we don't repair our system, we won't last long enough to know if our transmissions even went through."

"Then let me come to you," Johns interjected. "There's no reason for you to be running around solo."

"I'm not," Wendy argued. "Tootles is topside. He's got my back. I need you to finish your task. Even if we do get these parts, we're still going to need to send a message out. We can't do that if there's a bunch of space junk in our way."

"I don't like it," Johns growled.

"Noted," Wendy smirked into the looming darkness before her. "You can yell at me about it later," she said, continuing her trek toward the reactor. Her trembling breaths puffed in visible clouds inside her mask, fogging the visor with its condensation.

"Be careful, Captain," Dawes warned, her voice strained.

"Yet another reason I don't need Johns down here," Wendy rebutted with a whisper. "He'd come running around poking things with sticks."

Michaels snorted. "Remember, you need a piece that looks like your magRing."

"I've got it Michaels."

"Good," the tech pressed. "Because the panel is right in front of you."

Wendy crept toward the hulking reactor. The quiet room hushed as she walked, leaving only the muffled clang of her boots against the metal flooring. Alone in the bay, the tech waited, forgotten. Illuminated in her light, its small, silver hatch gleamed brightly while the rest of the room was shrouded in darkness.

A whisper whistled in her ear and she pressed her hand over the receiver, struggling to hear. "What was that, Michaels?"

"Uh, nothing?" Michaels responded in a question. "I didn't say anything. Dawes?"

"Nothing here, Captain," Dawes said. "Are you sure you're ok down there?"

"I'm fine," Wendy said, but she cast a nervous glance over her shoulder before she grasped the handle and pulled, revealing a tangled mass of webs. "Why is tech always such a mess, Michaels?" she grumbled. "For such intricate machinery, it sure gets tossed around a lot."

"What are you talking about?" Michaels spluttered. "It's beautiful! Not a single piece has been damaged. Look! There's the calefaction aperture *and* the oxidizer valve! If you disconnect that large gray cable you can release them both at the same time!"

Wendy grinned at the ardor in Michaels' voice and hurried to comply with his agitated directions. She tugged a tiny net of wires covering the pieces, then reached to cut through the heavy cabling. She hesitated only a moment when she pulled her blade from the hilt, remembering the moment Peter had given it to her.

Nah, you keep it. I'll get another. His grin deepened and he leaned toward her, his piercing gaze cutting through the cold wrapping her sopping skin...

Brushing the memory away, Wendy sawed at the cable until it succumbed to the blade's sharp edge. Pushing the heavy cord out of the way, she reached in and neatly plucked the valve and aperture from where they burrowed in the metallic nest. Lugging the weight, Wendy reached for the pack fitted to the back of her suit. She pushed aside the prepped supplies to make space for Michaels' parts and slipped them in, feeling the strain on her back as she returned to the mess of tech before her.

"Alright Michaels. Now what? I don't see the grid-thing you were talking about. Any ideas?"

"No," Michaels' voice tinged with disappointment before he let out an excited cry. "Wait, shine your light at the bottom corner! Do you see that piece over there?" Michaels choked in disbelief. "It's a perfectly preserved ion retractor. Those were only manufactured for four years before the Galactic Aviation Regulation Department banned them to keep pirates from utilizing the tech to rig ion bombs. Do you know what I could do with tech like that?"

"You want me to grab it for you?"

"Ahhh the good ol' GARD," Johns teased. "Be careful Darling, you should only grab that thing if you're prepared to leave Squints alone with it in his room."

"As opposed to my physio equipment?" Wendy clapped back, earning a spluttering laugh from Johns. "Do you need the equipment, Michaels?"

There was a pause before Michael's begrudging mumble. "Yes please."

Wendy snickered, but reached for the retractor. Her fingers fumbled in the dim lighting as she worked to unplug the piece. Disconnected from the cords, the tech was surprisingly light. She tucked it neatly into her pack, situating the piece before grabbing her dagger and turning to leave. The weapon slid from the floor, sending a grating clatter through the bay and up Wendy's spine as the blade scraped steel.

The tinny echo hovered in the room until a chittering whisper brushed through her ears. Wendy twisted to sound and let a startled cry as a billowing shadow swirled in front of her, reaching from the depths of the blackened room. She swung her arm, slashing with the blade, but her hand swept through air as the apparition faded with the ghost of a hissing laugh.

"Darling? What's going on down there?" Johns worried over the comm as Wendy searched the room, her gaze darting around the shadowed bay while her eyes strained against the dark. Gasping, Wendy tightened her grip and raised her blade defensively, blood thrumming through her veins. Her body coiled, ready to strike until the deafening buzz in her ears quieted and she registered Johns' panicked voice over the din. "I swear to God Darling, if you don't answer me now, I'm coming in there."

"I'm alright," she coughed over paralyzed vocal cords. "I'm alright."

"Then what the hell happened."

"I thought I saw something," Wendy ended her sentiment with a frustrated shake of her head. "But It was nothing. Just shadows playing tricks."

"Are you sure?" Dawes pressed. "Can we get you out of there?"

"Does she have the retractor?" Michaels' rebuttal was pragmatic.

Wendy barked a tense laugh. "Thanks for your concern Michaels," she jibed, although the tech's pragmatism strangely soothed her. She exhaled her nerves with a shaky laugh. "But yes, I'm fine. And so is the retractor. Is there anything else you se—"

"No." Johns' interjection clipped through the line, followed by Dawes' sigh of relief. "You're getting off that ship. *Now.*"

"But—" Michaels' protest was interrupted by Wendy's firm declaration.

"Not yet."

"What?" Dawes and Johns exploded in unison.

"I want to make sure we have everything. I don't want to come back later." She cast a wary glance around the creeping shadows before bolstering her voice. "Remind me, Michaels. What was the other part you wanted?"

There was a heavy pause before Michaels' strained reply. "The trajectory stabilizer grid," he prompted. "It should be in the same system you're already working in."

"Ok," Wendy nodded. She smoothed her uniform and returned to the port. "Talk me through it. I want to get out of here."

"The grid should be positioned near the bottom of the stack. You might have to crouch to see it." Michaels' thin voice crackled over the comm.

"Bottom of the stack. You got it," Wendy affirmed, then knelt to study the twisting pieces inside the reactor. She glanced over her shoulder to check for chasing phantoms. When the room was still, she refocused on her task. "Now what?"

"If it's down there, it should be easy enough to find. It might be tucked in though—look for a piece that has a coiled connector cable protruding from the side."

Wendy angled her neck to search for the piece. Tiny wires draped down the large silver box, crisscrossing over the tech in protective vines.

"X marks the spot," Wendy breathed, pulling the cording to reveal her buried treasure. "Michaels, I think I've got it!"

"Great. You just need to unplug it and bring it in."

Wendy worked to free the piece until a snap clicked through the room. The almost inaudible sound slithered through her audio receiver, sending a crawling shiver down her spine as it echoed the piece's release. With a final grunt, Wendy hoisted the tech and tucked it away, then turned toward the exit, her breath catching as her magbeam grazed the ladder's bottom rungs.

Crimson stains covered the bars, dripping from the metal like a macabre art piece. A terrible chill skittered up Wendy's spine, and she gripped the rungs to hoist herself up the hatch and leave the gruesome scene behind. She didn't slow until she reached the access point and found Tootles, stone-still as he strained, listening to the chilly silence.

"Tootles?"

The Boy turned a slow circle, his eyes narrow as he scanned the shrouded corridor. "I t-thought I heard s-something," he explained, his face pale. Behind him, a series of scratching chitters ricocheted through the corridor, swirling to meet her in the access hatch.

A shiver rippled down Wendy's spine. "Let's get out of here."

They hurried down the corridor, away from the frozen bay. Wendy ran in tense silence, straining to hear every sound outside her heaving breaths. Her chest hitched, but she pushed on, fear overpowering her fatigue to spur her onward until her knee buckled and she stumbled.

Hissing laughs swarmed her ears as the darkened corridor filled with excited whispers. Wendy's eyes widened and she cast her gaze toward Tootles, who slowed to search anxiously for the sound.

"Tootles, keep going," Wendy urged, the words like dust on her bone-dry tongue. She scrabbled to her feet and resumed her sprint, shepherding Tootles while she ran. Behind, the whispers grew louder and more belligerent as they whipped through her hair, tickling her ears while skittered claws scratched unseen inside the walls.

"You better be worth all this," Wendy grumbled to the tech cradled in her arms. She continued down the hall, her booted steps ringing through the metal corridor. Her knee protested with every step, but she ignored the pain as she fled. "Still with me Tootles?"

"R-right here,"

"Stick together," Michaels chimed, encouraging them from afar. "The exit is around the next bend. Get there, and you're home free."

"That's the best news I've heard all day," Wendy gasped, her voice ragged.

"You've got this Darling," Johns cheered. "Just a few more steps."

Pushing through the screaming pain in her knee, Wendy spurred Tootles forward, yelling her commands over the swelling voices scuttling through the edges of her mind. Each chilling whisper cut into her nerves, clawing at her until their ghostly tendrils darted in her peripheral, reaching to pull her back into the shadows.

"Almost there," Wendy whispered, her breath coming in shorter with every hurried stop. They hugged the corner tight and turned, revealing the entrance to the ship. The scratching noises filling the corridors were almost deafening as they closed in, invisible phantoms surrounding them from every side. With a ragged gasp, Wendy pushed Tootles ahead of her, boosting him toward the exit. He skidded down the stairs and Wendy followed close behind, as an icy claw swiped her neck, sending a frozen chill down her spine. It caught her hair and tugged backward, but Wendy screamed and pushed ahead, feeling the lock rip from her bun as she activated her mask, only waiting long enough for her breathing apparatus to latch before she leapt from the ship into the open arms of space.

Furious whispers screeched after her, echoing in her ears as she hovered in the air, gasping while her suit struggled to balance her oxygen levels and still her spinning head. When her breathing slowed, Wendy turned to Tootles, who watched with a pale face, and gave him a reassuring nod.

"Dawes?" she commed over the cotton in her mouth, "You all got pretty quiet. Tell Michaels we got his parts—if he doesn't use them to fix my ship, I'm going to haunt *him* for all eternity."

There was tense laughter on the other end before Johns exhaled a relieved sigh. "You did good, Darling."

"Thanks," she said. "Now we just need to get back to the ship, and we can all breathe easy for a bit."

"Don't celebrate yet Captain," Dawes' voice strained over the speaker, washing Wendy's exhausted body in a wave of cold dread. "We've got another situation."

19

FIDUCIA II (GROUNDED)

LEAD MECHANIC PETER PAN

"Get back Tinc, don't go too close," Peter warned, with murder in his voice. "You never know what Hooke is capable of."

At the sound of Peter's growl, Hooke stirred. A shiver wracked through his body, and the threadbare clothes clinging to his emaciated form fluttered like leaves on the wind. With a heavy wheeze, he turned, able only to move a fraction, but enough to pierce Peter with his icy blue gaze. Peter froze as he met his stare and realized the strength behind it had nearly depleted.

"Peter. Help me."

His hand lifted pitifully before it flopped lifelessly to the floor. Warring emotions stirred through Peter as he observed the miserable heap before him. Memories of a time long past, clashing with more recent recollections of betrayal. A heaving cough ripped from the captain's chest, thrashing his weakened body against the floor. Hooke groaned miserably, and Peter's jaw set as he turned to the Stjarnin.

"Help me take him."

Tiger Lily stared at the figure before her, her smooth features obscuring the fury in her obsidian eyes. "*This man is a murderer*," she accused, her voice thick with barely bridled emotion. "*He would have given my flesh to summon the demon.*"

Peter nodded, straining to mimic Tiger Lily's emotionless mask. "I know," he said, then motioned around the empty cave. "But the Shadow isn't here. We need answers, and right now Hooke is our best bet."

Tiger Lily glared at the captain, silently judging. Her hands clenched as she issued a terse order to her warriors, who rushed forward, their weapons drawn and menacing. Peter nearly cried for them to stop, when they knelt to pick up the captain.

He watched in shock as the Stjarnin rose, to lug Hooke to the boat. Reaching their destination, they dropped the captain unceremoniously into the craft where he landed with a pained gasp. Tiger Lily stifled a small smile at the captain's pain, then moved toward her vessel, which sat, rocking in the choppy waves.

"*You have your Captain*," she granted, her slate voice matching the flint in her eyes. "*Do not request any more favors.*"

Peter scrubbed his hands over his face. He wasn't sure what he was doing, risking his only ally to save the man responsible for their misfortune. If there was any justice, Peter would leave the captain to suffer the fate he had earned.

But a small niggling in the back of his mind whispered fervently, reminding him that once, a very long time ago, it was Hooke who rescued him.

His jaw tensed as he remembered the scrap of dust and torn clothes he had been when Hooke found him nicking parts to pawn. How the captain had brandished his szikra when he caught him in the alley, then sheathed it and extended his hand. That was the day Peter found his place.

And it was James Hooke who had given it to him.

Releasing a heavy sigh, Peter crossed to his boat, feeling the Stjarnin's impassive eyes on his back as he knelt to where Hooke lay shivering in a pathetic heap. His nose turned at the stench of despair surrounding the man, sweat mixed with urine and lingering sick. He stared stone faced, watching the haggard captain as he murmured unintelligibly.

" ...didn't... stop... voices..."

Towering over them, Jaxtara stiffened and cast a disdainful look at the wretch. Peter ignored the seething alien and leaned closer to listen, but Hooke's rasping voice faded with his shallow breaths, dissolving his message into an inaudible jumble.

"Did you hear that, Tinc?" he asked, hoping the bot's perceptive sensors could detect the garbled tones. Tinc hummed a negative as she hovered over the captain, casting his gaunt frame in her gentle glow. Hooke's pale skin was tinged sickly blue, which belied the fever radiating from his flesh. Peter glanced at the thick sheen of sweat collecting along the captain's thinning hairline, clinging to his stringy gray strands in trembling beads. His burning temperature oozed into the chill of the freezing cavern, draping him in a smothering humid backdraft. Peter worried they would return to the camp with a corpse and no answers, when suddenly, Hooke released a rasping wheeze.

"Take... her...next..."

The captain's faltering words piqued Peter's interest. He gripped the captain's sopping collar and yanked Hooke toward him, surprised at how frail the once strong man had become.

"What do you mean?" Peter demanded, his ears thrumming with pulsing blood. "Who wants her? Who is she?"

Hooke's vacant stare ambled around the cavern before settling unsteadily on Peter. A relieved smile washed over his face as his feeble body sagged weakly to the ground.

"Pan. Of course it would be you."

The last words escaped his lips and he released a ragged breath and collapsed to the floor, in a deep, feverish sleep.

"Hooke!" Peter shook the man until his head lolled. He could have been breaking the captain's bones, as weak as they were, but he didn't care. "Dammit Hooke! Wake up!"

"*He cannot hear you,*" Tiger Lily echoed through the cave. "*He has succumbed to the fever. He is very weak. It is a wonder he survived. He is strong, your Hooke.*"

Though she spoke with grudging admiration, she spat the name like a curse. Peter didn't wonder why. He was asking a great deal from people he barely knew, and only tenuously trusted.

Tinc emulated his thoughts, buzzing anxiously in his ear. He ignored her worried hums as he was pulled along the undertow of his thoughts, a swirling mess of anger, hurt, and fear. Because even in his weakened state, Hooke was a tangible thing before him, withered and alone, the consequences of which, Peter hadn't missed.

The Shadow wasn't in the Skull.

Itzala had escaped.

20

The return to the Stjarnin camp was tense. None of the party spoke, except for Hooke, who laid on the floor, moaning incoherently. Peter studied the captain as he slept, observing his restless struggle. Coarse, gray hairs covered the captain's strong jaw, obscuring it under a layer of stubble that matched the dingy strands straggling from his scalp. Under the grizzly coat, the hollow of his jaw sunk under his pallid skin. Though there was no definite way to tell how long it had been since the Shadow had stolen him from the *Roger*, it was clear, time had not been kind to his old friend.

Unsettled by the brittle bones protruding from Hooke's tattered clothing, Peter glanced at the princess to distract himself. She sat stiff-backed in the boat ahead, her face angled forward as they sliced across the Neversea's tilting waves. Tizari was not so poised. Peter noticed the worried glances she cast at them before her gaze darted to Jaxtara in a silent, wary exchange.

Ignoring their pointed stares, Peter continued his brooding, delving into his muddled thoughts until the boats docked in the hidden cavern. They tethered the crafts before moving to ascend the winding staircase, with Hooke hoisted over the Stjarnin's shoulders. Crestfallen, they climbed the stairs, a somber party returning defeated. For though they reclaimed the sorry captain, the Shadow was lost.

Peter glowered at Hooke's lolling form. James had a lot to answer for. One way or another, he was going to pay his penance.

When they reached the edge of the camp, they found an audience waiting, the Stjarnin village looking on curiously behind the stoic stares of the prince and chief. Tiger Lily met them proudly, her head held high before she motioned quickly to her warriors.

"Densani jando. Teani son tok ne na," she said brusquely, then as a bitter afterthought she translated to Peter. *"Take the prisoner."*

Peter's gaze darted to the princess, but he remained silent as he followed the Stjarnin to a tent on the outskirts of the village. They filed in to an empty chamber containing only a small table opposite a neatly made bed with a simple, woven blanket. Tiger Lily motioned to the bed, and the warriors laid Hooke down before stealing from the room, leaving them alone until a halting argument sounded outside and the prince pushed inside, followed calmly by the chief. The prince barreled inside, his features flushed with rage as he searched the room.

"Gandanse ne branju," he reigned in his shout to an elevated hiss. "Mene ke adi?"

Tiger Lily blinked slowly. "Sene graza anjara. *We need answers.*"

The prince waved his arms in a strangely human dismissal. "Henadi gandesa." He motioned to Hooke then turned to his father for support, but the chief simply looked on in silent observation. "Jintanti?" the prince urged.

The chief scanned the room. He took a long slow breath, then hobbled to where the captain twitched restlessly in his sleep. He placed his gnarled hands over Hooke's sternum and closed his eyes to release a low hum. His deep baritone rumbled from his chest with surprising strength. The note droned long and pure until, with a jerk of his hands, the chief withdrew from the captain and turned to face the others.

"Mene anjadi. Itzala ne ane."

The prince gaped from his father to his bride, shock lining his face. His mouth worked to speak, but the chief continued in his booming tenor.

"Lijadi ge." His command filled the room, impregnating the air with raw power. "Likansa ani menone," he murmured, then nodded at Tiger Lily, his lips formed in a somber stack before setting his endless gaze on Peter. "*Find Itzala.*"

He shuffled to the door, followed by the surly prince, who stopped at the door to face the princess. He caught her in his steady gaze, before touching his slender fingers to the tip of his forehead. The princess returned the gesture and the ghost of a smile flickered over his lips before he locked Peter in a withering glare. Peter's fingers twitched uncomfortably before he quickly emulated the Stjarnin's shared gesture. With a furious huff, the prince stormed from the room leaving Peter confounded by his reaction and the princess' hearty laugh.

Peter's brow pulled as he waited for the princess' shuddering shoulders to still.

"*You just told Prince Juntara that you hold him first in your heart and mind.*" Tiger Lily explained, fighting to suppress her smile. "*It is the equivalent of the human proclamation for love.*"

"What?" Peter choked. "But, I—no!" he exclaimed.

"*I know. As does Juntara,*" Tiger Lily assured. "*It does not make it any less amusing,*" she remarked as she moved to examine Hooke.

"Depends on who you're asking," Peter grumbled, joining the towering Stjarnin. She gazed at Hooke's shuddering form, her features smoothed back in their impassive mask.

"*Itzala has left him,*" she said gravely. "*And left the husk of a broken man.*" She fixed Peter with a pensive stare.

"*Who is this man to you? There is deep regard for him in your gaze, but it is fractured—tainted with distrust. How do you know the man who captured me?*"

Peter's hands scrubbed his copper hair. "Hooke and I go way back. Long before we arrived on Neverland."

"*You were travelling companions.*" Tiger Lily nodded. "*But I am not interested in time. I am interested in meaning. This man,*" she gestured to Hooke with dislike, "*is important to you. Even so, I have allied myself and consequently, my people, with your cause. For their sake, I would like to know why.*"

Peter glanced at the shrunken husk of the captain and released a heavy sigh. He rarely shared his past with anyone, but he doubted the princess would continue to supply her assistance without an explanation. She watched him patiently, evidence of a life spent on an ageless planet. When it was clear she was not going to renege, he scrubbed his face and sank into the carved wooden chair at Hooke's bedside.

"Before Neverland, I didn't have a family," he began, his voice tight. "The Boys—well, they're the only people I have. They have been for a long time," he steepled his fingers on his knees, preferring to focus on them instead of the princess' steady gaze. "But before them, I guess you could say Hooke was the next closest thing."

Tiger Lily frowned. "*Your people do not have parental units?*"

Peter barked a laugh. "My people do, but I didn't," he answered bitterly. "My *parental units* decided I wasn't much worth the effort." His jaw tightened as he remembered his mother's soft smile as she waved goodbye. A strawberry blonde curl fell in her face, and when she brushed it back, he had thought there was something on her cheek...

He waved his hand, dashing away the memory as it tugged painfully against his chest.

"I was alone," he continued, remembering the Hooke's arrogant smile as he sheathed his szikra. He had cornered Peter after chasing him through the lowstreets. Peter still remembered gaping at the fearsome captain when he beckoned for Peter to join him. "Until Hooke found me."

Understanding donned Tiger Lily's features, but she did not speak, allowing Peter to continue. He leaned in the chair, letting its stiff back support the weight tumbling off him.

"He didn't leave me there. He brought me to the Fleet to work on his ship, and trained me." Peter glanced at the captain, still sleeping fitfully on the bed. "He gave me a place to stay."

"*He was a good man once,*" Tiger Lily imparted.

Peter met her stare. His shoulders bunched in a sad shrug. "I don't know what happened."

"*Itzala,*" Tiger Lily asserted as she studied the captain's huddled form. Her jaw set in a tense frown, but as she ruminated, the anger in her eyes faded. "*The Darkness captured your friend. That is what changed.*"

Peter nodded. A nagging question hovered in the back of his mind, puzzling how the Shadow got its clutches into Hooke, but he supposed that would be a question for when the captain woke up—if he ever did. Hooke shuddered in his sleep, and Peter wondered if he was fighting demons of his own. Before he could consider further, Tiger Lily spoke again, pulling his attention from the captain's fitful slumber.

"*Now Itzala has gone,*" she continued gravely. "*And there is only one other place he would go.*"

Peter's gut twisted as he thought of Wendy, trapped with the Shadow closing in. His brow furrowed as he pictured her walking down the quiet corridor of the *Roger*, her graceful footsteps echoing through the paneling when a billowing cloud of blackened rage descended upon her.

"We have to get to them. Now." Peter moved toward the door, spinning through his final launch checklist while his conscience berated him for allowing the distraction from his original mission. Who knew what had already happened since the *Roger* left? He stormed across the room until a soft touch stalled his escape.

"*Not yet,*" Tiger Lily declared, ignoring Peter's impatient scowl.

"But I have a ship prepped and ready to launch—that would have *already* launched had you not sent me chasing ghosts."

"*A brazen attack against Itzala would be unwise. The Darkness thrives on fear and uncertainty. The only way to succeed—to truly succeed—*" she stopped Peter's argument with a raised hand, "*is if we understand our enemy.*"

"You've been chasing this thing for thousands of years and you still don't *understand* it?" Peter snapped, his impatience getting the better of him.

"*We understand parts,*" Tiger Lily retaliated. "*There is still much to be learned. And now,*" she looked meaningfully at Hooke, "*we have the very rare chance to do so.*"

Peter followed her gaze to where Hooke battled unseen monsters. Peter could guess what the captain was facing. He remembered his lingering terror after the Shadow left, and it had only been with him for a very short time.

Hooke would have nightmares for the rest of his life.

Peter's jaw clenched as he considered the princess' words. His every instinct screamed for action, but under it all, a soft, fierce voice urged caution. Wendy would go purposefully, with a clear plan in motion.

And she would succeed.

He remembered the fire in her eyes as she battled the mermaids and her fearlessness when she faced the Shadow. She was strong. She could protect herself until he got there.

And then, he would end it.

"Alright," Peter said tersely. "We'll set a plan. But it needs to be quick," he stipulated as he started toward the door. He pointed at Hooke as he continued toward the exit. "You do whatever you need to do to wake him up. I want him talking when I get back."

Tiger Lily nodded. *"Our best healers will see to your friend. His will is strong—he will need it to recover."*

Peter nodded. "Whatever it takes," he affirmed. "Hooke has a lot to answer for."

21

THE JOLLY ROGER

CAPTAIN WENDY DARLING

By the time Wendy and Tootles made it back from the Sweeper, Johns was waiting, with the others in tow. He helped her inside, grounding her to the ship until her heavy magboots linked to the metal paneling. Secured inside, Wendy waited until the creaking hatch crashed shut before ripping off her visor. Free from the stifling mask, she sucked a deep breath, feeling light headed as she gasped air that hadn't quite reached atmospheric equilibrium. It nettled her brain like a space junkie.

Scowling, she shook her head, casting off her dizziness, she quickly stripped from her atmosuit and rushed to meet Dawes. The pilot's panicked words whirred in her mind as she hurried to the loading bay, with Johns following close behind. The pilot had explicitly instructed them to report directly, though the clamor coming from behind the looming bay doors would have summoned them regardless. Exchanging an apprehensive glance with Johns, she activated the panel, opening to a scene that rivaled the Roman coliseums. Pirates lined the edges of their cell, forming a rioting wall around a violent brawl. SMEE circled outside, whirring in a tizzy as he shouted helplessly at the pirates flogging each other.

"What the hell is going on?" Johns bellowed as they rushed toward the cell.

"I don't know, Commander," SMEE said, his golden eyes wide. "I was alerted to a commotion in the bay. When I came to investigate, deckmate Noodler was displaying excessive aggression. I tried to stop him but—"

"Excessive aggression?" Johns balked before motioning to the wrestling pirates. "He's killing him!"

Wendy followed his gesture to the arena, where Mullins was pinned under the berserk deck hand. His hands raised protectively in front of his face, but they did little to defend from Noodler's crazed attack. The deck hand pummeled the aircraftsman, tearing bits of flesh with every clawed strike until Mullins' blood spewed across the room.

"Shyte," Johns growled. He ripped off his commander's jacket and flung it to the ground, his arms bulging under his tight gray tee. "I'm going in."

He tore the key card from where it hung behind his badge and smashed it to the lockpad. The latch clicked free with a tiny hum and he crashed through the heavy bars with Wendy following quickly behind. Unbothered by their presence, Noodler bore down on Mullins, who was barely unrecognizable under the stream of gore covering his face.

Skidding to the center of the poorly formed ring, Johns muscled the crazed pirate off his victim, allowing Wendy to pull Mullins free. She anchored her grip around the disfigured pirate and tugged, smearing a trail of blood as she dragged Mullins from the ring. His head lolled as he sagged against her, little more than dead weight in her arms. Blood flooded from his nose, running in thick streams over the angry bruises forming over his face. Wendy pulled him to the edge of the cell, then ventured a glance at Johns, who still crouched in the center, his muscles rippling as he struggled to restrain the crazed assailant.

Eyes wild, Noodler clawed at Johns, his bloodstained hands tearing at Johns' eyes. Johns parried the attack and drop-stepped back before slamming his knee into Noodler's gut. The deck hand grunted and toppled to the ground, where Johns dropped to pin him. Under the commander, the pirate struggled and bucked, but Johns was too strong. Trapped, Noodler let out another crazed shriek and lunged forward, gnashing his teeth. Johns reeled back from the wild attack, then crushed his hand into the pirate's sternum, hammering him to the ground. The deck hand's neck whipped back and he his skull smacked the metal with a sickening crack. Noodler finally stilled as he slumped to the ground and Johns hurried to bind his hands and feet. Sensing the end of the fight, the other pirates jeered, but Johns ignored them as he carried Noodler to the exit. The deck hand's stringy hair draped down the commander's shoulder as his head drooped lazily against him, his eyelashes fluttering while he mumbled incoherently under his breath.

"Back up," Johns boomed over the pirates, his voice carrying a venom Wendy hadn't known it to possess. The pirates complied and shrank away, granting them passage through the narrow opening where SMEE stood guard.

"Take him to the MedBay," Wendy grimaced at the unconscious deck hand before casting another glance at Mullins. He hung in her arms, his breath coming out in shallow, ragged gasps. "Mullins needs medical attention right away, and we don't have time to wait. We have to figure out what just happened." She glanced murderously at the pirates swarming the bars, their raucous cries adding to the room's chaos. Her stomach turned at the crimson stain seeping in the middle of the cell before she turned to SMEE. "Make sure everything calms down here, then comm Dawes. Tell her I want to see her immediately."

Tugging Mullins toward the door, she followed the path the Johns foraged with Noodler. They reached the MedBay, where DeLaCruz rushed to greet them. Her worried frown deepened at the bloodstains spattering Noodler's clothes before Wendy trailed in with Mullins in tow.

"*Que demonios,*" the medic rushed to help Wendy. "What happened?" she demanded as her eyes darted over the pirate's injuries.

"There was a fight," Wendy summarized. She let DeLaCruz lead her to the empty medtable, where they set Mullins, illuminating his pale form under the sterile light. His chest rose and fell feebly as he labored over shallow, wheezing breaths. The blood pooling from his nose had slowed, but bubbled with every shaking breath. Wendy met the medic's disbelieving stare and gave a helpless shrug. "We're trying to find out more."

She glanced out at the physio deck, where Johns strapped Noodler to the physiokinesis machine. It wasn't a perfect solution, but at least thick, banded straps secured the deck hand against any more wild outbursts. Wendy released a sigh, then turned to the medic.

"I need you to stabilize him. Make sure he doesn't die before we can get his account. We're gonna need it to figure this disaster out."

DeLaCruz nodded from where she leaned over Mullins, her fingers working deftly to assess the pirate's condition. Confident the situation was under control, Wendy stalked to join Johns. He hovered over Noodler, who had awoken to discover his restraints. He reclined in the stiff chair and leered murderously at the commander.

"Alright you crazy bastard, you've got our attention," Wendy announced. She anchored her hands on her hips as she stepped closer, venom dripping from every word. "So, tell me what the hell kind of crazy game you're playing at."

Noodler's rotten grin widened to issue a hissing laugh. He rocked forward, straining against the bindings until his cackle ended in a wheeze.

"Pretty Captain wants to play?" He crooned, his lecherous gaze piercing her through his cataracts. "I'll show her a game she never forgets."

The words hardly escaped his mouth before a sharp backhand cracked across his face. Wendy blinked at Johns, who stepped back, seething. "You *will not* speak to the Captain, or any woman on this ship, like that. Try it again, and I'll cut off every extremity your wrinkled ass has left."

Noodler's eyes flashed as he worked his stinging jaw. After a moment of sulky silence, he turned to Wendy, his ghoulish smile fixed firmly in place.

"Wosn't meanin' no harm, Captain," Noodler wheedled. "It's just so lonesome down in the barracks it is. Gets so quiet with no one to talk at whot wants to listen," his gaze darted to Johns before he leaned forward to whisper. "Makes it easy for the voices to get inside."

Ice flooded Wendy's veins, but Johns stepped forward. "Don't be ridiculous," the commander scoffed. "You have all your friends down there.

Just one big, happy turncoat family."

Noodler's gaze narrowed in annoyance, but he quickly returned his attention to Wendy, a witting smile on his face.

"Captain knows I be talking true," he wheezed a gritty laugh. "The voices, they get in and nettle ye so. Makes it hard to remember where you end and they begin. It's almost enough to make ye go mad."

Wendy's breath caught under the pirate's blurred stare. Her heart thumped against her chest as she remembered the chittering whispers that chased her through the *Lucky Day*. She pressed her lips and the pirate's horrible grin widened at her omission.

Johns glanced worriedly from Noodler to Wendy. "You're not really listening to this tinbucket are you, Darling?" When she didn't respond, he clasped his hands over her shoulders and forced her to meet his gaze. "Seriously, Captain. He's one mop short of a janitor's closet. I don't think even he knows what garbage he's spewing."

"Don't have to worry about words when the voices do the talking," Noodler trilled before he let out another wheezing laugh. "They take care of ye, so long as ye let them."

Johns released Wendy's shoulders and whirled toward the deckhand. "And it's clear you're really getting taken care of with your stank breath and permanent living quarters." His voice lowered to a murderous growl. "Now shut it before you damage my calm."

Noodler's hissing chuckle strengthened as he swayed against his restraints. "Threaten all ye want, Commander. Captain knows the truth," his murky gaze sharpened as he turned at Wendy, his expression dark as stone.

"The voices, they know too."

Wendy stepped back, unnerved by the deckhand's eerie accusation. She wanted nothing more than to escape the suddenly sweltering room and Noodler's prickling laugh, but she balled her hands into fists and leaned forward, closing the space between them. She grabbed a fistful of his tattered shirt, ignoring it greasy texture against her skin as she drew him toward her to issue a menacing whisper.

"You tell your voices to stay the hell off my ship," she warned, her voice acidic enough to curdle milk. "Your actions are your own and you will pay for the harm you've caused."

Noodler's demented gaze contorted in a brief flash of fear before his skeletal grin returned.

"Can't shut 'em out, Captain," he jeered, before breaking into an eerie croon. "Close your eyes, cover your ears, nothing's gonna bind 'em. Close your eyes, hide your lies, the Shadow's gonna find 'em."

The macabre song chilled Wendy to the bone, and she flung the deck hand back, stinging with satisfaction when his head cracked against the seat and he emitted a pained gasp. The victory was short lived, however, as Noodler's daze dissipated and he resumed his sinister song. Wendy turned to Johns, steeling her expression to conceal her unraveling nerves.

"I'm going to find Dawes. Stay with him until you find out what happened." She glanced at Noodler, ensuring she had the pirate's attention. "If he won't cooperate, send him out the hatch."

Johns' eyes widened at the weight of Wendy's threat, but he didn't argue as she pushed her way from the MedBay. She hurried out, her fingernails biting into the soft skin of her palms as she retreated from Noodler's fiendish serenade. The tune crawled under her skin to burrow deep in the recesses of her heart, filling her with a chill that she couldn't quite shake. The door whizzed shut after her escape, enclosing her in the silent corridor, with only Noodler's echoing taunts to accompany her.

Close your eyes, cover your ears, nothing's gonna bind 'em. Close your eyes, hide your lies, the Shadow's gonna find 'em.

Wendy stood in the corridor, her hands pressing her ears to silence the terrible cadence whirring through her mind. She was so lost in thought that she didn't hear Dawes' approach until the pilot's worried voice sounded lightly in her ear.

"Captain?"

"Dawes!" Wendy jerked from her reverie, heart racing as she met her friend's concerned stare. "I expected you to meet me in the bay."

"Sorry Captain, I had to wrap up everything with Michaels," she held up her comm to display the tech's image on her screen. Michaels glanced up to toss Wendy a wave before he buried his nose back in the *Roger's* switchboard. Lowering the comm, Dawes turned to Wendy, her expression pulled in a worried frown. "What happened out there?"

Wendy's jaw tightened against the memory of scratching claws and chittering voices.

"We don't know," she answered before directing her response in a safer vein. "SMEE said he heard a commotion, then hurried in and found the pirates trying to kill each other. We're still not sure why."

Dawes gazed at Wendy, her lips working silently before she issued a quick nod. "I'm sure we'll find out soon."

Wendy nodded, her stare unflinching from the pilot's curious expression. "You did good Dawes." She said, then raised her voice so Michaels could hear over the clamor in the hull. "You all did. Hopefully, it wasn't for nothing."

"It wasn't," Michaels distant voice crackled over the comm. He looked at Wendy as Dawes raised the handheld for him to see. His eyes glinted excitedly behind his glasses as thin lines of coding reflected in their frames. "Whatever Johns did out there was enough to clear a path." Furious tapping sounded in the background as he coded complex commands. "I can't confirm which have processed, but all of our transmissions have spooled out. Communications are back online."

22

Communications were back online, but nothing had changed, Wendy growled at the thought as she resumed her nervous pacing through the cabin. It had been days of radio silence, and she was getting anxious for results. Clutching the comm, she forced her legs to a stop as she abandoned her self-control and hailed the maintenance bay.

"Michaels, have you had any luck replacing the oxidizer valves?" She sucked a breath as the cabin lights weakly flickered overhead, as though they waited for his response as well. It had been three days since their return from their excursion to the *Lucky Day*, and the ship was quickly deteriorating. They had expended a lot of energy to get the parts, now Wendy prayed it was worth it.

"Still nothing," Michaels' channeled in, his strained patience barely concealed over the crackling intercom. "I'm making progress, but the wiring is ancient—and finicky. From what I can see, someone had already done a number of patch jobs before we inherited the ship. The work was solid, but it's all layers of repairs I have to sift through." His slow exhale whistled over the comm. "I'm sure I can fix it, it's just going to take some time."

"Alright," Wendy ceded. She scrubbed her face, glad Michaels couldn't see the strain his words placed on her nerves. "Comm me the second you make headway. Nothing else takes priority. Understand?"

"Better than most, Captain." He cut the line and Wendy dropped into her seat, fighting the urge to scrub her hands against her face. The repetitive motion was beginning to chafe her cheeks. Instead, she smoothed her hair before reviewing the transmission records for the hundredth time that day.

"No progress?" Dawes called from her pilot's chair. She picked the ends of her fishtail as she waited for Wendy's response, her lips pulled in a worried frown.

"No," Wendy swiveled to face her. "Nothing." She opened her mouth to say more, but hesitated at the deep purple bags under the pilot's eyes. Dawes had all but refused to leave her post since their entry into the graveyard, citing her role in the incident as just cause. Wendy relentlessly assured that it wasn't her fault, but Dawes didn't budge, save the few hours Wendy's threats of disciplinary action had earned. The repentant pilot didn't need any more stress. "He's optimistic we'll have something soon," she lied.

Dubious, Dawes scrutinized Wendy's forced mask, but instead of pressing for answers, she offered a small smile. "Optimistic is good."

"Indeed." Wendy nodded, then strode across the room as she fell into a pensive silence. Her mind whirred in a dizzying spiral until Dawes' bemused voice broke through her daunting thoughts.

"Captain. You're doing it again."

Wendy blinked, then followed the pilot's smirking gaze to the center of her worn footpath. She was about to respond when the transmission panel thrummed to life, signaling an incoming message. Wendy's jaw dropped and she darted across the room, her hands shaking in disbelief as she fumbled to accept the transmission. Crackling static swelled in her earpiece, drowning her in white noise until a familiar tenor trickled from the weak signal.

Initiating Communication code xv1543f7-9. This is Admiral Renee Toussant of the Expeditionary Fleet, hailing the Jolly Roger. *Report.*

"Admiral?" Wendy's voice broke with relief. She exchanged an elated glance with Dawes, who hovered over her shoulder, straining to hear the Admiral's words. She pressed her hand to the earpiece as another round of static washed through the comm. "Admiral, is that really you?"

Yes Darling. We received your distress signal. Our teams are working to pinpoint your location, but any intel you have will be immensely useful in assisting our endeavors. Do you know where you are?

"No Admiral," Wendy admitted, but even delivering the disappointing news couldn't stifle her smile. "Our systems have been compromised. We are unable to determine our whereabouts. It will likely be the case until we break from the graveyard."

Graveyard? The Admiral's stiff tone lilted in curiosity.

"We've encountered a collection of fallen vessels from unknown origin gathered in the Krawk Nebula," Wendy explained. "We made a brief excursion to explore, but the information we gathered was minimal. Other

J . M . SULLIVAN

situations claimed our immediate attention."

What situations, the Admiral demanded.

"The rapid deterioration of our vessel," Wendy answered simply. There was no use sugarcoating it. The Admiral was not a woman who minced words, and dressing up the truth would only result in the less assistance—which they absolutely couldn't afford. "And the assault of one of our prisoners. We are investigating both matters, but there are no definitive answers as of yet. The only thing I can confirm is that we need immediate assistance, and we are requesting it in earnest."

A heavy pause weighed over the line before the Admiral's throaty growl clipped through the speaker. *Of course, Darling. The Fleet will do everything we can to assist your vessel. I've already assembled a team dedicated to locating your position.*

"Thank you, Admiral," Wendy breathed.

Don't thank me just yet, the Admiral cautioned.

Wendy's brow furrowed. "Admiral?"

We will do our best, Darling, but without a precise location, there is no way of knowing when my team will reach you. At best, we're looking at a minimum of weeks, but in reality Captain, it could take months.

Wendy's blood ran cold. "With all due respect, that isn't enough. My men are working diligently to repair the ship and resume our course, but the fact of the matter is that we're dead in the water, and I don't know how much longer we'll stay afloat."

I understand, Captain. Unfortunately, until we have our sights set, there is nothing I can guarantee. We will prep for immediate launch while research works

220

to pinpoint your position. Our goal is to reach you in three weeks.

After another weighted pause, Wendy deflated. "Understood. My team will maintain our course of action. We will continue to update you on our progress."

That's what we need, Captain, the Admiral agreed. *Keep your men calm and occupied. I assure you, help is on the way.*

"Yes, Admiral," Wendy murmured before another thought jumped to mind. "And Admiral? When we departed Neverland, we were forced to leave a team member behind. One of the *Jolly Roger's* original crewmen, the mechanic Peter Pan. The vessel was compromised and he remained anchored to kickstart the launch. Our mission will not be complete until we retrieve him as well."

That's not the priority, Darling. First, we need to get your team. Then, I expect a full debriefing. After you share your intel—if we have the resources—I will consider it. But granting full disclosure, that planet has already claimed two of our finest ships. I am not inclined to hand it another.

Wendy swallowed to clear the tremor building in her voice. "I promised him we would return."

The line went quiet before the Admiral's brisk voice clipped in. *I sympathize, Captain, but that is just not a promise I can accommodate.*

"I realize this goes against protocol, but he saved us!" Wendy exploded against the pressure crushing her lungs. "Without Peter, we wouldn't have even made it this far! We owe him our lives!"

And you would repay his sacrifice by putting yourself in the same situation he freed you from? You have to know you were incredibly lucky to survive the first crash. It's nothing short of a miracle that both crews remained mostly intact after incurring such damage. I am not a gambling woman, Darling, but even if I was, the odds would be too high. I'm sorry. It's too much risk for far too little return.

Wendy's throat clenched, and she felt she might be sick. A dozen arguments bubbled against the blockage in her throat, but the Admiral continued in her detached tenor.

The Fleet is prepping a team now. I will inform you once they launch. We are coming for you, Captain. Stand fast until then.

Silence clipped Wendy's ear as the signal ended and she dropped the receiver, numb. Her head reeled as she considered the Admiral's briefing while a tiny whisper played an undercurrent to her dizzying thoughts.

Peter, Peter, Peter.

"Are you ok, Captain?" A soft touch sent a shock of electricity searing through her body. She whirled towards Dawes, while her dam of thoughts burst in a violent torrent. Tears pricked the corner of her eyes, but she faced the pilot, hoping her impassive mask would hold.

"Fine, Dawes." She tugged the corners of her jacket to busy her trembling fingers. "I just need to—" she fumbled for an excuse to escape the stifling room, "to speak with Michaels," she finished with a brisk nod. "He should be aware of our time constraints."

Without waiting for Dawes' response, she streamed toward the exit, the whir of the quarter doors needling through her crowded thoughts. She stormed through the halls, no goal in mind other than to escape the worried frowns and tired, sympathetic eyes. Dawes meant well, but she had too many questions that Wendy couldn't answer. Getting out of the room was imperative for her to retain her sanity. She had told Dawes she needed to talk to Michaels. She supposed that was as good a place as any to start.

Wendy stalked through the halls, wrapped in a haze of frustration until she slowed to a stop. Her knee throbbed, and cool air stung the tears collecting in her eyes. Brushing an icy droplet from her eyelashes, she bent to tend her irritated knee. It felt swollen, large and clunky as the pain radiating through her nerves responded to her touch. A frustrated growl escaped her throat and she pounded her fist against the corridor before slumping against the steel as the reverberations faded through the ship. She stood for a moment and listened to the silence, using the quiet to calm her hitched breathing until a passing breeze prickled the back of her neck.

Alarmed, Wendy whirled around, forcing her back to the wall. Her fists clenched defensively until her gaze settled on Commander Boyce. He looked questioningly at her before casting a quick glance over his shoulder.

"Expecting someone, Captain?"

Wendy released the tension in her stance before straightening her jacket. She stood at attention, abandoning her pain to address the crewman before her. "Not at all, Commander. You just startled me."

"Apologies. But you are standing in a common area," he pointed out, casting another glance over his shoulder before refocusing his distracted gaze on Wendy. "Should I leave you to your... what exactly was it you were doing? Meditation?"

"Beating my head against the wall is a more truthful answer," Wendy confessed. "Albeit, less dignified."

Boyce dipped his head in silent understanding, then leaned toward her conspiratorially. Tired lines etched into the commander's face, but nothing could deny his handsome features. His dark eyes stormed as he watched her, flitting from charcoal gray to piercing blue, enthralling her with his stare. "Only if someone sees you," he whispered, livening his gaunt features with a smirk.

"And what about you," Wendy challenged, staring into his pool blue eyes.

"I was never here," Boyce's breath tickled her ear as his smile brushed her cheek. He pulled away, leaving Wendy flushed at his brazen proximity. "Which stands to reason, considering you've not once come to visit since our departure."

"I've been extremely busy, Boyce. I—"

Boyce cut her off with a large grin. "You really need to learn how to take a joke, Captain."

A soft flush crept to Wendy's cheek as she forced a small, embarrassed laugh. "I didn't realize you told jokes, Commander. From what I recall you were always…" the end of Wendy's sentence evaporated into her mortified stare.

"An asshole?" Boyce finished, a low laugh rumbling from his chest. "That's fair I suppose."

"I'm sorry, I didn't mean to—" Wendy fumbled until Boyce smiled and raised a large, boxy hand.

"Of all things Captain, you are always one hundred percent genuine. Whether you like it or not." He drew nearer, then leaned in to whisper. "It's one of the things I have always admired about you."

Wendy tucked a loose curl behind her ear as she searched the hall for any point of focus besides the commander's intent stare. Finding nothing, she let out a nervous cough, ignoring Nana's chiding buzz as she fought to still the rapid acceleration of her pulse.

"Admired is not one of the words I would have expected," Wendy confessed, but Boyce's gaze held steady, drinking her in as though she was an anchor on the rocking sea. It sent a thrill coursing down Wendy's spine. She shivered and wrapped her arms around her chest, placing a blockade between her and Boyce's heat.

"The hallways are getting colder," she noted, "I really should speak with Michaels." She turned to leave, and a firm grip wrapped around her elbow. Boyce gazed at her, a perfectly chiseled statue, waiting unguarded for her response. Her mind veered into a dizzying spiral as he closer, his presence setting fire to every nerve in her skin. Wendy's breath hitched and the commander hesitated, his expression searching hers in a silent, hungry question.

Ears ringing, she returned Boyce's stare while her mind raced in a useless blur. Taking her hesitation as his answer, the commander surged forward, wrapping his powerful arms around the small of her back to draw her toward him, decimating the final inches between them as he crushed his lips to hers in a deep, searching kiss.

Wendy tensed, trapped in her mind's erratic whirlwind, until her body responded, short circuiting every thought until all she knew was Boyce. She sank into the kiss, allowing the fire radiating from his chest to burn his warmth into her.

Her concession strengthened Boyce's resolve and he clutched her tighter, deepening the kiss as he pressed her against the chilled panels of the *Roger*. Wendy fell into the commander, allowing his strong arms to cradle her as she freed herself from all her worry. For once, her mind wasn't focused on the ship, or the crew, or how they would survive—there was only Boyce's touch and the kiss he wrapped her in, a glorious escape that she wanted to hide inside forever. She moved her arms up Boyce's rippling muscles to knot her fingers in his hair, earning a throaty groan before the commander slipped his hand to trace his fingertips along the length of her spine.

Wendy's skin lit under the gentle brush of his touch and she pressed into him, reveling in the dizzying kiss until she pulled away, breathless as she searched the commander's storming gaze. It was so different from the open green stare she was used to looking into.

Her breath hitched as she thought of Peter and remembered the Admiral's decision about his fate.

"I should go," she extracted herself from the commander's warming grip. "I've been away from Commands too long, Dawes is probably wondering where I am," she choked over the lame excuse, but Boyce wrapped his hand around hers, stalling her escape.

"People often try to distract from the things they want the most, Captain," Boyce said, his voice husky. His free hand clasped and unclasped nervously before he finally reached to smooth her stray curls into formation. "Especially when it's something they cannot dare to have."

He pierced her with his sapphire stare, silently pleading for her to stay.

"I'm so sorry," Wendy murmured, reaching her hand toward his.

Boyce drew back, his chiseled jaw tightening to a carved stone mask. He dropped his hand, releasing her against the corridor wall and leaving her to the chill.

"Don't," he clipped, his voice colder than the icy chamber surrounding them. "I was a fool to think I could fight it."

"No Boyce, I—"

"I said don't!" Boyce's pool blue eyes darkened to pitch as he swatted her away. She reeled back as the commander grimaced then clapped his palms over his temples before turning to face her, his expression cold as stone. With an eerie calm, he straightened to face her, only his hands rebelling as they curled and uncurled in fists at his side. His eyes flashed again, and their ebony sheen faded to a dangerous metallic grey.

"Don't pretend. As I said before, Captain, it doesn't suit you."

Before she could respond, he whisked down the hall, anger rolling from his shoulders in palpable rage. Wendy stood long after the commander disappeared, until the ring of his furious steps stilled from the metal grating beneath her. Guilt and regret swirled around her heart in an intricate dance, swaying through every part of her conscience until she was only a husk of remorse, paralyzed between loyalty to her heart and duty to her crew. She tried to clear the wreckage Boyce's kiss left in her mind, but her clamoring thoughts refused to be silenced until a soft step whispered through the corridor.

"Tootles," Wendy breathed, glad only she could hear the thumping rhythm of her heart pounding too quick. "You startled me."

"S-sorry Captain," Tootles apologized. "I w-wasn't t-trying to," his brow furrowed at her tight expression. "Is everything o-ok?"

Wendy nodded, her lips pursing over her unsettled emotions. "I'm fine," she lied.

"D-did the commander u-upset you?"

Wendy's cheeks paled as her mind whirred through her interlude, wondering how much Tootles had seen—if anything. A fresh wave of guilt and embarrassment rolled through her and she nearly choked on the words she forced from her mouth.

"You saw the commander?"

"J-just leaving. He l-looked angry. A-are y-you ok?"

Relief flooded through Wendy so forcefully that it hurt. She nodded, but couldn't bring herself to meet the boy's gaze. "I'm fine," she assured, eager to change the topic, "the commander needs some rest. It's been a rough few weeks for everyone. I think it's taking its toll on all of us."

"Some m-more than o-others," Tootles murmured.

Wendy frowned as he pressed his lips in a firm line, silencing his thought. She tilted her head, and the boy let out a weighted sigh.

"It's so quiet now," he spoke slowly, measuring her response. "M-maybe he hears the voices."

"The voices?"

Tootles dropped his gaze. He kicked shyly across the paneling, making the metal grates sing with his bumpy soles before he confided, "L-like the ones on the o-other sh-ship. The o-one outside. It was s-so n-noisy. T-too m-many voices."

Wendy peered at his youthful face, clouded with worry. She reached for his shoulder, forcing a reassuring smile as she searched his storming gaze. "We'll be home soon. Then we can all get the rest we need."

"M-maybe," Tootles agreed, his voice distant. "Or m-maybe we never w-will."

"We are fixing the ship and going home," she declared, more bravely than she felt. "I made Peter a promise and so did you," she reminded him firmly. "You're not going to let him stay on Neverland forever, are you?"

Tootles shook his head so hard, Wendy was afraid it might wrench from his neck.

"Good," she nodded resolutely. "Then I don't want to hear any more talk about voices, understood?"

"Y-yes captain." Tootles raised his hand in a stiff salute. Fine lines of worry still traced his brow, but a budding smile replaced his somber frown. Wendy squeezed his shoulder.

"Peter would be proud," she commended, though it left lead in her heart. Pride would be the last thing he felt if he knew how she had spent her last moments. Clenching her jaw, she forced the damning thoughts from her mind. She needed to focus on her crew. Her ruinous love-life could wait until they had survived. "Now," she announced, "I have some urgent matters to see to. Is there anything else you need?"

Tootles shook his head and turned to leave, then paused and rushed back to crush her in a hug. His small arms wrapped around her waist as he nestled against her and released a tiny sigh. Wendy raised her arms, bewildered by the sudden display of affection before Tootles bounded off, his footsteps loudly ringing through the hall.

Alone again, Wendy shivered and rubbed her arms to warm them from the sudden chill. A gentle breeze circulated through the corridor, carrying ominous murmurs on the frigid air. Wendy whipped around, searching for the phantom murmurs until a crackle of static exploded from her comm, sending her from her skin.

"Captain, are you there?" Michaels' reedy voice crackled through the receiver.

Wendy forced her breathing to still the erratic cadence of her heart. "Here, Michaels," she confirmed. "Got any news?"

"None that you want to hear," he admitted. "But, if you have a minute, I have something you need to see."

"I'll be right down." Her comm clicked as she ended the connection and glanced around the empty hall. "Pull it together Darling," she scolded herself. "Be a captain."

She hurried to the maintenance bay, grateful the only sounds surrounding her were her own shallow breaths. Unwilling to test the occurence, she scurried down the ladder to the *Roger's* sweltering belly, where Michaels laid underneath a large metal frame, barely visible under its oversized paneling. As she approached, a loud ring ricocheted from deep below the tech followed by a string of colorful swears.

"I didn't know you could swear like that, Michaels," Wendy teased over the spluttering rig.

"Of course I can," Michaels' retort was muffled by the wrench in his teeth. "I'm also fluent in binary code and Vulcan swears, if you're looking for diversity." He grunted as a loud creak shrieked through the room, followed by a hiss of steam. "I have an extensive vocabulary."

"Apparently." Wendy grinned. "So tell me Webster, what did you need me for? It surely wasn't creative linguistics."

"Not today at least." Michaels scooted from the frame with a barking laugh. He wiped his blackened palms on his pants, staining what little clean fabric remained. "What I really need is more time, but I don't think that's something you can give me."

"That's actually what I need to talk to you about," Wendy deliberated. "I have good news, and some potentially bad news. Which do you want?"

Michaels wiped his face, leaving a smudge along the edge of his glasses. "You pick," he sighed.

Wendy cleared her throat. "Our transmission was recovered by the Fleet. We were just hailed by the Admiral."

"If that's the good news, I'm not sure I want the potentially bad stuff."

Wendy squirmed under his perceptive gaze. "You're probably right. But a lot of it depends on us. The Admiral assured me that a Fleet is coming, but it's going to take some time. Anywhere from a few weeks to possibly months. And that's being generous."

Michaels chucked his wrench to the ground, then dropped to a crouch as he buried his face in his hands to muffle another colorful round swearing.

"I know I asked for more time, Captain, but that wasn't really what I meant."

He exhaled ruefully, then stood and motioned for Wendy to follow. He led her around the system he had been working under then pointed at a gaping panel with a jungle of wires splaying from the inside.

"This is the calefaction system," he said, then gestured to a small silver cylinder resting on his small workbench. "And this is its crux. It's been deteriorating since we hit the graveyard. I've been trying to restore it with the parts we acquired. The tech's compatible, but nothing seems to be working."

Wendy studied the piece and the gaping cavity in the system it belonged to. "I know enough to realize that's all very bad, but give me layman's terms.

What does that mean?"

Michaels' face was grim. "The calefaction system regulates the temperature for the entire ship. It keeps us in stasis while we travel through extreme temperatures outside." He pulled his glasses to wipe them with the corner of his shirt. Wendy wasn't sure how the grimy cloth could be any sort of help to the smudged lenses, but she waited patiently for him to finish. When he was done, Michaels placed his glasses over the bridge of his nose and looked at her, his face drawn in a frown. "If we lose the system, we lose stasis." He paused to let the words sink in, then simplified further. "If we lose stasis, it's going to get really, really cold."

Wendy's stomach plummeted, hollowing her insides at the devastating prognosis. Gnawing dread seeped into her bones as she tried to comprehend the implications, but Michaels flinty gaze warned her there was more.

"But that's not the worst part," he elaborated with a derisive glare at the innocuous cylinder.

"Of course not," she groaned. "What's the worst part?"

Michaels ignored her scathing tone and continued his sterile analysis. "There are interference markers on the mainframe commands around the calefaction aperture," he said flatly. "They could only be put there by someone tampering with the system."

23

FIDUCIA II (GROUNDED)

LEAD MECHANIC PETER PAN

By the time Peter reached the ship, his breath was ragged and he felt light-headed. He leaned against the hull, then scowled as his translator registered Tinc's snarky jangle.

"That's a lot easier to say when you don't actually have to *breathe* to survive," he grumbled. He allowed three deep breaths, then opened the hatch, sending Seven tumbling to his feet, chastising him with warbling chirps as she wrapped around his ankles. Her downy fur tickled his exposed skin and he laughed as he stepped free from her twisting embrace.

"I wasn't gone that long," he protested.

The Neverfox only huffed through her narrow nose before she jumped into his arms. Gears whirring, Tinc shot inside with a string of snide remarks, but Peter cradled the beast closer and scratched her ears, feeling her contented purrs rumble in his chest.

"We're gonna get her Seven," he murmured. "We'll all be together soon."

He set Seven down and made his way to the helm, dropping into the high-backed chair he had installed from the original *Fiducia*. The chair adapted to his motion as he slid forward to check the main navigation panel, a small comm screen that was surrounded by a dozen control switches to commanded the compact vessel. All of the controls were deactivated, awaiting initiation, except for one. At the bottom of the screen, a tiny light blipped innocently, flashing bright against its sleeping comrades. Peter's breath caught as he looked at the blinking indicator, its pulsing beacon signaling a message received. He activated the transmission and a familiar voice broke through, clear as crystal, the same voice that banished the phantoms in his dreams.

This is Captain Darling of the Fede Fiducia—*but if you're listening Peter, it's just me, Wendy.*

Peter listened to the remainder of the transmission with his heart in his stomach. Wendy's voice was the same as he recalled, but hearing it spoken restored the rich timbre that his memory could never quite replicate. He smiled as her formality broke and gave way to the girl he found deep within the jungles of Neverland. The forest warrior who battled mermaids and tamed Neverbeasts with a halo of chestnut curls framing her lovely face.

The recording ended and a smile pulled the corner of his lips as her last words echoed in his ears. Of course she planned on coming back. He remembered the fire in her eyes as she made the vow before she escaped with the Boys and her crew.

And took the Shadow with her.

His fist clenched as he thought of the Darkness lurking in the *Roger*. Wendy didn't know the danger that followed her. She was in trouble. Now it was his turn to rescue her.

Swiveling in his chair, he quickly located his pack and began to rifle through it, shoving aside its various contents until he located the softened leather binding of Tootles' journal. Smiling, he ripped it out to thumb through its dusty pages. He flipped past dozens of illustrations and diagrams until he found the page he needed. Skull Rock leered up at him, swallowed by a thick black cloud. He didn't know what all Tootles had found on the Shadow, but if it would help him find Wendy, he'd share everything he knew.

"Come on Tinc. We've got a lot of catching up to do," he bid darkly to the bot fluttering over his shoulder.. "And I think the first place we need to start is with our old friend, James." He slammed the tattered book shut and shoved it in his pack. Though it was far from comprehensive, he hoped Tootles' lexicon would expound upon the Stjarnins' insight to the Shadow, and that Hooke could fill in the rest.

"Stay, Seven," he prompted, earning a quiet tail swish before he rushed from the ship. "I'll be back soon."

He sealed the *Fiducia II* and glanced at Tinc, his jaw tight with worry.

"If anything happens to her, I'll rip him limb from limb," he vowed. The nanobot's processor flickered as she reinforced his promise with a colorful string of threats. Peter's anxious frown gave way to a terse smile.

"Let's see what the codfish has to say first," he mused. "Then we'll decide from there."

He shot off with Tinc alongside him, her trail of golden sparks the only marker to their rushed path as they crashed up the mountain to the Stjarnin village. The posted guard watched curiously as they approached, but granted Peter's raging prowl to Hooke's chambers. Inside, Peter found the princess supervising with cool disdain as her medics tended the unwelcome guest.

"Is he awake? I need to speak w—" the medic hovering over the captain stepped back, revealing Hooke, awake and alert as he sat propped against the wall. His icy eyes flicked up from the shallow, wooden bowl he held from to meet Peter's gaze, and a small, sniffing laugh rasped through the room.

"Why Pan, I didn't think you cared."

His smarmy grin summoned a rumbling growl deep within Peter's chest. He shoved through the barricade of healers, ignoring their surprised protests as he knotted his fists in the loose fabric of the captain's tattered shirt.

"You know damn well I don't care about your sorry ass. You're lucky we didn't leave you to die on that godforsaken rock," he spat. "In fact, we would have if—"

"If you didn't need me," Hooke's infuriating smile hinged on his skeletal features. He glanced around the room. "Give me some credit, Pan. I'm no stranger to strategy."

Peter barked a scoffing laugh. "And what exactly was your strategy when you tried to tether a thousand-year old deity to your bidding? You had to know it would end badly. Not even you could be that delusional."

A flash of uncertainty undermined Hooke's haughty facade before he sagged wearily against the pillow. "Bad form to kick a man while he's down, don't you think Pan?"

Peter snorted at the sallow captain. "The way I see it, we're the only reason you're still alive," he cast a casual glance at Jaxtara, who surveilled stiffly from his post. "And if you decide not to cooperate, I'm sure the Stjarnin would be more than willing to remedy that. The princess has you here as a favor, but it seems to me, I'm not the only one you owe an apology to."

Hooke followed his wave to Tiger Lily's silent glare, then glanced at the medics gently tending his wounds. After a terse moment, he brought his hand slowly to his chest.

"I am indebted to you, Princess," he said humbly. "Your generosity is undeserved."

"Yes. It is." Peter affirmed, stepping closer to Hooke's dormant frame. "And it isn't free." He dropped his voice, pitching his snarl so only the captain could hear. "You're going to tell us everything you know about the Shadow, and then you're going to help me stop it."

Hooke grimaced, then shifted to a more comfortable position. He glanced around the room before returning his gaze to Peter with a weary nod.

"Fine, but only you, Pan." His concession provoked an indignant sparkstorm from Tinc, which the captain observed with keen interest before he offered a brusque amendment. "You and your bug." Tinc responded in a flurry of furious swears, but Hooke's attention had shifted. Peter followed his darting gaze from the medics tending him to the princess' silent glare.

"Your attendants can go, but the princess stays."

A bitter scoff erupted from the captain's throat. "Very well," he dipped his head in a weak nod. "I suppose it's only fair."

Tiger Lily's chin raised slightly, but she dismissed the medics before sinking regally into her chair, her onyx gaze unwavering. When the door whispered shut, Peter glared at Hooke.

"Start talking, James. And don't waste my time."

A smirk turned the corner of the captain's pallid lips. "Always so sure of yourself. Even as a scrawny little twig you were never afraid of a fight. You were a lot like me," he paused as his face darkened. "Before Hinson-Breahl's started taking over."

Peter's brow furrowed, but he refused to show sympathy. "Hinson-Braehl's? You're one of the Afflicted?"

Hooke sighed. "From my mother's side, I'm afraid. The only lasting thing the woman ever gave me. Genetics are a funny thing, Pan. A man can overcome almost any adversary except the ones genetically coded into his DNA." He read the shock on Peter's face, and gave a small knowing shake of his head. "The Fleet never knew. Until the onset of the disease, the markers are invisible, unless you know what to look for; and with enough money, you can hide just about anything."

Peter gaped at the captain. "But you never looked—" his voice trailed off as visions of end-stage Hinson-Braehl's victims swam across his vision. "You never..."

"Displayed any symptoms?" Hooke relinquished a wry smile. "Of course not. That wouldn't be good form. What kind of crew would hold to a captain whose own body won't even comply with his command?" He scoffed. "I invested a great deal in disguising my infirmity, and it worked. I was able to live the life I desired. But when I discovered a chance to defeat my affliction, it was too great a temptation to pass up."

Peter examined the captain's emaciated form. He searched for the tell-tale signs Hinson-Braehl's left on its victims, but only saw the wreckage laid waste by the Shadow.

Hooke let out a knowing laugh. "It does seem the gamble backfired a bit."

Rolling the loose fabric on his tattered sleeves, Hooke displayed the sickly green veins protruding from his biceps in that tracked yellow against his ashen skin.

"When we discovered Neverland, the Shadow's power halted the progression of the disease. How ironic that I was healed, but banned from living." Regret marred his rueful expression. "Itzala promised freedom from my affliction and this cursed planet in exchange for my fealty." He grimaced at the bones jutting under his withered skin. "I was blind to not realize my allegiance would cost much more."

The captain's eyes glazed and he stared into the distance, haunted as he plucked absently at his shirt. Peter exchanged a silent glance with Tinc, who hummed skeptically in his ear. He quirked a brow at her abrasive suggestion, and the nanobot jangled defensively, eliciting an amused smirk.

"Of course he's not forgiven, Tinc, but that doesn't change the facts." He turned to Tiger Lily. "What do you think Princess?"

Tiger Lily's expression remained neutral. "*The darkness can be very appealing to those who lose sight of the light.*"

Peter's lips pressed in a grim line as he returned his attention to the penitent captain. After a measured silence, he continued with slow, deliberate words. "You aren't forgiven for what you have done, James. Quite honestly, I don't know that you care to be. But that isn't why I'm here."

A sniffing laugh accompanied Hooke's defeated shrug. "And what, pray tell, is the reason you've deigned to honor me with your presence?" he challenged, the steel in his expression commanding every ounce of his retained pride.

A sly grin crept over Peter's lips. "We're going to find the Shadow," he said, "and you're coming, too."

A throaty laugh erupted from Hooke's chest with a strength belying the captain's weakened state. It ripped through the room until the captain calmed himself and the sound dissolved into lingering echoes resonating through the tiny room. Hooke let out a gasping breath, then leaned against the wall to fix Peter with a bemused stare.

"And how do you propose we do that, Pan?" The quirk in his lips disappeared as he sobered from his moment of glee. He shook his head, dismissing the question before Peter could respond. His mouth pulled in a frown, and Peter could almost see the traces of remorse flit across his stony expression. "If the Shadow has managed to escape, there is no way to find it."

"We already know where it is," Peter argued, "we just have to catch it."

Hooke released another small scoff. "Tenacity was always one of your greater virtues," he muttered. "So tell me. Even if what you're saying is true and you have, in fact, located the Shadow—a feat which seems highly unlikely—how exactly do you plan to catch the Darkness?"

"We believe the Shadow hitched a ride in the *Jolly Roger* when Wendy's crew departed. We're going to catch them and bring it down."

"The *Roger*?" Hooke's eyes flashed as his interest piqued.

Peter nodded and glanced at Tiger Lily, who slowly inched toward them as they continued their conversation. "Wendy's crew repaired the ship for their voyage home," he affirmed.

"And I take it these restorations included the resurrection of your bug," Hooke motioned to Tinc with a wry smile. "It looks healthy, all things considered." He sagged into the bed, his expression twisted in concentration as he deliberated, then straightened with a determined nod.

"It's possible," he allowed, "But it won't be easy. Without a host, Itzala's form is weakened, but not incapable. It only needs a host to grant it more power. From there, it will only grow in strength. The difference being that now, it has access to the galaxies." His musing ended with a small shake of his head.

"What," Peter demanded.

Hooke glanced at Peter, a ghostly smile tracing his lips. "I merely find it amusing," he answered, before elaborating under Peter's furious glare. "You resent me for my part in Itzala's rise, which, coincidentally, you foiled." He leaned weakly against the wall and released a tired sigh. "However, it seems your actions are the ones that have doomed us all."

Peter's jaw worked in rage against the captain's observation. His temper spiked, providing a solid handhold for his bitterness to overpower mercy.

"I'm sure you would like to believe that. It might even help you sleep at night, but color it however you want, Hooke, this is your doing. The only reason we ended up on this damned planet is because of your greed and pride. If you hadn't been chasing some fairy tale, we'd never have ended up here."

"And you and I would have long been turned to dust," Hooke mused.

A choked sound escaped Peter's throat as the captain's words sank in. Hooke was right. If his crazy whims hadn't brought them to the Star, they would have lived out a normal, complacent life. Peter would never have found his crew. And he would never have met Wendy.

"You don't get to wash your hands of this," Peter charged. "You're culpable. And if you have any shred of honor in your entire worthless being, you'll help bring an end to what you started."

Hooke glowered at Peter, the blue in his eyes transmuting to black sleet. After a poignant moment, he inclined his head in a terse nod, unrelenting in his stare.

"A man is nothing without honor, Pan," he clipped, "but those who pass judgment would do well to look to themselves first." He frosted the room with his icy threat, then slumped into his bed, his eyelids weakly fluttering. Peter made no move to assist as he waited for the captain's final verdict.

"I will help you," Hooke yielded. His ire ebbed, the captain had once again transformed to a deflated husk. He exhaled tiredly, his chest falling like the ocean tide. "But first we must enlist more men."

Hooke's eyes slipped shut, leaving Peter gaping as he sunk into a fitful sleep. Unaware of his audience's watchful gaze, the edges of Hooke's mouth pulled in a deep frown, exposing the sorrow he masked while awake.

"*He is shrouded in guilt,*" Tiger Lily's quiet observation murmured in

Peter's ear. She gently traced her finger over the shuddering arc in Hooke's brow. As her mossy fingers caressed his dampened skin, Hooke's tension evaporated, smoothing the deep creases forming in his skin. The princess removed her hand, and with the absence of her touch, the captain's invisible demons reclaimed their hold on his aged features. "*Whether his conscience allows him to comprehend it or not, regret clings to him like a silhouette.*"

Peter met the princess' somber gaze. "Regret doesn't change the things he's done," he growled.

Tiger Lily blinked slowly as she scoured Peter's face. "*No,*" she agreed, "*but perhaps it can change the way we judge him.*"

Peter's gaze darted to the captain, sleeping fitfully on the bed. His brow furrowed as the princess' statement echoed through his thoughts, inundating him with conflicting emotions.

"*We will help you,*" Tiger Lily's concession shocked through Peter's distress. "*Your captain's failures do not dismiss our own. Itzala's escape has entwined our fate.*"

Her declaration hovered heavy in the room until there was a quiet stir and Jaxtara breezed through the door. He bowed low when he arrived, then spoke quickly with the princess before skirting back to his post. Tiger Lily's lips pulled in a somber smile before she moved to the door and gestured for Peter to follow.

"*Jaxtara has informed me that our men are ready. You have your warriors, Pan. I will bring you to them.*"

24

Intrigued, Peter dashed after the princess. She didn't speak as she led him away from the small huts toward a large clearing tucked behind the mountain's shadow. As they approached, he made out the shape of a troop of warriors working furiously around a hovering disc. The Stars' rays glinted off the quicksilver material, cascading from the sharp edges like they were a rounded orb. Peter craned his neck, puzzling at the physical impossibility while the Stjarnin worked diligently, their swiping hands rippling the to shift and shape the surface of the disc.

Before he could stop himself, Peter reached for the liquid, then drew his hand back, surprised when the material felt solid to the touch. His eyes widened as he looked at Tiger Lily, who only smiled before she issued a quick command. She cast her arm out, pushing Peter back as the warriors surrounded the disc, then touched their hands to the edges, connecting in a large circle.

Dazed, Peter obediently staggered back as the Stjarnin began to hum and the quicksilver disc started to glow. Slowly, the warriors drew their circle wide, and the disc began to quiver and bubble until the manipulating material formed a sleek, crafted ship.

Peter shuffled forward, mouth gaping as he stared at the perfectly formed vessel. His fumbled over a hundred competing questions until he finally spluttered a single word.

"How?"

Tiger Lily laughed, a low rumble in her chest. "*We are an ancient race of people, long blessed by the Star. Did you really believe all we had was spears?*"

Peter's witty retort was lost in awe as he circled the ship, his mind still boggled. He caressed the mercury edges, each part perfectly fused together to create the seamless vessel. The *Fede Fiducia* had been impressive. This was glorious.

"*Our ship will take you to your captain,*" Tiger Lily echoed behind Peter as she slowly trailed his circling steps. "*My warriors are prepared to leave as soon as you are ready. They will ensure your safe passage through the Nebula and to your men.*"

Peter nodded. "Thank you," he said.

Tiger Lily's lips quirked in a wry smile. "*You are most welcome. My men will be most appreciative to be free from harboring our unwelcome guest.*" Tiger Lily smirked, then called to her warriors. "*We leave at Starfall.*"

Hovering anxiously outside the *Fiducia II*, Peter stood, waiting for Hooke's arrival. At Tiger Lily's suggestion, he had hurried back to the vessel to prepare for departure. It had taken a little creativity, but he managed to designate a secondary seat for the captain. After securing the last pieces, he ran an updated inventory and initiated a secondary systems check. The final results were calibrating results when Seven bristled at his feet, filling the cabin with her quiet rumble.

Peter followed her stare and saw Tizari in the doorway, leading two strapping warriors. They navigated Hooke through the narrow doorway before releasing him to hobble to his seat. The captain's feet shuffled heavily across the ground, but he held his head high as he crossed the cabin, only collapsing when he reached his destination.

Peter nodded to the Stjarnin, as they turned to leave, but Tizari lingered in the doorway, her gaze fixed where Seven wrapped around Peter's ankles. She looked thoughtfully at the beast then at Peter before her lips curved in a soft smile. She pressed her hand to her chest, then darted from the door to follow her companions.

"This is your rescue vessel?" Hooke's contempt cut through the quiet, as he scanned the *Fiducia II*'s cobbled panels. "I think I'm better off taking my chances with the aliens."

Peter scowled and turned to the sneering captain. "They didn't want you," he clipped. "Seems there's not a high market value for harbingers of destruction."

Hooke scoffed and leaned in his chair, the purpling skin under tired eyes revealing the strain the trip had placed on him. Seven sniffed curiously at his boots and he kicked to shoo her away before glancing where Tinc hovered over Peter's shoulder. His eyes narrowed at her flitting form, but his mouth pressed in a contemplative line before he cast a final glance around the room. "Should I expect more guests, or is this our crew?"

"All present and accounted for," Peter chirped. He flopped in his seat as he activated the visor screen. A wry smile crept to his lips as he noted how the Star's cast darkened the sky.

Starfall.

Tinc jangled excitedly over his shoulder and he bobbed his head, answering her garbled question. "And now, we fly."

He flipped the switches to the ship, initiating the launch. The *Fiducia* roared to life with a slow grumble, her thrusters vibrating through the entire ship as they prepared for takeoff. The cabin warmed as the core's energy built, swallowing the vessel until a sweeping hiss whistled through the air, propelling them into the atmosphere with a tremendous roar. Peter's stomach flipped as the rumbling *Fiducia II* struggled to break free from Neverland's greedy grip. The ship moaned under the pressure, but with a final whir, the thrusters reacted, launching them into the beckoning arms of space.

Peter sagged against his chair, the slow exhale of his chest at odds with the excited thrum in his heart. They had made it skyward.

He was going home.

THE CREW IS
CARRIED OFF

25

THE JOLLY ROGER

CAPTAIN WENDY DARLING

*S*omeone is tampering with the system. Michaels' warning played in Wendy's mind as scanned the tech in the maintenance bay, her eyes straining for signs of a disturbance. She walked along the looming machinery, each twisting piece dwarfing her in the sweltering room. Hot wisps of smoke steamed from open pores in the tech, stinging her face as she passed until she reached the end of the bay and found a large metal panel with a gaping hole slashed inside.

"Michaels, I found the problem," she said, turning to where the lieutenant-commander had been just moments before. Behind her, the empty room flickered, as the overhead lights groaned and a thick, dark cloud descended upon her from the rafters.

Wendy edged away from the writhing darkness, watching as the edges twisted into murky tendrils reaching for her ankles. She backtracked further until her feet bumped against a massive panel and she stopped, looking over her shoulder at the cratered barrier behind her. Shrill voices whispered in her ears, swarming her mind with wicked cackles before one of the wisps lashed out like a whip, roping her in its grasp. Wendy shrieked and jerked away, plunging through the panel's gaping hole to somersault into oblivion. Her screams ricocheted around her as a cackling laugh swelled around the void, trapping her in its echoes until she crashed to the bottom of the chasm and plunged into an icy pool.

Spluttering, she resurfaced and spun around, treading water as a cluster of bubbles splash up beside her. She turned toward the rippling disturbance, then screamed as a mermaid lunged from the water to plunge her far below. Wrestling against the undertow, Wendy thrashed in the creature's grip until another skeletal siren wrapped its gnarled hands around her legs, while a third clawed viciously at her hair. Wendy struggled against the wraiths, they streamed toward her in a neverending current until with a final bubbling scream, her lungs flooded and she sank into the darkness, while the mermaid's haunting song swirled over the Shadow's malicious laughter.

"Captain? Is everything alright?" Dawes' worried gaze was the first thing Wendy saw when she blinked awake, grimacing at the pain in her arms. She looked down and saw the pilot's white knuckles circling her biceps as she gave Wendy another forceful shake.

Freeing herself from Dawes' grip, Wendy rubbed her eyes, chasing the specter of her most recent nightmare with a shudder. Her hand played absently at her throat where the phantom's grip had bruised her skin as she shivered and started another lap around her quarters.

Before, her pacing provided an outlet for the nervous energy building in her body. Now, it was to combat the ever-creeping cold. It had been four days since Michaels' prognosis of the *Roger's* crashing calefaction system. Since then there had been no answers or solutions, only the steady failure of the ship's heating as the antiquated vessel struggled to compensate for its overloaded systems.

Nearly a week, and nothing but bad news.

Wendy exhaled and watched as her breath billowed in front of her. Just one more silent reminder that time was running out. Her eyes narrowed as she strode to the StarBoard. She scanned the blinking panel for the millionth time, but the softly blipping lights remained the same. Mainframe holding stasis. Internal temperature compromised. No incoming transmissions.

"Just thinking, Dawes," she answered, realizing the pilot still waited patiently for a response. She pursed her lips, then turned to her comrade. "You're sure nothing has come in from the Admiral?"

"Nothing, captain," Dawes' sigh revealed her wearing patience. "We're still waiting. I check about a thousand times a day too," she offered with a small smile.

Wendy's icy disposition thawed at the pilot's gentle demeanor. Relegated to the captain's quarters, Dawes bore the brunt of Wendy's stress. And as the captain's pent emotions continued to swell, her bedside demeanor got worse and worse.

"I'm sure you have, Dawes," Wendy assured. "I just don't understand what's taking so long. At the very least, I would have expected a status update. It's more than a little troubling."

"It is strange," Dawes agreed, her furrowed brow pulling the tiny scar under her hairline. "It definitely goes against protocol," she began, then bit down the remainder of her words.

The gesture wasn't lost on Wendy. "What?" she prompted, eyeing the pilot warily.

Dawes shook her head in a soft dismissal. "It's just—even if they hadn't had any progress, Fleet protocol dictates communications remain intact. The Admiral is aware of our situation, but even with consideration to the impact sending and receiving transmissions would have to our system, there is no reason they shouldn't have contacted us again. At the very least, they should have hailed several days ago."

Wendy gave a grim nod. "That was my thought too." She looked at the transmitter. Her fingers itched to grab the tech and scream into it, releasing every raging thought bouncing in her mind before launching them into space to free herself from the darkness swirling inside her. Instead, she smoothed her jacket.

"Michaels is working on the panel." she reaffirmed, as much for herself as for Dawes. "We'll give the Admiral twenty-four hours, and if we still haven't heard back, we'll send a signal. I'd like to conserve as much power as we can." She eyed the blanket Dawes settled over her lap. "We need to keep off the cold as long as possible."

"Do you think Michaels will be able to fix the panel before then?"

Wendy's lips pressed in a line. "I sure hope so," she said. "If he does, you'll be the first to know."

"The first to know what?" a boisterous call interrupted as Johns strolled through the room, his jacket zipped tightly under his chin. "When we're gonna start the first interstellar Ice Capades team? I'm telling you, if we just let the twins run some water across the kitchen floor, we'll have a Class A rink in no time."

Wendy rolled her eyes. "That's not what we're discussing, Johns, but thanks for the input."

"I'm just saying, I'd rock those sparkly tights." He shimmied his hips. "See what I mean?"

Wendy snorted. "Sparkly tights. You got it. I'll put in the uniform request once our ship is less likely to drop from the sky."

"Whoa, Darling, easy does it or you're gonna fall out of running for Captain of the Year."

"Yes. I'm sure they'll have to cancel quickly before they send me my pin," Wendy deadpanned before a harsh scoff erupted from her chest. "Don't be ridiculous."

Johns' teasing grin flickered. He crossed the room, concern softening his angular features.

"Stop that, Darling. You've done everything right. All things considered, I'd say you're far surpassing all those guys taking the easy road. Everything going to plan without any life-threatening catastrophes? They're not proving anything, if you ask me."

"Thanks," Wendy replied. A smile bubbled to her lips, but she smothered it with a tired sigh. "Speaking of catastrophes, what did you need? Have our balustrades fallen off the ship?"

"Not yet," Johns grinned, "But if you'd like another challenge, I'll see what I can do," he offered.

"No," Wendy stamped the idea. "I'm at capacity for bad news, so unless you're going to tell me you've discovered a way to convert ammunition into power, I really don't want to hear it."

"I can't just stop by to tell my favorite captain how much I love her?" Johns glanced at Dawes, "and my favorite pilot, too, of course."

"Of course," the pilot needled. "And what does your favorite medic have to say about these sentiments?"

"'Rissa is secure in our love," Johns boasted. "She knows who I come home to every night."

"Not on my ship you'd better not," Wendy threatened.

Johns coughed. "Figuratively speaking, of course."

Wendy fixed him with a pointed stare. "Keep it that way," she instructed, then smoothed her hair. "Was there something you wanted to tell me, Johns?"

Johns glanced at Wendy and his casual expression softened into concern. His hazel eyes scanned her tired face. "Are you ok, Darling?" he asked. "You've been so busy being a bad ass space captain, that I haven't had time to check on you. Are you getting enough sleep?"

"Not even close," Dawes mumbled under her breath.

Wendy scowled at the pilot, who suddenly became very interested in her charts. "I'm fine," she assured. "There are things more important than sleep."

"That's just your Type A talking," he mused, his smile widening under Wendy's narrowed stare before he sobered. "I mean it, Darling. Real, true, uninterrupted sleep is essential to optimum performance. You know it as well as I do. HE101: Principal Health Foundations," Johns cited as he steered her from her chair. "Now come on. Dawes can handle the ship while you take a break. A nap will do you—and those scary bags under your eyes—a world of good."

Wendy absently prodded her cheeks as Johns forced her from the command panel. Between her anxiety-induced insomnia and her nightmare riddled REM cycles, she couldn't even remember the last time she had gotten a decent night's sleep, but she wasn't about to admit that to Johns.

"My eyes are fine, Elias. When I need assistance with my beauty routine, I'll let you know," her quip had a biting edge. "Until then, unless you have something of substance to report, you should tend more astutely to your post."

Johns balked at the bite in her tone, but clamped his mouth shut, and pulled to attention. "Yes captain."

A pang of guilt rushed through Wendy, but she fixed Johns with a curt nod. "Thank you, commander," she clipped, bristling against her empathy. "How are the prisoners?"

Johns' jaw clenched. "Well, that's what I needed to talk to you about." He flexed his neck before he fixed her with a serious stare. "It's the old deckhand, Noodler. We were questioning him in the bay when the ship died. As soon as the lights went out, he lost it again. Started jabbering about those damned voices. Then all of a sudden, he went nuts." His face paled as he recounted the story, revealing freckles that his tawny skin normally disguised.

"I've never seen anything like it. We tried to calm him down, but he wouldn't have it. We had to restrain him. Barely got him contained before he ripped Curly's face off. Poor kid's gonna have a hell of a scar." The ghost of a smile trace Johns' jaw as he tried to make light of the situation, but it disappeared as he swallowed and his skin blanched.

"Even that didn't work though. Noodler—it was like he was possessed. I've never seen—" Johns stared into the distance, as the memory overtook him. "He started screaming and thrashing against the binds. I thought the geezer might actually break loose, but he jerked so hard, his heart stopped. I don't know if his bones were too brittle to handle it or what, but," a shiver rolled through the commander's body as he shrugged helplessly.

Wendy responded with a slow nod. "It's ok Johns, it wasn't your fault. Noodler was never quite right."

Johns' haunted stare met her gaze, "I'm telling you, Darling, something was seriously wrong." His eyes flitted from Wendy to Dawes, who watched intently from her chair, and he cleared his throat, realizing his audience. "I'll file the report, but I'd like you to look over it before I submit."

"That's fine, Elias. Document what you can, and I'll approve. In the meantime, have DeLaCruz help you wrap the body, and seal it in a cryobed. I'll have her perform an autopsy once we have less life-threatening issues to worry about."

Johns nodded and excused himself, then exited the room, the bounce in his step subdued. Wendy waited for the door to hum shut then turned to the pilot, her jaw set.

"Dawes, have you made any headway on pinpointing our position?"

"Yes, Captain." She pointed to the map's upper right corner. "See this cluster over here? I recognize it. I can't remember where, but the pattern looks familiar. If we can get the ship just a bit closer, we can cast the map to see more of the constellation, and then maybe use it as a point of reference."

Wendy followed Dawes' finger. The pilot was right, the pattern looked familiar, but she couldn't quite place it. She sifted through her memories of charting assignments and her interstellar travels classes, but the origin of the cluster evaded her.

"It's as good a place as any," she agreed with a sigh. "As soon as we're operational, chart the course."

"Already programmed," Dawes chirped. "Just give me the green light, and we're on our way."

"Ok," Wendy agreed, caught in distant thoughts. "I'll take a look when I get back." She waited for Dawes' nod, then hurried to the door, her mental task list growing with every step. It mounted as she walked through the chilled halls, her eyes slowly adjusting to the dim light. She was so lost in thought that when she rounded through the corridor, she nearly stumbled over a large pile on the ground. Catching her balance, Wendy stepped back to peer at the strange heap, and her hand flew to her mouth to stifle her scream.

A dark black puddle seeped from the mass to pool around her feet. It filled the hall with a tinny, electric smell that stung her nose. There was a labored wheeze, then SMEE's crisp voice called weakly up to her.

"Captain, is that you?"

"SMEE!" Wendy cried, kneeling toward the synth. "What happened to you?"

"I-I don't know," SMEE began, then broke off with a rattling cough. "I-I-I-I jjjuuuuuuuu"

"Shh, don't talk." She stilled the synth's glitch with a gentle press of her hand then activated her comm. "Michaels, report to Corridor 4b. I need you here now!" She screamed, then cast off the device to study the wreckage before her.

SMEE's manicured body lay in shambles, as if something had attempted to dismantle him bit by bit. His appendages hung from their joint-sockets, their exposed fiber-wires cracking with a still fizzling current. His head rested at a disjointed angle, and a large hole gaped in his chest where his heart should have been. Gallons of multifaceted oil spilled from the jagged crevices gored in his body, surrounding him in a pool of simulated blood. Though it was all manufactured, Wendy's stomach churned as she looked at the carnage before her—the equivalent of synthetic viscera. A tiny cry escaped her throat, and SMEE's head lolled toward the sound, emanating a soft whir as his gears spun uselessly, their laborious efforts giving the synth a too-human wheeze as his golden eyes stared sadly into hers.

"I'm dreadfully sorry to report like this, Captain," SMEE said, and his severed hand flexed as though to smooth his disheveled hair. "I'm quite the mess."

Tears sprang to Wendy's eyes as she forced a smile, although the damage to the synth was worse than anything she had ever seen done to a human. She crouched to her first mate, moving to tame the golden flyaways at his crown. She patted them smooth, then straightened his broken glasses, earning a grateful smile from the automaton. "Mr. SMEE there has never been one cylinder on your person that has ever been less than a perfect gentleman."

SMEE's fractured smile widened, then with a heavy whir, his golden eyes flickered and dimmed as the remaining power in his core fizzled, leaving only the chilled shell of his cybernetic frame. Wendy bowed her head and a tear slipped down her check as footsteps rumbled down the hall, thundering until they screeched to a sudden halt.

"What happened?" Michaels leaned over his knees, struggling to breathe as he examined the mutilated synth before him. Wendy met his stunned stare and a single tear slipped down her cheek. She pressed her palm to the synth's fine, copper hair and smoothed it one last time before standing to address the lieutenant-commander.

"I don't know," she said, the numbness in her voice reflecting her emotions. "This is how I found him."

Michaels knelt beside her, his eyes glinting behind his glass frames as he scanned the damage to SMEE's frame. They darted over the first mate, then roved down the corridor, following the dark liquid seeping across the floor. "There's a trail of bl—synth oil," he corrected himself with a grimace. "It looks like he dragged himself a fair ways. His shoulders slumped, and he looked at Wendy helplessly. "Who would do something like this?"

Wendy stared at the mangled synth, her lips drawn in a tight line. The shock of discovering his massacred figure had slowly begun to ebb away, leaving her to process the ramifications of the situation.

"I don't know," she murmured. "But I promise I'll find out." Her stare hardened as she looked at SMEE. "Michaels, I need you to finish up here. If you need help, call DeLaCruz. Maybe her anatomy expertise will come in handy. I'm going to handle this."

She didn't wait for Michaels response as she hurried to Commands. She was too preoccupied with her next steps.

"Everything sorted, Captain?"

Wendy let out a sarcastic snort. "You don't know the half of it," she said darkly.

"What's wrong?"

"There's been a situation," Wendy stated, not knowing how else to classify the disaster that swallowed the ship. "The ship has been compromised. W—" She yelped as the *Roger* trembled and let out a massive groan. Stumbling for her footing, she reached for the receiver, its weight heavy on her leaden arms. Her message couldn't be long, but it was worth the power it would expend. She inhaled a shaky breath as the *Roger* bucked again, shying under her feet as it cried for help.

Wendy didn't need Michaels to know there was little time left.

Steeling her voice, she initiated the transmission and channeled a calm she didn't possess. Nerves held no place in crisis, and the Admiral needed to think she was keeping her head.

No one could know how terrified she truly was.

"This is Captain Wendy Darling of the *Jolly Roger* requesting immediate assistance. During our last correspondence with Fleet Admiral Toussant we were given the directive to stay the course and await further instruction. It has been four days, and we have received no contact. Our ship is rapidly deteriorating and as our repair attempts continue to fail, so does the crew's morale. If anyone can help us—" her voice broke and she dipped her head to bolster her nerves, then took a deep breath before continuing.

"The ship is not sustainable. Requesting immediate and urgent assistance, this is Captain Wendy Darling. Godspeed."

26

FIDUCIA II

LEAD MECHANIC PETER PAN

"Confound it, Pan! Tell your cursed bug to keep its blasted sparks away from my prosthetic!" Hooke massaged his metallic arm where Tinc's glowing trail of embers singed into the wiring.

Peter watched as the captain batted Tinc's fluttering figure and tried to suppress a grin. Tinc's teasing was the least of Hooke's atonement for all the trouble he caused, but Peter wasn't about to point that out to the sullen captain.

"If you keep talking like that, she's going to think you don't love her," he needled. Tinc buzzed a smart retort in his ear that Peter was sure would earn an earful from the recuperating pirate had he understood. As it was, Hooke scowled and twisted in his seat, cursing as he flexed his stiff limb.

"What kind of first mate is a glittering pixie anyway," Hooke grumbled, eyeing Tinc as she buzzed around the cramped cabin. He covered his prosthetic, protecting its exposed wires from her golden sparks cascading from the rafters.

"Tinc is an advanced, highly customized piece of tech," Peter argued. "Her capabilities are uniquely suited to assist me in any tasks I might require. And," he added with a wry grin, "she's got a great sense of humor."

Hooke scowled. "A mechanical bug with *jokes*. The ideal companion."

Peter's eyes narrowed. "Better her than a half-keeled pirate with a god complex. And yet," he gestured to Hooke, allowing his hanging silence to prove his point.

"And yet." Hooke sighed and glanced around the room, his face pinched in steely disapproval. "Not that it's accomplished much," he groused, bitterly expounding on Peter's point. "Trapped on a half-rate barge with a gear-grinder at the helm while I sit, demoted to a tinned sardine. At very least, you could let me study the charts. Captains need to be useful, Pan. It's in our blood."

Peter arched a brow at Hooke's criticism. "Why Captain, it almost sounds as though you don't appreciate the challenge," he mocked. "Bad form."

Hooke bristled. "A challenge does not have to be appreciated to be overcome, Pan," he grumbled, wincing as he flexed his metallic fingers. Although the captain had been slowly recovering his strength, he had struggled with the prosthetic since the onset of their voyage. Peter glanced over at the metal limb, rusted and tarnished with age.

"I could take a look at that, you know," he offered grudgingly. Hooke glanced up, surprised, and Peter shrugged. "If it will get you to stop whining."

"Gentlemen never whine, Pan. They express distaste."

Peter rolled his eyes. "Whatever helps you sleep at night," he scoffed, but peered at the rusting prosthetic as he prodded the ridges of the tech to assess what he could easily adjust. He reached in his pocket to retrieve his screwdriver, then deftly tightened and loosened some of the sticking pieces and stepped back with a triumphant smile.

"Odds bobs." Hooke wiggled his clunky fingers. The movements were still slow, but they were less stiff. "You never did disappoint when it came to machinery."

Peter bristled at the backhanded compliment. A handful of snide retorts rushed to his lips, but he bit them back and nodded. "Tech doesn't keep secrets. It tells you where it stands. What you see is what you get." He met the captain's gaze with a challenging stare, then swiveled toward the navigation panel. "You don't have to worry about being lied to," he finished under his breath.

He looked at their progress. According to the trajectory, they had made good time, and with their Stjarnin escort, he was confident they would close the gap between their vessel and Wendy's.

He just hoped it would be soon enough.

Peter slumped in his seat, ignoring Tinc's reassuring hum as he caught Hooke's cool stare. "I suppose you have something you'd like to say?"

Hooke shrugged innocently. "I was merely wondering if you'd considered all outcomes before you launched your ambitious rescue mission."

Peter's glower darkened. "Only one outcome matters: that I get to Wendy."

"And what if you don't?"

"Is that some sort of a threat?" Peter was across the room in a flash. Before he realized it, he had Hooke pinned against the wall, his fist buried in the old captain's jacket, his knuckles crushing into his windpipe.

Hooke's eyes widened, but even though his breaths came in ragged gasps against Peter's grip, his expression remained detached. "The only threat I see currently, is you," he lectured. "Now why don't you put me down so we can continue like reasonable gentlemen?"

"Reasonable," Peter scoffed, but loosened his grip. Hooke brushed the wrinkles from his tattered shirt while Peter tromped to his seat and flopped sullenly in his chair. An amused snort flared the captain's nostrils.

"Obviously, the best case is we rescue the crew, and no one is worse for the wear," Hooke began. "But," he continued, his expression shrewd, "it's exceedingly likely that's not going to happen."

"I know that," Peter was petulant. "I just prefer to focus on the positive."

"But have you prepared yourself for the reverse? Do you have means in mind for fighting the Shadow and stopping the demon? Or are you going to handle it the way you did your last great crisis and fling the ship headlong into the first astral body you happen to run into?" He arched a pointed brow, forcing Peter to look away.

"I'm not going to tank the ship," Peter grumbled.

"At least you've learned that much." Hooke glanced at their charted course. "Odds are, it will take some time to catch the *Roger*. How long will that leave Captain Darling and her crew alone? Do you really think the Shadow will be content waiting patiently for them to arrive? It is wounded and hungry. What will you do if you reach your captain and you are too late?"

Hooke asked, his voice clinical.

Peter's hands knotted. "It won't get Wendy," he proclaimed defiantly, "she's too strong."

Hooke bobbed his head. "So the Shadow won't take the captain. What of the rest of her crew? Or are they impervious to its dangers as well? I suppose being led by such a woman of virtue—"

"You'd be the expert," Peter barbed. "I wonder, what exactly *did* the Shadow see in you? Was it your dishonesty? Or perhaps your willingness to abandon those who trusted you to their deaths. I imagine your black-hearted regard for the world helped you bond. It probably found a nice dark corner and snuggled right in. Didn't even have to paint the walls," his voice dripped venom. "Tell me James, did it hurt? Or is your soul so empty that you didn't even notice?"

Hooke's icy eyes glinted as his jaw worked over his response. Finally, he released a poisonous breath. "I am not here for your absolution. I have sins to atone for, but they are mine alone. It is not from kindness or fond regard that I have offered my assistance. Our end goal may be the same, but it does not make us a team, and it most assuredly does not give a lowly mechanic the right nor the standing to address me as such. I am a Fleet Captain. Commandeering a set of steel scraps does no more to your position than crown you king of a junk heap," his lip turned at the cramped cabin, "and a miniscule one at that. It's no accomplishment I would boast."

Peter glowered at Hooke's disdain. "Ex-captain," he seethed.

"Pardon?" Hooke raised his prosthetic to his ear. "Come boy, do speak up. We all know you are quite capable of crowing when the mood strikes."

Peter's chest swelled as he stepped closer to the captain. Nose to nose, he realized just how sunken the captain's frame had become. Though Hooke stood with all the bravado of his former glory, his shoulders stooped and age blemishes revealed time's claim on its stolen years.

"*Ex* Fleet captain," he repeated more forcefully. "You're a turncoat. I may be just a mechanic, but your actions have made you a doxy Benedict. You have no more claim to a captain's title than I do. Less than, if training serves."

Hooke recoiled from the verbal blow, but fitted a scathing grin before sweeping in an elegant bow. "Forgive me, *commander*. I had no idea you were such an expert. Especially in uncharted territory." He lowered his breath to a deadly growl, and inched forward, his voice carrying every bit of power the once-captain retained. "Out of respect for your assistance, I will grant this one courtesy, Pan. I can be a beneficial ally or a formidable opponent. The terms are up to you. Speak to me in that tone again, and I'll see personally that you won't have the ability to worry about the Shadow's claim on your fair captain."

Hooke allowed his words to sink in before he turned towards the door. "I'm done serving whatever penance you think you might have earned. I may not be your captain, but you are most certainly not mine. I owe you nothing, and it would serve you well to remember the terms of our alliance." He smashed his hand against the panel and stalked into the narrow corridor. The door whisked shut behind him, leaving Peter seething after him, with only Tinc's soft hums to soothe the violent storm in his mind.

27

"Five points!" Peter crowed as his balled sock bounced off the roof to land in his makeshift hoop. He glanced expectantly at his Tinc and Seven, and his victory pose drooped in disappointment.

"Aww come on guys," Peter moaned, spinning in his chair. He leaned back to watch the roof as he spun, and the dark metal grating blurred in a dizzying circular pattern. "Let's play again. I'll go easy on you this time, I swear."

Tinc's sassy retort showered in a short flare of sparks.

Peter grinned. "Someone's a sore loser."

Tinc burrowed further into her nest, muffling her stream of angry buzzes. Peter's lips pursed before he turned to the Neverfox. "Am I right, Seven?" He probed, hoping to stir the sleepy beast. Hearing her name, Seven thumped her tail before standing and circling her back to Peter.

Peter flopped in his chair dramatically. He was going stir crazy. It wasn't that he was opposed to confined spaces, working the *Roger* had quickly remedied that. But on the *Roger*, he was always busy running the rig— and back then, he hadn't minded being alone. His time on Neverland, had accustomed him to having company. In the treehouse, he couldn't hardly breathe without one of the boys tackling him, and there was always someone to talk to, whether he wanted it or not. Even the first days after the *Roger* left, with his build to occupy him, being stuck on Neverland hadn't been so bad. But being trapped on the tiny *Fiducia II* with no one else to talk to made him achingly aware of lonely he had become.

He sighed and turned toward the navigation panel, lazily using his foot to rock his chair as he surveyed the map. It had been a few days since the Stjarnin had commed, but he could track their progress on the charts. He wasn't sure how, but they were making good time—excellent time, really. They had covered more distance in the past few days than he had any regular Fleet cruiser could have in weeks. And while he was immensely proud of his handiwork, he wasn't delusional enough to think the *Fiducia II's* speed had anything to do with his tinkering. He wondered again just how advanced the Stjarnin's systems were, and how much they had given up to protect the galaxies from the Shadow. Certainly, if it hadn't been for Itzala, they would be leading the charge in technology and who knew what else. Instead, they remained on Neverland, fighting to keep its evil at bay. And with just a few brash decisions, all their sacrifices had been shot through the latrine. It was no wonder the Stjarnin were less than enthused when humans crashed onto their planet. They had proved every threat they posed to the ancient race, and then some. Not only had they let the Shadow escape, they had helped it.

Peter ran his hands through his hair as his rueful thoughts tumbled over him. What else had he barreled into that he had no right to? He had been offered his position on the *Roger*, and earned his keep. After the crash, he took the Boys, but it was to free them from the pirates' mistreatment. And they had mostly kept to themselves on Neverland, preferring to stay out of the way, until he met Wendy. Peter paused.

Wendy.

A dozen images flashed through his mind as he thought of the beautiful captain. Strong and brave, and fiercely determined, she fit the role perfectly, and it was clear that it was everything she wanted. He remembered the fire in her eyes as she worked to save her men, and her gentleness when she had adopted his Boys as part of her own crew. She would return to Earth a hero, having vanquished a demon and saved a crew thought lost to time and space. With her accomplishments, she would be granted any opportunity she wanted, but had promised herself to him.

He looked at his hands. They were worker's hands, cracked and covered with grease and grime that would never quite wash out, and the rest of him wasn't much better. He was a mechanic, and as much as he hated giving weight to Hooke's words, the old pirate was right. He wasn't a captain, and manning the *Fiducia II* didn't make him one. His station wouldn't change when he returned. His place was buried in boats, turning the gears.

That was no place for a captain.

Wendy deserved better. She deserved someone who could walk beside her as an equal. Someone who could stand proudly beside her and understand the world she belonged in—not some derelict cabin boy who hadn't been part of society for over a hundred years. What did he even know about the world anymore? From what he'd seen of the *Fiducia's* tech alone made it clear things had changed drastically—and not just in machines, which he understood. Did he really think he would fit into Wendy's civilization? Navigating Neverland was one thing. New London, with its politics and societal structures was something else entirely.

Balling his fists, Peter pounded the navigation panel. The screen bowed under the pressure, and the chart flickered fuchsia before it faded back to its sleek chromatic hues. They would reach the *Roger* soon. They had to. He would stop the Shadow, and then his debt to Wendy would be paid. He could set her free to do all the things he knew she could. His gut twisted miserably at the thought, but he knew it was right.

"You're going to veer course if you don't adjust the trajectory inclination," Hooke's curt voice cut through his preoccupied thoughts. "You have to keep your hands on the board, or you'll lose valuable time."

Peter turned to the captain, surprised. The salty pirate had been avoiding him since their argument. He wondered what made Hooke come around. He glanced back at the panel to inspect the charted course.

"But navigation has the trajectory charted," he protested. "The tech has it under control."

"You rely too heavily on machines," Hooke admonished as he approached the panel. He gazed at the charts, considering the map like an old friend. "Technology has its merits, but some things are better handled manually."

He pointed to the coordinates at the top corner of the screen. There were three bright white sets—one to tell velocity, one for the thrust and the last for propulsion, each rounded to the nearest ten thousandth. Peter was familiar enough to know that if the number deviated too high off course, the white would transition from yellow to orange, and then, if you were really lost, it would flare red. Outside of that, he hadn't given the specs much thought.

"Most people think they can chart a course on a rig, then sit back and enjoy the ride. I can't tell you how many fleetmen started service looking for easy glory with dreams of being a pilot. The thing is—and any true pilot will tell you—that's not how it works. Charting is an imperative part of the job, but staying the course is where you separate men from the doxies."

Peter's brow furrowed and Hooke gestured to the coordinates. His metal hand scraped the screen as he traced the heavy appendage over the decimal values in the top coordinate.

"An amateur will chart using the whole value, but any soldier worth his szikra will tell you—good piloting is in the fractions." He lowered his hand to allow Peter to study the numbers as the values shifted and change. He observed until it inclined almost five thousandths, and Hooke trailed his hand back to the thin mark outlining the *Roger's* course.

"The big numbers won't tell you when you start to go off course. It happens after the decimal. If you wait until your front values start to change, you've already moved too far."

Hooke leaned over and typed in several swift commands. It was almost imperceptible, but the screen flashed and rerouted the trajectory, placing a new line under the old. Where the ship sat, the difference was hardly discernible, but as Peter followed the indicated paths, they broke and gapped, creating a significant distance between the two.

Peter gaped at Hooke. "How did you know to fix the alignment when the software didn't? The tech is configured to auto-adjust to maintain course integrity."

Hooke smirked. "The machine would figure it out eventually," he admitted, "and it would recalibrate. But it would take time. Relying on systems to do your calculations puts your life in the hands of a machine. And for all the advanced calculations and postulated outcomes it can give, a machine can't factor split-second decisions, and it doesn't understand instinct. A truly gifted pilot has a firm grasp on both."

Peter considered Hooke's words as he studied their course. He didn't know why Hooke was telling him this, but it was valuable knowledge. He glanced at the captain, who still studied the charts thoughtfully.

"Did you miss it?" he asked.

Hooke turned to Peter with a frown. "Miss what?"

"Freedom." Peter answered, gazing at the star charts before him. Dozens of unnamed constellations streamed before him, dazzling in their beauty, but only a small piece of the galaxies yet to be explored. Long ago, Hooke had told Peter the skies were the only place that man could be truly free; that the wilds of space were the only place tethers couldn't hold. And yet, looking at the tired lines etched into the captain's face, Peter couldn't help but wonder if perhaps Hooke had been very wrong.

After a moment's thought, Hooke turned to Peter with a tired smile. "Sometimes you don't really know you've lost your freedom until you've found it again." His hand played absently where his coat buttons should have been. When his fingers found nothing, he glanced down and Peter saw the thin webbed stain peeking underneath his shirt. He recognized the marks all too well.

Hooke coughed and dropped his hands in a natural captain's stance.

"But yes," he continued. "To answer your question, I have quite missed the open skies. I will enjoy my time here while I can." He nodded quietly, then turned to go. Peter watched him leave, once again resembling the proud captain who had taken him in over a century ago.

"James, wait," he called, then paused as pride caught his voice.

"Yes, Pan?"

"Would you like to monitor the panels?" Peter offered. "You know more about the millimeters or whatever they are, and I probably should run a systems check. You can make sure we don't slow down again while I'm gone."

Hooke blinked in surprise, then gave a deep nod, but he couldn't hide the smile lighting his features. "Aye, Pan," he said, "I'll keep you flying true."

Peter jerked his head in quick thanks, then hurried to escape. He had never been one for emotional moments, and this was quickly beginning to feel like one. He had nearly stepped through the heavy doors when a high-pitched beep rang through the room. Screeching to a stop, he turned to the transmission panel and activated the incoming message, his heart in his throat.

"*Fiducia II*. This is Pan. Requesting identification credentials."

Pan.

Peter's heart dropped as he registered Tiger Lily's deep, cool voice.

Our monitors indicate we are approaching a foreign vessel. My men believe we have found your ship.

Peter gripped the comm and glanced at his chart, which registered only their charted course through painfully empty skies. His brow furrowed.

"How long until we reach them," he asked, though his question manifested as a demand.

If the vessel we are receiving truly is your missing ship, our projections place convergence in two of your human days. If it is not, I have no prediction.

Peter's chest thumped. Two days. His mind blurred as a myriad of possibilities settled over him. Before any could form into a coherent thought, Tiger Lily's calm voice interrupted through the comm.

As I am inclined to believe it is your ship, I feel now is the proper time to remind you. My men will not allow Itzala to escape. If the Shadow cannot be contained, we will destroy the vessel.

"But what about the crew?" Peter asked, knowing as he spoke, that it wouldn't make a difference. The Stjarnin had sacrificed much more in the past. Of course, they would see the lives of a few crewmen as expendable.

I do not mean to upset you. I only find it necessary to address the unpleasant possibility now, so it does not come as a shock later, should misfortune arise. The princess' voice registered cold in the comm, but it would have sounded the same had she been standing at his side. He exchanged a silent glance with Hooke, whose face remained tightly neutral, only his glinting eyes revealing his displeasure. When Peter didn't respond, the princess continued.

Hopefully it will not come to that. We have moved quickly. We can only hope Itzala has not done the same.

The comm disconnected, leaving a soft buzz in Peter's ear followed Tinc's weight lighting on his shoulder.

"I'm guessing you heard all that?" His bitter question earned a despondent hum as the nanobot fluttered her tiny wings. He glanced at Hooke, fighting the urge to divulge his true thoughts. The captain may have been a temporary ally, but it didn't mean he trusted the rehabilitating pirate. Instead, he rapped his knuckles against the navigation panel.

"Well. Bad news doesn't change the status of our ship," he announced with a nod. "James, man the charts. I still need to make sure we don't drop from the sky."

He stalked across the room, his shoulders tense as the thoughts he barricaded beat angrily against the dam in his mind. He nearly made it to the door when Hooke's coarse voice slowed his escape.

"The Shadow doesn't care about relationships," Hooke mused, his eyes fixed on the screen before him. "Even the relationship between itself and its host. Its power is tantalizing, and its appeal is great. Fighting the Shadow's touch is not something most men can do." He turned to Peter meaningfully.

"Well, Wendy isn't like most men," Peter snapped.

A knowing smile pulled Hooke's lips. "Perhaps," he ceded, "but the captain isn't the only one on the ship."

Peter's face tightened. "My Boys won't fall for the Shadow's lies. We told them what went down in the *Roger*. They know what could happen."

Hooke shrugged. "Knowing and experiencing are very different. And still, you aren't accounting the full crew. There are many on board that have hidden desires. The Shadow is skilled at finding and exploiting what you want most." He lifted the base of his shirt to reveal his torso. Peter's eyes widened as he looked at the devastation on the captain's pale skin. What once had been smooth, clear flesh was marred and blackened, creating a grisly web that spidered his entire front, all emanating from a thick spot directly over his heart. The marks were raised and mottled like a sick gray bruise that wrapped his entire body. After a moment's exposure, the captain lowered his shirt and his gaze. "Take it on good authority."

Peter's lips pressed together as he deliberated what to say. Finally, he resumed his course to the belly of the ship, his anxious thoughts nettling in his mind like bees.

"Stay the course," he ordered as he fled. "We need to stop the Shadow before it makes things any more difficult."

28

"That's everything, Tinc. Bright and shiny, just like we like it."

Tinc jangled as Peter wiped the grease from his fingers and frowned at the stains on his calloused hands. Hooke was right, just a glance and you could easily identify his station. It had never bothered him before, but now he wondered if maybe he wanted more. He brushed the thought aside as he chucked his towel in the bin. The *Fiducia II* was running smoothly. Right now, that was all that mattered. He scanned the hull and couldn't help the swell of pride that blossomed in his chest. For all the thousands of miles they had travelled, his little rig had held its own. He patted the sleek walls with a smile.

"Atta girl," he said, then leaned in to whisper, "Captains don't know everything."

A small laugh bounced from his chest before Tinc swooped in, jangling impatiently.

"Yes, Tinc, you're pretty too," Peter sighed. Tinc buzzed irritably, but drifted to settle on his collar. Sparks fizzled from her core as she nuzzled in, singeing tiny spots into the fabric. "Everything look good up there?"

Tinc hummed her affirmation and Peter nodded. "Good. Let's go make sure ol' James isn't getting too comfortable on his own." Tinc swooped around his shoulders in a quick circle, wrapping him in golden sparks before shooting toward Commands. "Showoff," he grumbled, but followed briskly after, eager to return.

When they reached the cabin, Peter found Hooke where he left him, his face drawn in a troubled line.

"What's wrong?" he pressed.

Hooke studied Peter in silent contemplation before swiveling his chair to press a small, blinking orange button and filled the cabin with the crackle of a corrupted signal. Peter's brow furrowed as the static faded into a high-pitched whine, then slowly cleared as a faint audio recording struggled to fight its way through.

...It has been four days, and we have received no contact. Our ship is rapidly deteriorating and as our repair attempts continue to fail, so does the crew's morale. If anyone can help us—

Peter smashed the receiver to pause the transmission. He stared at the screen, his throbbing pulse matching the flashing beat of the message indicator light.

"When did you get this?" he demanded, whirling on Hooke.

"It came in a few moments ago, I—"

"Why didn't you notify me immediately?" Peter seethed.

Hooke's eyes flashed. "I believe that's what I just did."

Peter slapped the panel. "Don't patronize me, Hooke! You heard her—Wendy is in trouble! We—"

His tirade was cut off as the *Fiducia II* rocked and a loud clunk ricocheted from outside of the ship. Peter clutched the navigation panel to steady his stumbling as the ship swayed violently, and its regulation system fought to recover from the hit.

"What was that," Peter demanded, lunging to code open the visor. His eyes widened in shock as the sleek, holographic cover faded, revealing the open space before them.

Except, it wasn't open. Space that should have been empty for thousands upon thousands of miles was instead filled with crumpled bits of scrap littering the sky.

"I'd assume it was a large piece of space junk," Hooke mused, turning to Peter. "Unless you have another guess?"

Disregarding the Captain's snark, Peter moved forward to peer at the scene. Fragmented hulls of once fantastic ships drifted across the nothingness, filling the void with a fleet of capsized ghost ships. Throughout the larger bodies, smaller pieces of debris flitted, tiny galaxies of scrap in mechanical constellation of death.

"What happened here?" he whispered, noting dozens of body styles and markings covering the wrecked ships.

"Nothing good," Hooke murmured. He stared out at the broken ships, his icy eyes bright as he studied the army of downed vessels, stuck in an endless orbit of waste.

"Do you think Wendy is out there?" Peter scanned the broken ships for a familiar bird. If the *Roger* ran into the wasteland before them, there was no way the battered old ship would have escaped unscathed.

...If anyone can help us—the ship is not sustainable...

A frustrated sigh ripped from Peter's chest as he pressed the transmission button again. The receiver bit his hand as he gripped the device, hoping the tech wouldn't register the waver in his voice.

"Hailing the *Jolly Roger*. Hailing the *Roger*. Wendy, it's Peter. We received your transmission. We'v—"

Peter paused as the line went dead. Confused, he glanced at the receiver buzzing in his hand as the holoscreen flickered over the visor, revealing Tiger Lily's somber mask.

Pan. You cannot contact your Captain.

"What do you mean I can't contact them?" Peter gestured wildly with the dead receiver. "They're in trouble!"

My men intercepted the message as well. We know their ship is failing.

"But they'll get creamed out there!" Peter choked over his shock as he stared desperately out the visor. "One rogue barge and they're done for!"

Tiger Lily's face was grim. *Itzala cannot escape. We will not allow it the chance. I sympathize with your friends' plight, but if Itzala were freed, their fate would be worse. This is a kindness.*

"Leaving them is a *kindness*?" Peter erupted, "No wonder the Shadow took up with you, you're all insane! There are innocent people on that ship! Some of them are barely older than children! You trapped them there—if you don't help, you're *murdering* them."

The princess' lips pulled in a troubled frown as she blinked at the screen. *I am sorry, Pan. We cannot help you.*

The screen blipped, and the visor cleared of everything but the broken vessels drifting before them. Peter's chest heaved as he stared at the screen, trembling until Tinc's nervous hums drew him from his sea of rage.

Slowly, he turned, his back to the screen as he faced his old friend; the captain who betrayed him. He stood for a moment, wrapped in boiling energy, before he inhaled a sharp breath.

"We have to help them. I won't stand by waiting for their death," his voice was brittle as he considered the road the Stjarnin's actions would force them to take. He peered over his shoulder at the now empty visor. A large piece of shrapnel floated across the bottom of the screen and he pressed his lips together, sure what he had to do.

"We have to get through to them," he said, his fists clenching in determined balls. "Will you help me?"

Hooke gazed at Peter, his expression unreadable before it flitted to the visor screen and his hand pressed the stain on his chest. With a slow nod, the captain released a roguish grin.

"On my honor as a pirate."

Peter grinned. "That's exactly what we'll need. We're gonna do some fancy flying."

29

THE JOLLY ROGER

CAPTAIN WENDY DARLING

Wendy finished the transmission and the ship rocked again, this time blacking out the entire cabin before the lights flickered to cast the room in a weak haze. Wendy glanced around, noting the burgeoning shadows lingering in the dimmed corners.

"Dawes, that chart you programmed, are there any nearby planets on course?"

"Nearby meaning?"

"Near enough that if things get hairy we have a backup plan," Wendy answered, her voice grim.

Dawes turned an apologetic frown. "You know I hate lying to you, Captain."

Wendy pinched the bridge of her nose to stifle her throbbing headache. "That's what I thought," she sighed.

"What are we going to do?"

"Find Tootles and round up the Lost Boys. Take them to their quarters, then secure your position. If you find Commander Boyce, take him with you. Once you are in position, do not leave until I give the all clear. Until then, we are running a security lockdown. Understood?"

Dawes' brushed her brow in a quick salute. "Yes, Captain."

"Good," Wendy said. "You are dismissed. Get everyone in position and tell them to prepare for an emergency landing. Hopefully it doesn't come to that, but at this point, I think we need to prepare for the worst."

Dawes clenched her jaw to still her trembling lips. "Take care of yourself, Captain."

Wendy watched as the pilot hurried through the door, then glanced around the darkened cabin. The weakened lights flickered overhead in an erratic pattern, plunging the room into darkness before illuminating it with a tired hum. As the light faded, the shadows elongated, creeping toward her, their greedy fingers outstretched while scratching whispers clawed above the buzzing drone of the emergency lights.

Soon, very soon...

Wendy whirled around, searching for the phantom voice, but the frozen room was still; silent except for her ragged breathing. She exhaled a deep breath, stifling the hitch in her chest as she strained to listen to the *Roger*, hoping for the familiar sound of its smooth whir as it sliced through the air, but she was wrapped in only silence. The steady thrum of the engines no longer drowned the whispers of the temperature regulation systems.

The ship was completely dead in the air.

Heart pounding, Wendy initiated a comm, then held her breath as the tech clicked through the connection sequence and erupted in a wave of static, washing her earpiece in a wave of white noise. Frustrated, Wendy slammed her palm against the receiver, hoping the force would jar something into place. It was a crude solution, and she knew almost certainly it wouldn't work, but tech had never been her strong suit. She needed Michaels.

Or Peter.

Unbidden, the mechanic's roguish smile flashed through her memory, washing over her in a swirling wave of despair and regret. She had promised Peter she would return. What a fool she had been to think she could keep her word.

She threw the device against the wall and slumped to the ground as the weight of her guilt pressed down on her. A cold tear trickled down her cheek, then dropped on her necklace, making the tiny acorn glisten in the dim light. Wendy glanced at the charm and a rebellious surge of anger flared in her chest. She reactivated the comm, her heart in her throat until another wave of static exploded in her ears. Flinging the device, the comm skittered across the floor and to a stop, filling the cabin with hushed silence. Wendy's chest heaved in rage as she glared at the useless tech, until the room began to resonate with another wave of skittering whispers. A surge of panic welled in the pit of Wendy's stomach, and she scoured the room for the source of the ghostly noise. Lingering shadows darted from the edge of her vision with every turn, while the chilling murmurs twisted to devious laughter.

Not long now, they slithered in her ears. *He won't resist much longer...*

Wendy stilled in the middle of the room, her chest constricting as understanding crashed over her in horror. *The whispers,* she thought, remembering the phrase. Her mind reeled as she thought back to what Noodler said about the ominous sounds. *Captain knows,* the addled pirate had said, his whitewashed gaze completely sober. *The voices, get in and nettle ye so. Makes it hard to remember where you end and they begin.*

He had warned her. All this time, all the clues she hadn't seen it until it was too late. She broke into a run, allowing her last brief seconds of panic to ebb before she began her trek through the *Roger.* The nightmares, the shadows, and always, the voices. Growing stronger every day, while everything else spiraled hopelessly out of control.

Captain knows... the voices whispered again, but this time, they didn't frighten her, because they were right. The captain did know. And now she had to act.

Wendy hurtled through the corridor, her head ringing with every step until she reached her destination. She paused outside, her skin prickling as she raised a trembling hand to the jarred door. Quashing her fear, she clamped both hands to the default handle and tugged, listening to the familiar hum as the panel slid on its familiar track, revealing Boyce's room. She stepped inside, studying the commander's meticulous space. Nothing was out of place; his bed was neatly made, and his secondary uniform hung ready for use. Wendy released a nervous laugh and mentally chided herself for worrying until she saw the Records Log on the commander's table.

Wendy retrieved the abandoned techpad and gripped it in her hands. The Fleet's insignia shone innocently from the screen. She brushed her thumb over the glassy surface, and the display shimmered to a new page, requesting her identification. With a few quick taps, Wendy entered her security code, and the device stamped a notification prompt over the new screen.

Last entry not saved. Please verify activity.

Wendy cleared the notification, removing the box in front of the log. She scanned the last entry, and the sinking feeling in her chest hardened to lead.

The darkness grows stronger every day. It hides in the shadows, waiting, hoping. It won't be long now until it catches us all. It won't be long until they are mine.

Her pulse thrummed against her temples as she abandoned the entry to access the menu. She read through Boyce's catalogued messages, each one solidifying her fears. Finally, she pulled her gaze from the screen and abruptly dropped the log. A lump bulged in her throat as she fought the urge to be sick. She needed to find Boyce. He needed to explain.

She was turning to leave when her eyes landed on a tilted panel in the commander's wall. Stomach writhing, she stepped forward and reached for the thin metal sheet. It creaked as she pushed, slipping on a worn groove in the floor. Wendy peered past the shoved the panel to a narrow compartment carved into the side of the ship, just large enough to step in.

Creeping forward, Wendy's thumping pulse shifted to screaming sirens. An assortment of crude sketches plastered the wall, each more gruesome than the last. Harsh, angry brush strokes created swirling images of darkness looming over a shrouded form, settling over its shoulders in a seething black mass. There was a progression to the images, moving from the prominence of the smaller figure under a soft, blurred shadow until the shadowy figure billowed to overtake the form. As Wendy moved from one image to another, the penmanship transformed as well. The early drawings were controlled and delicate with a refined artistry—but as the sketches evolved, the line work became harsh and erratic, composing the images from a collection of thick scratches carved into the page.

Slowly, Wendy picked up the last one, her hands trembling as she studied the writhing mass seeping from the smaller figure's shoulders as it lay on the ground, staring up with a vacant gaze . She brushed her thumb across the surface and pulled back in surprise when the image smudged, staining her finger with still-wet ink.

Heart pounding, she replaced the sketch and crept back as quietly as she could. She had almost cleared the small compartment when her gaze caught a large item buried deep in the crossing wires. Her instincts screamed for her to leave, but Wendy ignored it and reached for the hidden item and tugged, releasing it from the wall. It jerked loose, falling heavy in her hand as she untangled it from the wires to examine it. Her brow furrowed as she studied the long, narrow piece of tech and its jagged ends covered in thick oil. Puzzled, she peered closer, and her eyes rounded in horror as she saw a clump of golden synthetic hair stuck to the piece.

Disgusted, she discarded the part in the tangled wires and backpedaled from the compartment of horrors, her mind finally working in unison with her jarred nerves. As she retreated, her comm buzzed, and she fumbled for the receiver, blinking at the foreign display code illuminating the screen.

"Captain Wendy Darling," she whispered, the rest of her formal greeting evaporating into her parched throat.

Wendy? A relieved voice sounded on the other end of the Comm. *Cap, is it really you?*

"Peter?"

Yeah. It's me. Peter let out a nervous laugh. *You don't know how good it is to hear your voice. I've been trying—*

"Peter," Wendy cut him off with a hushed exhortation. "We're in trouble." She spoke urgently, unsure how much time she had. She didn't know how Peter had even reached her, but she forced away her rapidly spiraling questions to focus on imperatives. "Our ship is dead—"

We know, Cap. We got your message. We—

"No. Peter. *Listen.*" she hissed, "Something is wrong." She glanced at the sketches covering the wall, and dread billowed in her chest. "There's someone—"

A searing pain lanced the back of her head and she slumped forward, releasing the comm with a yelp as her body went slack. Static filled her ears as pain bloomed from her skull and the world around her turned black.

THE
NIGHTMARE
COME TRUE

30

FIDUCIA II

LEAD MECHANIC PETER PAN

"Cap?" Peter's breath hitched as the faint line clicked and went dead. "Cap, are you there?"

He pressed the comm to his ear, straining for any sign of life, but there was only dead air. He tried to reconnect, but only static sounded where Wendy's tight voice had once been.

She was in trouble.

Peter's mind whirred as he mentally replayed their conversation and relived the terror in her voice. Why had she been whispering?

She was trying to tell him something. But what? He scrubbed his fingers through his hair and let out a frustrated growl. He didn't know. He hadn't shut up long enough to let her tell him. He unclenched his fists, to relieve the tension from his scalp and turned to Hooke, who watched with the same, detached look on his face.

Peter's temper flared as he met the captain's blank stare. He surged forward, wrapping his arms around Hooke's neck, his vision going red as he released a strangled cry. "What have you done?"

Hooke's face twisted in rage as he clamped his hands over Peter's clenched fists and struggled to release the mechanic's hold. The metal ligaments in his prosthetic whined as they cinched against Peter's knuckles, crushing his bones under their steel. With a yelp, Peter released his hold and shoved the captain into the wall before checking the damage to his hand. He winced and flexed his fingers, then lunged for Hooke again, his fists swinging wildly. Caught in his momentum, Peter surged into the wall of the small cabin, and released a furious roar before he cratered his fists into the wall.

Chest heaving, he slumped against the cool paneling until his burst of rage ebbed, leaving him with the ability to reason. He let out a few slow breaths, then ground his palms into his eyes as he turned to Hooke, who watched from a safe distance, his expression twisted in a bemused grin.

"Feel better?"

Peter's features twitched into an embarrassed scowl. "Of course I don't feel better," he grumbled. "The *Roger* is dying, and if we don't find it soon, she'll bury our crew with her!"

"*Our* crew?"

Peter let out an exasperated sigh as he pushed his hair from him eyes. "You heard her, James! We have to go now!"

Hooke straightened his spine, his joints creaking on a still tired frame. He glanced at the visor where the Princess' image had appeared, his mouth drawn in a long, hard line. Finally, he loosed a sigh that ended in a stiff nod. "On my—"

"On your bloody pirate honor!" Peter crowed, interrupting the captain, who fixed him with a pointed glare. Momentarily cowed, he fell back, his hands pulling naturally into attention, surprising him with how easily the familiar action came back. Satisfied, the captain continued.

"This is not going to be easy, Pan. We have to move quick and sure. There is no margin for error. The Stjarnin meant what they said." He motioned to the floating graveyard before them. "If we don't do this right, we're going to become the newest addition to their collection."

Peter's face pulled in a grim line. Hooke was right, but there was no other choice.

"What are we going to do?"

"I don't think you understand what you are asking Pan," Hooke groused as he strapped himself behind the navigation panel. He scanned the screen before him for the fourth time in the past two minutes, his look of apprehension lit by the screen's faint glow. Soft beams illuminated the tired lines on his face, which had slowly begun to fade, along with the heavy stoop of his shoulders, revealing his former strength and poise.

"Don't think you can handle it, Hooke?" Peter challenged from where he bolted a thick leather strap to the floor. He tugged the band with a few quick jerks to test its hold. The band twanged dully, but held fast in place. Satisfied,

Peter brushed his knees before facing the captain. "I guess you really have lost your touch."

Hooke's icy glare narrowed in contempt before he turned to scour the boards before him with a scoff. He searched the screen, his face drawn in consideration. "By my calculation, there's a ninety percent chance we won't survive."

Peter's mouth formed a line. "That's ten percent more chance than the *Roger* has if we don't try."

Hooke studied him thoughtfully, then nodded before he twisted to the board. The *Fiducia II* lurched as he slammed the controls forward, spurring the ship to a hurtling roar. It rocked the ship, tumbling the loose cabin items to the floor with a deafening crash. Tinc's angry jangles thrummed in Peter's ears as dove to the ground and scrambled to Seven and secured her to the band he had tethered to the floor. The Neverfox issued a frightened chirp and burrowed into his arms, hiding from the thundering rumble that surrounded the ship. Once Seven was secured, he stood unsteadily, swaying as Hooke swerved between the hulking pieces of space scrap surrounding them to disappear further into the field.

"A little warning would have been nice," Peter grumbled as he strapped in, adding more stability to the bumpy ride. Hooke paid him no mind as he focused on path, his arms tensed on the controls.

"I told you the window was small," Hooke retorted, his gaze unmoving. "You were the one who was unprepared."

Peter scowled as he conjured a snarky retort, but before he could unleash it, Tiger Lily's image flickered over the floating scraps in the visor's lower corner. Her shoulders tensed in silent fury as she regarded them before her fleet of glowering warriors.

Pan.

Peter busied himself with studying the switches and buttons on the navigation panel, pointedly ignoring the princess' address.

It is never easy to hear a loved one is hurting, the princess stated, then paused until Peter finally met her gaze. *I am sorry, but you cannot go to her.*

"Not sure what you mean, Princess," Peter responded flippantly.

Your Captain is already gone, Tiger Lily's plea softened in sympathy. *If Itzala has laid claim to her ship, he will have his way.*

Peter's eyes flashed a challenge. "See, that's where you're wrong. There's still a chance we can save her."

And what of the Shadow? Tiger Lily asked. *We had this discussion once before. Your promises were made.*

Peter's jaw clenched. Tiger Lily was right. He had agreed not to risk freeing the Shadow, but the thought of turning back and leaving Wendy and the crew to fend for themselves made his blood run cold.

"Sorry Princess, but things have changed."

Tiger Lily's onyx gaze burned from the screen. *You are making a grievous mistake,* she said. *You must stop this now, or we will stop it for you.*

Peter met the worry in her ebony eyes. "Sorry Princess," he repeated curtly. "But I have somewhere to be." He deactivated the visor, and Tiger Lily's image flickered and disappeared, revealing a massive asteroid coursing toward them. Peter gasped as Hooke executed a hasty barrel roll, and the *Fiducia* narrowly swooped out of its trajectory. He braced himself, waiting for the jarring impact as the rock hurtled past them, then let out a shaky breath when he realized the rock had sailed neatly underneath them. His shoulders loosened as he glanced at Hooke. "Well that was clos—"

His words ended in a sharp yelp as the ship bucked and rocked dangerously. Seven's panicked howl drowned Tinc's frightened jangles as the tiny cabin was bathed in flashing red warning lights while the *Fiducia II* spiraled through the air. Peter reached wildly for the nanobot and stuffed her in his pocket before ducking for cover. He glanced at Hooke, whose face pulled in fierce determination as he commanded the ship through the chaos. The *Fiducia II* continued to scream as she hurtled through the air, but the captain didn't seem to notice. Beads of sweat formed over his brows as he continued to navigate her from the dangers surrounding her exterior.

Peter's stomach plummeted as their violent dive lurched and Hooke eased the barge into a quick loop before evening into a smooth glide. A tenuous calm settled over the cabin as the ship's blaring alarm dulled behind the smooth hum of the *Fiducia II's* engine. Peter sunk into his chair, his heart slowly settling to match the ship's smoothing path before he cast an impressed look at Hooke.

"Not bad for a pirate." he murmured, reaching to activate the transmitter. His heartbeat echoed in his ears as he waited for the visor screen to reimage. The screen adjusted, revealing the Stjarnin princess, surrounded by her fleet of warriors, seething in silent fury at his unabashed defiance.

Pan. His name was bitter on the princess' tongue. *Turn back now. If you continue down this path, my men will be unable and unwilling to help you.*

Peter returned her gaze with a tight-lipped smile. "If it's all the same,

Princess, we told you our decision last time." He glanced at Hooke, who gripped the navigation controls under white knuckles. "We've got people to save."

The princess blinked then nodded, her fury ebbing to sadness. "It seems we are at an impasse," she mused, then glanced at Hooke's coiled frame before returning to Peter. "Heed this warning. Though your agreement has changed, ours has not wavered. We will give you the chance to obtain your men, but if you fail, your lives, and deaths, are bound to theirs."

Peter stepped toward the visor, his eyes wide. "You're letting us go?"

The princess' shoulders stiffened. *Know the repercussions of your actions*, she warned. *If you fail to retrieve your captain, my men will destroy your ship.*

The princess held his gaze for another silent moment, then the screen blipped, leaving only the image of the *Jolly Roger* floating lifelessly before them. The ship waited peacefully for them on the outskirts of the graveyard, its hulking frame battered and scarred. Peter looked from the ship to Hooke, who sat stoically beside him, his face unreadable as he studied the ship.

"Think we can do it?"

"It seems we don't have any other choice." Hooke met Peter's searching question, his piercing eyes alight with the challenge. "With death before us and behind us, the only chance for life is victory." He looked at Peter, the ghost of his former glory strengthening from within. "Which shall we embrace?"

Peter met Hooke's challenge with a devilish grin.

"To live will be an awfully great adventure," he answered, remembering the farewell he had given Wendy. The captain's beautiful face flashed through his memory, her curls tumbling wildly about as she gazed up at him, her lips still flushed from their kiss. Tinc jangled in his ear, commanding his attention with a snarky remark. "Tinc," his eyes widened as he faced the bot in feigned offense. "That was rude."

Tinc buzzed a laugh and swooped around the cramped cabin to land lightly on the navigation panel. Golden sparks cascaded over the panel's screen to the floor as Peter moved to study Hooke's map. "How are we gonna do this thing?"

Hooke's eyes glinted as he tightened his grip on the navigation controls. "Don't get cocky yet, Pan," Hooke warned as they steered into the *Roger's* gravity field. He looked at the ship's battered hull, scarred with darkened dents. He reached for the wall, his pale hand brushing gently against the *Roger's* panels before he caught Peter's stare. He stepped back and dropped his palm with an irritated sigh. "We have to find them first."

Peter glanced at the visor and his face peeled in a wide grin. "That shouldn't be too hard," he pointed at the screen to a small window in the *Roger's* looming frame. A tiny figure with a golden halo bobbed from the bottom of the window, its brown eyes wide as it waved frantically at them. "Someone knows we're here."

He lunged for the transmitter, and clenched it in his hand as he scanned for an available signal. Static spat from the speaker, followed by a low hum that faded into a faint voice.

"Th-this i-is th-the c-c-crew of th-the *J-jolly Roger*," Tootles' soft voice sounded across the thin signal. "I-identify y-your v-vessel."

"Tootles!" Peter's throat warbled with overwhelming relief. "Tootles, we need to board the ship."

P-peter, is that y-you?

"It sure isn't the Queen," Peter retorted. "Of course it's me—who else would be fool enough to travel the 'verse to save your scrawny neck?"

Tootles small laugh dipped in a wash of static. *N-noone I g-guess.*

"That's right, no-one," Peter confirmed. "Now, open the dock and let us in."

A rushed whisper sounded in the background before a scuffle rustled through the receiver and a new voice trickled in.

Hello?

Peter's brow furrowed. "Who's this?"

Commander Jensen Michaels, the reedy voice introduced, before resolving dryly. *We've met before.*

A small smile crept to Peter's lips. He remembered the thin mechanic. He was quiet, but had proven himself skilled with tech. Most importantly, Wendy had made it clear that she trusted him implicitly. "Michaels," he grinned. "I remember. Are you the one who's gonna get me back on board?"

I'll do what I can, Michaels' offered over the static. *Are you close enough that you can dock quickly?*

Peter's features twisted in a confused frown. "How quickly are we talking?"

I can probably spark enough life to hold the rig open for about five minutes before the pressure stabilizer collapses. If you can't get in by then, you don't get in at all.

Peter gnawed his lip and glanced at Hooke, who gave a terse, silent nod. He drew a quick breath and raised the comm. "We can make it," he said.

There was a brief pause before Michaels' thin voice crackled over the speaker. *Alright then. See you soon.* He disappeared with a quick click, hanging silence in the air. Peter turned to Hooke.

"Five minutes."

31

THE JOLLY ROGER

CAPTAIN WENDY DARLING

Wendy woke with a raging headache blossoming in the base of her skull. Still groggy, her head lolled as her eyes fluttered and adjusted to the dim light. Every sway summoned a fresh wave of pain radiating from her skull. She tried to bring her hand to check the wound, but her arm couldn't complete the motion—it was bound behind her back.

Her mind suddenly alert, Wendy struggled against the bindings, fighting through the throbbing pain. She glanced around the dim space and recognized her quarters, sitting quietly as though nothing was wrong. She blinked again, half expecting the scene to shift, but it was the same as before. She sat in her Captain's chair, her back cradled softly by the firm seat, everything perfectly normal except the tightly wound wire tethering her in place.

Wendy tugged the binding to loosen its hold and let out a soft yelp as the frayed endings of bit into her skin. Stubbornly, she continued to work the bindings, tingeing the room with the faint scent of copper until a shadowed motion caught the corner of her eye and she craned her neck toward the source.

At the edge of the room, Boyce stood, pacing by the bookshelf. His hair was disheveled as he rushed back and forth, muttering unintelligibly as he paced, his speech becoming more frenzied with every step. Wendy's brow furrowed as she observed his manic motions, but Boyce, consumed in his own thoughts, continued his twitching pace as his hand scratched absently at the base of his wrist.

"Commander?" Wendy rasped, then swallowed to relieve her dry throat. The commander whirled at the sound, his eyes widening in worry as he examined at her bound figure. He stepped toward her, then hesitated before gripping his head and spinning to resume his pace while scratching furiously under his cuff. Wendy's forehead creased in worry and she pulled toward him, but her bindings tightened as she pulled against the corded restraint. "Boyce," she called, "What's wrong?"

Boyce's anxious pace stilled at her use of his name, and he stopped across the room, his shoulders tensing as he turned around to gaze at her, his once sapphire eyes a churning, onyx storm.

"Oh Captain," he purred, his smile widening to an eerie grin. "I thought you'd never ask."

32

FIDUCIA II

LEAD MECHANIC PETER PAN

"This is your warning, Pan," Hooke's grumble gave Peter enough time to strap himself to the chair and stash Tinc in his pocket before the *Fiducia II* lurched in a sickening drop. Sirens shrieked in his ears as the captain's uncharted maneuver flung him against the seat, pinning him with the force of the captain's neatly executed dive.

Gritting his teeth, Hooke clutched the controls and whipped the *Fiducia II* again, drafting around the *Roger's* bulky form in a neat noose. Small pieces of debris assailed the ship as it hurtled toward the *Roger's* landing dock, and Peter grimaced, praying they didn't encounter anything larger. His neck jarred as the *Fiducia II* jerked against the impact and began to tremble under the strain. The ship moaned and vibrated, filling his ears with a deafening groan that he was certain was going to be the last thing he heard before the ship imploded and sent him careening into space. His eyes clamped shut as there was another jarring rock followed by a crashing boom.

"You can open your eyes now, Pan," Hooke's grumble was laced with amusement. "We've survived. Not that pinching your lids shut would have helped you anyway."

Peter peered into the now quiet ship, then fixed Hooke with a scowl. "I asked you to get us on the ship, not try and shishkebab us on the way in."

"Always complaining," Hooke groused. "You got your warning, be grateful for that." He leaned back and exhaled, the shaky tinge of his breath revealing his true apprehension as the *Fiducia II's* rumble was drowned by the *Roger's* closing bay. Seven whimpered at the noise and curled around Peter's legs, reinforcing the thrumming vibrations in his legs with the trembling in her chest. Peter's own chest tightened as he listened to the creaky groans, waiting for the final whoosh of the pressure seal as it restabilized the bay. After another silent beat, he turned to Hooke.

"Well that was close."

"I've had worse," Hooke mused. "Remind me to tell you about my expedition to the Starling Quadrant to visit the Regata Outpost," a devilish grin crept to his lips. "The Base Director wasn't a fan of mine. Damned doxie tried to bar my entry completely. His daughter on the other hand—"

Peter rolled his eyes. "I'm sure it was very impressive," he said, before scanning the visor again. Only the empty bay was visible on screen. "How much time do we have?"

Hooke scoffed. "Until the boat-monkey closes the rig or until the hostile aliens use us for target practice?"

"Good point," Peter snorted. He strode to the door, with Tinc trailing over his shoulder. When Hooke moved to follow, he held up his hand in a stalling gesture.

"Stay here."

The captain bristled at the command, but Peter met his glare with an innocent shrug. "Someone has to watch Seven," he quipped, then sobered his smarmy expression. "And I've got enough news to break without—" he gestured at Hooke's waiting form. "I'm sure there will be questions."

Hooke scowled, but didn't argue as Peter exited the cabin. Tinc buzzed and flitted to accompany him, landing quickly on his shoulder. She hummed quietly in his ear as he waited for the hatch to slide free, his insides writhing in restless apprehension. The door opened and he held his breath, puffing his cheeks before stepping tentatively into the darkened dock. He had barely touched down before a small, solid form rushed from the shadows, tackling him to the ground with a bout of happy laughter.

Peter glanced down at Tootles' bouncing, golden curls as the boy tightened his grip around his middle. A slow smile spread across his face as he sank into his fierce hug before addressing the others waiting outside the ship. Several members of Wendy's crew hovered in a loose group, Michaels and the other commander Wendy was close to, Johns. Beside them the small, pretty pilot—Dawes—looked on, anxiously twisting her long red hair. Peter nodded respectfully, then turned back to Tootles, whose laughter had morphed into heaving sobs of relief. He wrapped his arms around the boy's small body to still his shuddering breaths. Peter allowed Tootles a moment to settle his heaving shoulders before slowly pulling away. He looked at the others standing in the bay, each watching with worried expressions.

"What's going on?"

The crewmen looked at each other, then Dawes stepped forward, her fingers working her braid as she talked. "We don't know," she admitted. "The captain gave orders to round up the crew, and then the ship died." She glanced around at the others. "I found Tootles and the other Boys, then took them to the MedBay where Michaels and DeLaCruz were working to stabilize SMEE." She turned to Michaels, the furrow in her brow deepening. "Someone tried to rip him in half," she finished weakly.

Peter grimaced, but before he could inquire more, Michaels stepped forward, his muddy gaze piqued in curiosity. "How did you get here?"

Peter shrugged. "I built a ship." He motioned to the *Fiducia II* with a smirk.

Johns crossed his arms over his broad chest. "And you knew where to find us because?"

Peter scratched his head as he thought of the best way to explain. He cleared his throat, but before he could continue, Hooke's voice rippled from the ship, his raspy tone pinched in annoyance.

"I would think there are more pressing matters than the third degree of your rescuers," he snipped as he jumped from the *Fiducia II* to land on the *Roger*. The metal paneling clanged and emptied in a soft echo while the *Roger's* residents gaped at the former captain. Johns surged forward, stretching his arms in front of Tootles to barricade the boy as he looked from Hooke to Peter, distrust painting his face as he loosed a low, threatening growl.

"What is he doing here?"

Hooke fixed the commander with a withering smile. "I should think that's obvious," he flexed his prosthetic and glanced around the dead dock. "You've wrecked my ship."

"*Your* ship?" Johns spluttered. He looked to Peter incredulously, but Hooke just released a superior laugh as he stepped towards the commander, his stare filled with withering condescension. "It's been a hundred years, and nothing has changed. The Fleet still prefers bulk to brains."

Johns' chest puffed as he towered toward the captain, murder in his gaze. "Last I checked, the Fleet doesn't take kindly to murderous psychopaths running point on missions." He glanced around at the others. "Hell, knowing what you did, I could probably kill you right now and they'd call me a hero when we got home."

Hooke's eyes flashed. "But that wouldn't make you much better than me, would it, Commander?"

John's chest deflated. "No," he spat. "I guess it wouldn't." His looked bitterly at Peter, as he hovered protectively over Tootles, tension coiling his posture. "This is your responsibility," he hissed. "Anything happens, it's on you."

Hooke snorted, "Anything more than the disaster you've already put yourselves in?"

Johns hands balled into fists, but Peter stepped in as a blockade.

"I've got Hooke," he promised. "Now, tell me what happened to Wendy."

Dawes flipped her braid. "She went to secure the ship. She said she would meet up with us after, but," she cast a worried glance at Michaels, and Peter noticed her small hand wrapped in his. "It's been almost an hour and we can't reach her."

The weight in Peter's stomach grew. "Do you know where she went?"

Dawes shook her head. "She was going to wire the Admiral then scan the ship. She could be anywhere."

"We'll start at the helm then," Hooke declared. He looked to Peter for approval, and Peter nodded.

"Agreed. If she's not there, we'll work our way back." He glanced at Dawes, his brow quirked. "Have you been in contact with the Admiral long?"

Dawes frowned. "No. We only reached them recently, and even that was only once. They said they were sending help, but it's been days with nothing but radio silence."

Peter's lips pressed in a thoughtful line. Hopefully the Fleet didn't show up with the Stjarnin waiting in the wings. The last thing they needed to add to this catastrophe was an intergalactic showdown. He glanced at Hooke. "Clock's ticking."

"Something I'm still getting used to," Hooke remarked.

Peter coughed a harsh laugh and fixed the captain with a grave grin. "Let's just make sure it doesn't catch us." He started toward the exit, with Tinc and Hooke on his heels before a hurried cry called after them. Johns rushed toward them, with Dawes and Tootles sticking close behind.

"I'm coming too."

Peter shook his head. "No," he said firmly. "We'll get the front of the ship, you make sure all personnel are accounted for. Is anyone missing?"

Dawes shook her head. "We just checked on the pi—" Dawes' response died in a cough. "Hooke's men."

Peter followed her gaze to the stoic captain. His icy glare glinted as the pilot corrected herself, but his expression remained cool.

"And?"

"They're secure. We have them contained in the holding bay." She glanced at Johns before her gaze flickered back to Hooke. "They aren't happy, but they're safe."

Peter nodded as Hooke released an almost imperceptible sigh. "Anyone else?"

Dawes gnawed her lip. "Only Commander Boyce. We've been trying to reach him, but his comms are down. Should we try to locate him?"

Peter shook his head. "Secure your position with the others. Wendy wanted you all together for a reason. Hooke and I will find Wendy. We need you working on a solution for once we've got her." He turned to Johns. "Can you do that, Commander?"

Johns gave a terse nod. "Find Darling," he gripped Peter's hand. "We'll handle things down here." Peter winced as the hulking commander tightened his hold around his knuckles. "Don't come back without her," he warned.

"There'd be no reason to," Peter replied honestly.

Johns' lips pulled in a tight smile, and he released his hold. He turned to stand tall as he faced the crew. "Tootles, take Dawes and report to the others. You're pointman until I get back. Tell DeLaCruz I'll be there soon."

Tootles saluted the commander, but his eyes darted to Peter. Johns saw the boy's stare and waved his arm with a relenting sigh. Tootles' smile widened gratefully before he dashed across the empty dock to wrap Peter in a final hug. "B-be c-careful P-peter," he whispered.

Peter returned the boy's embrace. "Keep the Boys safe for me," he whispered. "I'm counting on you."

Tootles pulled back, his face beaming before he bobbed his head and bounded off with Dawes, chest swelling as he hurried to complete his mission. Peter watched him proudly and nodded a silent thank you to Johns, who returned the gesture before turning to the tech.

"Michaels, the only one who has any chance at fixing this ship's busted-ass is you. We need you below deck, and I'll help however I can." He cast a sour glance at Hooke. "I may not know much, but I can do the heavy lifting." Michaels nodded, and the commander issued a tight salute.

"Wait," Peter turned to Tinc and gave her a meaningful look. She hummed anxiously, but slowly flitted to Michaels when Peter shook his head. "Take Tinc," he offered. "She can help. She knows the *Roger* inside and out, and she's really good with small spaces."

Michaels gaped as Tinc jangled proudly from his shoulder while Johns raised his hand in a tight salute.

"Alright," the commander announced. "Our men are sorted," he cast a challenging glare at Hooke before ending his stare with Peter. "Now it's up to you." He tapped Michaels on the shoulder and spurred him down the corridor. Peter watched as the trio hurried down the darkened hall until only Tinc's faint green glow could be seen bobbing through the dim. When they finally disappeared, Peter turned grimly to Hooke.

"That's twice now I've stuck my neck out for you," he pointed out.

"And you said you didn't care," Hooke retorted, flexing the joints on his stiff prosthetic.

Peter scoffed. "Just don't make me regret it," he said. "Now, let's get you back to your quarters."

"I'm not that kind of girl," Hooke said dryly.

Peter rolled his eyes. "If I can access the backup transmission system, I may be able to redirect its power to help generate the ship. It was installed as a stealth system so it needed its own independent power source." He glanced at the weak glow cast from the faint white emergency lights. "It won't be a lot, but it will give us something to work with."

Hooke nodded and pointed down the opposite corridor Johns and Michaels had disappeared into. "Just so long as your Captain hasn't done anything to my port wine."

Peter snorted. "Because *that's* our biggest concern."

"That wine has been aging for a hundred years, Pan. If we survive, I'm going to need a drink."

Peter laughed as he started down the hall, but as their pounding footsteps thundered through the narrow corridors, Hooke's ominous sentiment echoed through his mind.

If we survive.

33

THE JOLLY ROGER

CAPTAIN WENDY DARLING

Wendy watched as the commander turned to the mirror and smoothed his hair. She blinked to clear her eyes as Boyce's reflected image rippled and contorted in the smooth glass, creating a strange shadowed version of her liaison officer.

"You never could see me, Captain," he said, his handsome features tightening to match the wound coils of his body. "Like my father." He averted his gaze, but not fast enough to conceal the flash of pain in his eyes. "No matter what I did, or how many achievements I earned, it was never enough for the General." He glanced over his shoulder to fix Wendy with a bitter smile. "I was hoping you would be different."

"Commander," Wendy demanded. "What's going on?"

A harsh laugh escaped Boyce's chest as he nervously scratched the cuff of his wrist. The erratic motion lifted his sleeve, revealing a dark mark spreading from the base of his wrist up under his uniform.

"Boyce," Wendy's voice was an octave too high as she stared at the commander's black rash. "What happened to your arm?"

Boyce jerked his arm from her view and twirled to face her, fleeting panic lacing his features. When he saw Wendy's worried look, his fear was replaced with a slow, curling sneer.

"I would have been perfect for you, Captain," he said. "We are equals. Near perfect matches, one would say—and many have, might I add. But you were always preoccupied. You never showed any interest in anything until *him*." He spoke the last word like a curse. "Your career I could respect, but the mechanic?" His nose curled in a pompous sneer that rivaled her father's. "What could he possibly offer you that I couldn't?"

Wendy's mouth dropped as she fumbled over what to say. Boyce watched her with narrowed, thundering eyes, the angles of his face pulled into a steel trap.

"Nothing!" Boyce answered his own question and stalked toward her. His chest heaved as he stared at her, the churning sea in his gaze roiling to a tsunami. "There is nothing that shiprat could do for you that I couldn't a thousand times over! He is uneducated, under-classed, and unimpressive. I thought perhaps it might have been pity that you would overcome once the wretch was out of range," his gaze held for another furious moment before Boyce's shoulders drooped and the churning darkness faded to a smooth sapphire blue. He watched her quietly, then reached to softly cradle her chin. "But even here, you could not see me."

Tempered from his rage, Boyce gazed at her earnestly. His eyes bored hopefully into hers, clear and vulnerable. Wendy's tongue froze, heavy as lead. Seeing her hesitation, lightning flashed through Boyce's stare, roiling it into a storm. He ripped his hands through his golden hair, disheveling it even further. His face contorted before he returned to stand calmly before Wendy, his features eerily smooth.

"You chose him."

Boyce's chest slowed its erratic heaving as he watched her, holding her in his swirling trance. He scratched the darkened mark on his wrist and studied her thoughtfully. He took a step closer, his breath hitching with emotion. "Why?"

Wendy's mind reeled as she analyzed the captain's erratic behavior. Crackling tension rippled from his coiled body, so intense she could practically feel the aggression sloughing from his skin. She needed to calm the commander so she could reason with him.

"I didn't choose anyone," she said.

Boyce straightened his spine and stepped back, his anger replaced with a startled stare.

"What?"

Boyce knelt to meet her gaze, his body trembling against the war within. His steely stare lightened every second he held her gaze, and the soft pulse in his throat slowed, allowing a faint edge of hope to restore the handsome features on his face.

Wendy allowed a calming moment before firmly repeating, "I didn't *choose* anyone."

"But you pushed me away."

Wendy studied her lap as her hands twisted nervously behind her. Her hand jerked in surprise as a sharp edge poked the soft pad of her fingers but she gripped the stray end firmly and began to work the frayed edge. She forced her gaze to Boyce, who knelt, still waiting for her response. She softened her features into an apologetic expression as she met the commander's expectant stare.

"I didn't know what to think," she used the honesty of the statement to bolster her deceit. "There was so much happening so fast, and so much at stake..." she trailed off as her mind coaxed her fingers through the knots tethering her hands. Boyce inched closer and set his hands on her knees, his warm touch pulling her attention. His grip was gentle, fierce and desperate as he held her, as though she was the only thing tethering his tenuous sanity. Behind her, Wendy felt the ties loosening around her wrists, but she needed more time.

"And then when the Stjarnin took you, all I knew was that I needed you back," she confessed, channeling her guilt from the commander's capture. Her gut twisted at the words that sprang to her throat as she looked at Boyce and whispered, "I couldn't lose you."

Boyce's sapphire gaze widened at her admission, and before Wendy knew what was happening, the commander crashed into her, his mouth searching hers, desperate and pleading as he fell into her like a boat on a summer storm. He pulled her in, and Wendy allowed the kiss to deepen, letting Boyce lose himself while she pulled her hands free and quickly unraveled the cord from around her wrists. The wire loosened, releasing the tight hold around her ribs as the commander's kiss turned hungry and he wrapped his arms around her in a crushing embrace. His muscles contracted, drawing her to him as his teeth grabbed hold of her lip and bit down. Wendy yelped and jerked back, her eyes wide as she looked at the commander, who had released his hold and leered at her, his eyes smoldering coals over a bloody smile. A shocked gasp escaped Wendy's chest as she recoiled, her arms thrashing against his hold, but Boyce's taut grip only constricted tighter, forcing her breath in a choked gasp. A harsh, grating laugh escaped his lips, bubbling through the pooling blood staining his teeth as he spoke in a distorted hiss.

"Come now, Captain, you didn't really think I'd let the commander's pathetic feelings allow you to escape me again, did you?"

Wendy's eyes widened in terror as she met the Shadow's malicious stare. It sneered down at her from Boyce's face, salivating a thin line of blood.

"It's you," she whispered breathlessly, as everything clicked slowly into place. The voices, the attacks, everything. It had all been in front of her the whole time, and she had been too dumb to see it. "What did you do with Boyce?"

The Shadow released a wretched, hissing laugh that crawled under her skin. "The commander is here," it declared. "Though not for much longer. He served his purpose well, but now," it paused as to leer at her through Boyce's face, distorting his handsome features with pure malice. "I'm ready for something *sweeter*."

Wendy's stomach lurched as she tried to pull free from the Shadow's hold, but it wrapped her tighter in its clawing embrace. It leaned in, its wicked smile curling Boyce's lips in an unnatural angle when a furious growl murmured through the freezing room.

"I hope I'm not interrupting."

34

THE JOLLY ROGER

LEAD MECHANIC PETER PAN

"Ah Peter," the commander's words slithered from his throat in a sinister whisper as he turned and fixed him with a chilling grin. His lips twisted in an exaggerated crescent moon as his eyes narrowed, and Peter could have sworn he saw dark wisps slink from his shoulders. Boyce scanned the cabin and his wicked smile deepened. "And look. You've brought my old friend."

Peter glared at the figure before him, a sickening mixture of Wendy's commanding liaison officer entwined with the wicked, writhing tendrils of the Shadow. He looked from the creature to Wendy, who met his shocked snarl, her beautiful eyes widened in absolute terror.

"Peter," she cried, "You shouldn't have come." She squared her shoulders, as if her petite form could protect him from the billowing evil behind her.

"Get the crew and *leave.*" She commanded, only the tremble in her voice defying her determined stare.

Peter's brow furrowed as he looked at the beautiful captain, still reeling from all he had witnessed in the past moments, Wendy in the arms of the handsome commander, entangled in a passionate kiss before she pulled away and the man caressing her face transformed into the coiling shadow-demon before him. It curled around Wendy's limbs, its viscous appendages licking hungrily at the captain's exposed skin before slowly seeping back to its undulating body. The vision wrestled against his bludgeoned heart, which crumpled under the weight of seeing his captain with another.

"Pan," Hooke's growl rumbled in his ears, interrupting the calamitous ringing echoing in his mind. His face etched in stone as he glared at Boyce, while his metal hand clenched menacingly. "Make your decision."

Peter followed Hooke's gaze as he looked meaningfully to where Wendy struggled in the Shadow's grip, still trying to form a barricade between him and the writhing monster. Her eyes widened as she registered Hooke, standing with Peter, once again strong and proud, with only the faint gray tinge of his hair evidencing the devastation the Shadow had wreaked on his body.

"Stay or go, Pan," Hooke prompted, his low growl pitched so only Peter could hear. "Save your captain or follow her command, but you need to choose before the decision is made for you." His gaze darted to the looming commander towering hungrily over Wendy, the dark shroud emanating from its body matching its midnight leer.

Peter's hand clenched in a fist. "No," he said.

The Shadow's expression twisted in amusement while Wendy jerked desperately against its grip, her head shaking wildly. "Don't Peter, it's too strong, it's—" her words ended in a pained scream as Shadow-Boyce tightened its grip and crushed her in its menacing embrace.

Peter lurched forward and the Shadow grasped Wendy's neck and yanked her sideways, clutching her body like nothing more than a terrified rag doll. Its gruesome laugh ricocheted through the cabin and slithered up Peter's spine as Boyce's lips pressed to Wendy's ear.

"Now, now, Captain," the Shadow hissed, "let's not spoil the fun. Our friends have just gotten here." The Shadow circled Boyce's flexed arm around her chest, revealing the inky black stain bleeding from the commander's wrist to the length of his forearm.

The Shadow's Mark.

Wendy groaned as the Shadow tightened its grip, crushing her with its superhuman strength. A flare of wicked tendrils shivered from the Shadow's stolen form, delighting in Wendy's pain. Peter's heart wrenched as a raw cry ripped from her throat until the monster released her and she sagged forward, panting as she struggled to meet his gaze.

"Get them home," she begged.

Peter surged forward, his hands outstretched and ready to rip her from the Shadow's grip when the creature twisted and snarled, whipping the captain's wilted body behind him.

"It's nice to see you again, Pan. You look well," the Shadow taunted then turned to Hooke, its smile curling into an evil crescent moon. "And you, Captain. For now."

Hooke's lips pulled in a taut line as he met the Shadow's challenging glare. The harsh ridges on his face stood out, highlighted in the dim glow of the cabin, revealing the lingering effects of the Shadow's stay.

"Let them go, demon," he ordered. "You are no longer welcome."

Peter watched in surprise as Hooke stepped forward with slow, deliberate steps and stretched his arms wide, revealing wiry, corded muscles under his paled skin. His storming gaze flashed as he strode toward the Shadow and began to speak, delivering his words in a sure, steady tone. They were stuttered and jilted, but Peter recognized the Stjarnin's harsh dialect streaming from Hooke's unsteady incantation.

The Shadow recoiled, twisting Boyce's features in horror as Hooke continued the chant, his commands strengthening until the mock-horror on Boyce's face erupted in a gleeful smile before it loosed another malicious laugh.

"Once invited, always a guest," the Shadow whispered in a mirthful hiss. Its smirk widened at Hooke's shock. "You're going to have to do better than that, I'm afraid." It said, then backhanded the flummoxed captain, sending him crashing into the towering bookshelf along the cabin wall. There was a sickening crack as Hooke's withered body slid to the ground, followed by a shower of gilded leather books as the heavy shelves rocked against the attack. The creature looked from the captain's slumped form to its raised arm in delighted surprise. A sly grin skittered over its face as it flexed Boyce's muscular arm.

"You see, Captain, I've grown much stronger in our time apart." Dark tendrils rippled from the commander as the Shadow writhed in delight. "Once I escaped your weakness, I was able to claim a superior host. It wasn't easy, but with a little patience I soon found my way in."

Peter's furious glare shifted to a silent question as he considered the Shadow's admission. It met his curious gaze and Boyce's face curled in a sickening sneer as it continued its gloating.

"You see, the commander fought me for a long time," the Shadow explained, it flexed Boyce's boxy fingers and watched with its inky gaze. "When I first stumbled upon him, half-broken and mangled, he almost pushed me away completely. I might have been wandering forever had I not found a foothold to burrow in."

The Shadow quirked Boyce's brow in a calculating glance at Wendy, who returned his leer with a tiny shake of her head. A distorted laugh escaped the commander's chest as the Shadow pulled her closer, its taunting gaze fixed on Peter as it tenderly caressed her face.

"Our fair captain has such an interesting effect on human hearts."

35

THE JOLLY ROGER

CAPTAIN WENDY DARLING

A startled jolt rocked through Wendy, and the Shadow let out another slow, curdling laugh at the anguish on her face.

"Jealousy is my favorite human emotion, I think," he mused, watching the pain churning between Peter and Wendy. "So much sorrow, rage, and guilt carried along with it. So much delicious hate to feed from." He looked hungrily at Wendy. "His pain made me strong, and once he discovered my presence, it was too late. The commander was helpless to fight, no matter how hard he tried." A brief flash of anger flitted over Boyce's face as the Shadow let out a low, furious growl. "And try he did."

Wendy's eyes widened as she looked at Boyce's stolen body and saw the ghost of her commander. She thought to Boyce's erratic behavior before their kiss and the Shadow's revelation, but it hadn't been just then. Boyce had been battling the Shadow since they disembarked and she had been too self-absorbed to realize he had been in trouble. She glared at Boyce, filled with bubbling rage as she thought of all the pain the demon had put him through. Her hands curled and she threw herself into the Shadow, earning a fleeting sense of satisfaction when she landed a sure punch against the distracted monster's face.

Black tendrils of rage flared from Boyce's shoulders as the Shadow rippled from his body before quickly seeping back to burrow deeper inside the commander. The brief flash that flared in Boyce's eyes was gone, replaced with the ebony void of the monster's glare.

Seething, the Shadow swung a powerful backhand, sending Wendy reeling. She let out a surprised cry and staggered to regain her footing, then clamped a hand against her flaming cheek. Tender flesh throbbed under her fingertips, but she loosed a furious yell and rushed the Shadow again. She blitzed across the room, spurred by her fury, but it dodged nimbly and dropped to kick her legs from under her. The commander's muscular leg smashed into the back of her knee, hammering her injured tendon.

Wendy's elbows jarred as she hit the ground, but she gritted her teeth and quickly rolled to face her assailant. She flung her arms to defend her face, barricading the commander's fist as the Shadow directed a powerful blow to Wendy's midsection. The Shadow laughed and took another menacing step forward, its muscles bunching the commander's body as it prepared to attack. Wendy scrabbled back, watching the monster grow more powerful before her eyes, its strength revealed by the tendrils of rage slithering from Boyce's body, wrapping him in a writhing cloud of evil. The Shadow sneered and let out a wicked laugh that ricocheted through the freezing room.

"Try as you will, Captain. It will make no difference. You will fall to me, just as your commander."

Inky coils flared from the Shadow's possessed figure as it flexed the commander's arms to showcase its power, sending thick tendrils curling in the air before they dissipated into the dark. The Shadow's malicious laughter stilled as it slowly refocused on Wendy, its onyx stare completely overtaking Boyce's pooled gaze. "Now Captain, let's see what you can really do."

36

THE JOLLY ROGER

LEAD MECHANIC PETER PAN

Peter watched as the Shadow loomed over Wendy, his head spinning until the captain's pained cry cut through the churning mass of bitter emotions overtaking his thoughts. He gripped his dagger from its sheath and with an anguished cry leapt toward the Shadow, burying the blade deep in the monster's shoulder.

The monster issued a hissing gasp as Peter's blade plunged into the commander's skin, drawing a rushing line of crimson mottled with an inky stain. With an anguished howl, it smashed its fist into Peter's chest, casting him across the room. Grimacing, it gripped the embedded blade, and slowly wrenched the dagger free to twirl the blood-stained steel in the dim cabin light. Mottled rivulets of blood coursed down the metal, Boyce's bright red essence mixing with the Shadow's evil. The Shadow studied it with intrigue, as though it had never seen its physical effects manifested. Its smile deepened as it slowly rubbed the blade across its chest, eyeing Peter devilishly as it wiped his dagger clean.

"Still determined to protect a love that so willingly denounces you," the Shadow hissed. "It's been a long, cold ride these past weeks, and you weren't the one there to keep the captain war—"

Peter's furious scream cut the Shadow's words short as he rushed the demon. His vision red, Peter attacked, pummeling the commander's face as he tackled the monster to the ground. He grinned in vengeful glee as he registered the shock on Boyce's face before he crashed his fist down, bloodying the commander's wicked smile. He pressed forward, striking the monster again and again until with a surge of power, the Shadow exploded a wave of seething energy, and flipped him to the ground, pinning him under the commander's weight before it retaliated, repaying him blow for blow. Peter blocked his face as best he could until the Shadow landed an explosive punch, shattering its knuckles against his jaws. Peter released a pained groan that evolved into an agonized cry when the Shadow raised his dagger and plunged it into his collarbone. Metal rang in Peter's ears as the force of the blow dug the blade from the front of his chest to pin him to the floor. The Shadow let out terrible laugh as it looked at Peter, its clawed fist poised to attack. Peter's eyes widened as a wave of black evil surged from the commander and rolled, his mind screaming in pain as he ripped his body off the dagger. His head rolled just in time for the commander's fist to pummel the ground, cratering the floor where his face had been not milliseconds before.

The Shadow released an agitated growl, bu straightened the commander's posture to seethe at Peter, the traces of another wicked smile slowly repositioning on his features.

"You won't beat me again, Pan. Not in this body. The commander's jealousy and anguish have made me too strong. Even now, I feel my power manifesting. This physique gives no resistance against you."

Ignoring the Shadow's haughty taunts, Peter staggered to his feet, with an agonized groan. His hand clasped the wound on his shoulder, but it did little to slow the river of blood sopping through his shirt. Still, he stood fast, his jaw clenched proudly, even as his eyesight blurred the image of the shadow-swathed commander. Swaying perilously on his feet, Peter met the Shadow's wicked gaze, holding it with contempt. The demon's leer only widened as it stepped closer, seeping malice and hatred.

"Try as you might Pan, it will always end the same. With you under my heel, right where you belong."

Peter keeled over to stop the spinning room before he peered up at the Shadow. Damp strands of his coarse red hair stuck to his forehead, plastered in place by the sweat pooling around his temples. His breathing was ragged, and his legs trembled under his efforts to stand, but as he peered at the Shadow through graying vision, he quirked an arrogant smile.

"That might be true," he whispered, his voice rasping through dust-dry lips. "Except there's still three of us."

The Shadow's eyes widened and he whirled to where Hooke stood behind him, brandishing his szikra. Peter grinned as the captain's blade hummed to life, sending crackling electricity sizzling through the length of the deadly blade. After the Shadow had abandoned the 'weak' Captain and turned his attention to Wendy, Hooke had slowly begun to crawl across the room toward the decorative urn still holding his weapons. Peter then moved to the Shadow, positioning himself to keep the pirate out of sight. Hooke's moves were stiff and slow, but with the Shadow's attention fixed on Peter and Wendy, the captain had crossed the room undetected. Now, he stood before the Shadow, the beaming energy from the blade illuminating his face as he glowered at the creature, the tension in his body crackling like the electricity coursing his weapon.

The Shadow fumbled in shock and Hooke lunged, using the surprise he had earned to bolster his attack. He surged forward and slashed, the szikra a deadly extension of his arm that sliced a deep burn across Boyce's chest. The Shadow shrieked as the cabin filled with the scent of burning flesh and fabric as a line of singed blood dotted the commander's uniform. The Shadow fell back, but Hooke struck with another quick swipe, this time drawing a burning line from the commander's left shoulder blade down to his hip. Boyce trembled and dropped, sending a trembling groan through the metal panels as he hovered on shaky knees while the Shadow's leeching form slowly billowed over its weakened host. A large black mass formed a hovering cloud that clung to the commander from thin vines, connecting him to his parasite.

"Perhaps I underestimated you," the Shadow's hiss bubbled deep within the commander's chest. Its words slithered against Boyce's heaving breaths like a bad ventriloquist.

"A mistake I won't suffer you to make again," Hooke growled.

With another flash of the szikra's glowing energy, Hooke attacked, this time slicing through the large shadowy form of the creature hovering over Boyce. The Shadow shrieked as the surging blade severed its anchored appendages, sending them fluttering to the cabin roof before they dissipated into nothing. Hooke slashed again, this time aiming at the Shadow's bulk, earning another screech as he neatly severed a thick segment of the Shadow's exposed form. The captain pressed forward for another attack, but his weakened legs buckled and he dropped breathing heavily with the exertion.

The Shadow's frightened stare twisted to a menacing sneer as it observed Hooke's exhausted frame. A crawling, hissing laugh whispered through the cabin as it sank its claws back into the commander, the thin strands of darkness swelling to thick ropes before Boyce's head slowly pulled to stare at Hooke like a sick puppet, his expression kinked to match the Shadow's wicked smile, and his eyes dark as the billowing pitch above him.

In a deadly flash, the Shadow struck, barreling Boyce's fist into Hooke's prosthetic wrist. The tech crumpled under the blow and issued a whirring hiss as it glitched and released the szikra. Before Hooke could react, the Shadow retrieved the discarded weapon and whirled in a graceful arc, spinning the still searing blade until it plunged deep into the captain's gut. Hooke staggered back, his eyes wide as he clutched the searing wound, then sagged to the ground as the cabin filled with the stench of burning flesh.

"No!" Peter lunged forward, his dagger slashing as he tried to continue Hooke's work, but the Shadow twisted and pulled Boyce on its perverted marionette strings, sending Peter sailing past. Furious, Peter growled and whirled around before lunging forward again. The Shadow tried to dance away, but was met by Wendy, who had crawled from the corner to attack from the other side. The monster struggled, but Wendy gripped its host, pinning Boyce's arms in a skilled bind. The Shadow roared and lashed out again, this time driving the commander's foot into Peter's chest, sending him staggering as it wrestled against the captain.

She let out a loud shriek as Boyce's eyes closed and the Shadow surged out, mauling her with raw power. Wendy's face contorted in a grimace as she tightened her hold, contending its wicked fury. The Shadow narrowed its eyes as it fixed her with a lecherous grin.

"Oh Captain," it hissed, its dead eyes scouring her body. "Still the same as last we met. You fight so fervently to protect the ones you love." It released an evil laugh, then looked from Wendy to meet Peter's horrified gaze. "But I wonder. When your loyalties lie in two different places, what would your true heart's desire really show?"

Suddenly, the roiling tendrils seeping from Boyce's shoulders dissipated as the commander's body went slack, and Boyce blinked, his words thick as he turned to Wendy.

"Captain?" he curled in on himself and let out a pained scream. When his body stopped trembling, he pushed himself roughly to his knees and looked back up in Wendy, agony and confusion lacing his features. "What's happening?"

Peter watched as Wendy's face twisted in horror and pain as she looked at the commander. His heart lurched at the warring emotions in her gaze, the pain of her hesitation greater than any damage the Shadow had inflicted on his body. The shock loosened her grip and in a flash the commander's clear blue gaze washed as a soul-curdling grin slithered across his features.

An anguished cry stalled in Peter's chest as the Shadow burst from Wendy's grip and used her hesitation to unsheathe a large, hidden kitchen knife and plunge it deep into her shoulder. Peter's trapped cry ripped from his lips, exploding across the metallic chamber as the captain's body arched in a pained spasm and she slumped to her knees, her eyes wide with shock.

"Wendy!"

37

THE JOLLY ROGER

CAPTAIN WENDY DARLING

Peter's worried cry soaked thick through Wendy's ears. She blinked at the strange sensation, intrigued how everything sounded as though she had been plunged into a pool of molasses. She blinked around the cabin, noting everything from the thin wafting tendrils of darkness slithering around her limbs to the damp strands of red falling in Peter's frightened green eyes, but movement was difficult. Boyce's sleek sleeve slipped through her numb fingers and she fell for an eternity before crashing against the hard metal floor. She looked up at the Shadow, her head lolling to meet the demon as he leered at her through the commander's once-handsome features. Now, they rippled in vindictive glee, contorting Boyce's dapper smile in a gruesome mask that sent shivers through her frozen limbs.

Why did everything have to be so cold, she thought as her gaze drifted from

Boyce's stolen face to scan the quickly dimming room. Her heavy eyelids fluttered as the Shadow knelt beside her, relishing his moment of victory. She turned to the monster, her body still tensing on instinct, though the motion was sluggish and delayed.

The Shadow's grin deepened as it leaned in, its breath hot on her face as it hissed its wicked laugh. Wendy could barely recognize the dedicated soldier she had grown up with through its vile facade. A pang of remorse flitted through her at the thought, briefly overwhelming the cold pain lacing her body.

"Boyce," she whispered, bringing her fingertips to gently touch the strong angles of his cheek. "I'm so sorry."

A tiny tremor ricocheted through the Shadow as Wendy cupped the commander's face. His body went rigid as Boyce blinked, and as his gaze cleared, the ebony stain washed away by the sapphire blue in his stare. Wendy's eyes widened as Boyce's boxy hand gripped tight against her wrist and he fixed her with a weak, pure smile.

"No," he drew his hand to mimic her action. His rough fingers brushed against the smooth skin of her cheek, but the warmth coursing through them returned some of the heat dissipating from her body. "I am." He gazed at her, his still clear eyes filled with longing and regret. "I should have told you a long time ago."

A brief film of black flashed over his gaze, and Boyce shuddered before they slowly shimmered back to blue. His hand trembled, but he smoothed his thumb against her cheek, sending another wave of warmth through her as his gaze hardened in fierce determination.

"None of this is your fault." Wendy moved to speak, but the commander gently touched her lips, tenderly stilling her words before he looked at her meaningfully. *"It's ok."*

Wendy's stomach lurched, and her head shook in silent defiance as she stared into Boyce's peaceful gaze, filled with depths of emotion before he wrapped her in a tender kiss. His arms tightened around her back, cradling her for a fleeting moment before he released his hold and drew away, a mournful expression as his eyes clouded with onyx. His grip constricted before he forcefully released his grip, dropping her to the floor, while his body buckled against an unseen force.

"Boyce!" Wendy cried, trying to reclaim her fading soldier. Boyce quirked his head before he gripped his stomach as a low moan escaped his lips. He issued a pained grimace and extended his hand in a warding movement, panic tracing his quickly darkening features.

"Let me go, Darling," he murmured, before brushing his fingers along her cheek in one final, tender caress. "Let someone else take care of you for once."

"*No*. Boyce," Wendy pushed on unsteady feet to reach the struggling commander, but she only crossed a few steps when Boyce's arms swept in a wide-reaching arc. An agonized bellow ripped from his chest, harsh and grating as it throttled through the enclosed cabin. The noise lanced in Wendy's ears, beating against the throbbing pain already pulsating her body. The scream continued until it expelled all of Boyce's oxygen, leaving the commander to slumped and gasping. His golden hair dangled in disheveled tangles as he stared at the floor until his heavy gasps stilled and turned into manic, heaving laughs. They slithered through the room and up Wendy's spine as Boyce raised his head and fixed her with an obsidian stare. Seething hatred seeped from the commander's gaze as he searched the room, while thick shadows wriggled possessively around his arms and legs.

"Boyce," Wendy whispered, her hand shaking as she reached for the commander.

"Boyce. Is. GONE!" the Shadow roared and swiped at Wendy, slamming its fist into her stomach. A wheezing gasp whooshed through her lips as she sailed back, her vision covered in blackened dots as pain seeped through her broken body. Agony racked her chest as she twisted to face the looming Shadow, its face lined in fury as it knelt to plunge its fist in her hair. It gripped her curls and yanked her to her feet while her body screamed against the abuse. She tried to struggle against the force, but her efforts were little more than a puppet facing a tsunami. The Shadow grinned and drew her nearer, exposing her jugular to its bared, gnashing teeth.

"And soon, you will be mine."

Wendy pulled away, her gaze darting around the cabin for a way to free herself, when Peter surged forward and the Shadow loosed a powerful backhanded, sending him into the wall with a sickening crack. His head lolled, and Wendy cast another desperate glance for anything to use against the monster. Her eyes flitted over the holographic visor Dawes used to display her faux beach. An idea slowly began to form in the fuzzy recesses of her brain until another vice like squeeze crushed her ribs, deafening her with the sound of her own fracturing bones. Vision fading, Wendy forced her trembling hand to the sheathed gun on the side of her thigh. She had already found her mark. She gripped the weapon and glanced at Peter, her eyes filled with regret.

"I'm sorry," she mouthed, then pulled her gaze from his pained expression to redirect all of her remaining strength to lunge forward and wrap Boyce in an unyielding bear hug. She pinned the commander's arms to his torso and kicked, knocking his legs from underneath him. The Shadow crashed to the ground, and the metal panel beneath them trembled with the impact, but Wendy didn't notice. She was too busy positioning her shot.

"Peter, Hooke, strap in!" She yelled, then squeezed the trigger to release two neat shots into the visor before them. The material shimmered and absorbed the first shot, then buckled under the pressure from the second. A thin fracture splintered the screen, taunting the room until a whooshing groan drowned the cabin. Wendy dove under her captain's chair, fumbling to loosen her belt as the untethered items in the cabin began to shake and pull toward the visor's vortex. With a deafening boom, the shards imploded, shattering the visor to nothing more than obliterated scrap floating in the void of space.

Wendy gritted her teeth and secured her restraint, hoping it would hold. She searched for Peter and Hooke, but she couldn't fight the force swirling around the cabin. She held her breath, her head spinning as she protected her last reserves of oxygen against the suffocating emptiness of space and the sounds of the eternal abyss. Something jerked her leg and she glanced over, her eyes widening as the Shadow clawed up her pants, its fingers stabbing desperately into skin as it clung for life. Its face contorted in a furious grimace, its eyes wild with fury while its wispy tendrils careened into the void.

"Not again," the Shadow fumed, crushing her in its grip. Wendy almost cried out against the pain, before she bit down and kicked to shake her body free of the clawing monster. Spots danced across her vision as her lungs bucked in her chest, but Wendy choked back her breath, denying them to save herself. She twisted and kicked, but the Shadow climbed higher, clamping its vice-like fingers around her damaged knee.

Wendy yelped, releasing the last of her air into the vortex before them. The Shadow curled a wicked grin as panic washed over Wendy's features. It raised its hand one final time, prepared to latch its claws into her femoral artery when suddenly, its eyes widened and Peter's wiry frame crashed into the monster, knocking it loose and sending its untethered figure hurtling into space. The Shadow screamed and scrabbled for a handhold, but Wendy only saw its terrified expression as it disappeared into the black before her vision slowly faded. She felt another tug on her leg and her eyelids fluttered open to Peter, clinging to her, his head ducked to avoid the hurtling items being sucked into space.

Summoning the last of her strength, Wendy lunged for Peter, her arms interlocking with his as she gazed at him in a tight-lipped smile, then fell slack, feeling a pleasant buzz course through her mind as the absence of oxygen overtook her system. Through the haze of her fuzzy mind, she saw Peter lunge forward and smash his hand on the navigation panel before the groaning sound of closing metal hummed her to sleep.

WHEN
WENDY
WOKE UP

38

THE JOLLY ROGER

CAPTAIN WENDY DARLING

Wendy woke squinting against bright fluorescent lights beaming down on her. The humming bulbs nettled her ears as she raised her hand to cover her face. Her muscles protested the movement, and she winced as the motion jarred the wound in her shoulder.

Pushing into a sitting position, the thin sheet covering her torso slid down, exposing her to the cool air. Goosebumps prickled her flesh against the sudden temperature shift, but as she examined the bandaging secured over her chest and hips, she realized her breath no longer condensed in warm clouds. Noting the change, she continued her personal inventory, examining the pristine strips binding her ribs and her injured shoulder. Spots of red splashed through the bandaging, marking where she had been hit, but as she prodded each wound, she only felt the tingling numbness of an anesthetic.

Gingerly, she stretched her arms and a surprised gasp tugged her tender ribs as she peered at her exposed stomach, which was stained by an ugly map of mottled bruises. Splashes of purple blended into blotches of dark blue and sickly green stamped across her skin, marking her abuse. Abandoning her center, Wendy moved her attention to her legs. She slid them flat, feeling her muscles tense and contract to obey her commands. Her injured knee throbbed, and when she removed the blanket, she saw the bandaging had been reinforced with a large, mechanic brace. It wrapped from her shin to the middle of her thigh and pressed against her skin, compacting the joints in a tight cast that held everything in place.

Her personal assessment complete, Wendy scanned the room as her muddied mind worked to orient her current position. As she twisted, her elbow knocked a small package, and she flinched as it clattered across her bedside table. Intrigued, Wendy picked it up and twirled it in her hands. It was SMEE's gift. She hadn't ever gotten around to opening it.

Tears pricked the corners of her eyes as she tore carefully at the clumsy wrapping. With a soft rip, the paper tore free, revealing a small butterfly figurine crafted from tiny metal parts. She clutched the gift to her chest and allowed the tears she was holding back to slip down her cheeks as she mourned for everything that had happened. For SMEE, for Boyce, for her heart.

A soft shuffle behind her sounded, and she moved quickly to wipe her tearstained face. Her movements were stiff and abrupt, stopped short by the pain lancing through her. She sucked in a sharp hiss, then bit her wince when a husky voice broke through the quiet.

"Wendy," her name was a gasp of air carried on a wave of sweet relief. Peter quirked a crooked smile as he drank her in, his earthy irises scouring her as though afraid he'd never see her again. He frowned as his gaze drifted over the violent bruising on her ribs, and Wendy pulled the covers to hide the mottled marks. Realizing his lingering stare, Peter's cheeks washed in a bright pink flush. Wendy's face flamed in response, and she dropped her gaze, acutely aware of the tension between them. She knotted her hands in the sheet, then slowly smoothed them, ironing the folds with her palms. When the flush in her face cooled, she met Peter's guarded stare with a warm grin.

"I missed you," she said.

Peter returned her smile with a roguish grin and rushed to wrap her in his arms. Her muscles flinched against the sudden touch, but soon relaxed in his gentle embrace. Warmth filtered into her body where Peter cradled her, and as she sank into his touch, his fingers slowly drifted across her back, drawing chills with every gentle stroke. A contented sigh escaped her lips as the pain that wrapped her body slowly dissipated, leaving only her and Peter. After a quiet moment, she angled her face toward his. Peter's breath hitched as he met her gaze, but it didn't still his accelerating heartbeat thrumming its unsteady rhythm against her chest.

"Not as much as I missed you," he said. His thumb caressed the arc of her cheek and he drew her closer. His head dipped toward hers, stirring her heart as the scent of cloves filled the dwindling space between them. Her stomach flipped in a pleasant ache as she prepared for his kiss, her lips burning for his familiar touch.

"Darling! You're awake!" Johns' exclamation boomed through the room, bursting the intimate moment as Peter dropped to stand sentry while Wendy quickly reclaimed her fallen sheet, trying to remember when she had lost it. The thought sent another warm tinge rushing to her cheeks, but she quashed it to face the commander as he hurried over, his face split in an eager grin. "We gotta stop meeting like this. Your near-death experiences are doing nothing for my nerves."

Wendy laughed as Peter sidestepped to allow Johns to wrap her in a crushing bear hug. Though his embrace was worlds different than Peter's, to Wendy, the commander's brawny arms were home. She nestled under Johns' boxy chin, inhaling his mint aftershave as she buried her face in his chest, grounding herself in his embrace before she pulled back to return his grin.

"I don't suppose it's doing anything for mine either," she admitted. Johns' smile widened and he gave her a quick squeeze before releasing her. Wendy grimaced, but plastered her smile as the commander inspected the bandages tucked expertly around her.

"You do know mortal injuries aren't part of your job description, right? I know how dedicated you are and all, but this seems excessive."

Wendy laughed. "Thanks for the heads up. Next time an evil entity tries to take over and kill us all I'll just step aside and let it." The words slipped from her tongue, and her face fell as she dropped into a terse silence. Her gaze darted guiltily around the room, her eyes flitting sorrowfully to Peter, then Johns, before trailing to the door where Dawes stood protectively beside Tootles. Their presence warmed her icy chest, helping to settle her remorse for Boyce as a heavy weight at the bottom of her heart. She accepted its crushing pressure. It was the least of what she deserved. Penance would come later. For now, they needed to celebrate the living.

Her smile returned as she nodded at Dawes. "Another exceptional job, Lieutenant. Keep this up, and you'll be captain soon enough."

"All respect, Captain," Dawes grinned. "I wouldn't touch your job with a ten-foot pole."

A laugh reverberated from Wendy's chest, and she winced against her twinging muscles. "Make it look that easy, do I?"

"Something like that," Dawes offered, then crossed the room to give Wendy a hug, with Tootles stuck to her side.

"I-I'm g-glad yo-you're ok, Captain." He swept a formal salute before Wendy motioned him at ease.

"Me too, Tootles," she admitted. "But I think there's someone who is even more excited to see you." Her eyes flitted to Peter and the Boy's face lit. He rushed to Peter and wrapped him in a tight embrace, laughing delightedly until his giggles dissolved into soft sniffles. Wendy watched until Peter's eyes misted over and he turned away from the room. She wiped the moisture around her own eyes, then looked at her team, who stiffened to attention.

"What do I need to know." It was a statement rather than a question, but still Johns and Dawes exchanged uncertain glances.

"Darling, we don't need to do this right now," Johns started, but Wendy waved his protest with a flick of her hand.

"I'm not dead, Johns, nor do I have any intention to be anytime soon. As such, I need to be briefed on the status of the ship." She passed a stern look from him to Dawes. "Thank you for handling things while I was incapacitated, but it's high time I get back to business."

"But 'Rissa said," Johns' dispute was quelled by Wendy's furious glower.

"While I appreciate DeLaCruz' skill and attentiveness Johns, she is the ship's medic and not your captain." Her eyes flashed before she evened her voice to a less steely tone. "I would like to know if there was anything of significance that happened in my absence."

"Really Darling, you need to rest." Johns laid a firm hand on her shoulder. Wendy's temper flared, but the concern in his gaze fizzled it to a low simmer. She placed her hand over his with a sigh.

"I appreciate your concern, Johns, but you of all people should realize that's just not gonna happen," she finished with a smile.

Johns shook his head. "No, I don't suppose it is," he said wryly before glancing at Peter. "Just make sure she doesn't overdo it. Darling doesn't tend to know when enough is enough."

Peter stepped forward and nodded. "I'll do my best," he said, "but I'm not in the mind of telling her what she can and can't do." He fixed Wendy with a pointed look. "It's not like she'd listen anyway."

Johns guffawed. "No, it's not." He slapped Peter on the back. "Just be careful and don't go falling in love with her. Captain's too busy for things like that, and I like you. I'd hate to think I might have to wring your neck if you tried something funny." His broad hand rested amiably around Peter's shoulder, but Wendy couldn't help but notice Peter's nervous glance at the commander's tightened grip.

Peter's eyes darted to her meaningfully and she quickly shrugged into her captain's coat. "Thanks Johns," she clipped, then straightened her jacket and hurried to the door, with Peter following suit, while Johns watched with a puzzled expression.

"Was it something I said?" His confused murmur was followed by Dawes' hushed whisper.

"Wait. What?" Johns' gleeful bellow pursued them, but the rest of his words were quieted by the swish of the bay doors. "Darling and the *mechanic*?"

Peter snickered behind her while Wendy rolled her eyes. "Add one more thing to list of explaining I'm going to have to do," she rubbed the budding headache needling her temples.

Peter grasped her hand in his. "Or, you can add it to the list of things that are nobody else's business."

"Clearly you haven't spent enough time with Johns," Wendy deadpanned.

"And that's something I assume I'll have to remedy," Peter declared as he brushed her hair behind her ear. "But it's not something to worry about today."

Wendy's grin widened as she pressed her forehead to Peter's, holding her hands in his. As they stood in the quiet space of the MedBay, her mind clamored with busy thoughts of the ship and its crew until Peter pulled her face to meet his earthy gaze. The warmth in his eyes stirred the thrumming of her heart, drowning her worries as he leaned in, building the heat between them until a throat cleared in the dark.

"You're not as alone as you think you are," a voice gruffed from the corner.

Wendy jerked back, once again releasing herself from Peter's grip as disappointment rippled through her keying nerves. The sharp motion triggered the sensor and lights flickered on, allowing her to focus her narrowed gaze at Hooke's strained form resting in another recovery bed. Wendy scanned the sleek machinery, noticing the tethers circling the disgraced captain's wrists.

"Not the welcome I'd hoped," Hooke mused, watching Wendy's stare. "But not one I can say I didn't expect."

"Then why are you here?" Wendy frowned, searching the Captain's tired face. Stubble lined his cheeks, dotting his jaw with a peppered shadow that matched his wiry hair.

Hooke met her challenge with a reckless smirk, then looked from her to Peter, his bemused expression widening as he drawled, "Would you like to tell her, or should I?"

Wendy turned to Peter, her face pinched in a stern glare. "What is he talking about?"

A nervous laugh escaped the mechanic's lips as he scratched his head, his shoulders shrugging in feigned innocence. His gaze landed everywhere in the room except where Wendy stood, holding her fierce posture, towering in her fury.

"Hooke and I, sort of, made a deal," Peter breezed, before sheepishly meeting her raging gaze.

"What sort of deal?" Wendy forced her face to stone as her mind conjured Hooke's possible demands. Certainly none of the imaginings she envisioned could be done. No matter how she felt for Peter, there were some things that just couldn't be promised. Hooke's betrayal of the Fleet would, at the very least, require he stand trial for his actions. The Brigade had rights to him and the punishment served. Anything less would be an infraction against the Fleet and would deserve its own punishment.

"I wanted to serve penance," Hooke interjected. The timbre of his voice matched the sincerity in his stare enough to trick anyone into believing his cause was noble. "I still have a lifetime ahead of me, but I thought helping Pan was a good place to begin."

Wendy's eyes narrowed. "And what's in it for you?"

Hooke stretched his arms, emphasizing his binds. "If I had bartered my freedom, do you think I'd be sitting here now?"

An indignant huff whistled through Wendy's nostrils. "You would if my crew had any sense," she snapped, then motioned to the restraints. "Which, apparently, they do."

Hooke's icy eyes flashed in the light, revealing clear blue orbs unmarred by shadows. "Tethers only bind the flesh, Captain. The claim to my soul is mine alone."

Hooke's words twisted in her stomach as he held her gaze, unrelenting until the bay's whirring doors announced the room's newest guest.

"Captain, you're awake. And, up." DeLaCruz' surprise quickly faded to exasperation. "I told Johns I would only let him visit if he promised to keep you in bed."

"He tried," Peter tattled over Wendy's shoulder. "She didn't listen."

DeLaCruz scoffed. "I don't know why I assumed she would." She set down the stack of blankets she was carrying, then walked to Wendy, armed with her micriatry pen. "At least let me do a final assessment." She clicked a button at the end of the metallic wand and a light shimmered into Wendy's eye. Wendy squinted into the beam and held her breath as the medic prodded her with deft fingertips. She nearly made it through the prodding until DeLaCruz examined her ribs. Wendy flinched then grinned sheepishly as she allowed the stern medic to complete her exam. She mentally braced herself as DeLaCruz rotated her injured shoulder, then checked the bandaging around her collarbone before squatting to check her knee.

"No major pain?" the medic's doe eyes searched her for dishonesty. Wendy shook her head, biting against the fiery pain where DeLaCruz' iron fingers burrowed into her knee.

"Nothing I can't handle," she said stiffly before stepping out of the medic's reach. DeLaCruz nodded and straightened, then returned to her stack of blankets. As Wendy watched, she realized the white linens weren't blankets, but clean strips of bandaging.

"What are those for?" Wendy eyed the supplies warily while her hand darted to r the wrappings around her neck.

DeLaCruz huffed a laugh. "Don't worry, they're not for you," she said as she crossed to stand over Hooke. She checked the restraints around his wrists, then diligently began tending to the detained Captain. "Since you're all sorted, I thought I'd see to my other patient." She pulled his blanket, revealing taut crimson-stained wrappings. Wendy's eyes widened as the medic slowly unraveled the stained linens to reveal a large, blackened gash spanning the base of his ribs to the crest of his hips. The szikra had cut clean through his skin, burning his flesh as it cooked the organs inside. Hooke sat patiently, his face twisted in a silent grimace as DeLaCruz applied a topical anesthetic to ease the pain. When she finally stepped away, he lowered himself against the bed, his face tinged puce while he situated his blankets then met Wendy's stare.

"If there's nothing else you need to say, Captain, I'd ask that you take your leave." The ice in his voice breezed through Wendy, its licking chill jolting her into motion.

"No," she clipped, before quickly smoothing her hair. "That will be all for now." She inclined her head to Peter, silently urging him forward before excusing herself from the room. The door whirred open as they arrived, and Wendy stepped through the threshold before turning back to DeLaCruz, who stood beside Hooke, deftly tapping an entry to his MediRecs.

"Commander?" Wendy asked, earning DeLaCruz' interested stare. "Please ensure the captain is stable, then move him to holding with the others." She turned to leave, then hesitated once more. "Provide him with his own space if necessary, and please, make sure he is comfortable."

She heard Peter's spluttered protests behind her, but ignored them as she looked at Hooke. The pirate's face paled in the dim glow of the Bay, but as he peeked his eyes a soft smile splayed across his lips and he gave a fleeting nod before quickly drifting to sleep. Wendy's mouth twitched and she crossed the threshold into the *Roger's* chambered corridors. Peter stood in the corridor, his lips pulled in a stifled frown.

"He saved our lives, Wendy."

"Not before he endangered all of them," she countered. "There has to be some sort of accountability set for his actions. I trusted Hooke once and it nearly cost my entire crew. I won't make the same mistake twice."

"And what if it was Boyce?" Peter challenged bitterly. His green eyes flashed to meet her with a surly stare.

"That's different," Wendy murmured. "The Shadow *took* him. He didn't go searching for it like some lunatic! In fact, the only reason it even *found* Boyce was because James Hooke set it free!" Her chest hitched as the scathing words tumbled loose, releasing emotions she hadn't allowed herself to process. She looked at the handsome mechanic before her, his piercing green gaze scouring her beneath a mop of flaming hair. His appearance fit him so perfectly—spirited, daring, and untamed, but for the briefest moment she wished it was a golden-haired boy with a pristine suit standing before her. A steady, dependable boy who understood her world.

But that boy was gone.

She crushed her eyelids to chase the Commander's phantom, then opened them with a heavy sigh. "I can appreciate all that Hooke risked to assist to our plight," she offered diplomatically. "However, condemning or absolving a fellow Captain falls far outside my rank. I am acting in accordance with Brigade regulations. We will return Hooke and allow the Fleet to decide the proper way to proceed. I will not disregard protocol."

She stared at Peter, who stood silently before her, the crease in his brows the last of his protests. He gave a terse nod.

Wendy offered him with a tired smile. "Let's not worry about it yet," she suggested. "There's still a lot of space between us and the Fleet. "I'm sure there are more pressing matters at hand." She sighed as her daunting responsibilities mounted in her brain while they continued to Navs. Peter walked beside her, soothing her bubbling nerves with his steady presence until they approached her quarters and a loud clang sounded from within.

She cast a wary glance at Peter, who grimaced, then turned to face her.

"Listen, Cap, before you go in, there's something I should probably tell you. Navs took a pretty good beating when the Shadow reared its ugly head. We're working on it, but, well, let's just say it's like a rough draft."

Wendy snickered. "I'm pretty sure I can handle a little mess." She pressed forward, triggering the sensored panels. The door whirred on its hinges revealing the cabin inside, and Wendy's jaw dropped. She stepped inside, her jaw wide as she observed the disarray in her pristine living space.

"You ok there, Cap?" Peter teased.

"You said it was a mess. You didn't say it was the eighth level of hell."

Peter snickered. "Exaggerate much?"

Wendy shrugged. "If cleanliness is next to godliness, then one could only assume," she gestured helplessly to the mess. "We're in the fourth, maybe fifth level of hell?" she asked wryly.

Peter laughed. "It doesn't get fun until you're in at least the sixth," Peter winked, then strode purposefully into the room. Wendy followed, and a cascade of orange sparks zoomed across her vision.

"Tinc?" she asked, unable to hide her bewilderment as the bossy bot flitted around the room to buzz orders at Curly and the Twins as they sorted the wreckage. "How did you fix her?"

Peter grinned. "You know what they say, Cap." He held out his hand for Tinc to perch. She flitted down with happy hum and a shimmer of pink sparks. "All it takes is faith and trust." He patted the bot fondly before she swooped off to jangle another series of garbled commands at Curly, who peered out under a heavy bandage as he worked. Seven sniffed behind him, following his steps until she heard Wendy's delighted gasp, then chittered and bounded to her arms. The Neverfox's happy chirrups were drowned in her lilting coos as she burrowed around Wendy's neck. Her face flushed, Wendy turned to Peter.

"You brought Seven?"

"The dang thing followed me home," Peter groused, but his act was betrayed by his contented grin. Realizing his ruse was up, a sheepish laugh rumbled from his chest. "I thought you'd want to see her," he admitted in a husky murmur.

Wendy looked up at Peter as she stroked Seven's downy fur. "I missed her almost as much as you," she teased, before nuzzling the beast and setting her down continue her exploration of the cabin.

A wry smile curled Peter's lips. "Tied with an animal," he muttered, before he looked back around the disheveled cabin. "Maybe fixing this room up will boost my ranking," he winked, then pointed to the Boys as they continued sifting through the mess. "The Boys have been working almost nonstop. They're gonna deserve a medal after all this is done."

"And a vacation," piped one of the Twins, before he was echoed by his brother, "with a fancy dinner we don't have to cook."

Wendy chuckled. "I'll see what I can do," she promised. She looked at the books, and her face fell. The heavy tomes lay open and bent, washed in a sea of ripped pages, their gilded bindings cracked as they splayed across the floor.

Wendy frowned at the damaged works, then raised her gaze, saddened by the lost art. The mahogany shelves loomed in front of her, a trail of thick gashes in the floor paneling revealing where the heavy furniture scraped the floor against the pull of space. Hooke really had made an investment in the pieces, the craftsmanship had survived the vortex unscathed. She smiled at the thought, then paused when her gaze caught an intricate carving etched in the back of the shelf.

Wendy's brow furrowed as her fingers brushed the ridges. Rough, uneven edges jutted against her fingertips as she traced the poorly hewn etchings. Blunt, jagged edges formed clumsy lines and swirling whorls splaying across the back of the shelf and adorned it with a scattering of dots. She peered closer, enthralled by the markings and the mystery they revealed and turned to Peter, a question on her face. "Have you ever seen these?"

Peter's brow furrowed as he moved beside her, his emerald eyes burning with curiosity as he followed the intricate, swirling pattern. "No," he said, thinly concealing the wonder in his voice. "I don't know what it is."

"Me either," Wendy admitted absently, still tracing the hewn edges. Although she'd never noticed the strange, hidden markings before, she couldn't shake the feeling that they were somehow familiar. She bit her lip as she considered, then forced the murmuring thoughts from her mind. It was a mystery better served for later. A quick glance around her cabin assured as much. She smoothed her hair, then leaned to help Curly continue his makeshift tower. Peter joined in, and together, they worked quietly to restore order to the chaos. It seemed a small gesture, but in the wake of the devastation, even the smallest move could help. She was about to move to another pile when the cabin whirred open to admit a creaky trolley.

Wendy turned and the heavy purple book she held tumbled from her hands. Behind the cart, a slender figure with golden hair and beaming eyes jaunted merrily in, trilling mechanical notes as he hummed with each step.

"SMEE?"

The first mate stumbled to a stop, clinking and sloshing the crystal goblets on the trolley's surface. He glanced around, his blinking almost comical as he squared toward Wendy and raised his arms in a delighted span.

"Oh Captain! You're alright!" He exclaimed, dashing around the cart to rest his hands on Wendy's shoulders. His golden eyes gleamed as he fixed her with a warmer smile than she ever received from her father. "We were so worried about you!"

"Me?" Wendy laughed and a loose tear cascaded down her cheek. She looked at SMEE, marveling at his immaculate condition. Freshly suited in a clean-pressed uniform, with his hair and cap neatly in place, the synth looked just as he had before the attack. She smiled before drawing her hand to a small cut at the edge of his eye, where his faux skin was replaced with a shimmering layer of thin, fabricated material. "I thought we lost you."

SMEE chuckled as his fingers proudly prodded his synthetic scar. "You know, most models don't come with scars. It makes me look rather dashing, don't you think?"

Another happy laughed bubbled from Wendy's chest. "If I didn't know any better, I'd think you were a real boy."

SMEE's gears whirred as he let out a delighted chuckle. Wendy stared at the resurrected first mate in wonder. "How were you fixed?" she asked before motioning to the patched StarBoard. "How was *any* of this fixed?"

SMEE's chest swelled under her attention as he prepared to his explanation, but Peter's voice piped from behind as he stepped forward, hands in his pockets as he bit a guilty smile.

"Well Cap, there's something else I have to tell you."

39

THE JOLLY ROGER

LEAD MECHANIC PETER PAN

Peter hesitated as Wendy turned to face him, her hazel eyes lighting with a tempered flare, turning them into fleeting solar flares in an endless galaxy of light. She was beautiful—this strong, independent woman who bore the weight of her crew on her shoulders and fought fiercely to protect them. His breath caught under her spell, so innocently cast, before she blinked, releasing him from her trance and restoring him to his senses. He raked his fingers through his hair, pushing the coarse strands to flop back in place.

"I didn't get here on my own," he admitted, fixing her with a sheepish grin.

Wendy's brow furrowed. "I know," she admonished, "you brought Hooke. For reasons still mostly unknown," she added wryly.

"No," Peter countered, as the cabin door whirred behind him. He held his gaze on Wendy, as he worked out his words. "I mean, yes, I *did* bring Hooke, but he wasn't the only one who helped me get to you."

"The Stjarnin," Wendy answered, her eyes sliding over his shoulder.

Peter frowned. "How did you kn—"

"Pan." Tiger Lily's cool voice resounded through the cabin like waves against the shore. Peter turned to the princess standing inside, her lean body towering high above the door's metallic frame. Behind her Tizari and Jaxtara waited, expressions blank as they scanned the wreckage. Around the room, the Lost Boys stalled their work, their gaze wary as they looked from Peter to the waiting Stjarnin.

"Princess," Peter dipped his head. "I see you've figured your way around the ship."

Tiger Lily nodded. "It wasn't difficult. The vessel is primitive." Her lips curved in a wry smile at the shared joke before she stepped aside and gestured at Michaels, who had been obscured behind her looming stature. "And the intelligent one was most eager to see our technology. He was very helpful."

Michaels gave a humble wave, but his ears tinged pink with delight. Wendy smiled and rushed forward to wrap him in a soft hug, then laughed at the streaked grease on his lenses as he studied her through his shrewd gaze. "Are you ok?"

Wendy's head bobbed as she gave a veiled smile. "A little sore, but I'll live."

Michaels held her gaze, the small dent in his brow hinting his disbelief, before he conceded a nod of his own.

Wendy smiled, then drew back and glanced around the room. "You guys had some party while I was gone."

Michaels snickered. "While I don't doubt Johns' capacity to elicit this sort of damage, even he wouldn't be dumb enough to do it under your watch."

"Good to know he's got *some* common sense," Wendy grinned, but Peter noticed how her gaze flit uneasily to the waiting Stjarnin. She tugged her jacket before she flattened her jumbled curls and straightened to address their guests.

"Princess Tiger Lily," she bowed to the princess, then nodded to acknowledge each of her escorts, "Welcome aboard," she offered a diplomatic smile as her eyes darted to Peter. "I'm surprised you're here."

Peter offered a nervous cough as Tiger Lily returned Wendy's greeting, then turned her deep gaze patiently toward his. He looked between the two women, each powerful in her own right, and suddenly felt very small. His throat cleared and he stepped closer to Wendy, feeling the princess' stare drift behind him. He gripped Wendy's hands, his thumbs brushing softly over her smooth skin as he thought about where to begin, and realized nearly another lifetime had passed in the time they had been apart. He sucked a slow breath and glanced at his captain and the galaxies in her eyes. Wendy would get a full explanation later, but for now he figured simple was best.

"While I was still on Neverland, the Stjarnin approached me. They shared their fear that the Shadow might have escaped. At first, I didn't believe them, but when we found Hooke, our fears were confirmed. The Shadow had left him for dead, and apparently," he paused as Wendy's face fell to push away the gnawing tug of jealousy writhing inside, "found someone else." He tightened his hold on Wendy's hands to pull her distant gaze back to him.

"The Stjarnin agreed to come with us. The princess guessed the Shadow had stowed away on the *Roger* and volunteered her assistance to find and recapture it." His eyes darted to Wendy's. "We made it in time to save the ship, but . . ." he fell into silence. There was no need to say the rest. The flaring storm passing through the captain's troubled gaze told the end.

The room quieted, and Wendy's face hardened to chase her haunted stare. "But the Shadow has been handled," she finished curtly. She glanced at the princess. "I am sorry we were unable to reclaim Itzala, but I can assure you, he is no longer a threat." She turned to her navigation panel, her shoulders tight as she gazed at the now open visor. Peter watched as she searched the stars dotting the screen, mirroring the scene before them. With the ship repaired, Dawes had successfully navigated the *Roger* from the Dengara Enstjarni to the smooth expanse of space. She stood like that for a moment before turning to face the princess.

"And you fixed our ship."

Her guess was confirmed by the princess' solemn nod. Her response much more dignified than Michaels' eager head bob behind her. Peter suppressed a smirk as the mechanic gaped at the Stjarnin in awe.

"Then we owe you a great debt. Not just thanks, but our lives," Wendy dipped her head in a respectful bow, then rose, her brow furrowed at Peter. "I didn't realize your people were so advanced. All of our intel indicated otherwise," she trailed off as Tiger Lily's lips curved in a knowing grin.

"*Humans,*" her head swayed as she issued a low, throaty laugh and looked meaningfully at Peter. "*Always so certain of their superiority.*"

Peter chuckled and scratched his hand through his hair before answering with a helpless shrug. He didn't miss the confusion that flitted across Wendy's face, but she waited patiently with a poised smile.

Tiger Lily crossed the room and placed her hand on Wendy's shoulder, wrapping her long, slender fingers around the Captain's petite frame. She dipped her head in a respectful bow before murmuring a single word, her harsh syllables smoothing into clear English in Peter's ear.

"The princess says thank you," Peter translated, looking from Tiger Lily's stately form to Wendy's determined stance. Wendy extended her hand, replicating the princess' gesture.

"No," Wendy responded. "Thank *you*," she said softly. "You saved my men."

Tiger Lily blinked slowly then spoke, her throaty voice tumbling in fragmented English, "but you saved us all."

A single tear coursed Wendy's cheek as she offered the princess a trembling smile. They stood in place, silently regarding each other, holding themselves with grace and poise in silent understanding, while a wave of thrumming energy stirred the room. Finally, Tiger Lily stepped back, breaking the moment as she looked to her warriors.

"*Tizari, Jaxtara, it is time to leave. Our people have long awaited our freedom from Itzala. We should not make them wait any longer.*" She said, then turned to Peter. She regarded him solemnly, holding him in her endless gaze.

"*Pan,*" she touched her hand to her chest, "*my people owe you a great debt. I see now why the ancients entrusted you.*" She stepped toward Peter, her lips curving in a stacked smile. "*You have become a friend to the Stjarnin, and to me.*" She reached for a beaded strand of hair, then tugged on the intricately carved stones. She extended her hand, offering him the decorated jewel. "*Take this gift with my thanks. Should you ever need to reach us, this will help you do so.*"

Peter glanced at the princess' gift. The thin carved lines flared turquoise then faded, leaving only the beautifully etched stone. He closed his fist, and winked.

"Sure thing, Princess."

Tiger Lily sniffed a laugh, then turned to leave, Tizari and Jaxtara trailing silently behind her. Tizari beamed at Peter as they passed, and even Jaxtara allowed a grudging nod of thanks. Peter grinned as he watched them leave, until the doors whirred behind them, leaving the remaining crew staring at him in stunned silence.

Peter glanced around, his cheeks flaring at their shocked expressions. He coughed a laugh, then scratched his hands through his hair as he gave a helpless shrug. "We're friends now," he explained.

"I gathered," Wendy retorted, her features hosting a thousand silent questions. Peter braced for her interrogation, but it was interrupted by a droning beep before the flickering image of an imposing woman appeared on the visor. Her silver hair matched her piercing gaze, a stark contrast against the deep hue of her skin. She scanned the room through the screen, her tight stance perfected to razor sharp edges. Wendy saluted, her body gone rigid in perfect imitation.

"Admiral Toussant," Wendy's eyes boggled, but she quickly recovered and swept a sharp salute. "It's good to see you, Admiral."

40

THE JOLLY ROGER

CAPTAIN WENDY DARLING

"At ease, Darling," Admiral Toussant's brusque command rippled through the cabin as she glanced from Wendy to the crew, her sharp eyes narrowing at the unfamiliar faces. "Report, Captain. We've been trying to contact you for days, but our transmissions were never received. It seems as though the signal was blocked." The harsh lines tracing her mouth softened and she spoke again, a tinge of relief wrapping her words, "Is everything alright?"

Wendy's chest tightened as she looked at the Admiral. Perfectly pressed in her seamless uniform, Wendy could only imagine how her own tattered presentation appeared to the esteemed commander. She pulled self-consciously at the edges of her jacket before she smoothed over her untamed curls, forcing them into compliance.

"Everything is stable, Admiral," she responded, meeting the Toussant's even stare. "We were awaiting your correspondence when our internal power was cut. During the outage, we discovered our ship had been infiltrated. The Shadow followed us from Neverland."

Toussant's brows met her peppered crown. "The entity followed you?"

Wendy nodded, hoping hear bobbing head hid the lump forming in her throat. "Yes," she affirmed. "The Shadow claimed a host and hid alongside the crew. We were unaware of its presence until it revealed itself during the outage."

"You encountered the Shadow," Admiral Toussant stated, confirming her understanding through the shock on her face. "Where is it now?"

Wendy pulled a troubled frown. "It has been destroyed. It tried to overtake the ship, but we were able to overpower it." She motioned to Peter, who stood silently beside her, bolstering her with his presence. "With the help of Lead Mechanic Pan and Captain Hooke, we subdued and expelled the Shadow from the ship. There's no way it could have survived."

"And its host?" Admiral Toussant inquired shrewdly.

Wendy dropped her eyes to hide her brimming tears. Once they quelled, she raised her gaze, her face a mask of shame and regret. "Commander Boyce fought the Shadow as best he could. His sacrifice allowed us to finally defeat the Shadow. Without his selflessness, we all would have been lost."

The Admiral's lips pressed in a hard line. "A devastating loss," she declared, her voice grim. "He will be missed greatly." She glanced around the room, meeting each individual with her sharp gaze before addressing the cabin with clipped professionalism. "Thank you, Captain, for the update. Of course, I will expect a full briefing upon your return. Please prepare your statement, and those of your crew, as well as your guests." She looked at Peter with a wry expression. "Pan, I take it?"

Peter executed a flawless salute, impressing Wendy with his propriety. "Yes, Ma'am."

Admiral Toussant waved him at ease. "Glad to see you made it on board," she fixed him with her piercing stare. "I'll be most interested to hear how you accomplished such a feat."

Peter nodded. "It would be my pleasure, Admiral."

The Admiral's lips twitched in a quick smile before she stamped her mouth in a hard line. Her steely gaze glinted before she returned to Wendy. "Well Captain, once again you've seemed to prevail against staggering odds. Your crew is very lucky to have you. Our team is on their way. They will provide you with supplies and begin your escort home. In the meantime, please prepare your mission briefing. I'm sure it will provide most insightful." The Admiral grinned before she raised her hand in a proud salute. "Well flown Darling, and smooth sails onward."

The screen blipped, leaving only the galaxies before them. Wendy stared at the stars, her heart drifting through the vast expanse of space. The Admiral was proud of her. The ship had survived, and her crew was safe. But Wendy couldn't help the niggling feeling that none of it was because of her. The familiar pull of stress pressed down on her, cording a thick line of tension down her back. She would press on. She had to. For the Admiral, for her crew.

For Boyce.

A thin trailing star flitted across the visor screen, its sapphire tail glittering in the night. Wendy watched it fade as the commander's words lingered in her mind. *You have to let me go.* Her hand pressed to her lips, her trembling fingers meeting the ghost of Boyce's touch. Grief welled in her heart, manifesting in tiny crystalline tears. Behind her, a stifled cough sounded, reminding her of her duty. Quickly, she brushed the moisture from her cheeks and turned to face her crew.

Her team stood before her, waiting patiently for what she had to say. Wendy met each member's gaze in turn, from Curly's nervous shifting and the twins' matching expressions to Dawes' encouraging smile ending in Peter's handsome smirk. Finally, she breathed an exhausted sigh.

"It's been a hell of a day," she chuckled helplessly at the meager sentiment, but the statement broke the tension in the room, earning a swell of relieved laughter. It pulled a tiny laugh from the barrel of Wendy's chest, lifting some of the weight crushing her lungs. She allowed the moment of levity to end before straightening to meet the stares before her.

"You've all done an excellent job. Our return may not be easy, but I know that with your help, we can make it through anything." She turned to Dawes and Michaels, the members of her original crew. "Round up the rest of the team. We have a lot to talk about, and we'll all need to be on the same page moving forward."

Dawes and Michaels nodded and saluted, then Wendy turned to Peter's men. "Find the other Boys and bring them with you. Like it or not, we're all in this together now," she glanced at Peter before slipping her hand in his. "This is our crew."

Peter tightened his callused hands around hers, wrapping it in his warmth. His roguish grin smoothed into a genuine smile as he looked at her, then back at his boys.

"You heard the captain," he announced. "Round up the men!" he released a whooping crow, then wrapped Wendy in his arms and spun her triumphantly as the crew moved to follow her orders. Wendy's head spun in giddy delight as Peter twirled her once more before gently setting her to the ground. He stepped closer, drawing her into his strong embrace as she recentered her balance, her cheeks flushed in exhilaration. She glanced around the room, quiet now that the two of them were alone. Peter's shallow breaths whispered in her ears and she gazed back at the faithful mechanic who had crossed the galaxies to find her and who watched her like she was the most precious jewel in the 'verse.

"You didn't have to come," she murmured. "I told you I would be back."

Peter grinned and pushed a loose curl behind her ear. His green eyes searched hers as he stared at her, thrilling her with their endless emerald depths. A wry smile pulled his lips before he drew his fingers down her cheek in a sweet caress.

"I didn't want to miss you that long," he said, then drew her lips to his in a soft, gentle kiss that surprised Wendy with its tender touch. His hands trailed her skin, sending thrilling waves coursing through her until he slowly pulled away, allowing a chill to trickle through their warm embrace. She pressed her hand to his cheek as she looked up at him, and all their wonderful moments tumbled through her mind. Her heart thumped in an unsteady rhythm against her chest, matching the erratic emotions stirring through it. Being with Peter had never been easy, but as she met his open gaze, she was certain her feelings were true.

"I missed you too," Wendy murmured, her fingers toying with the coarse hairs drifting over his eyes. She brushed them away, leaving only his forest stare, grounding her in his steady presence. She pressed on her tiptoes to close the distance between them once more and leaned in, ready to vanish into his touch when the visor flashed in a brilliant flare of gold.

Wendy's brow furrowed as she pulled away to walk toward the screen. In the corner of the monitor, a golden flare burst within a distant constellation before fading into the void.

"What was that?" Peter asked.

"I'm not sure," Wendy admitted. She pointed to the visor, her eyes dotted with the remains of the mysterious beacon. She stared into the screen, but only stars and planets remained, unworried by the disturbance. "I don't remember seeing that constellation before." Her fingers trailed after the scattered astral bodies. "It looks like a neighboring planet. Maybe it's experiencing some sort of atmospheric disturbance."

Peter's face pulled in a curious frown before he shrugged and pulled Wendy into his arms. "Well, I'm going to take advantage of our time before we have an inevitable disturbance of our own."

He kissed her again, wiping away her doubts and fears. Her muscles and joints ached against the pressure of his crushing embrace, but as she spiraled into the dizzying bliss of Peter's lips all her pain ebbed into a warm, shining moment of peace.

Guilt could wait. Fear could wait. The Admiral's report could wait. Everything outside of this moment could wait. Peter was here, and wrapped in his arms, that was all that really mattered.

EPILOGUE

COMMANDER AIDAN BOYCE

I'm not sure what day it is. Time slips by erratically these...weeks? Months? I doubt it's been that long, but it would be unforthcoming to deny that I find it unsettling. I wonder if it is an aftereffect of my stay on Neverland. Perhaps time is making up for her stolen moments. She keeps strict records. I imagine she doesn't like to be cheated.

Neither do I.

If I had to wager, I'd estimate it has been a few weeks since I departed the *Roger*. I don't know my exact location, I only know that somehow, I survived. Through agony and endless pleas for merciful death as I travelled the depths of what I was sure was hell, I awoke in what seems a vessel of some sort. I have run inventory to figure out what is needed to make it operational, but my knowledge of most crafts doesn't extend beyond basic operations. Restoration was not part of my training—even for modern vessels—and my current residence is a far cry from cutting edge technology. But it is secure.

Thankfully, there are enough supplies that I have been able to sustain myself. Food, clothing, and an assortment of personal belongings have been left to my disposal. I even found a box of handcrafted toys in an abandoned crate. It makes me wonder what happened to the previous residents, but that cannot be my concern.

I must find a way back. The supplies were a boon, but even with strict rationing, they are quickly dwindling. I may not know how long I have been on board, but I do know that I cannot stay much longer.

I am hungry.

I do my best to distract myself from the gnawing pangs, but one can only find so many ways to entertain oneself whittling wires and gears. It is tedious work that echoes in the silence. Reverberations of tools against metal throb in my ears until they are swallowed in palpable silence. It wraps in waves, enveloping me in a deafening lull. I hope soon someone will find me, set me free from this silent shell and return me to myself. But with each passing day, my fear grows that I soon will go mad without anyone to talk to.

Except for me.

ACKNOWLEDGEMENTS

First and foremost, I thank God for blessing me with the opportunity and ability to share my stories with the world. Without your gracious gifts, I would truly be lost.

Next, I want to thank my family. For my husband and children, thank you for the countless hours you allow me to dedicate to my work and for encouraging, listening to, and loving me through it all. I love you all to the moon and back.

For my parents, thank you for always believing in me and encouraging me to follow my dreams. I hope I've made you proud. For my mother and father-in-law, thank you for being a second sounding board. I'm so grateful you've chosen to love me, too.

For the rest of my family and friends—my inner circle—thank you for being the best support group a girl could ever ask for. You make my life complete.

For the dreamers who jumped headfirst into Neverland with me Jessica, my bestie—girl this acknowledgement would be six pages long if I listed all your amazingness. I don't know where this book would even be without you. I'm so lucky to have you. Katie, thank you for always making time to listen and offer advice in anything and everything. You're a queen. Ethan, the most gracious editor EVER, thank you for your encouragement and patience and willingness to make my story better and convince me it was (mostly) not a hot garbage fire.

Of course, for Jon and Sherry; Thank you so much for believing in my work and continuing to turn it into something truly magical. Without your grace and support, our boy might still be lost.

And last, but definitely not least, I thank YOU, dear reader. Without you, there would be no reason to continue Peter and Wendy's story. They may be a piece of my heart, but now they belong to you.

Thank you.